Jokerman 8

Jokerman 8

Richard Melo

Hey Doug —
cool to meet
you at Orca Books.
All my best!

Richard Melo

Soft Skull Press • Brooklyn, New York • 2004

Jokerman 8
1-932360-34-4

© Richard Melo, 2004

Cover design by Kevin Jahnsen

Published by Soft Skull Press
71 Bond Street, Brooklyn, NY 11217

Distributed by Publishers Group West
www.pgw.com • 1.800.788.3123

Printed in Canada

Cataloging-in-Publication Data available from the Library of Congress.

Jokerman 8 is dedicated to
Carrie Jessen
(1973–2004)

Amelia & I will always love you

Prologue: 1991

We are Jokerman, environmental pranksters, a high-fiving wingnut tribe hanging out on the idiot fringe of the green movement, charged with inciting umpteen laugh riots, painters of the have-a-nice-day yellow happy face across the vast trunk of old growth eco radicalism & drinkers of beer. We are Jokerman c/o The Joshua Tree, 867 Font St., San Francisco, CA 94132, attn. Eleanor Cookee. We are green buffoons—laughter fills our bag of tricks with pacifist bombs. Instead of things that go boom in the night, we are full of flags that pop out & say bang! We are not the arrogant, murky, doomsaying, mad bombing—those lone-wolf, off-kilter, blackbearded & unshowered, aging, bum-knees-&-all New Left eco-revolutionaries of old. We are a newly evolved & different breed of animal.

1967—*Please, love, do turn up the radio*, says the soon-to-be mother to the soon-to-be father on that cool October evening inside the bedroom of the second-story shoebox of an apartment they rent in San Francisco. The lights are off already. Curtains flap against the wall, moving with a breeze flowing through an open window.

Turning up the radio seems like the right idea—an instant solution. It has nothing to do with the song that's playing. Neither one of them has heard the song before—neither one knows who sings it—neither one will remember it later. The reason they turn it up is because these walls are thin & Uncle Richard—who is not yet an uncle, although we have never known him as anything other than Uncle Richard—is creaking back & forth in the rocking chair on just the other side of the bedroom door. The last thing we want is for Uncle Richard to hear—or, even worse, the neighbors.

Seconds later, it happens—it goes.

We begin & here we are. Born in the sixties, we are the babies in the blinking sun in home movies, our images captured in the horse-fenced backyards of the tiny ranch-style houses of our early lives where we play pretend to be Scooby Doo & Josie & the Pussycats. We see ourselves wading in green plastic, frog-shaped swimming pools—then cut to flying kites in Kodachrome color against a backdrop of the sky's clean blue fabric. Everything flickers on the milky white bedsheet hanging on the door where these moving images play, the lamp & motor of the super-8 projector dying more with every passing frame. A fan in an open window blows waves across the makeshift movie screen—the rippling distorts our baby faces resplendent in their childhood smiles. We see more of us—images falling in quick succession: climbing trees in the park, feeding ducks, chasing seagulls, building sandcastles at the beach on vacation in south California, eating from a box of Kellogg's Corn Flakes, throwing sticks for a dog named Alfie, playing outside at someone's wedding, wandering through the park looking for a place to pee.

We are anything but self-conscious; we do not feel the heat of the camera following us. We do not yet know what cameras do—our childhood smiles become us.

Then come scenes where our parents show themselves. One at a time they appear, while the other handles the camera. Our mothers wear their hair long, straight, parted down the middle, their jeans faded bell-bottoms with butterfly & ladybug patches. The funny faces they make before the camera bring tear-spilling laughter to us now. Our fathers step inside the frame with thick sideburns & dark sunglasses, an orange shirt with vertical blue stripes—a wide collar—sandals covering hairy-toed feet. They talk to the camera even though it records no sound & reading lips only lets us glimmer together pieces of what they are saying. Our parents look younger & less gray than we ever remember them—not to mention, happier. Mostly, yes, they seem happier.

It's funny to see our parents like that—together, carefree—in love with the world, with each other & with us. Was everybody really that happy once upon a time? Or do people just make themselves smile big like that for the camera?

The truth is we can't remember—we were babies at the time—1969.

The father-to-be, whose name is Carl Seldom, stumbles through the dark room, his fingers reaching for the radio, pinching air clumsily in search of its volume knob. Finding it, he turns it up—too loud—the speaker rattles & distorts. Too much volume will spoil the mood. The neighbors next door will pound on the other side of your bedroom wall, shouting at the two of you to *turn it down!* So Carl Seldom does just that—but now it's too soft & what about the neighbors downstairs? Too soft means they might hear. They will pound on their ceiling, your floor, yelling at you two to knock it off! [Life ain't easy when you're newlyweds, especially in the middle to late sixties when fuses are short & people are so in love with shouting.]

Up again Carl turns the knob gradually, then fades it down, then up slightly more, then tweaks it back down. Sooner or later, he'll get it right.

1991—Here comes Jokerman.

We are open—we are close. We are conjoined—we are growing together at the shoulder. We come in peace—yes, all of us.

Far away now from our parents, we creep toward adulthood, though never getting more than halfway there. We are less shaped by our childhoods than by the world as we now see it, feel it, touch it & heal it.

We have something new on our mind—something other than ourselves—something we wish to lay waste: the scraping of the flora & fauna off the planet's surface by the masters of conspicuous consumption. We stand against those who for the sake of their own upward mobility have brought you dwindling fish counts & chemical rain, who are causing global frog populations to disappear, who have waved bye-bye to one woodland species after another, who have cut down as much of our ancient treeful heritage as the government has allowed them & then some, who have poisoned children & adults alike who don't know where their cancer comes from & find a way to blame their ancestors.

Nothing we own is worth any of this. We would rather own nothing & have it all.

We are Jokerman, an International Collective, hangers on of the Joshua Tree & we wish to remind you, when you tread, tread lightly & when you drink, save some for the fish.

Who we are now: We have seen enough of the world to report back that the difference between the person sitting next to you & a leaf of grass is in name only. Sound ridiculous? Life is life — whatever you choose to call it. Whatever you choose to call it is only a name. Death is life. Rocks are life. We all get together in the shape & spin of things.

Interconnectedness: It could happen to you.

Biodiversity: It is yours alone & all of ours together.

We are tangling in the fallen vines & picking up punch lines.

We are ordinary & everyday—though some might call us young.

We are ordinary & everyday—you hear a good joke & pass it on.

We are revolutionaries of the spirit—bent less on revolution than on revolving evolution.

We are laughing all the way to the bank of a river near you.

We are a generation of accidents.

Our conception was ill conceived.

We were born of the moment.

We are accidents waiting to happen.

We are people who are not sure who our parents are, because our parents themselves to this day don't know who they are.

We are the children of the sixties—born to children in the sixties.

We have seen the best minds of our parents' generation destroyed by plastics.

America—take it or leave it.

Let's trust ourselves never to turn thirty.

Growing up in the mighty shadow of our parents' generation, we missed out on the sun. Beginning our twenties, we want to feel sunlight on our face.

We are evolving spontaneously—learning & growing at every turn, leaning gently upon one another.

We are free spirits, every one—radiant & cometlike—sleek & catlike.

We are standing sideways & in between.

We breathe—we wander.

We fall asleep standing up.

We are all winged mammals. The problem is that some of us don't feel our wings yet. [*I don't know, love—they still feel like arms to me.*]

We bend like reeds in the wind—we shimmer like cottonwoods in August.

We are all parts of the same body—between us, we can live a million years.

We are the sum of our ancestral voices, speaking all at once. We are a group effort.

We taste like water.

We are large & we are real—we are small & ethereal.

Do we contradict ourselves? Fine, then—we contain multitudes.

We oscillate. We twist & turn in the shape & spin.

We winnow along the rill—we awaken covered in rime.

We are the bricoleurs of ecotage.

We are about time & losing it every step of the way.

We are Americans, every last one—the person sitting next to you & the leaf of grass alike.

We are bound to taking the world less seriously.

We ask you to stop & see how silly all this is.

Smiling is fine—but laughter is key. We are Jokerman. Here we are.

We walk—shoulder touching shoulder—all together & all by our-selves—to the western edge of the continent, amid constant reminders that we don't know really where we are or how high. I mean, the con-tinent ends where the water begins, but the water keeps rolling in & out, never holding still. Not to mention, some will have us believe Earth's surface rises & falls by twelve inches over the course of a day depending upon the position of the moon—but if that's true, why isn't the ground now breaking beneath us? Maybe it's already broken. [*We lost our train of thought.*]

Ankle deep in sea foam, we keep walking—staring out as far as we can see—until the planet's bend veers down & away from you & you can see no farther without filling in what's out there with your imagination—I think I see Japan.

We've been to the ocean before, but never feeling it this way. The Pacific Ocean doesn't care how old you are & today someone says to her-self, *all I can think about is I'm turning twenty-two & wondering if I'll start to feel old.*

Press us to make some sense of this. Make us describe what is happen-ing. Say you'll stop listening if we don't put it all together in this instant. In that case, we will tell you this: We see what's going on as a sense of renewal—a sudden rejuvenation—a finding of the energy to go back & face the world more ocean-like—a sense of recovering something description defying & longtime lost. When we're here, it's almost like we have it back: our childhood smile.

Part I

Smile

Chapter 1: In which we give our soul to you

Live happy.

Chapter 2: 1968

1968—The time, its sights & sounds—Stop! Look! Listen! *NOW VIBRATE!* Lavender Pop Tarts & Mr. Magoo—raspberry faces swirl in you. Open up your eyes, the skies above your head are real & kaleido-scope streetlights measure what you feel.

1967—Outside their tiny apartment on Fell Street along the Panhandle of Golden Gate Park, autumn is the song that plays along with the sea-sonal changes it brings, which are hardly noticeable in the City where the trees scarcely shed & the seasons blend into one another. With the exception of the cool, foggy months of July & August, San Francisco is suspended in a state of endless spring. If there is anything here that sets this fall apart from the other seasons, it is that the streets smell slightly more like eucalyptus than usual. The smell sticks to your shoes after you walk through the park & later when you get home, you wonder if the neighbor's cat might have pissed on them.

Even louder, love, Molly Seldom asks Carl Seldom in their tiny room.

Neither one is comfortable if anyone can hear them. Carl trips over air once more in the dark in search of the radio volume knob.

Carl's older brother—whom we call Uncle Richard, even though he is still more than nine months away from becoming an uncle—arrived a few days earlier out of the clear baby blue with two wadded up pieces of paper clutched tightly in his hand. *At first, we thought he's gone AWOL from the U.S. Army—from Fort Bragg, from Vietnam—but one of the slips of paper he brings us cites medical reasons for his honorable discharge, though it doesn't mention what his condition is. The second wad was torn from an envelope—the Christmas card we sent him last year—the part of the envelope with the label for our return address. This is how he found where we live. Have we been married a year already?*

I don't know, he's—Molly searches for the word least likely to offend Carl, she & her husband sneaking off into the kitchen together to talk about the outward demeanor & slow speech of their sudden visitor. At last, she finds the word she wants & it slips out of her—*funny*. She says it sighing, with kid gloves. He is her husband's brother, after all.

But she's right—Uncle Richard returns from the Army with a different soul than he had when he left. Carl Seldom, too, is at a loss to explain why Uncle Richard now seems other than himself. Neither Molly nor Carl know what else to say, though Molly asks the question that matters most at the moment: *So how long is he going to stay?*

The *funny*, as Molly thinks of them, hear voices. If Uncle Richard is hearing voices, they are singing rather than speaking. They sing bouncy *yeah-yeah* songs in Merseyside accents.

Uncle Richard returns from the Army hungry—not for food or for lovin—but for the radio. The radio, too, is not enough to satisfy Uncle Richard until it plays something Beatles. You can almost hear his heart racing & see the hair on the back of his neck stand on end as the Beatles over the radio waft in through his ears.

So where there is hardly enough space for Molly & Carl in their tiny Fell Street apartment, Uncle Richard cramps everything—disrupting much of the newlyweds' privacy. They ask him if he will be staying much longer & he replies by humming a tune neither one of them can recognize. After his first week of sleeping on the raggedy, third-maybe-fourth-hand sofa, he gives no signs of leaving anytime soon. He sits, staring blankly at walls that Molly & Carl are still too new to their apartment (despite having lived there a year) to have decorated.

He sits there, jumpy, nervous; he has no idea why. He sits & listens to the transistor radio hour after hour, waiting for them to play the Beatles again. Weeks will pass, then months & mysterious government checks will arrive for him at their address & he will cash them & buy a hi-fi record player from Sears & some Beatle LPs & 45s, which he will then spin endlessly. He will mouth the words to the songs, lying on the floor, staring at the ceiling late into the night. He drifts & dreams & recalls fondly *summers on the Isle of Wight & grandchildren on your knee*, even though nothing of the sort—nothing Beatles—ever really happened to him.

[After midnight, Carl Seldom, stumbling through the room in the dark looking for a light switch so he can turn off the hi-fi, will trip over his brother. He never would see Uncle Richard lying there or even hear him breathing. The fall will throw Carl's back out & he will spend the rest of the week in bed with sciatica.]

When does it happen? When do we reach the point when we stop being polite? When do we decide to throw him out?

Love, I can't imagine him wanting to stay much longer. I'm sure he'll catch our drift soon enough—relax about it.

Interlude: Radio is for free

When you set the record on the turntable a spinnin & drop the stylus onto its outer groove, sounds lined within the vinyl surrender to electronic amplification on the hi-fi in your room. You fill your space with music. The record plays into you & you alone—meeting your rhythm halfway & occupying your space & time—becoming you. The record you play is your choice & sound only travels so far. It's different with radio. When the radio turns on, the radio plays itself into everyone—all the people listening in. The radio plays the same to all; radio plays what it damn well likes & it reaches all over town. Radio lets you feel the pulse of the city. Radio lets you know the world outside your door & window is still out there. Radio has a pulse of its own. Radio never blinks. It's not like the rich have one radio & the poor have another. Radio doesn't care that way. You can turn off the radio & still hear the last song you heard playing in your head—like an afterimage burnt temporarily onto the inside of your eyelids, so you can see the sun even once you turn away & close your eyes.

Chapter 3: Up

Then comes the night when it happens. While Uncle Richard appears to be asleep in the rocking chair, Carl & Molly steal away with the transistor radio into their tiny bedroom. They turn off the light. They turn on the radio. They stand kissing beside the bed. Molly asks Carl, *Please, love—do turn up the radio.* Despite being married, they are still self-conscious about people knowing what they do in their room alone with the lights off & radio on. It takes him a seeming eternity to find the volume knob in the dark. He finds it, turns it up, then she: *Even louder, love.*

They carry on, picking up where they left off—*this feels so good*—rubs & caresses, clothing falling on the floor, stepping out of it.

The song that plays on the radio is not by the Beatles, though the group sounds like the Beatles—maybe it's the Left Banke or the Knickerbockers. Uncle Richard who is just now stirring in the room on the other side of the bedroom door can hear nothing other than a low rumble. He listens & listens until he convinces himself that it's something he wants to hear—something he needs to hear.

The bedroom door bursts open, light fills the room & Uncle Richard flies in—

Aaaaaaaaaaaaaaaaaaaaaaaaaaaaaaaaaaaaaaaaaaaaaaaaaaaaaaaaaaaaaaaaaaaaa aaaaaaaaaaaaaaaaaaaaaaaaaaaaaaaaaaaaaaaaaaaaaaaaaaaaaaaaaaack!

Shut the door!

Sometimes life happens this way, folks.

Chapter 4: The movement you need is on your shoulder

1968—One thousand miles to the north, the father of Jude, our econaut sister, pushes the envelope in a government-issue black sedan—speeding through April's slashing midday rain on Interstate-5 North near the Puget Sound—on his way to witness the birth of his second child. He can't seem to get it right—always running late, missing the birth of his children—but because it's wartime everyone understands. Guilt is creeping inside of him. He's been letting his thoughts revolve more around his second tour of Vietnam than his upcoming second tour of fatherhood. He's neglected the pregnancy this time. Funny how he thought he still had a few weeks left. *It seems like we found out she was pregnant just a few weeks ago*, he says to himself, *just a few days ago*. Time flies. Guilt creeps & time flies.

Jude's father now drives even faster in hopes of making it to the base hospital before the baby makes it into the world. Today, his mood seems strange to him—owing largely, he imagines, to a touch of influenza—that & the impending birth he is on the verge of missing. He knows that even if he gets there late, the child will never know, because he knows children just don't remember the day they are born.

He knows his wife will forgive him, because she understands what is happening in the world—she understands how important all this is. He knows his child would understand, too, if only it were old enough to understand. Outside the car window, evergreens blur with the rain & incandescent gray sky. He goes over them again—the phrases he makes himself remember, his *mantras*, even though *mantra* is a word he himself would never use. The word mantra sounds too hippie for his own personal scene.

Preparedness is how we win the war over there.

Preparedness is your best bet for coming home alive.

We are fighting the war for our children—no one wants them to grow up under a Communist sun.

We are fighting so that other dominoes will not fall.

There are more that he cannot remember just now—he has them all written down somewhere. Suddenly, it all seems hollow. They are just words, after all & he can't keep his mind on what they mean. Then he remembers—the reason he makes himself remember all this: the family ghosts, the ones back in St. Augustine. At the dawn of the nineteenth century, the family's itchy, Massachusetts boot heels began leading them away, not to the west with the popular migration, but rather southward. They left vestigial traces in Virginia, the Carolinas & Georgia & kept moving—generation after generation—a slow progression farther south, closer to the sun. Some bought fishing boats & went as far as the Florida Keys—to Key West, the southernmost point in the United States. Jude's father's branch of the family tree decided against going all the way & remained in northern Florida along the Atlantic side in St. Augustine. Jude's father grew up believing that the family ghosts were worth dying for; his American ancestors had made sacrifices so that he could live & raise a family in this world—in this time—1968. The least he can do is return the favor. But now he lives near the Puget Sound & prepares himself to fly further bombing missions over Southeast Asia. The family ghosts are far away. The enemy is even farther. Voices inside him are telling him to break ties with his past. They tell him to live in brazen disregard of his family ghosts. They tell him to live happily as an airline pilot in Seattle, which is a far cry from St. Augustine, with his wife & son & new child whose birth is taking place at that very moment. The voices tell him, *to hell with Vietnam.*

The rain battens down the world—it confuses everything & makes you inarticulate—even to yourself. He is driving too fast, his heart beating impatiently—wildly—in & out of sync with the rhythm of the windshield wipers. Trucks passing by in the oncoming lane shower dirty water all over the sedan. Then as if directed by angels, the radio plays a new one by the Beatles. For the song's duration, Jude's father loses himself completely in the song's calming piano part, its tambourine playing & drumming, its cowbell ringing, its absence of electricity, its seemingly everlasting fade out of na, na, na na-na-na-nas. He is surprised to hear a Beatles song he can listen to without instantly wanting to turn off the radio—as the band's music has become so strange to him in recent years. This, though, is a song he enjoys already—a song he senses himself falling in love with. Now he's wondering if the old record player works so he can pick up the 45 of this & play it at home.

He dreams for a moment about ditching everything except his wife & children. He dreams of letting his hair grow out, splitting for San Francisco, smoking marijuana & grooving on music like this all the time. He would never do it, but when he thinks about it, a laugh slips out of him. He nonchalantly raises his hand to his mouth to cover the laugh. He is alone in his car & there is hardly any other traffic on the road this afternoon & even if there were more traffic, no one would see him because the rain shields anyone outside from seeing in.

Still he is carefully self-conscious. He never lets himself smile too much, or laugh, especially not while in uniform. *That's no way for civilians to perceive their fighting men—it makes light of the present situation.* He conceals joy even when the only people who can see him are the ones inside his head—the family ghosts—the voices he must keep reminding himself to remember—far away in St. Augustine.

In the following moment, he forgets it all—lets go. He finds himself lilting off into the freeway exit, falling in touch with the world—the billboards & buildings along the side of the freeway, the misty evergreen Olympics to the northeast, the blanched sunlight filtering through the clouds, the damp air he is breathing. Then on the radio, they are playing that new Beatles song again as an encore performance. The station had been deluged with telephone requests to play the song once more; the people want to hear it. It's an all right song for these haywire times, they say, a soothing influence speaking to the internal & the external—calm & peace.

Yet these days the word *peace* has a hollow ring. These days the word *peace* is overused. It's a way for boys with long hair to meet girls in beads.

Later on, he will not remember anything else they played on the radio that day. Nor will he remember anything else he was thinking about. Jude's father arrives at the McChord AFB hospital ten minutes after the birth. This time, *it's a daughter*. The nurses have washed her; her mother is holding her; the baby is not crying. They even tell you she never cried. When her father first holds her, she looks as if she wants to cry, then doesn't. All he feels is happiness & that new Beatles song is not far from his mind—he can't seem to shake that song out of his head.

When it comes time to name their newborn daughter, he wants to give her the not-exactly-run-of-the-mill name Jude in appreciation of his moment in the car, driving as fast as he could through the rain to welcome her into the world & hearing the Beatles on the radio. While Jude's mother has a list of names she would rather give her daughter, she mistakenly thinks Jude is a family name on the St. Augustine side. Knowing how important her husband's family is to him, she easily agrees on Jude as the baby's name.

Jude is a Catholic name, *though we are not Catholic*—a boy's name, *though she is not a boy*—but none of that matters. Naming her Jude is a spontaneous act—one of his first & one of his last.

The world is not at peace. MLK is gone & RFK has only a few days left. Leave it to the Beatles, however, to take a sad song & make it better.

August 1971—On his third tour of Vietnam, Jude's father's plane goes down over Xiangkhoang. His body since then is forever missing, lost somewhere in the Laotian jungle countryside. He is presumed to have died in the fire following the crash, though that presumes there was a crash & fire. One moment his plane is on radar—the next moment, it isn't.

Jude's father will never know that she wears her straight red hair shoulder length—just long enough for a ponytail. He will never know that she becomes a high school track star in Puyallup, Washington who never loses a race in high school & wins three state championships. He will never know that she attends Stanford not for sports but on a full-ride academic scholarship to study molecular biology, although she has no intention of becoming a doctor. He will never know about her escapades in spiking trees, her escapades in sinking Icelandic whaling ships, or her escapades in parachuting into snow-covered British Columbia wilderness on a bend to keep the wolf out of harm's way. He will never know how fine she can do without any trace of him in her life, except her name.

Interlude: Help

The Beatles are like chocolate & ice cream & make you happy. The Beatles are about love. The Beatles keep you young; the Beatles keep you going. When they were together, they were about togetherness. You can see it in their photographs. We have never seen a picture of four people who look as good together as the Beatles & that says nothing for their sound. Where would any of them have been without the others? The Beatles are about the help they gave one another, about crafting music none of them could ever have made alone—the four of them improving each other's songs beyond measure. The Beatles compare to none who came before them, except maybe the Marx Brothers who magically performed together as four. With the Marx Brothers, though, it wasn't like everyone in America went out & grew Harpo hair. Harpo hair didn't come into style until the Beatles & none of the Beatles themselves ever wore curls. The Beatles remind us we do nothing alone & together all we ever do is ascend.

Chapter 5: Oregon dreams & flying pentagons

1968—*Let's go, honey, to a place in the country where our baby child can run across meadows of tall grass alongside a black lab. Where come autumn, Canadian geese fly overhead on their way to Mexico. Let's move ourselves far away from all this—let's fly away from here.*

Oh, Carl! Why are you saying this? Why are you doing this now?

Carl Seldom already has it in his mind to move—no direction other than north will do. Convincing Molly, who is just now pregnant, is the first step. In explaining to his wife why he is choosing for them to relocate so suddenly, he tells her about a peace protest in Washington, DC that he learned about in an article in a beat-up, doctor's office copy of *Time* magazine that he read in the waiting room in the moments before finding out whether or not a baby was coming. By the time Carl read about the protest, it was already old news, people were hardly talking about it anymore. To Carl, though, the news was new & stirred a startling & unshakable impression. Lying in bed for yet another week with yet another bout of sciatica that settled in just after he learned his wife was having a baby, all he could do was think about it. The *Time* article detailed a plan by people, who the reporters described as hippies to storm the Pentagon, encircle it between 50 & 500 thousand strong & chant, in unison, ancient Aramaic exorcism rites, which would then cause the world's largest office building to levitate high above a tuned-in world & cause it to swoop into the sky & hang there. [Carl knows what hippies are—they are the people with long hair & painted faces in the park. *If they are raising the Pentagon*, Carl explains to Molly, *there is no telling what hippies might do—right here in San Francisco.*]

Perhaps what is most disturbing about *Time*'s coverage of the peace march is its failure to answer the fundamental question the article itself so poignantly raises: The Pentagon—did it levitate or not? Perhaps not having an answer to this question is what is rousing in Carl a desire to unroot. Perhaps Carl is right—the clock has just struck 1968—maybe the world really is coming apart at the seams & what's best for him is to take his young family & up & go, for safety's sake.

So what exactly went down at the Pentagon that day? Let us for a moment leave Carl Seldom & the pages of *Time* & hear for ourselves the voices of people who attended Pentagon Saturday: What happened when they looked up into that blindingly overcast Virginia sky in 1967 when the world was watching?

It's all true—if you blinked, though, you missed it.

It went up, turned orange, spun around & came back down on its very foundation—amazing!

As soon as it rose up, people rushed in, filling the space where the Pentagon used to squat, craning their necks upward to watch it fly away. The land they walked upon instantly returned to its natural state—a swamp—& people got their shoes stuck in the muck.

I was glad to see it come down gently & not hurt anybody.

One gentleman had been in a first floor restroom when the building separated from the floor. There he was—suspended in the air, dangling from the ceramic urinal, hanging on for dear life, his trousers hanging off his ankles & change dropping from his pockets, keys & a lighter. I stare up & he stares down. For an instant, we make eye contact & I recognize him, the secretary of defense.

I was at home watching the spectacle on television. I saw the Pentagon fly from right behind a TV reporter's back. It scuttled away—it turned five cart-

wheels—it flipped & flopped back & forth. The reporter didn't even notice, carrying on with what he considered breaking news—breaking news, my eye! All he had to do was turn around & see the real news breaking all over the place. They caught it all on live TV & never again said a word about it.

Yes, the Pentagon levitated, but it was not nearly so amazing to me as the birth of my two children, Alex & Winnie.

But these are not voices Carl Seldom hears. All he has is the memory of a beat-up, doctor's-office copy of *Time* & *Time* is laughing behind his back, coyly concealing what Pentagon Saturday was all about, even though *Time* was there & *Time* should know.

The voices carry on:

Altogether now: Pen-ta-gon! Has-to-go! Pen-ta-gon! Has-to-go!

We encircle the Pentagon & draw one collective breath. We let go all at once & that is enough to do the trick. The resulting gale shoots the Pentagon skyward.

The Pentagon floats up into the atmosphere like a helium balloon, the knot attached to a child's wrist having slipped.

The deal was that the war was supposed to end if the Pentagon levitated. LBJ even went on TV agreeing to those conditions: If you levitate the Pentagon, I will end your war forthrightly, I remember him saying. Obviously, though, if we were smart enough to make the baby fly, the Powers That Be were smart enough to make it seem like it never happened, so they could blitz out on their end of the deal. What people don't realize is that the Pentagon never stopped levitating. The Defense brass was embarrassed—I mean, we levitated their shotgun shack right there in front of God, the Media & Everyone & there was nothing they could do about it. So government creeps working for Nixon hypnotized everybody in the country into believing that the Pentagon never left the ground. It's still up there, though & will never land until they figure out a way to bring it back down & yes, we are all still under a government spell.

What we did was nothing really. Breaking the law of gravity is one thing— breaking the law of humanity is wholly another.

Yes, it rose up slowly—in the name of love.

It lifted up & went reaching skyward until it was just a little dot.

It sparkled; it was pretty.

My story is credible; I am a certified public accountant.

I am a blind person, so naturally I didn't see anything. I'll tell you what: something was in the air, hovering & eclipsing the sun up there. A wave of shade crossed my bare arms, bringing on a chill. Something overhead was lingering.

If we ever decide to do this again, rather than levitate the ugly beast, let's try a shrinking down. I will put our little friend in my pocket, take him home & plant him in my garden among the wildflowers. [Hey! I'm afraid if you did that, you would grow the ugliest & most vicious weed colony anyone has ever seen.]

Eleanor Cookee (who does so much for Jokerman: getting to the bottom of things, setting things straight, turning off the lights when all the others have left the room) remembers a professor of hers mentioning in class that he had attended the Pentagon Saturday march. She visits Professor Kahn-Hut during his office hour. [His door cracked open, she pushes it all the way.]
Why, Ms. Cookee — how can I help you?

Eleanor Cookee is direct to the point: *I remember you saying once that you were at the protest march on the Pentagon in October, 1967. There was a levitation attempt. I was wondering—did you notice anything peculiar that day?*

His eyes bug. He closes the office door. The answer spills out of him, like a longtime bottled-up confession that is dying to breathe. *Yes, it levitated. Let's leave it at that.* He then goes on, fidgeting, touching his hand to his face. He clears his throat, then rambles: *If you don't have the language to describe something, you won't even try. Saying a levitation never happened fits nicely into an acceptable view of how people want to see the world. The truth here (as it is anywhere) is always in the eye of the beholder. To answer your question, on Pentagon Saturday, I decided to give up engineering & take up philosophy, because when I saw that freakin motherfucker leave the ground, without question, it blew sky high every freakin conception—violated in an absolute sense all the laws of physics I knew & loved & left me realizing that there were further laws of physics that I could never, for the life of me, understand. I might as well have burned my engineering degree right there on the Pentagon lawn, like so many draft cards. (As an aside, I had a student draft deferment.) After Pentagon Saturday, all I could do was throw my hands up in the air & go home & live each day, resigning myself to a life of chasing my tail in circles like a dog, which is still preferable to designing highway overpasses & bridges. So again to answer your question, to say a levitation of the Pentagon took place is yes, the most accurate form of verbal expression I can drum to match my experience in Washington that day.* He comes back down. *I must say, however, that the highlight of Pentagon Saturday for me is still the Fugs.*

1968—Five months we've been married & now my wife is pregnant. I know this is how life happens sometimes—a part of the human experience. So why do I feel so unready? Why do I feel so uncertain about my place in the world? The world just suddenly isn't a safe place to live anymore.

Someone somewhere recently had said something to Carl Seldom—made a mention of Oregon: the state just north of California where cities lie along rivers, where the license plates spell out P-A-C-I-F-I-C W-O-N-D-E-R-L-A-N-D, though in very small letters. Something about Oregon is drawing him there—to a place he has never visited & can only imagine. Molly wishes she knew what it was, because nothing about the so-called Rainy Day Land sounds appealing to her.

Oregon is a place far & away from all this —a land of sense restored— a foregone conclusion.

Oregon is where money doesn't grow on trees, but the trees grow on you.

Oregon is where there is no tourist appeal, no Disneyland or Grand Canyon or Miami Beach, where people go only because they know someone or heard something or dreamed something. It's a place where literally a million or so Californian refugees will sooner or later follow in the Carl Seldom family footsteps.

Oregon is where maybe they will forget to forward your mail to you.

Oregon is calamine lotion, baby oil, eyelashes & lens caps; it is woolen gray leggings & green plastic boots, fool's cap pads, a dime store hairdo, Cleverset locks, ranking file, safety belts, knobby knees. Oregon is a drive-in movie in the rain. Oregon is notifying the next of kin. Oregon is a person who smells like a leaking tire, a dog named Jane, the deepest shade of green you will ever see under an overcast winter sky.

In Oregon, when the people leave the store, the animals talk among themselves.

Oregon has many sea cliffs & capes & the rainstorms here last for years. Oregon is the wetness behind your ear.

Oregon is a place to go & live quietly—to hide out from the world.

San Francisco is unnatural, unreal. *Just look at the hippies: they have no sense of what they look like & if only they could see themselves through all that hair, they would die in a fit of laughter.*

Oregon welcomes you, the sign says. *Come back soon.*

You think you know a man well enough to marry him & next thing you know he tells you he wants you to move with him to Oregon! My God! All of this sounds like crap to me. Why are we really moving? I'm so pregnant that I'm ready to burst & your sciatica is so bad that you have hardly been out of bed in months. A fine pair, we are. How the hell are we going to make this work?

We'll raise a beautiful Oregon farm child: a boy in Osh Kosh overalls, a girl in a pink dress & sandals. Just share this vision with me, love—a child running across a hillside meadow alongside his dog & geese flying overhead.

But why Oregon? Molly who is now seven & a half months pregnant asks aloud during the bumpy ride in the orange & white U-Haul as they make the journey toward Rill, Oregon—a town nestled between Portland & the Pacific Ocean on the Columbia River—an area where land is cheap despite its scenic beauty. As they leave Shasta & roll toward state border, all she can see ahead are rain clouds. *If we have to move, can't we just settle for Sacramento?*

Chapter 6: Tangled up & blue

1968—Rain drizzles on the early summer night when at the hospital the child is born. The birth has complications: the umbilical cord wraps around the baby's throat, forcing the doctor's hand to perform an emergency cesarean section. The child is born blue (although some might say *purple*), taking several seconds after the cord is untangled from his throat to begin breathing.

Years later, those of us who know him will imagine the scene: The obstetrician cuts the cord & the baby can see himself floating in the air in slow motion, hovering above his mother's bloody navel, from which he just exited, drifting above the hands of the hospital staff attending the birth. It looks something like a scene from a 1960s-era NASA spacewalk mission, a lone astronaut floating in orbit attached to a mother ship capsule by a hose, which provides the astronaut oxygen. It is the hose that keeps these pioneering astronauts connected to the ship & from drifting away into the vastness of space, alone with their breathing. It wasn't until the 1980s that NASA designed a space suit that didn't require the oxygen hose, allowing astronauts a greater degree of freedom during spacewalks & to become more detached. But by then, the solitude barrier of space had already been broken.

For Theo Seldom, birth is like floating in orbit in a clumsy space suit, his babyhood body, still attached to the mother ship capsule by the hose, the hose strangling him. Then it's cut; he can breathe & is set free. A hand then reaches out into the air slowly & grasps for him but misses. The hand tries again & wraps its fingery self around TS's leg & plucks him out of the air. Yes, the first touch from a nurse's hand gives TS the gravity that has kept him on the ground ever since.

They now live in another state—a newborn just home from the hospital rocks in the chair in his mother's arms. Then suddenly, there's a knock at the front door. Uncle Richard has arrived again, knocking more fervently the longer it takes them to answer. He waits for them, standing outside in the drenching rain, a bag slung over his shoulder. He's found them again & come this time to stay. They can tell by knock who it is & take as long as they can before answering.

Chapter 7: Our baby in the blinking sun

1971—Baby Theo Seldom passes through life three to four years of age growing up like most small, healthy & ordinary children sleeping, drinking, eating & playing. He is forever wallowing in dirt, covering his nose with filth & begriming his face. He wears his shoes down to rags, lies in the grass with his mouth gaping to catch who knows what & delights in chasing butterflies. His best friend is the family dog, a lab mix named Andy Kaufman—no relation to the other Andy Kaufman.

Theo piddles on his shoes, wipes his nose on his sleeve, blows his nose into his chocolate milk & dives headfirst into the foulest muck at hand. He collects wooly caterpillars in a jar with leaves in it & airholes poked into the cap. Later, he sets the butterflies free.

He hides underwater from the rain.

He scratches himself where it itches.

He tickles himself to make himself laugh.

He weeps for dead possums along the side of the road.

He chases cows & goats in a neighbor's pasture.

He falls asleep in tall grass.

He eats from the same dish as Andy Kaufman.

He believes he can teach himself to fly.

He pisses fullbladdered at the sun.

He is everywhere, into everything, but speech escapes him. He says nothing.

Chapter 8: Earth calling Doctor Spock

Dig the slowness, dig the stillness—the near silence except for an arousal of wind & leaves. Leaves in the creekside cottonwoods glimmer in the morning sun—dewy grass—a two-story farmhouse recently painted white; all this, seen by you shortly after dawn. Nearly inaudible sounds of doors opening & closing, footsteps: you hear clues there is life happening inside. The people are awake: brushing teeth, making coffee, drinking orange juice, eating Life cereal, changing the baby, changing the baby, changing the baby. Then, through an open second-story window, music plays—the room's sleeper having just awakened with Beatles on his mind. His first movements of the day are to spin a record on his portable player, drop the needle into the vinyl's groove, it sounds like a jet landing amid heavy guitar & drums like they do back in the USSR.

Early on, Carl Seldom experiences difficulty in fatherhood. He cannot feed the baby from a bottle without nearly accidentally choking his son to death. He cannot burp the child in a way that doesn't make Molly nervous. She whisks Baby away, afraid that he might drop him. He cannot change the baby without getting shit all over his hands, all over himself, all over the table & walls.

He is trying his best at being a dad, but nothing comes naturally. His ineptitude begins with the fright he experiences at his son's birth—a birth that takes place while Molly is sleeping, knocked out on anesthesia—while Carl sits in the waiting room reading *2001: A Space Odyssey* & imagining the horror taking place on the other side of the hospital walls. *No more babies*, Carl pledges to himself midway through his book, *not now, not ever*.

His wife is able to see past his clumsiness. She takes on more responsibility herself & shoos her husband away when the baby needs care. She worries & not because of Carl's ineptitude as a father but rather because something about her baby does not seem right.

The two parents do their best to understand certain aspects of their baby boy's behavior: why he seems so preoccupied with his childhood body, why he seems so preoccupied with his bodily functions, why he seems so oblivious to the world, why he always seems so happy for no reason, why he seems to think the dog is a person & he is a dog—& most of all, why he is not yet using words.

Children of other parents, it seems to Molly, are talking moments after birth, often giving a review of the experience: *Bravo! Good form, Mother! Pip-pip!* All the Seldom baby ever does is wheedle & gulp, sneeze & cough, smile & make noises from the other end.

Baby, say mama, say papa. Please say something that will show us that you can say anything.

Rather than say anything, the child sighs & adopts a serious air as if he is infinitely wise beyond his two-&-a-half going-on-three years & understands the value of silence. Other times, Theo seems disoriented, as if he knows something is expected of him & if he only knew what it was, he would do it. When this happens, he becomes visibly frustrated. Then he breathes, lets it go & becomes happy again. He rolls around with the dog.

Molly & Carl both fear all along that their child will turn out funny— in the worst, Uncle Richard sense. How tough do you need to be at times like these, when you are in the process of discovering that the child you brought into the world has a handicap? It blinds you— nothing else matters.

They avoid speaking about their child's silence. It is as if they are refraining from admitting to one another that Baby Theo still isn't talking—that maybe the problem will just go away on its own. They begin to second-guess one another, reading each other's minds without really knowing what the other is thinking. The silence between them is suffocating. Uncle Richard living under the same roof playing Beatles songs day & night only makes everything worse.

Finally, they have to talk to one another.

He gurgles. In a way, that's talking, isn't it? I mean, what if he's trying to say something? What if he's gurgling to say I'm hungry, Mom. *Maybe his gurgling is saying,* I'm cold, Mom. *Maybe he's saying,* I'm tired of all the rain, Mom. *Maybe he's saying,* I love you, Mom.

Carl Seldom just looks at his wife.

It's only gurgling, his look says to her, which is actually not what he is thinking at all. Rather Carl's thoughts are placing the blame inward. *She blames me because of my brother, believing that whatever is wrong with the boy, it must run on my side of the family. What can I do? How can I help what runs in the family? Sweetheart, I'm so sorry. I never meant for this to happen.*

Months pass & still Theo is silent. Life for the parents becomes worse, but still they try.

We can find a silver lining in that he speaks in body language.

Yes, he communicates in ways other than speaking.

We always know what he wants & he's happy. The most important thing is that he's happy.

That he is happy, yes.

He never complains.

He likes people.

We give him everything he needs.

There's nothing more we can give.

With this, the parents embrace, though later they cannot help falling again into their earlier fears & ambivalence toward one another.

Let's face it. The boy can't talk & probably never will.

That's the worst fear; it becomes even worse when one of them says it.

A sunny, spring afternoon & Theo naps while Uncle Richard is in the living room playing *Rubber Soul* on the hi-fi set, listening intently, concentrating deeply, while Molly cleans, sweeps, vacuums, and walks back & forth past him. Every two minutes & forty-two seconds, Uncle Richard rises from his chair, picks up the record needle & sets it again at the beginning of "In My Life." He listens to the song five times in a row. He returns to his chair. She carries on vacuuming, then stops, turns & asks, *What are you hearing? I mean, when you listen to the record over & over like that, just what do you hear that makes you want to hear it again?*

He looks up at her in disbelief that she had spoken to him at all. She never speaks to him. Then he responds: *The drumming mostly—I hear the drumming mostly.*

She rolls her eyes.

He looks up at her, realizing that she expects him to say more. Can I start it over for you? He lifts the needle & sets it again at the song's beginning. *Listen—*

Molly, who over the last few months has developed an intense hatred toward everything Beatles, becomes hypnotized not by the harmony or harpsichord interlude or even the lovely lyrics—but, yes, because of the drumming. She's hearing the song as if for the first time, even though he's played it over & over today & umpteen times yesterday & as often the day before. She curses that damn Ringo for drumming like that. Then as soon as the song ends, Molly retreats back into her world, vacuuming another room, outwardly bemoaning Uncle Richard's Beatles fascination all over again but now with much less bluster.

For Uncle Richard's birthday, Molly gives him a headphone set so he can listen to the Beatles in his own private world (which, in a sense, he is doing already). Headphones on, he lies on his back singing the songs at the top of his lungs. All he can hear is his own voice blending in with John, Paul, George & Ringo.

The rest of the family hears his horrible, off-key, howling whine, singing lines about *a hard day's yeah-yeah-yeah & love is all you need & I can't tell you but I know it's mine—in summer, meanwhile back.* Molly becomes so annoyed, she asks Carl to sneak into the living room at night & break the headphones. Carl waits until Uncle Richard is asleep & smashes the headphones into tiny pieces, sweeps them up & dumps them in the trash & in the process, inexplicably throws out his back.

When Uncle Richard awakens & finds his headphones destroyed, he begins to sob. This causes Molly & Carl to sympathize with him & bemoan whoever would think of breaking the man's headphones, as if forgetting they are the ones responsible.

Uncle Richard's sobbing goes on & on for days, its volume ever-intensifying. After three days, Carl & Molly can't bear it any longer, they are on the verge of going to Radio Shack to buy Uncle Richard a new headphone set. Then suddenly, the sobbing stops & Uncle Richard is back to normal as if he had no idea what had set him to sobbing in the first place & he again listens to his 45s & LPs from early morning until late at night at full-room volume.

The parents take the child to one specialist after another, the best their insurance will afford them. The doctors don't know what to say. They check his ears—he's not deaf. *You can see that for yourself. Clap loudly when his eyes are closed & he flinches. He thinks you are going to hit him.*

[*Now wouldn't it be nice if he were nothing but deaf. We could teach each other sign language, Honey & in turn, teach it to the boy.* Molly looks at her husband glumly. *We already know he's not deaf.*]

The doctors can't find anything to diagnose.

Some doctors say, *He's all right, he's just a slow learner, that's all. Give him time & he'll surprise you. I bet by the time he starts school, he talks just as well as all the other children.*

Home again at the kitchen table, Molly sits across from her son showing him flash cards & with great self-consciousness, repeats the names of the things pictured on the cards.

Dog,

Dog,

Dog,

Dog, Molly says, elongating the syllable to the point that the word hardly sounds like dog anymore. She hopes that Theo will get it—*it's a dog, like our own Andy Kaufman.*

TS watches his mother as she tries & tries. He doesn't get it.

They take him to other specialists, who, in turn, give a less optimistic prognosis: *Brace yourself for a life with a child forever silent. It happens sometimes.* [No.] That wasn't the opinion they wanted to hear, either. Who are you going to believe while the child still doesn't speak?

It would be different if he were choosing not to speak—but he's too young to choose!

Looking back, love, were we in any shape to become parents?

Let's not answer that—please, let's not.

If only he had died at birth—if he had died, we would have always grieved, but his troubles would have ended. It's a much more difficult life for him to go on living.

Please don't say that. She bursts into tears.

I'm sorry. I never meant for it to be like this.

They remain seated, both looking down at the kitchen table & not at each other.

In the moments when he laughs, she says, holding back sobs, *we are all happy.*

Yes, we are. Very much so.

Next morning, Molly Seldom wakes up at dawn as a beam of sunlight pierces a hole through the bedroom window blinds. Her husband is lying asleep next to her, snoring. She whispers in his ear, *I hate you,* not loudly enough to wake him. Then she says it again, keeping herself from crying, her hand flat on his chest, her head on her hand. The words erase nearly all of the times she had said *I love you.* A third time would wipe them all away—thousands of I love you's falling off the edge of Earth, dissipating into the wild blue, relocating & letting go.

Carl says nothing; he's asleep.

The dandruff flakes on his pillow become more visible as light seeps into the room & makes her hate him even more.

Interlude: This is here

Jude says she remembers being born. *Say what? Is that even possible?* When you are born, you have never seen the world before & wouldn't it all seem strange to you? Wouldn't everything be too weird for you to know what anything was, who those people were? How would you register faces? How would you recognize voices? Yet Jude matter-of-factly recounts word for word the conversation her mother & father had in the base hospital when deciding what name to give her. She remembers details she couldn't possibly have made up or heard from someone else: the rainy weather, the windows & the trees outside, the creaking door in the delivery room, the mole on the cheek of the nurse named Norma—it's amazing. Babies don't know they're supposed to remember & they have no need for remembering, for recognizing. Other people are doing all of their remembering & recognizing for them.

The Jokerman curious, always wondering about the lives of others, once asked Theo Seldom (who we will always know as TS) his earliest childhood memory. He replied that he remembers his mother once bathing him in the kitchen sink. Another time, he tells us he remembers watching dust in a shaft of light in his parents' otherwise dark bedroom one summer morning. He remembers sitting outside & seeing a bank of dark clouds approaching over the horizon & wondering how the Pacific Ocean got stuck in the sky. He remembers it raining inside the house one winter, meteor showers inside the house one summer. He cannot remember anything else, other than running up & down hills with the dog, Andy Kaufman. But then TS can't be sure of any of it; memories are all he has to show for his early life & if we know anything, we know that people have a way of remembering life other than the way it happens. TS is the kind of person who never looks back at his childhood, which is why he's forgotten so much of it & which, in turn, makes him seem like he comes from nowhere & his childhood becomes all the more interesting to us.

TS will begin talking soon enough. It has never been that he cannot speak—he's just reluctant. Even now, TS waits until he has something to say. All TS tells us he can remember from tonight is the joy of the flight, the arc. He could have stayed in motion, circling Earth forever in a continuous loop had the wall not stood in the way. The next thing he knows he's suddenly much older—the same age as the rest of us & aboard the Greenpeace goodship *Caliban* & sailing into the North Sea.

Chapter 9: A hundred-millionth bird flies away

The scene is a sweet summer evening under a sapphire sky & full of sound: moonless, windless & hot. The adults—four of them—sit in lawn chairs in the home's side yard where the grass is growing exceedingly tall from Carl's neglect. (*What the hell! Let it grow the way it wants! It's just grass!*) The four of them are tuning in to a shortwave radio & gazing up into the sky.

The night becomes too dark for any of them to see how much of the wine they have drunk & how many empty bottles are strewn along the ground underfoot. (*Watch out that you don't trip when going to the bathroom.*) The night becomes too dark for them to notice that the radio has lost its signal from Radio Sao Paulo & is now generating nothing more than static. The night becomes too dark for any of them to see Theo as he stands in the lawn beside them, looking at them, wondering what it is they are all about tonight. The night is too dark for anything; you might as well turn your eyes to the sky.

Carl & Molly are seeing satellites for the first time. Their visitor, Carl Seldom's college friend is pointing them out. He knows about such things. The satellites they see seem like stars—only if you watch them long enough do you notice they are moving—creeping—crawling slowly across the night sky—then finally seemingly touching down in the Douglas fir treetops that line the horizon in every direction.

Interlude: Acid in the moonlight

When the sky is clear in summer, you can watch satellites all night. The night critters are watching them already. As for you, forget watching for shooting stars. Instead keep your eyes opened & your necks craned for satellites. Trace them across the sky until they fall over the edge of the horizon—then go & find another. Then by day, when nothing else is visible in the sky other than its blueness, the sun, drifting clouds of the cumulonimbus sort, birds, jet aircraft leaving long vapor trails behind them, those same satellites you can see only at night are now watching you. Boo!

The invasion of space by satellites like those seen by Carl & Molly is a recent phenomenon. It happened in our lifetime, folks. Satellites will mean that the view of the stars as seen from earth will never be the same. Our view of space will be forever obscured. Stars in the past were fixed points of light that would rise & fall over the course of an evening. You would see them rotate on an axis around Polaris, the North Star. Planets were distinguished by retrograde motion as they would charge back & forth between points in the sky over days & weeks. Now throw into the mix these new counterfeits—filthy satellites. The ghost is in the machine & they move as if with a plan of their own & you can watch them while the real stars in the real heavens remain unchanging.

1989—The night of the San Francisco earthquake. The world turns simple then. We love the sky—drunk & lying on our backs on the roof of the Joshua Tree, knowing that tomorrow's midterms are going to be postponed indefinitely. All the world has been shaken up & returned to its natural state. There is not a street light for a hundred miles. We had forgotten that night is supposed to be so dark, so used to the City we have become.

Tonight you can see the stars, all the stars—the sky as seen by settlers & ancients alike. It's a John Muir kind of sky, but the moment loses its purity because among the stars you can see satellites, too, drifting along their way & ruining the enchantment—satellites & an occasional news helicopter.

39

Chapter 10: Response & responsibility

1971—Earlier that same day, Theo formed his first word. It was in the morning, after breakfast. *All right*, Baby says. He says it, though, not within any kind of context—not as a comment or response to anything in particular. Does anyone even know if Theo knows what *all right* means?

The first time he says it, his father could call it an accident: Baby is making a sound that this time happens to be a word, but since Baby makes a number of sounds—none of which happen to be words—this is probably not anything.

Theo then says it again—*all right*—pronouncing the word perfectly— as if to confirm his father's sentiments, though by confirming them, he contradicts them.

Suddenly, it occurs to the father (& the mother, who is there in the room as well) that this is something other than random sound making. The question now is where does this phrase come from? *All right* is a phrase neither parent uses frequently. Nor does the child have any interest in television or radio where newscasters & disk jockeys might say *all right.* Nor is *all right* a phrase on one of the flash cards Molly uses in hopes of drilling words like cat into their child's not-yet-existent vocabulary. (For first words he picks difficult ones, as the l & r sounds upon which all right are built around are notoriously difficult for young speakers & Theo says the phrase perfectly. Carl just wants to know where the word comes from.)

All right. Theo says it once more, but this time the parents notice something: an aspect of the inflection, something subtle: *Why, I never—it's a trace of a British accent.*

Now they know the source of Theo's all right. Knowing the source hurts. Beatles songs are working their way into Theo's head. Beatles songs are working their way into Baby's head even before we have a chance to teach him his name or to say *cat* or to say *I love you, Mom.*

As parents, you blame each other & you blame yourselves & you bring yourselves to the point where you cannot bear to say anything to one another again.

So the house falls again into silence, which lasts a mere few hours until that afternoon when Carl Seldom's college friend drops by, appearing from out of the blue. His arrival has the family speaking again, except for Theo who is now no longer saying anything—not even *all right.* They grin & laugh & give off the air of being happy when they greet their guest.

It's when Carl greets his old chum on the front lawn between the driveway & the filbert tree that Molly begins to notice how her husband's appearance has changed these past few years. He now wears his hair longer & a wild mustache hides his mouth completely when he's grinning, though his eyes still give him away—they curl up & grin for him. Carl is someone who laughs through his eyes & he's so happy his friend who he hasn't seen in forever drove all this way just to surprise him. *Yes, how nice it is to have company. How much nicer it would have been (for me) to know about it beforehand—I would have cleaned the house.*

How much nicer it would be if they include me in their conversation. Instead they huddle, as if everything between them is so secret. I understand that it's been ages since they've seen each other, but please understand where I'm coming from. I'm here, too. It's not fair to treat me as if I'm not. We are living so by ourselves here; I never asked for this. I miss seeing the faces of other

*people. You pass them on the street & wonder just what it is a person is about.
I miss watching people. I miss California & the City. What exactly was Carl
running from? He freaked out because he thought the world was freaking
out. Now we're here & life goes on. Now we've been here a while & we're
losing the sense of why we came. Was there ever a reason, really? Is it too late
for us to go home?*

That night on the lawn while the adults drink wine & gaze skyward,
Theo roams among them all looking into the adult faces in the dark.
The dog, Andy Kaufman, is his constant companion, always at his side.
Even without any other light than what is radiating from the stars, he
sees how dark the wine is making the lips of his mother & father & the
college friend & Uncle Richard. Their voices sound funny. They seem
funny. He can smell wine any time anyone breathes. He & Andy
Kaufman are now alone in the world wondering where the others have
gone, even though they're still here.

Off alone now, several feet away from the others, Theo blows soap bubbles in the dark. On occasion, stray light from who knows where—
maybe from stars & satellites—catches the bubbles. Starlight glistens
through the bubble's fragile rainbow shell as they float away into the
dark air. The others—the adults—continue sitting in their lawn chairs
sharing silence between them. All the other summer evening sounds—
the insects & the frogs—have died down. The only sounds now comes
from the bubbles as they burst after catching a draft of air that doesn't
like them & the stationless radio nobody seems to remember to turn off.

Every so often, Baby will climb atop people's laps. Sometimes he will try
to climb over them as if he were using people as a ladder to climb somewhere higher. You have to catch him before he crawls over your shoulder & up into the air. Then he will go away for a spell & blow more soap
bubbles in the dark. Then he will linger around the adults again, not
doing anything & not saying anything.

Molly? Molly? Molly? Molly?

Molly cannot hear you just now. She's tuning in elsewhere. Off she flies
into her own world—the world of what's on her mind, where it's daylight & she is sitting at the kitchen table reading the morning's mail that
has just now arrived. Over the past several months, Molly has been cor-
responding regularly with a friend of hers from college who also lives
in Oregon—though 300 miles away in the southern part of the state—
on, of all places, a commune. Yes, it's a farm where women & men live
together as family, forsaking their own real parents & siblings & hus-

42

bands & wives. [They are important words: *Live. Together. Family. Real.*] In college, Molly's friend was called Meg, but now that she is living a dramatically different lifestyle, she doesn't want to be known as Meg anymore. She signs the letters she writes to Molly, *Love Shyla*. Shyla has two curly-haired children, Athena & Daniel; she sent pictures of them in a letter a few months earlier. Shyla writes that she doesn't know for certain who the father is or even if the two children have the same father. She further writes that raising children without a father for her is a liberating experience, that the children are happy & healthy (in their photos, they seem so) & that she, too, is happy & healthy. She writes that she is on a path that is both spiritual & fulfilling & that she doesn't care how anyone judges her, but in a sense, the act alone of writing to Molly is a plea for acceptance. Molly breathes in & out while reading the letter from her friend. In the last letter she had written, Molly confided to Meg (Molly can't get the hang of calling her Shyla) her deepest secret: her fear that Theo will never speak. Molly's family is older & in the process of dying away. She has no one else to turn to, no one else whom she trusts to ask advice on being a parent & Carl can't so much as hold the baby without nearly dropping him.

Molly waited anxiously for her friend to write back, eager for her letter. She wanted advice, perspective, anything. Shyla's letter had arrived early that day, shortly before the episode of Baby speaking his first words. The letter went on & on about Shyla's own children, seemingly ignoring that Molly had written her about the trials & tribulations of raising a non-speaking child. It was becoming apparent to Molly that Shyla didn't listen to her. Shyla's letters revolved around Shyla's own world. Not until Molly came to the end of the letter did she find what she wanted in the postscript & the advice was brief:

PS Just love your child. It's the best you can do.

That was it. That was all the letter said. [*Why can't Meg seem to get it? I already love my child. I love my child with every thread of my being. It's just never enough.*] But there was something more in the letter a second post-script, an answer to another question Molly had forgotten she asked. Ages ago, Molly had written about the teenagers who park their fathers' pickup trucks alongside the road & roam in nearby cow pastures on rainy days when the mist hangs low. They stare at the ground, searching for something. Molly even joked in her letter that the kids seem as if they are on an Easter egg hunt. In the second postscript of her letter, it became painfully apparent that Shyla knew exactly what the teenagers are doing:

PPS By the way, the teenagers you see in that field are looking for mushrooms, the kind that turns you on.

Molly's stomach turns over. She had seen those kids so often & it never once occurred to her that these are the type of kids who would do that, who would turn on. They don't seem like they have a single hippie bone in their bodies. They seem like the kinds of kids Molly hopes Baby will grow up to be like. She has spent so many afternoons wondering about them, wondering if Baby will grow up to be friends with them, wondering if they'll take Baby on their trips to the pasture with them, wondering if they'll like Baby even if he doesn't talk. [*Oh yes, Theo does talk. When she closes her eyes she can hear Carl Seldom reminding her, He quotes the freakin Beatles.*] Now she doesn't know what she wants Baby to grow up like anymore. She knows she will have to stop calling him Baby. She just wants Baby to talk, to say anything other than Beatle words. She just wants her husband to understand.

If you see Uncle Richard sitting in his lawn chair apart from the interaction of the other three adults, who are hardly interacting at all, you might say he's fallen asleep. Position yourself close enough to him & it's plain to see, he's not asleep, rather that he's humming to himself. Lean over closer & you can hear that he's not humming— rather he's singing quietly under his breath [*mumble, mumble*]. You can't make out a word until you hear a string of them all together: *Somebody spoke & I went into a dream.* He carries on, singing drawn-out *ahhh-ahhh-ahhh-ahhh*'s that sound almost like snoring, but, to himself, he sounds just like the Beatles layered beneath a psychedelic forty-piece orchestra playing out the rhythm inside his head.

Carl Seldom's college friend is wondering about Uncle Richard, who sits on a lawn chair across from him, quietly drinking his wine & now craning his neck upward toward the satellites & stars & carrying on humming to himself.

How are you, there?

In disbelief that anyone is speaking to him, Uncle Richard spills his thoughts of the moment—however incongruent they are with everything else that has been tossed out for discussion that evening, however incongruent they are with everything else in the world. His speech, slow & measured, is running out of sync with his thoughts: *We are revolving like a record, turning at thirty-three & a third revolutions per minute. Sometimes we can't feel them, we revolve so fast. We are always curving inward. Did you know the Beatles almost called their Rubber Soul album*

The Magic Circle? They got it—they knew what we are about. They told everyone. Just listen —

This surprises Carl. It now appears that Uncle Richard can hear the Beatles without even a record player or radio. [The secret that Uncle Richard knows is that in 1971, the air itself still clings to Beatles songs; they roll in with the breeze.]

Although Uncle Richard is addressing him, the college friend is not listening. Instead, he's staring at the house through an open screen door & peering inside. No one notices him staring through the screen door at the macramé on the walls & the handmade candles in wine bottles. He recalls earlier, touring the grounds with Carl, seeing Molly's watercolor paintings of forests & the Pacific Ocean in every room. [*It's not a bad life Carl Seldom has carved out for himself here*, the college friend thinks.]

What trippy notion was it that got you to come up & live out here in the boonies? The college friend asks of Carl.

Carl wonders about the answer, then remembers. It was *Time* magazine's report on the Pentagon protest, the levitation attempt & the whole world seemingly freaking out. Looking back now, those times were both weird & wonderful: weird because that was the mood back then & wonderful because they were the times when he & Molly were first married & the baby was born. Carl decided to move here with his family so that their future could be different. That's the story he tells himself. None of that, though, is how he responds to the question asked of him. *Following my dreams—I was following my dreams.* He says *following my dreams* the second time because he likes the way his voice sounds when he says it the first time.

The only person who notices this is Molly whose mood suddenly slips. Carl will never admit they might have been happier if they had remained in California where it rains less & the wind blows with less bluster, that Theo might talk more in a place where there is more to talk about & we can take a family day trip to Disneyland. *My husband thinks he's a dreamer & calls himself a dreamer. I love my dreams, too, but I can't live mine. I can't dream about moving someplace & just up & move my family there like he did. We will move again tomorrow to another place— Alaska, if he takes a mind to it. Rather than have dreams that matter in our life, I have responsibility: changing the baby, changing the baby, changing the baby. Carl is the only man I have ever let know me; I used to love his sense of purpose. He saw life so clearly & he saw me in it. So I obliged him. He believed I was the one—I remember that now—I remember him saying that. I never took the time to decide for myself whether he was the one for me as well. Now here I go, off to pick up the dishes from dinner, even though it's past midnight, because if I don't, no one will. It is my responsibility. Responsibility first, dreams later.*

The conversation ebbing, Carl's eyes follow his wife as she stands up & walks inside. He watches her through an open window as she picks up the plates & silverware from the kitchen table. [*My wife loathes me—secretly, silently—she thinks I don't know. She's gone to pick up the dishes, angry at me under her breath. How can I let her know that the dishes can wait until tomorrow?*]

Moments pass; no one speaks. Now perhaps feeling the effects of the red wine, Uncle Richard sings to himself more loudly & with greater confidence than before, [audible even above the ever-present din of early-morning summer sounds & the damn radio still on.]

Dig the stillness, dig the slowness, groove on Uncle Richard's shaky-voiced singing—some of the words aren't even in English!

Jai Guru Deva
Om
No one's gonna turn my world
No one's gonna turn my world
No one's gonna turn my world
No one's
gonna
turn
my
w
o
r
l
d
.

Now is the moment when TS's memory awakens: His mother, having finished picking up the dishes returns outside & pulls Theo aside & takes him into the house to discover that he's shit his pants—again. *You're a grown boy. I thought we were over this with you.* He looks at her as if he doesn't understand. He says nothing in response. It's a stinky, sticky mess—her eyes water—she holds back vomit. While she's changing him, the shit gets all over everything: the kitchen sink, the wall, the mirror. Somehow in this moment, she forgets who he is, she forgets what he is; then most importantly, she forgets who she is. With energy she is unaware that she has, she picks him up by the leg, swings him around & lets go. He splats against the wall upside-down; everything he sees turns willy nilly. He begins to drip headfirst down the wall, leaving a trail of shit on the wall behind him while his mother looks on in horror at what she's done.

Forgive me, please forgive me—

Gravity kicks in. He slides crashing downward onto the floor.

Chapter 11: Iceland summer

1989—At times people appear with no past behind them—you look up
& there they are. This week, the Jokerman 3 (for that is how many of us
there are on this trip) are on summer vacation & blown by the wind
under a blue sky sailing across the dolphin'd Atlantic aboard the
Greenpeace goodship *Caliban*. Embarking now are Willie Shoman,
Jude & TS, the Johnny-Come-Lately of the bunch, who just walked up
one day with no past behind him & there he was. It was as if he had been
with us all along.

The three are playing on the ship's deck. Cottonball clouds sail along
overhead. Jude & her Greenpeace friend, Katy, are showing off with signal flags, making their best impersonation of the faceless figure in the
How to Use Signal Flags manual & spelling out whatever words come
to mind. First, Jude spells out her word: R-E-A-C-T. Then it's Katy's
turn: M-I-S-B-E-H-A-V-E. The two of them get the hang of it, having
memorized the alphabet & their next words fall in quick succession: R-
E-C-K-O-N, B-E-N-D, P-A-S-S-A-G-E, I-N-T-E-R-L-O-A-F-E, S-
U-M-M-E-R, E-S-C-A-P-A-D-E, C-R-E-S-T-F-A-L-L-E-N, R-I-B-
O-F-L-A-V-I-N, D-I-L-L-Y D-A-L-L-Y . . . & of course, M-E-G-A-D-

E-A-T-H, for Katy is airy & educated & a terrific fan of heavy metal music, the more gnarled & yellow toothed the better.

Then Jude takes off like a jazz saxophone player flying solo:

VIVA JACQUES COUSTEAU
VIVA HD THOREAU
VIVA SEBASTIAN COE
VIVA BRIGITTE BARDOT
VIVA INSPECTOR CLOUSEAU
YOU SAY GOODBYE & I SAY HELLO

Rhyming with signal flags! Signal flag poetry! Now I've seen it all!

So off we sail to twist & turn away together with U2, whose songs flow into us, rattling us through to the hum. The purpose of the voyage is to make a scene with toxic waste, dropping a number of cracked & leaching canisters on the gravelly Irish shore less than 1,000 meters from the plutonium-producing plant from where they came. The waste is a highly carcinogenic by product of plutonium production & was jettisoned at a makeshift holding facility along the beach forty-five miles down the Irish seaboard where the local people lack the influence & affluence to protest effectively. All they can do is bury their children who die of cancer at a higher rate than almost anywhere else in the world & keep themselves in the face of the plant's parent corporation who deny that the barrels pose any danger whatsoever. Our idea is to begin where the barrels are dumped, don hazmat space suits, retrieve as many toxic canisters as our as our comfort zone will allow & then make our way upcoast where we will re-dump them in plain sight of the plutonium plant. What makes this a gig of gargantuan scope is that when our Greenpeace team removes its space helmets, four of us will be members of U2. In our line of activism, you don't get that every day. With U2 on board, God, the Media & Everyone will be watching. Satellites will beam the images & audio all over the planet & in particular, to our compats back home who will be looking closely at the TV screen, over the shoulders of Bono & the Edge, hoping to see us. A point will be made: The smile you send out returns to you—the same can be said of toxic waste.

The name of love is what U2 was about. U2 was not exactly the happiest, go luckiest of bands—Katrina & the Waves, U2 was not. U2 wore black & gray & never smiled. U2 tended to take themselves & their message seriously, believing that justice & freedom were no laughing matter & neither was the name of love.

"With or Without You" is a ghost cowboy song, if you listen just right.

"With or Without You" is a song about breathing.

"With or Without You" is a song about deciding whether to get it together or go it alone & realizing that whichever you choose, you will do both.

"With or Without You" is about trees not needing us & living on in spite of us, like the 4,000-year-old Bristlecone pines growing in Northern California that could blink & miss us completely.

I like the way the song starts—it lifts you gently.

The beginning is ticklish—there's a dowdy desert dog, a slow talker, dusty fur & face, settin about a-whistlin.

With or Without You is about free will & freedom.

With or Without You is about the universe & our place in it.

With or Without You is about God & letting go.

With or Without You is about surrender.

With or Without You is about my boyfriend who dumped me when he went away to college in 1987 & I was stuck with one more year of high school. I cried & broke out in pimples. I spent my senior year proving to myself that I can live.

Joshua Tree is an album like any other, made from the same stuff, vinyl. The needle falls into its groove, the record spins, music comes out of the hi-fi speakers. It is also an album like no other. *Joshua Tree* is an album you can plant yourself inside. You will sprout roots & feel sunlight on your face. In the sun's light or the undershine of a rising moon, you will grow. You can fall into *Joshua Tree*'s vision. You can trip through its wires. You can close your eyes & it will work its spell over your optical centers — it plays out like a dream, it plays out like a movie—it's the soundtrack of our lives & all our outlaw escapades. Set us to film & play U2 in the back. You can always hear *Joshua Tree* playing here. Someone has left the hallway door open, *Joshua Tree* wanders in to meet you. That's how college is for us—straying through sleeping corridors of dorm buildings at 4 A.M., when no one is supposed to be awake, not even the post-Letterman lush crowd or the early morning runners. You wander, restless from sleepless dreaming & then hear faint playing from behind someone's door—U2. San Francisco State University in 1987 is a university that never sleeps—someone is always awake—the all-night laughers & the insomniacs, the twice crazy & the less loved & not to forget the ones who are enrolled in too many course hours & are trying to get their studying done. SFSU in 1987 is a community where the doors are always open: To hear *Joshua Tree* anywhere, anytime on campus, all you need is to keep still & turn off the fan in your open window.

Joshua Tree is about co-ed bathrooms & being naked & not caring one iota.

Joshua Tree is about the moon turning red in grieving for the Disappeared—wherever they may be right now.

Joshua Tree is about how lucky we are to live & how lucky we will be to die.

Joshua Tree is an album that knows what it is about & even worse, it's not telling.

Joshua Tree is an album that stares you in the eyes & asks you if you yourself know what you are about. [We didn't then, but now we do, or do we?]

[Joshua Tree *came out around the time my dad died. He liked it more than I ever did. I listen to it now to remember him: the way he used to play it while his fingers danced over the keys of his IBM Selectric, he was a writer.*]

If you haven't listened to your *Joshua Tree* album in a long time, we hope you listen in again sometime soon; it's still there where you left it. If you can't find it, don't worry—it's still in print & reasonably priced for what it is. You might even be able to find yourself a used copy with fingerprints circa 1987 on the shiny, black dust jacket. You turn up the volume & place your hand on top of the speakers, feeling through your fingers the rumble U2 makes—quite unbelievable—the opening strains of "Where the Streets Have No Name." If when listening to *Joshua Tree*, you find it overly pretentious, or for whatever reason, you just don't like it, we respect your opinion. *Joshua Tree* is about 1987—we are turning nineteen—we are evolving at this moment into who we are today. We cannot change who we were, who we are & the part U2 played.

We have become the Joshua Tree & we're not changin back!
[Those last four words are spoken in Bono's trademark, desperate Irish brogue.]

It isn't the anticipation of meeting U2 that gives this voyage its allure. Back at school, wasn't it always someone else's U2 album playing & never our own? We are in this for the thrill of the voyage itself, the desire to gig while seeing sights & breathing air new to our eyes & lungs. The toxic waste stunt is okay, I guess; we are all about doing more on our own when left to our own devices & clearly, clearly, clearly, clearly, with less hoopla surrounding us.

Not long after we set sail from the Gulf Coast of Texas down around the Horn of Florida, dolphins swim alongside our ship. It's as if they know we're Greenpeace (even though we ourselves, the Jokerman 3, are not Greenpeace) & they know our opinions about tuna boats & they're cheering us on. Maybe dolphins are always this upbeat. They make us wish we went about more dolphinlike.

Willie Shoman, the only one of the three who likes to talk, asks his two Jokerman compats, *Ever see the movie where the team of scientists teach a dolphin to talk? Not just clicks & whistles, either but real, fullblown human speech—North American English, no less—in a cute little kitten voice. I think it starred George C. Scott.* When Willie talks, Jude & TS laugh—it's all they can do—their social preference is to remain quiet, but laughing is all right. This is the lingering image that people keep of the three of them when they were together: Willie talking, the other two laughing.

The best is when Willie busts himself up too. Willie is not necessarily funny: You can laugh at his stuff if you are in the mood; or you can laugh if there is no other way you would like to respond, just to show you're listening; or you can choose not to laugh but rather to reply to him directly; but engaging in dialogue is not what he prefers — he has become so used to being the only one speaking. It's almost as if all his talking is to himself—he thinks loudly—& the presence of others helps keep him from looking like he's just another lost soul on the loose.

Maybe dolphins always seem so happy because they are laughing at us. We must be hysterical to them: the hair falling down & covering our eyes; our flat, button up noses; our arms & legs sticking out; our opposable thumbs. Do they see us & think of us as what they could have become had they not gone back to the water? Or should we look at them & wonder what might have happened if we followed them into the water? That, to me, has always been the oddest bit about Darwin: *Why did dolphins & whales go back to the water after making it on land. Maybe it's something we should try? Maybe it's not too late for us? What I have always wondered is this: Was the decision to go back & chase fish around the water a conscious one? That a decision was made, does that not in itself imply a consciousness?* [The others do not answer. Willie's questions are rhetorical & Jude & TS are falling over themselves laughing. It's the picture we keep of them together.] *Here's another question: If evolution gave back to whales & dolphins their fins, tails, & snouts, why did it not restore their underwater breathing apparatus? Is it not hugely inconvenient for them to need to return to the surface to breathe? Here's even another question: Why do dolphins sleep with one eye open? You've heard that haven't you? I mean, if I went to sleep with one eye open, I wouldn't sleep at all. For me the first condition of sleep is two eyes closed. Even if I could stand to sleep with an eye open, the eye would dry out overnight, which is why, I imagine, we have eyelids. You would think, though, that dolphins, considering all the time they spend in the water, would have evolved right out of eyelids. They have no need for them. Unless . . . keeping their eyelids is just a way of keeping their options open . . . you know?* [As always, Willie then ties together everything on his mind to the subject of dreams.] *Maybe humans & dolphins have eyelids for no other reason than having built in movie screens for projecting their dreams onto.* [Now Willie becomes quiet as he gives his thoughts consideration, wondering if eyes are a source of light that shines only when the eyelids close, like the light in the refrigerator but opposite. The insides of eyelids as screens where dream movies play—this explains so much—rapid eye movement & the like.]

Willie, a biology major at SFSU, is hardly a devoted student. He frequently overloads himself with units, then counts the days down from the beginning to the end of a semester, finishing up with a low C average. All he wants from a report card is to see the words at the bottom: Academic status—undergraduate good standing. That way he could get the financial aid that would allow him to keep going to school. Then at the last minute before the new semester starts, he would give the financial aid money back & take off the next semester to camp for three months—to live wildly—to hike sections of the Pacific Crest trail he has never ventured into before, following in the footsteps of the inimitable John Muir.

He loves telling people about what he calls the wilderness gene. According to Willie, there will come a day when scientists will be able to trace the wilderness gene through a person's DNA; but that will be a worthless activity because it won't help anyone sell anything, except maybe trail mix. People who have the wilderness gene know it without any testing of their DNA because they can feel it in their bones. The wilderness gene gives people a burning desire to sleep outside as if sleeping indoors would cause you to suffocate. You sleep at night with the window cracked open, even during winter in Michigan. Gas heat seems strange. Air conditioning is unspeakable; it tampers with oxygen &

gives you a sore throat. The wilderness gene draws you outside, into the wild, where you can live. The wilderness gene also gives people a feeling when they are out in the wilderness that it is not the same as it once was. You have visions of the way it used to be: wild lands teeming with life. This is not to say they aren't teeming now—you just imagine the wildlife of today exponentially magnified. You can see it projected onto the insides of your eyelids: day turns into night as 100 million geese fly overhead & eclipse the sun's light. When millions of animals die because of human disruptions to their habitat, you feel ripples in the shape & spin. The wilderness gene lets you feel it. You want to change what you can or run away from everything.

As if Willie hasn't already talked your ear off about God knows what, he carries on, now telling you about a dream gene. He never explains it in such a way that we fully understand what he is saying. More than likely, he doesn't understand half of what he is saying either—figuring out everything while the words are flowing out of his mouth. In rare moments, he becomes tired of hearing himself & he grins & lets you do all the talking; he wants to hear what you think about the dream gene & if you don't talk to him, he will just grin at you & imagine what you might say if you were saying anything. From what we gather, the dream gene causes those who have it to wish to keep their dreams close to them, to care about what they dream. Willie values dreams the way others might value fancy cars or real estate. Willie understands that dreams revolve around whatever is on your mind. If you chase buses all day & breathe in car exhaust trying to make your next appointment on time, trying to make it to work so that they don't fire you, this is sooner or later what you will dream about. He says them over to himself again, his dream gene mantras:

Live the life you want & your dreams will follow.

Pursue the dreams you like having. Keep your friends & dreams close to you.

Own your life, carry not much else with you & live happy.

The nice thing about the dream gene is that everyone has it — what you do with it is up to you. Willie chooses not to have bus-chasing dreams. Willie every night dreams instead about forests & running, bird songs & wolf tracks in the mud. Call him a selfish bastard; he wants to keep it that way.

All of us aboard the *Caliban* keep busy. By day, Willie, Jude & TS paint rows of the ship's railings, tie & retie knots in heavy rope, carry on monkeying around with signal flags & read from a box of old paperbacks: Dell Classics, Signet, Pocket Book & Penguin. At night, there are stars; beer & whisky, if we want; more paperbacks to read; Shakespeare's *Twelfth Night*. Crew members & guests alike keep loose in the sun, finding ways to laugh at everything—seagulls. Dolphins swim alongside the ship & laugh at us & we laugh right back. We are beginning to know what they know. We are on to them & their secrets.

Blustery, North Sea storms are suddenly on top of the *Caliban* for days on end. The world at sea turns tumultuous & gray. At night, the fog lifts; then the wind & rain batten down. Damp, thick air finds its way to meet our skin no matter what we do to cover ourselves. Clouds hold out lightning strikes. First, there is the flash, then a gradual dying of the light lasting long enough for us to read the expressions of wonder & surprise on the faces of the others. If the light would last just an instant longer, we would have time to re-read baseball scores from two weeks ago. Walk along the deck & the wind pastes you to the ship's walls. Over dinner, crew members yell across tables in order to hear each other over the phantom knocking, the slamming open & shut of doors that the wind finds a way to unlatch. Our forks slant away from our knives & spoons & Brussels sprouts roll back & forth across our plates. All day we bounce & imagine ourselves as baked potatoes inside the stomach of a galloping horse. Every waking hour is a rollicking, high-sea adventure —neverending.

Then late at night, the sea quiets & we sleep as snug as babies in the hammocks of our cabin the Atlantic seems to pause to snore & sleep herself. First mate Chris Corner, whose dogs named Sleuth & Leonard Skinnard always follow at her side, pays our cabin a visit. Her words come to us half as a dream. Before we even begin to register, she seems to be checking items off a list as she reads them. *We just had a call from New York. This cabin where you live, these hammocks where you sleep, the food that you eat, the water that you drink, the air that you breathe are all being given to a writer & photographer from* Rolling Stone. *My apologies.*

[*Whoa, whoa, whoa! Can you run us through that again? We were sleeping after all. Sleep is still running through us & our swimming skills are not that great. Can we wait until morning to discuss this? Do we have to leave right now?*]

My apologies. First mate Chris Corner wants to make sure we know how sorry she is.

Then she repeats herself: *My apologies*.

My apologies—My apologies—My apologies.

First mate Chris Corner & her two dogs leave our cabin & the three of us, wide awake, stare at the ceiling. Only Willie speaks, picking up as if tonight were several days ago, as if he had awakened from dreaming the answer of his most self-troubling questions. *Since dolphins need to breathe air from above the water's surface, I believe what they must do is sleep on their side, floating upon the surface. If they sleep on their side, it makes sense that they keep the eye above the surface closed to keep it from drying out. I knew there was a reason why dolphins sleep with one eye open—a reason why dolphins have eyelids. Imagine, everything you need to know about biology is already inside you & all you need is to ask yourself. All you need is to go to sleep & dream.*

So the new plan is to dock in Iceland, at the the harbor of Reykjavik. There, the *Rolling Stone* crew will board ship & the three of us will, in a manner of speaking, walk the plank. Disembark. Surrender. Dislocate. The *Caliban* will then sail directly to Ireland, meet up with U2 & pull the gig—a week later than originally planned in order to accommodate *Rolling Stone* deadlines. Afterward, the *Caliban* will return to Iceland, drop off the media types, bring us back on board & sail back to the States. Sounds easy enough—

We would like to think that our Jokerman 3 are having far too much fun together for a change of plans, no matter how sudden & drastic, to dampen their spirits. A farflung soul, Willie Shoman, though, can change moods in a flicker. Rather than embrace the new plan as a chance to see Iceland & to take ourselves out of what could easily become a rock & roll fiasco, Willie's mood swings low.

The Greenpeace crew shortly after sunrise, with the Iceland harbor on the horizon, contritely tells us they will return for us in nine days' time. Willie tells them matter-of-factly that we might not want to sail back with you in nine days' time. They say that will be all right, that they will return for us anyway & that if we are not here when they arrive, they will assume we did something else & will see us again stateside. [*Willie, why are you doing this? They're our free ticket home!*]

Goodbye, Greenpeace. Goodbye first mate Chris Corner & your dogs, Sleuth & Leonard Skinnard. Goodbye, Lilliput & Salmon Dan; Aleutian Sam & Beachy Kimber; Frieda, Evinrude Everglade, Nadine, Diamondback Cat & Rapid Eye; Katy & your heavy metal music. We will miss you all! See you in nine days!

[*Is that all of you? Good. Hopefully,* Rolling Stone *will have space to write you up after they fill up their entire next issue with slick, full-page Calvin Klein ads!*]

Then as we are about to walk off the ship, Willie hands them a note he had written to them while TS & Jude had their backs turned. The crew saves it to read after we are gone; they know ahead of time that it will be an earful:

June 23, 1989

To all our Greenpeace pals:

Despite all your good intentions, you place yourselves in the hands of a system we have always distrusted—the same system you too used to mistrust. When you raise millions by sending out legions of college students to pedal your eco-ideology door to door, something happens to you. You begin to lose your sense of having fun with it. Your hair starts falling out & not because of the toxins in the drinking water. You have money; you spend it. The people who gave it to you want something back. You are suddenly held accountable.

Dearest Greenpeace! Can't you see what you put at stake? Your sense of humor & your ability to laugh at yourselves! You have become responsible—Madison Avenue—you may as well wear a suit & tie. You have lost yourself despite your best intentions, become too big for your own britches—too big for the John Birches. You have turned yourselves into a breeding ground for wild-eyed expectations. You give yourselves away.

We at JOKERMAN, Intl. are a group of backwater birds. Our organizational budget consists of no more than the change in our pockets & a few dollars credit on some university library copy cards. Are we happy? Yes, thank you. All we ever do is go out & pull gigs on our own, with or without you.

Go ahead & gig with U2. See if we care. Ask yourselves who are you leaving to reach out & touch the flame. The ones you leave behind, that's who.

Your darling bud,

Willie Shoman

After reading Willie's note aloud so everyone can hear it, the Greenpeace crew breaks into laughter. They know Willie Shoman well enough not to take him too seriously. They also notice that only Willie had signed it; he had neither shown it to TS & Jude, nor would they have signed it had they seen it. This is Willie's way of letting off steam. He's a human pressure cooker, or he can be.

Ah, Willie—we are only doing our best. Our most terrible fault is that someone in an office in New York is making decisions for us. Do you think anyone here wants to be accountable to Rolling Stone? *We know it's a rag. Please don't blame us for that. Greenpeace ultimately is about saving whales. That's why we are here. We will get back to that as soon as this* U2 *gig is over . . . & on our next mission, we will bring a music cassette rather than the band itself. You can't just go out & save whales without boats. If you don't raise funds, how else will you pay for your boats? We know deep down you understand. We love you, Willie Dilly. See you on the up-and-up.*

Off the *Caliban* & down the gangplank, we spill onto Icelandic soil. Daylight shines through endless blue sky every summer hour here in Reykjavik, the Sundhofn Harbor. At this time of year, night never falls & people must find a way to sleep other than waiting for darkness. The three of us dazed, we nearly walk away from the boat in three different directions—to each our own stranding.

Together, what do we know about where we are? We know about crags & volcanicity & not much else, really. Just how far will we go on a combined seven semesters of college French, a year of high school German & a semester's course on the Latin names for plants?

I am glad you brought your credit card, TS, even though it was a con job when they signed you up for it. Can we afford three fares home while keeping under the credit limit?

Hey! When we're ready to go home, we'll stow away! Even better, let's build our own boat out of barrels. Even better, let's swim.
Senses regained, we walk away together lost in a world that seems at once wholly familiar & wonderfully alien. We have seen older, volcanic rock formations before, up & down the west coast of North America. Everything we see here, though, seems no more than two weeks old & new moss has not yet had time to find its way into crevices in the rock, in the joints between stone. Everything here is hot to the touch. Willie becomes calm—the ground itself will let off steam for you. We seem to know what to do—we walk. Wherever walking takes us is where we are going.

Away from the dockside now, we pass an industrial, harborside district, a section of town built from corrugated iron rusting in the heavy sea air, concrete & somber-colored buildings, fishing boat equipment piled under tarps along the side of buildings, crab traps, l'essence de rotting fish & a salty sea cat wishing for night, pausing to stretch out before us. We go, farther, along streets made from stone, passing people who never seem to speak—not to us & not to each other. We walk on.

We laugh & stop & smell a flower, then walk more. We see a café, stop & drink an espresso (coffee is the international language of love) without saying so much as boo! to one another, the air having made us sleepy & again we are walking, past the Salvation Army Youth Hostel. We stop briefly at the bank to exchange what little American money we have for *ore* & *kronur*, then pay a visit to the Stat-Tourist Bureau where we purchase a copy of *The Primer of Modern Icelandic for English Speakers*. We see American tourists & quickly duck the other way; there is no sense in taking the easy way out. We pass the RC Church, a theatre, a jazz-band dance hall. We carry on: away from the ocean, over hills, past the gingerbread-style houses where people live.

Oh, my—I just realized it's turned into evening while we were walking. That's why we are encountering no one. That's why the only people we see are like zombies.

Then the country opens up, the town peters out, giving way to rusty brown lava fields. Low-lying mist weighs heavily on the ground, gray air & no trees within sight, but light birds flicker & flaunt—there must be trees around here somewhere; terns & wild ducks—there must be lakes, too. We walk: rocks & more rocks, everything volcanic, an issue of steam from a cleft. Then at last: the trees—each in solitude—gargantuan distances between them. We see glimmering glaciers on the horizon, sterile mountains, clean air, clean sky, all the world seemingly steam cleaned—sanitized—Sunday sober.

No one is saying anything; even Willie is now quiet. Yet we are deeply in touch with one another. When all of your communication becomes nonverbal, you know how close the three of you have become. We camp that night between crags, laughing it off that we cannot find a site soft enough to sink the tent's spikes into the ground. Without spikes anchoring the tent in place, a huge gust of wind can come along in the night & relocate us to another part of Iceland . . . & that would hardly matter to us—as we don't know where we are & we didn't bring a compass—not that it would matter. We are north enough as it is.

Iceland is a place where you can reach out & touch the flame: its molten center, its seething volcanicity, its world oh so seeped in mysteriosity— heat welling beneath the surface. Iceland itself is a reminder that earth is not quite finished—evolution ain't done with her yet. [Nor us, when you get down to it.] We thought we could feel the pulse of volcanoes in the Cascades, around Mt. St. Helens, but it's nothing like here.

My boots stick to the ground, the ground melting the rubber.

I kneel down & place my hand on the stones, burning the fingertips just slightly.

If the land beneath our feet opens up, then what will we do?

[Go with it.]

We see steam popping from the ground at every turn, black rock & scarce vegetation—shrubs we do not recognize. Let's go back & get a rental car & go. Into the hills & far away from town, into the mountains. This is a sign, perhaps, to stop working so much, to stop worrying so much, to take some time off, to fall off the edge of the world, to read some of the paperbacks we bobbed from Greenpeace, to enjoy the twenty-four-hour daylight, to camp in the cliffs. Fuck the car — let's rent mountain bikes! We've been too restless to relax. If we want, we never have to leave. No one has even asked to see our passports since we have been here.

Next morning, we find again down by the dockside, beating ourselves up at the sight of two fishing ships newly returned to port & the type of cargo they bear. Horrified, we wish we could close our eyes & make it go away. In 1986, a consortium of nations banned whaling worldwide. Yet here in Iceland, a few feet in front of us, workers load their bounty of five dead animals off two ships into trucks. People pass by along the docks—no one seems to notice—not the way we do. We have fallen somewhere along the cultural divide. There has always been whaling here. There have always been whales.

We believe that whales need us to leave them alone so they can keep on living. We understand that whalers want us to leave them alone so they can keep food on their tables. But still, nothing can lessen our outrage, nothing can soften our reaction. Whaling is illegal internationally & the law goes without enforcement. Perhaps we are wearing our culture on our heart sleeve, but something is rotten in the state of Iceland & although we are here at random, we now have a purpose.

The least we can do is pull a wingnut job to damage these two ships at night, Jude & Willie both suggest, thinking alike & behaving calmly. *It's easy enough.*

TS, sugar sweet, laughs at them & then makes a suggestion of his own: *What's stopping us from sinking the boats?*

TS is one of those rare people who you meet & you want to remake yourself more like him. He inspires the best in us. Knowing him makes us want to become better people: more gentle & genuinely in awe of one another & in love with the world as it fills us through our eyes. This is not TS's doing. He doesn't try to win anyone's affection or change anyone. He doesn't try anything. All he is, is who he is. It sounds strange to hear TS talk this way, yet the suggestion is his.

What's stopping us from sinking the boats?

We have no answer. Nothing is stopping us.

We will need flashlights, bolt cutters, two heavy wrenches—how much damage can we inflict with a Swiss Army knife?

Interlude: Disquietude

1989—Jokerman follows no rules until Eleanor Cookee, who leads us by doing all the work no one else wants to do, establishes a code, posts it on the wall in the Joshua Tree office. She keeps the code simple as possible—the code is what we are doing anyway, although no one is articulating it. The code gives form to our former formlessness:

Avoid capture.

Hurt no one.

Detonate nothing.

[That's all.]

We careen in a free for all, swaying from side to side along the road as if pulled by a runaway horse. All that matters to us in the shape & spin is that no one gets hurt. When someone gets hurt, it's not funny any-more. Burning a tractor is all right, when the tractor is intended as a tool for the building of a timber road. Breaking the windows & pouring day-old coffee into computers at a primate research center is all right— we can only imagine worse horrors inflicted inside.

[*I will not confine myself to anyone's rules. Obviously, I am not about to go out & set off bombs. I am offended that someone is telling me not to, because that tells me she suspects I might.*

But what if you go & hurt somebody?

Listen: I do not need a rule to tell me not to hurt anyone. If someone gets hurt, it will be an accident or in self-defense. If someone gets hurt, it will most likely be me. I may have a long way to go before turning 30, but I am an adult & I know better than to play with lives recklessly.]

Chapter 12: Cast your fate to the wind

Your view is what's real. It's all you have when you are standing 8,000 feet high above Oregon & peering down into the gorge at glacial land formations, coiling strings of rivers & a large, unbroken canopy of trees. When you return a few years later, it's as if you have come to a different place. You peer below to discover nickel-, dime- & quarter-size patches of green missing from the view. The last time you were here, you couldn't see the ground itself—the bare, exposed earth—not below you, not anywhere—maybe rocks but not soil.

Today, Louisiana-Pacific & Weyerhauser are leaving patches of earth exposed to heaven that seem so small from here, though they stretch on & on when you are standing in the middle of one. Unless you hike the 22 miles it takes to get here to see for yourself, you might never notice—at least not right away. Barren patches spread like an incurable skin disease. Timber companies say that they will reforest & that will do the trick. They will pour more money into public relations than they will into the seedlings' survival. It's all a boondoggle, a hoodwinking of America. Newly planted seedlings are not an adequate replacement for old growth ecosystems that are complex beyond human understanding. [Reforestation never works when all you plant are Wal-Marts.]

1987—Willie Shoman, Jokerman provocateur, gets busted for spiking ancient trees in the Siskiyou National Forest, but that's not what makes his face fall. At home at his San Francisco address after his release from jail, a registered letter arrives for him, which he signs for, opens & reads. It's an official correspondence from the Department of Interior, the federal agency that oversees the U.S. Forest Service. The letter is signed by the Secretary himself, although the typist's initials are *JMB*.

What does Willie say? Well, nothing. Willie is not the kind to talk to himself when no one else is around. When he's in the company of others, he talks to himself incessantly. He talks to himself so much in the presence of others that those around him pretend to listen while their minds wander elsewhere.

The Forest Service thought Willie's quote-unquote conviction was, in a word, *soft*, so it decided to mete out a punishment of its own. The letter to Willie informs him of his lifetime ban from the National Forests of the United States of America.

Banned for life? From the forests?

[When Willie becomes confused his eyes cross & he stares blankly ahead.]

Willie's eyes cross & he stares blankly ahead.

The Forest Service shows it has a sense of humor after all—banning him—as if Willie posed any threat to the forest whatsoever. Willie never litters, always covers his tracks, never plays with matches & by golly, the last thing he would ever do is fly out old growth logs with helicopters, the last thing he would ever do is build a logging road. All Willie ever does is visit, breathe & thoroughly fall in the love with life & the world all around him & occasionally leave some fifty penny nails cozily nestled inside some of the statelier trees. He's not hurting anyone; he's not hurting anything. Banishment from the thousands of square miles of national forest land is unthinkable. The government wishes to use its hold over the law to force the Willie Shomans of the world into extinction, like so many a gray wolf or marbled murrelet. Willie won't stand for this.

We breathe in the view; we camp. *Camping fixes my back. The rocks under my sleeping bag hitting the pressure points just right.* Rain beats loudly on the tent, pitter-pattering; our food & toothpaste hang from trees so bears cannot get to them. We hike; we spend hours studying the native plants that we cannot find in our field guide. We follow animal tracks & recreate the story of the critters who passed through this way before us. We pick up after ourselves so well that no one will know we were ever there.

The trip nearing its end, the three of us return to the tree in the heart of the valley where we hid the bag of tools, glue & fifty penny nails that we drive into ancient trees in the National Forest marked for cutting.

The way it works is this: One Jokerman stands on another's shoulders, while a third stands watch. We stand on each other's shoulders to make the spikes harder to find & to keep the logger out of harm's way if, indeed, this is a tree that does get cut. With a Leatherman tool, the top monkey scrapes a small circle of bark roughly four inches in diameter off of the tree. Then she uses a battery-powered Makita drill to pierce the tree's soft, wet flank by six inches. Into the hole, the top monkey pushes a fifty penny nail in as far as it will go with her thumb, then hammers it in the rest of the way so that the head is nearly flush with the tree's skin. Then she uses a small pair of bolt cutters to snip off the nail's head so that anyone bent on removing the spike from the tree will have a bear of a time of it. She covers up the tree's wound, coating the inside of the piece of bark with waterproof Elmer's & then wedging it back into place, so that to the naked eye, it will appear as if nothing happened there. We are used to it: the entire procedure takes two or three minutes. We can spike fifty to seventy trees on a good day. The trees will carry on as if nothing happened. Trees can live with spikes in them.

The idea is to delay the cut. Maybe if we delay it long enough, the cut will never happen. We are not alone, either. A rogue contingent of USFS employees are on the side of the trees, which seems obvious; it's why they become foresters in the first place—& no, they are not on the side of the timber companies. These employees do not always move up through the Forest Service ranks & are assigned the grunt task of checking out trees for spikes. They help us out in nonchalance. They take their own sweet time in checking the trees & pulling the spikes & in the end, delay the cutting even longer. The timber companies live in a world where time is money. We are glad we live someplace else.

[One day, the earth opened up & squeezing themselves out of a hole in the mud & slop were Jude & Willie. They are manifestations of a planet that refuses silent submission & produces a Jude & Willie to fight back.]

Despite repeated attempts by the timber lobby to make this as dire an offense as murder, tree spikers do not get arrested. Then again, there was the time back in '87 when Willie turned an ankle & an instant later, two baseball-bat wielding Chevron attendants caught him in the act— seemingly redhanded—& subjected him to a citizen's arrest, which led, eventually, to Willie's stateside forest banishment. They tied up his wrists with twine & drove him down to the Wakonda County sheriff's office. They kept the handle of the baseball bat in a stranglehold around his neck should he try to escape. His ankle throbbing & swelling, Willie wasn't going anywhere.

Jude, meanwhile, was left behind at the scene. She is a current Pac-10, middle-distance track champion & for all her world-class quickness, can outrun nearly everyone. Willie Shoman, though, running for dear life can almost keep up with her. God knows they ran in the past—more than once hearing gunfire with their names on it. Bullets give you no other choice but to outrun them. This time, though, neither ran. Willie had hurt himself & couldn't run & Jude wasn't going to leave him there alone. For whatever reason, the two Chevron boys didn't even notice her & instead hauled just Willie away.

Riding over the bumpy county roads en route to the sheriff's office, Willie becomes peaceful. He considers not his pending loss of free-dom—meaning in a word, *jail*. Rather he thinks about baseball.

Baseball is a way of comparing Willie Shoman to Fidel Castro. Both had dreamed of becoming star baseball players. Castro had been a semi-professional, southpaw pitcher, dreaming of playing in the American pro leagues. His baseball dream withering, he turned his thoughts toward revolution. As an American youth growing up in Marin & play-ing sports, Willie became not Fidel Castro but rather Charlie Brown. Baseballs were always landing on Willie's head, footballs were flying directly into his balls, basketballs were jamming his fingers & all too often, he was lying on his back staring at the sky, an opponent's blow having knocked the wind out of him.

During Willie's childhood baseball career, he could not swing the bat so it would hit the ball—he could not hit to save his life. Meanwhile, all the other kids in Marin County Babe Ruth League who could hit the ball did hit the ball while Willie rode the pines. Willie then decided to become a pitcher & spent the winter determined to build up his arm strength so that he could whiz fast pitches by opposing batters. When spring baseball time rolled around, those kids who could hit now hit Willie's curveball—hard. Trying once again, Willie now went to work learning to field an infield position in hopes that he could keep playing as a light-hitting defensive star—the goal was to keep playing—to make it to the next level. One day while playing third base, a line drive smashed hard into Willie's mouth. After that, he played third base defensively, tentatively, pee shy—lithely getting out of the way of any ball hit his way & letting it dribble into left field. That season turned out to be his last. He learned humility. He lost his desire to compete against others. After that, he grew his hair out & back at his Marin high school during the early eighties when his classmates were wearing business suits with suspenders & matting their hair down with pomade, people called him a hippie.

Ease up, Jimmy—I don't think he can breathe like that. I think he wants to say something. Let the dogfucker breathe.

Jimmy—his name is—loosens the bat's grip around Willie's throat.

Willie gags, unable to get the air he needs into his lungs fast enough. As soon as he can muster up words, he has a question for the two fellers— not an apology, not an excuse, not any *sweet talkin* with an eye toward changing their minds into letting him go—rather just a question.

Gasp, gasp, Willie gasps. Then his breath is caught. *Ever play ball?* Willie asks.

[Why did the dumb cuss go & ask us about playing ball?

It's because we have that bat in the rig.

Shoothow, I remember back in high school when we were playing & carried a bat with us because we had to go to practice. These days, we carry the bat just in case of trouble. The dumb cuss really did want to talk about baseball. I liked him better before I knew he used to play.]

Off they drive with Willie, leaving Jude standing alone in the parking lot behind the service station, carrying in her backpack a bag of nails & tree-spiking gear. She's the one who is redhanded; Willie is whistle clean. Because the gear is not on Willie's person when he arrives at the sheriff's office & they have no evidence linking Willie to tree spiking other than the testimony of the Chevron attendants who did not actually see anything other than Willie & Jude stepping out of the forest & who know what they were doing by nothing other than speculation, county sheriffs venture into the forest & discover freshly spiked trees but find no tracks or other evidence linking Willie to them. Willie, meanwhile, is saying nothing. Taking the Fifth confirms to everyone that he is guilty, but his silence, too, cannot be used against him. [Everybody else at the station house, Chevron attendants, deputies, jailers, etc., are talking about baseball, about their high school playing days & last year's World Series. Willie has a knack for getting people to talk.]

Without other evidence, Wakonda County charges Willie with criminal trespassing—pure & simple—a misdemeanor for which those convicted rarely spend time in jail, a misdemeanor for which those out-of-towners who are guilty usually receive a ticket & firm warning not to come back.

Willie's case is different. While the charge may be trespassing, everyone knows that tree spiking is his crime. After Eleanor Cookee, who handles the books at Jokerman HQ, posts his bail, Willie is free to go. He then returns two months later for his nonjury trial, which wraps up in less than an hour. The judge convicts him of misdemeanor trespassing & sentences him to six months in the county jail. Four months of his sentence are suspended & should Willie participate in the Inmate Work Program, he can be released in as few as fourteen days. *Yippee skippee!*

[*Why can't you do something about goddamn tree spikes?* Timber company executives whine to Reagan appointees at the Department of the Interior. The bureaucrats make haste, drafting a letter to the only known offender on the books: one Willie Shoman of San Francisco, California USA. *This letter will surely send a message.*]

Chapter 13: A little doghouse in your soul

His reputation spreads by word of mouth & from the sign down by the highway. So wonderful are his doghouses, they become an international phenomenon—last month he even had an order from Japan! Bill Taylor lives with his family along Highway 20 in Eddyville, a nook of land along Oregon's Coastal Range. In these parts romp many of the mangiest dogs in the state—stinky, sloppy, mud-footed dogs made mangier because of all the rain. Some years it rains 200 inches. Shelter here is a basic need for human & dog alike. It makes sense that everyone here owns a doghouse. Since Bill Taylor is best at making them, it makes sense that everyone owns a Bill Taylor™ Signature Doghouse. It starts off with the customized shed business he runs out of his home. Next comes the sign along the road: *Customized sheds. Low-low prices.* The finer print below says more: *Also Available: Genuine! Truly Top-Flight Doghouses!* The traveler passing through between Corvallis & Newport stops at the red, blinking light near the train tracks in Eddyville. On days when the rain ebbs enough to see some of the world beyond the windshield, the traveler may take a look around at people's property—not too different from anyone else's along this stretch of highway: the washing machines in the front yard, the clothing on lines waving gently in the coast wind, tires on the roof holding down tarps (patchwork repairs to prevent rain from falling in the living room & bedroom), chain link fences & always a number of kids glowing in their wild-cherry Kool-Aid smiles, running around dirty & barefoot with a dog in the light rain. Then you see it: *There!—along the side of the yard, the dog's house—Will you take a look at that one?* It's the kind of doghouse that catches your eye & will not let go. The next thing you know, you are forgetting your hurrying ways, your 75 miles per hour through the curves & turning the rig around, heading back a mile or so to the place where you thought you saw a sign. You are going to see a man about a doghouse & you don't even have a dog—not since the last one ran off. You meet him—Bill Taylor & he says he can set you up with one custom designed to fit your dog & match your homesiding, paint & all. *Shoot, I can load one of the prefabs in your Suburban right now if you like, or I can deliver it to you anywhere in the state—for a small extra charge. [Of course, our own two doghouses don't get much use. Our dogs sleep inside, in the kids' rooms. The way I see it, no one should ever have to sleep alone, but damned if we will let the kids sleep with us anymore & damned if we will let them sleep with each other, being kids from different marriages & all. A dog curled up behind a child's knees while asleep at night—that's the way I grew up & damned if my kids don't get the same.]*

You are living a lucky life when your joy is how people come to know you. Bill Taylor is a cut above; he can hardly keep up with back orders for his Bill Taylor ™ Signature Doghouses. His shed business is falling by the wayside, but his bottom line is steadily on the rise. Life is good.

1986—The doghouses here come in handy for Willie Shoman & Jude that soggy day in February in the Eddyville backwoods when gunfire came calling for them. The two of them find doghouses, hide out & keep dry until the shooters themselves decide to take cover from the rain & cuss themselves a blue streak & let Willie & Jude get away.

1989—Life gets better for the others in Eddyville. A rumor spreads: A timber sale is going through. They are going to let the cutting go on after all.

Down in Waldport, I heard on the radio that Oregon has more ghost towns than any other state.

I know. I've seen them.

It got me thinking: Eddyville is a ghost town, even though we're still livin here.

Can you call this livin? David, it rained more than 180 inches last year.

The rain doesn't matter if the sale goes through. It will be like the old days again when we all had money in our pockets & the Eugene radio station had enough power that we could get good reception.

Not so fast. The Willie Shomans of the world are still out there. I don't understand those people. Don't they know wood is the best product there is? It's not like tobacco, which kills people. Wood is for people to build things— the covered playground at the elementary school. Wood gives us the paper for the books that children read, the newspapers that keep us in touch with the world. People sit—that's what they do. Wood gives them chairs to sit on.

[People shit—that's what they do. Wood gives them the paper for wiping their asses clean.]

Interlude: Saddest dusk

1987—Sitting on the roof of the house in the Haight, we gather & watch the sun as it sets. The sky glows red thanks to out-of-control wildfires in the Sierras & a train wreck & chemical spill outside of Oakland.

Willie is in jail & the judge rules to allow the contested timber road to go through in the Siskiyou National Forest in southwestern Oregon— within six freakin inches of the Kalmiopsis Wilderness Boundary.

What a waste of time this is—sitting still, closing eyes. Yet there's nowhere to go at the moment & nothing we can do.

We have seen the future & we do not like the way it looks. We are one or two Ronald Reagans away from losing it all—the green scraped clean—mudslides after every rainfall & worse. Think of dying slowly—painfully—by poison & you don't even realize you're dying until you are already dead & by the time you're dead, you're not realizing much of anything.

You cannot scrape the land bare without making it scream.
Listen—it's deafening. You can hear it all the way from here.

Chapter 14: The Willie Shomans of the world

Loss of freedom hits Willie hard. It's not that he ever took freedom for granted; it's just that losing it feels worse than he ever imagined. At first, the work crew doesn't sound so bad: picking up litter along the side of Highway 37. Then Willie finds out what the work really is: cleaning up a bingo parlor.

On the third day of his jail hitch, Willie refuses to go back with the work crew & clean up the bingo parlor again, choosing instead to remain in his cell & sleep all day. Because of his refusal to work, he spends the next nine days in solitary confinement, which is fine with him because all he wants to do is sleep.

Twenty-eight days later, Willie's newly appointed probation officer pays the prisoner a visit. During introductions, the probation officer refuses to shake Willie's hand. Word about Willie has spread all through the county. The locals know of Willie's kind but are never sure what to call them. Still they try:

Tree Spikers.

Eco-Troublemakers.

Forest Degenerates.

Interlopers. Outlaws. Scum.

Californians.

Jerks.

None of these names, however, fit *Willie Shoman* as well as the name *Willie Shoman*. What's more, the name Willie Shoman has the power of reaching far beyond Willie Shoman. It's not a name they see in print or hear on television or know how to spell, but it's a name they can use when communicating with one another—a code to signify all that is evil in the world.

Willie Shoman becomes Wakonda County's ultimate scapegoat.

Meeting lowlifes is a regular part of the probation officer's job, but as far as lowlifes go, this one takes the cake—Willie Shoman. He's not just another of the *Willie Shomans of the world*, he is the Willie Shoman. [He utters Willie's name as if he were uttering the name of the devil himself.]

The probation officer reads through the terms of Willie's release to the prisoner as quickly as he can, so he will not have to spend any more time than necessary in Willie's presence—as if whatever Willie has is catching. *You will have to keep a regular job, regular hours & report to your probation officer anytime you are going to cross state lines.*

[All Willie can think of is how probation sounds worse than incarceration: *I spend half my time where the state lines have no markings!*]

The probation officer hands Willie a pen to sign his terms of release.

Back in court to explain why he refuses to sign his probation agreement, Willie stands before the bench & speaks into the microphone: *Your Honor, please don't make me tell you where you can stick this* [the next two word he utters as if he were uttering the name of the devil himself] *probation agreement.*

The room collectively gasps. An audience of drunk drivers & petty thieves wonders quietly, *What is this moron about?*

So Willie goes back to jail to serve out the remaining four & a half months of his sentence. Word breaks on the back pages of Pacific Northwest newspapers, on NPR & in environmental circles that a wingnut has gone to jail. During his jail stay, Willie receives ninety letters from all over the country. These keep him busy; he answers each one at length. He writes songs on his harmonica. His ankle heals. He looks forward to being free again & rejoining the other Willie Shomans of the world—free & clear.

Interlude: The ties that break

Stumbling upon traps happens, often. The traps themselves never catch us, as we are tall enough to see them from several feet away. If the trap is empty, we can destroy it & bury its broken pieces where the trapper will never find them. Still traps catch us, because they are not always empty. If the captured animal is still alive, there is nothing we can do other than attempt to set the animal free. A live animal in a trap will frequently twist, tug & chew the limb that is stuck, often amputating the leg, foot or toe in a desperate attempt to flee. Some of the animals do escape & survive by hobbling around for years. Others die soon afterward from infection or starvation due to their now-impaired hunting ability. The dead animals that we find, we bury where the trapper will never find them. Most traps belong to amateurs & school kids—people out to make a few dollars off of pelts. Trappers frequently locate their steel-teethed contraptions near the road, so that they don't have to walk far from the truck in order to check them. By law, trappers are required to check their traps frequently. Often they don't in hopes that exposure to the elements or starvation will kill the animal. Freezing to death will leave the pelt undamaged & eliminate the need to kill the animal with a gun or baseball bat. When a trapper finds a live animal captured in the trap, the general practice is first to beat the animal upon the head, causing unconsciousness & then kneel on the chest cavity, crushing the rib cage so that the animal will die from internal bleeding as blood pours into the lungs.

[The soft eyes close.]

Willie Shoman does this once—the kneeling—having discovered in a trap a gray fox so near death that Willie wants only to give the animal release. The pain of having killed the animal, even as an act of mercy, stays with Willie. When he comes back he is not the same.

Chapter 15: Please stop turning the wolf from its home

1987—Jude slides open the airplane door & in the same motion, jumps out into what must be the coldest air she has ever felt. She pulls the cord for her parachute & floats downward, her senses overwhelmed by the white noise of the wind in her ears & the bright whiteness of the snow toward which she is falling. The horizon seems unsteady, topsy-turvy. Can she fall any faster into the cold than this?

In British Columbia, hunters cry wolf. Wolves are killing thousands of elk, caribou & moose & leaving none for the hunters. Fearing a loss in hunting license revenues & tourist dollars, the province's minister of environment calmly decides upon a plan of action: Hunt down the wolves & kill them.

Alongside two other women, Jude jumps from a plane into the Muskwa River Valley of British Columbia in the middle of February, the white parachute becoming indistinguishable from the winter sky. The three compats had outfitted themselves for the harshest weather imaginable, which is exactly what they are diving into. Once they are safely on the ground, the plane circles back & makes another drop—bundles of their food & gear. The plan: to remain in the forest until the BC government's Wolf Eradication Project ends. Jude & her compats bring supplies to last them a week a half; they will stay longer if they can have more supplies dropped to them. The key is making the wolf hunt stop.

Now a distant glimmer in the American eye, the wolf population in British Columbia is one of the last remaining on the continent. The plan drafted by the minister of environment would eliminate half of the wolves living in the province.

Jude is just a person who can see what is happening to animals in the wild & can think of nothing better to do with herself than to do whatever she can to save them. She holds no delusions about saving the world, rather she moves from the desire to save what she can. She knows the meaning of sacrifice—without thinking she has made one.

[*We aim less to move the world as we do to budge it.*]

[When called upon to answer why we care & why we act, we become infants: our speech escapes us—the heart is always inarticulate. It is just something we feel, like sunlight.

Animals are already in their heaven. They rise, they run.

We as human beings can create ourselves an afterlife—this life is theirs.

We as human beings find our place in life's plan, as it spins.

Animals only find themselves in life.

We find ourselves unable to help ourselves & unable to explain why.]

Women & the wolf—the media makes a big deal out of that. This time is different than in Mother Goose: the girls & the big bad wolf are on the same side & the woodsman turns villain. The night when Jude & her comsoeurs come on during the evening news, people watching at home can't understand why three women would risk their hides to save a few measly wolves. Why jump from airplanes when it's so cold? Why not write angry letters to the editor & to Parliament? When the story gains interest & piecing together the symbolic connection between the women & the wolf becomes old, the press wants faces & bodies, eventually finding & televising high school pictures of the three women. [You want anonymity, but someone out there has your high school yearbook & the girl in the picture hardly looks like you anymore.]

Piles of caribou meat lay steaming in a clearing covered in the fresh, white snow of the Muskwa Valley. Behind the trees a helicopter full of shooters is hovering low. They wait with their binoculars & rifles for the wolves to discover the bounty. Once the smell of the meat draws the wolves out in the open, the shooting will begin.

Waiting for wolves, the shooters instead hear *plink-plink-plink*—what sounds like the repeated hammering of a note on an out-of-tune toy piano. Over there, they see them—three figures in bright colors—two blues & a red—people obviously: *Why the hell are they out there?* Through the binoculars, they take a closer look to see that one of the people, too bundled to determine a gender, is holding a gun, the pistol almost too small for the hand & pointing the gun skyward: *Plink-plink-plink*. The little gun firing in the air is scaring the wolves off. The wolves want the meat but aren't stupid.

[When the truth comes out, it turns out the gun used to scare the wolves wasn't a gun at all but rather a starter's pistol, a souvenir from Jude's days in track & field.]

Turning the chopper around & heading back to Vancouver will mean losing the caribou meat, for as soon as they are gone, the wolves will eat & the problem goes unsolved. The wolves are still out there. *What else can we do? We can't risk shooting one of those assholes on the ground.*

Interlude: Ol Cypress's Jokerman Chronicles

If you would learn the genealogy of the movement that produced us, then I'd refer you to *Ol Cypress's Jokerman Chronicles*. This volume will provide you & your fellow readers with greater detail on how the great agencies of the environmental New Left were born in this world & how Jokerman descended directly from them.

Cy, your writerly host & one of approximately ten million Jokerman currently living in the contiguous United States, will lead you from the days of Noah's celebrated ark down to the present, capsulizing for you the years we spent together & some of what are the strangest things we've seen. Funny how they're always the little things: the dummyless ventriloquist talking to himself in the twilight shadows of a San Francisco streetcorner; the *real* black bear trying on a stolen, Forest Service Smokey the Bear costume in the woods outside Missoula; the night we all slept in a musty, seashore haunted house with a flatulent ghost. *It's true. I say this because in the morning, I caught the ghost drinking milk from the cat's saucer.*

Unfortunately, while the manuscript was in storage in the damp basement of Cy's aunty's house near Cascade Head, rats & weasels nibbled off the beginning. The winter rain falls in torrents on the Oregon Coast. It weighs down your shoulders when you walk in it. It leaves craters on your face & forehead. It sheers the skin off of your hands. Feral creatures nibble off the beginnings of things.

Let's take a glimpse now of what remains:

Barbed wire has withstood the cruelty test of time; anyone who's seen a wolf or coyote impaled onto a barbed wire fence & died there will understand this.

Historically speaking, the advent of barbed wire has kept wolfkind from killing livestock. Still some wolves saw the barbed wire as a challenge but not an insurmountable obstacle standing between them & their rightful place on the food chain. These crafty wolves left settlers & ranchers up to their American problem-solving ingenuity. The Americans defeated the wolf not mano et mano but by traps, poison & shotgun fire. The wolf has since this time virtually disappeared from the lower forty-eight.

What earthly creatures can survive an onslaught of shotguns, traps & poisons? We measure our progress by our cheating ways. With such tools at your disposal, you can strike down all of heaven's angels just the same.

Wild lands know freedom, a certain etiquette & American human beings seem to have lost their sense of it. Guns, traps & poison don't belong here. They throw off the balance. The wolf reminds us of the absurdity of the notion of owning sheep & cattle, of penning up animals & calling them your own. The wolf reminds us of the absurdity of the notion of owning land. Just because you can put up a fence, does that mean what's underneath can ever belong to you? These ideas are what push America forward & what push the wolf against the wall. The wolf reminds us that life & land are held in common, belonging to no one & to everyone & I mean in the best Woody Guthrie sense. The wolf will take what it can get—controlled ranges at Glacier &

Yellowstone. The wolf reminds us of the necessity of knowing your place in the shape & spin & taking it, though not exceeding it.

Over the last one-hundred years, communities of the West have combined their resources to kill off the last of their local wolves—or the danger to their chickens & sheep will never end. They hunt them down until they kill the very last one. We applaud the renegade wolves who continued their attack on cattle & sheep in America after the advent of barbed wire & gunfire & managed to get away with it. Slipshod Dixon killed sixty-five sheep one night. Rags the Digger ruined traplines by digging them up without tripping them. Other wolves who made such a mark that they were given English names include Maybelline, Hobbler, Two Toes, Three-Toe Clyde, Peg Leg, Plucker, Ol Blue Eyes, Crip, Lefty & Swimmer the Magnificent.

[Cy's writing is so nebulous—cumulonimbus. Do you know what I mean? I like never know if he's being serious, or if he's poking fun at everything & if he is poking fun, then he's poking fun at us.

He knows better than to anthropomorphize. It's an unwritten tenet of the theory of deep ecology: You make your case without identifying too closely the traits of people with animals or trees. You respect the differences. If you go & say you love the wolf, then love the wolf for its wolfness & nothing else, especially not its humanness.

It's not like Cy goes out & Disneyfied the wolf or anything. It's not like they're talking wolves—singing & dancing.

I like what Cy has written. He gives the wolf a sense of history. It's more interesting than a history of ourselves. Can I tell you how sick I am of the name Jokerman? Jokerman *is a sexist name. I am surprised no one has noticed the* man *hanging out there at the end.*

I just wish I could tell whether or not Cy was serious, but I have an advantage, knowing him personally.

Cy is coming from a disadvantage. Writing is hard. I myself have never heard a compelling, logical explanation for the preservation of species. The species-decimation-leads-to-inevitable-apocalypse theories all ring hollow to me. The reasons we love & preserve species is spiritual & the spiritual defies tidy encapsulations in language. Do you know what I mean?]

Chapter 16

Helicopters swoop down low, flying ridiculously close to where the women are standing. The force of the choppers' blades pastes them to the snow & causes powder to swirl violently all around them. A helicopter's door slides open; the man inside takes aim & shoots. Later the TV news shows images of three women walking fast in severe wind— the instant storm conditions are the chopper's own making, but no one can see that on TV & the cloudy sky diffuses the sun's light so the chopper's shadow does not fall upon them. Eleanor Cookee is doing everything she can to give the media what they want, so that they will spread the message.

Eleanor Cookee is always outside the inner group, which consists of Willie Shoman, Jude & TS, though Cy & Squirrel are becoming more & more vocal & familiar. Yet in many ways, the group is nothing other than Eleanor Cookee. In her freshman year at San Francisco State University, just after she turns eighteen, she launches a nonprofit organization in which environmentally concerned lawyers make contributions toward mounting a charge against legally dubious timber sales & other land uses that adversely affect animal habitat, particularly the habitat of animals protected under the Endangered Species Act. All that is needed to prevent the sales from going through in many cases is a smart, legal challenge (or the legitimate threat of one). Eleanor realizes this & decides what she needs to do is find a way to unite lawyers who care about endangered species with evidence of abuses of the law. She names her organization the Wildlife Legal Cooperative.

It starts with a few phone calls & then gains momentum.

Eleanor Cookee can't find lawyers in California who will donate their time; for them time is money. She does find, however, lawyers who are willing to donate money, which is, in turn, used to hire lawyers. Frequently, she hires back the same lawyers who donated the money in the first place. The machine is in place & soon Eleanor Cookee herself is not even needed.

The WLC grows & becomes self-perpetuating. It takes an office in San Francisco's Business District & Eleanor Cookee loses confidence in her ability to run the organization. She is eighteen & has no idea how to maintain the organization's nonprofit tax-exempt status now that business is going gangbusters. So she leaves the WLC to attend school & study humanities at SFSU. To Eleanor, it is just as well, because she was ready to move on shortly after founding the WLC. The last thing she wants to do is endless fundraising.

As soon as school begins, she organizes another grassroots troupe, out of her dorm room single, that collects signatures for initiative ballots. Within months, she meets Spokes (an activist with a trust fund who will soon burn out & begin riding his bicycle back & forth across North America) & Willie Shoman & Jude & Cy & Squirrel & the troupe transforms itself into the Jokerman we know today.

Eleanor Cookee goes to Canada alongside Jude, though not following Jude into the February Canadian wilderness. Instead, Eleanor sets up camp in a motel room with members of the British Columbia chapter of the Sierra Club. She works nonstop—typing & sending out press releases, talking on the phone with every reporter who will answer her call.

Jude's approach to saving the wolves of Muskwa Valley is just to go out there, place herself between the shooters & the wolves & trust that that will be enough to let the wolves live. No one else needs to be involved. Jude is smart enough to know what works most simply. Jude isn't about making statements, posturing. Rather, she is about blocking the flow at the source.

Eleanor Cookee is different. She wants everybody involved; she wants all the world to know about it. The publicity, she believes, will evoke sympathy & change. Once that happens, protecting wolves will occur at a policy level.

The wolf hunt helicopter turns back, returning to Vancouver having shot no wolves. The pilot & shooters stand by, awaiting word that they can resume the mission. Live TV news covers the standoff during the five o'clock hour. The next day, calls pour in at the minister of environment's office, because it is he who was responsible for ordering the slaughter. Instant pressure from the local media exposure causes him to call off the hunt until the women are no longer in the forests surrounding the hunting zone. A lawsuit is filed on Friday. The court denies an injunction to stop the hunt over the weekend, but for as long as Jude & the two others remain in the forests, the minister of environment ordered the shooting to stop. The case is to be heard the following Monday. In the meantime, Jude & her compats camp out. The media attention provides a flush of monetary support & public sympathy for the women. Then come hundreds of letters to the Parliament & the minister of environment's office. On Monday, Justice Caroline Stoppard grants an injunction against shooting over the duration in which the case is heard. It is safe for Jude to come out of the woods. Eleanor Cookee sends a helicopter in to airlift Jude & the others out. Jude quickly returns to California rather than participate in the ensuing legal & media circus. A week later, Justice Stoppard rules that the hunt is illegal based upon a technicality in the way the paperwork was filled out in the Office of Environment. Thus the hunt is called off, not on principle, but due to an error in a government office. The end result is the same: No wolf hunt, not this year. Time to move on.

Interlude

TS is new & maybe doesn't understand all of what is at stake. He comes to Jokerman after meeting Jude & liking her. Eleanor Cookee, in turn, meets TS & begins to like his face, his smile, his seeming innocence, his mid 1960s haircut. She begins to think about him when he isn't around. When people ask her why she sacrificed what she did in order to do what she does, she always thinks of TS while answering something else. Jude & Willie, too, are taken in by TS's sweet essence.

So why don't we just sink the boats? TS asks.

It seems so simple that the others cannot think of a reason why not.

Chapter 17: Stinkin boat sinkin

We sank them whalin boats jes fine, dint we, darlin sugar lumps?

We did jes fine, Peppy.

1988—Saturday night begins with smashing radios & pouring leftover coffee into computers at a whaling station a few miles away from the harbor where the carcasses are taken for butchering before shipping to Japan—oh & for scientific research.

Through a warehouse door, we find a mountain of whale meat under refrigeration. We turn off the power so that the meat will spoil; it is midsummer, after all, & warm outside. Then it is off to the harbor where the two whaling ships are at dock, side by side.

First a siren—then two more on top of the first. We would run out into the street. Cars would come roaring onto the pier—Saabs & Volvos with the Icelandic word for police painted on the side. Spotlights would come on as we would run to hide in the scrap yards across from the harbor. Little men in white hats & black & yellow armbands would pour onto the pier. Three alert revelers would appear from nowhere along the port side of the first ship, throwing gangplanks into the water.

But when it happens, it doesn't happen that way at all.

Keep watch on the security guard, TS. It's the only thing you have to do. Surveillance cameras become useless on nights like this when thick fog beaches itself atop the harbor. Fog is as close as you come to darkness in the middle of an Icelandic summer. Tonight, all of Iceland seems asleep & if you listen closely, you can hear the world snoring. For the last half hour, the security guard has not stirred from his post inside a harbor side shack set up with video monitors showing scenes from various camera stations. According to protocol (which we had determined by spending five nights hanging out around the perimeter, watching for every shift change & nuance of security routine), when the fog renders the video watch system useless, the guard is to make continual rounds. We know tonight's guard well enough to know he is less vigilant; it's as if he figures that since he can't be everywhere at once, he might as well be nowhere at once. He might as well stay comfortable in the security shack, his legs up on the break table & a hot cup of coffee in his mitt. Watch him through the small window & see him falling in & out of sleep.

TS is to keep his eye on the door of the shack & if the guard decides to make rounds or begins to act suspicious, TS is to blow a whistle & then run—maybe even draw the attention to himself & then run. No way around it, running is involved. Swimming can become involved, too, if need be.

You understand what you do if anything happens?

Yes.

The rest is up to Jude & Willie.

A saltwater pumping system cools the engines of ships such as these. When a ship is in dry dock & the need arises to perform maintenance to the ship's cooling system, workers can open the saltwater cooling valve. It's an invaluable piece of knowledge for anyone who wants to scuttle a seacraft. Why? Because opening the valve when the ship is afloat will cause water to burst into hull & if it is not immediately closed, the ship will quickly sink.

Jude & Willie sneak aboard the first of the two ships & descend into the hull. With their flashlights piercing the dark, they find the heavy steel plates that make up the floor of the engine room. The salt-water cooling valve must be underneath. Jude uses a ratchet to undo the bolts that hold the manhole-sized steel cover in place, then a bolt cutter to cut through the lock that keeps the valve from unauthorized or accidental opening. Willie turns the valve; they hear the sound of water gushing. Water begins to fill in over the tops of their boots, drenching their pant legs.

The ship becomes an hourglass. How much time will it take to perform the same operation on the second ship? Can we do it before the first one sinks?

Moments later, both ships are sinking & it becomes a furious scramble. Swiftly, Jude & Willie fly back to the dock. Willie uses the bolt cutters on the thick ropes that anchor the ships to the dock, then tosses the bolt cutters into the harbor. TS joins them & they run quickly back to the rental car parked two blocks away. Without a squeal of tires—for haste would draw attention—they make a getaway as the two whaling ships sink quietly into the night.

En route to the airport, we look ahead to see a police checkpoint. We stop. We envision ourselves spending the rest of our lives in an Icelandic jail. *Please stay calm.* Police shine flashlights in at us. They ask us to step outside the car. What concerns them is whether we have been drinking. We haven't. They see that & let us go. They never ask why our clothes are dirty, why our pant legs are wet. Apparently, word of the scuttling is not yet out. To them, we are cleancut American tourists, heading back to the airport to catch an early flight. They are glad we have come to their country to support their local economy. They don't see us as the stinkin boat sinkers we truly are. We are on our way.

[Long stretches of silence ensue—then one of the three speaks:

Next summer let's go to the Barrier Reef.

Yes, let's.

Sounds good to me.]

We lift off, then touch down in Luxembourg. We hitchhike through Belgium & catch a ferry to Dover. From there, it's a cheap flight to Atlanta on Willie's mom's credit card. We make a connection & have a layover in Denver. From there, it's homeward.

The Greenpeace goodship *Caliban*, fresh from the U2 gig, is just off the Icelandic coast returning to drop off the *Rolling Stone* reporters & to see if we want transport back to the States when news breaks that two whaling ships (belonging to Choracorp, a Scandinavian company traded publicly on the NYSE) have been scuttled. At dock side when informed of the scuttling, crew members praise the action—even laugh about it—but claim no credit whatsoever. Those aboard the ship would have loved to say they took part, but their alibi aired last night on MTV.

We had forgotten about Greenpeace. It had never occurred to us that the Icelandic authorities might implicate Greenpeace in the scuttling. It is just as well, because no one implicated them. Iceland was never keen on having a whaling industry & never expended much energy in seeking out the culprits.

The question remains: Can you pull something like this off without being haunted by its ghosts later? We wonder if Choracorp will ever send a corporate goon squad to find us. What do Icelandic assassins look like? (The idea of that thrills Willie; he can outrun them all.)

We decidedly avoid news coverage of the event; we pulled what we pulled less for the media world to talk about & hash out (then move on & forget it ever happened) than we did to take a bite out of the whaling industry. Monkey see it's broke. Monkey make it fixed. We hear that Greenpeace, from its headquarters in New York, eventually issued an official statement regarding the Icelandic whaleboat scuttling in which the organization uncharacteristically condemned the action & vehemently denied all blame. They must have missed the word that no one was blaming them.

Several months later, a ghost appears; we knew from the start this would haunt us. The apparition took the human form of Captain Paul Shepard of the Pacific Pandora. The cap'n gave us more information about the sinking than we wanted to know. As a veteran of many run-ins on the high seas with whaling vessels the cap'n had no trouble deducing who was responsible for the double, boat scuttling even though we kept a low profile. The cap'n also told us how the scuttling was perceived in Europe (*favorably*) & the ultimate effect it has on the Icelandic whaling industry (*staggering*). His only wish was that he could have been there.

Then he shared his bad news—a dauble of spit elegantly hung from his lower lip. From talking with us, it was obvious we didn't know already.

Don't know what? The sound of gushing water had awakened the security guard. Intent not to allow boat scuttling to happen in his harbor on his shift, the guard boarded one of the ships & attempted to close the saltwater cooling valve after the ship was already halfway under. He went down with it. He drowned. *Sorry, kids—I thought you knew already. It was an accident, after all.*

Our heart nearly stops.

We had claimed no pride, no outward satisfaction in what we had done. We had never wanted to kill anyone. How are we going to live with ourselves?

But then there is a twinkling in the good cap'n's eye.

I am shittin you, kiddos. The scuttling wasn't discovered until just before church on Sunday morning & at that time, they found the security guard safe & sleeping.

Chapter 18: They pull your legs out from under you

1989—When Willie Shoman finally gets dragged to the hospital—dragged mostly because he no longer has the physical strength to resist his draggers—the nurse practitioner seats him in a wheel chair & rolls him away into an x-ray room. Glimpsing quickly at the pictures, the NP diagnoses him with a fractured leg & two cracked ribs, even though the reasons for Willie's visit are an aching hip & the loss of feeling in his left arm.

Lose a fight, Willie?

Nope.

Crash your motorcycle?
No, sir—don't ride one.

Hours later & after a seemingly infinite wait while the lab runs tests on Willie's blood & the doctors discuss the early results with him in private, two orderlies wheel Willie back into the waiting room. We ask him what they found out.

I'm pregnant, Willie tells us.

As of late, Willie is slowing down—sleeping more, doing less—though never, complaining of anything other than muscle & bone cramps. He will walk away & shut the door before showing you his discomfort. He rides his mountain bike & goes about his daily business until the day when the pain becomes so severe that he cannot ride anymore & his friends drag him to St. Mary's. Not all the test results are yet back, but he decides to call his family—for the first time in a long time—to tell them what's happening. How much easier this would be if he could just call & tell them he is in a family way. At least everyone could laugh at that.

He already knows how they will react when they find out.

Back at the Joshua Tree, phones ring. This time, it's Willie's grandmother, who happens to own the Joshua Tree. She lets us keep the house rent free. Before this happened to Willie, none of us knew whose house this is. *This is our house. That is all we know.* Today, though, Willie's grandmother is on the phone & she's not calling about the house.

As soon as the family on Willie's mother's side & his sisters & brother hear the news, they begin calling to see if there is anything they can do for him, asking if there is anything he needs. They know him well enough from his childhood—since he has hardly had contact with them since then—to know how independent he is & how difficult it is for him to rely on others & to ask for help.

Chemotherapy begins right away & the search goes out for a bone-marrow donor. All in a caravan, the family members go to the hospital to see if they can donate bone marrow to him. None of the family members match nor does any Jokerman bone marrow match. Willie is made from a different clay than the rest of us.

I'm a goner, he says to people when first telling them about the cancer.

At first it seems like a joke—he is only twenty-one. He had smoked pot when he was seventeen but stopped when he started having trouble remembering numbers. He has lived cleanly ever since. The doctors say that his teenage drug use is not responsible for the cancer. Something is, but finding out what matters less than keeping alive.

The thought of Willie dying—no one can imagine it.

You're going to live through this, Eleanor Cookee tells Willie, feeling dumb right after saying it. When she said it, she believed it. As soon as she says it, she realizes that maybe that will not be the case.

Willie himself rather than spend his energy fighting death, which he knows is inevitable no matter what kind of fight he puts up, decides instead to let himself die gracefully. He refuses to complain; he refrains from thinking negative thoughts about anyone. He becomes the person we all wish we were.

Willie Shoman—riding shotgun from the hospital alongside his mother, notices everything outside the car window—billboards advertising movies that have not yet come out.

I'm dying & none of this seems real.

Seeing random people along the sides of the street, inside their cars, he wonders what their lives are about—wonders what experiences they are having—ones that he will miss out on having, never have a choice of having. He will spend the rest of his life dying. He has no other choice. He will die & the radio will play new songs. He might not eat his favorite Mexican food again. He will never know where this baseball season leads—to a World Series played by the Giants & A's. He will miss it all—everything—the earthquake.

What he will really miss in the world, though are the things that never change—the mountains—streams—the places he dreams about, then goes out to find. When people describe an afterlife, they make it sound as if there will be mountains & streams & air. Willie worries there won't be. Willie worries the afterlife might be a clear cut.

Then Willie stops worrying & lets everything go. Suddenly, he's more lucid & happy. He even agrees to go to confession.

It's my mother's idea. She wants me to go, Willie tells us. This amuses him; he loves the idea of it. *I have nothing to confess, really. There isn't anything I've done I would take back. When I've sinned, I've sinned with gusto. But*

I am going to go. I guess I will need to fess up to the few & the proud times I have fornicated. If I have anything to confess it's maybe that I would have liked to have had more sex.

Tonight his little sister will take him to a high school production of *Godspell* at St. Ignatius. She has a crush on the kid who plays John the Baptist. The music is sweet & uplifting & Willie enjoys himself but thinks that if any member of the cast is worth keeping an eye on, it's the one who plays Jesus.

Family members now stop by the Joshua Tree with bags of food for Willie & the rest of us. Willie has slowed down enough to take up residence at the Joshua Tree rather than his usual hey-like-go-mad lifestyle of finding places every night to set up & sleep in his tent. Sensing we are undernourished & understanding that we are picky eaters, they accommodate everyone & they always bring us apples.

Willie's young nephew, Isaiah, never says anything during his visit as if it frightens him to say anything around older people. His eyes always glisten as if he were a moment away from tears. He pulls his T-shirt forward to make it a carrier for apples. He passes through every room at the Tree, with his mother & offers apples from his kangaroo pouch to everyone he finds.

Willie's family, for the most part, lives on the other side of the Golden Gate Bridge in Marin County. Considering how often Willie has communicated with them these past few years, they might as well live half a world away.

Before Willie gets cancer, his family feels intimidated by us as if they believe we are a bad influence on him. They think we are the reason he never calls them. They think we egged Willie on when he decided to stay in jail rather than accept probation. They had tried not to forgive us for that. Cancer has a way of throwing the world off kilter. Now they bring us food.

When one of Willie's relatives calls, he is often out already with another relative. The relative on the phone then asks how he is doing, how his spirits are. *Then the relative asks, how am I doing? What am I studying in school? Do I like the film program at State? The next thing I know, the relative is off & telling me a story about the time at Disneyland when he saw Francis Ford Coppola out of the blue on the Pirates of the Caribbean.*

They like us the more they come to know us.

RICHARD MELO

We are a part of Willie that will not die anytime soon.

Though no one says it, they are in love with us & we are in love with them.

In turn, the love his family gives him during this time catches Willie up in it; he becomes more carefree & happy than we have ever seen him. He loves to laugh with them & with us; the laughter cleanses the soul. We spend those months laughing together as much as we can.

We have never really stopped to consider it—not one of us had come from an ideal family situation—& certainly not Willie. Something clicks inside of us: *this is how family works*. We make peace with ourselves & our parents—the near ones & dear ones, the ones far away & the ones no longer living.

Willie moves into his old bedroom at his mother's house & we rarely see him. He is too ill to see us. When we do see him, he is antsy to go out into the woods, though less to spoil traps & spike trees than to just get out there & be.

All through Willie's illness, his father is living in Germany—if you can call it living. Passing through is more like it. Willie Sr. grew up in a generation where sons & daughters rebelled against their parents' generation. Willie Sr. rebels against the opposite—his wife & children. He decided that he simply did not want to turn out like his kids when he grew up. But how do you expect your children to take that? When the inheritance came in, he figured he could still provide for them in absentia. They would have all the money they needed & the last thing they needed was him. He chose to move to Europe & ride his bike. There, he could forget about everything he left behind. He could live as the person he wanted to be. These days, he knows he is still providing for them; the inheritance takes care of that. What he needs is to provide for himself. That means riding his bike back & forth across Europe during the summer & hitting the slopes in the winter.

Willie's older sister, Ruth, decides that their father needed to know about Willie's illness—to know that if he doesn't come home soon, he might never see his son again. Last year, he missed the wedding of his daughter, Helen. He did send a note, though, that said, *I wish you well*. Not to knock Helen's wedding, but he needs to come home for this. Ruth then finds how tough it will be to get a message to him; no one knows where to find him. The last we knew he was riding his bicycle up & down Europe & although he has a PO box in Munich, who knows

93

how often he actually checks it? When strapped for cash, he uses his American Express card & the bills go to the family house in Marin, but by the time the bills arrive & they can see an itemization of the places where he's been, he is already someplace else. Ruth realizes how much effort it will take just for her to get herself to Europe & how lost she will be when she gets there. She becomes discouraged & decides not to go.

Then Greenpeace rides to the rescue. Having heard from friends of friends about Willie's illness & of his sister's desire to find his father in Europe, Greenpeace volunteers in Germany offer to help out, willing to look around & ask some questions—enjoying the idea of playing private detective in their own country. They take off on bicycles to scour the countryside & forests. To all the cyclists they encounter, they show photographs of Willie's father & ask if they have seen him.

Reluctant, thinking the Greenpeace people might actually be the police, the strangers ask, *What's your interest in finding this man?*

His son is dying & he doesn't know.

By following promising leads & with the help of strangers, Greenpeace tracks him down & catches up with him in France. He looks nothing like his photograph anymore; he has become more gaunt & hollow.

At a campsite, three riders give him a letter written by Ruth.

[Before he looks at it, he asks what it's all about.

It's from your family.

Oh, them.]

He reads it while they linger nearby. He wishes he could be alone. He knows they are anticipating his reaction; he knows they want to take a message from him back with them. He writes a note to Willie on a page of his journal, tears it out & hands it to them for them to deliver back to Ruth in the states.

Returning home is so complicated; he cannot do that right now. Returning home means more than boarding a plane & flying home. It means facing them again, facing them & watching his son die. It means erasing the life he has drawn for himself here. He wouldn't be able to— he needs to ride. He would have to answer to people; he would have to answer to them. He is too young to watch his son die. Willie Sr.'s forty-

94

eighth birthday comes & goes without him even noticing. *Returning home shows them I was wrong. I am not going back.*

The summer in San Francisco is cold. Mostly it feels cold because people wear their summer clothes on days when it is less than hot. They remember what August is like in other parts of California & other parts of America. When we think back to the summer of 1989, we remember seeing Willie's mother in her winter jacket.

[There is no pain in life worse than being a mother & seeing your child become ill.]

It's the harshest winter in memory for Willie Shoman's mother. A harsh & bitter cold pierces her winter jacket, going straight to the bones. How tiny she seems & how alone in the world she looks even with her family all around her. [*That settles the question—I am never having kids.*]

Arriving at Willie's mother's house earlier than expected but too late no less, you walk up as the slow ambulance pulls away. You run after it. As slow as it goes, you can't keep up. It's a motorized vehicle & your legs can't hold pace. The adrenaline delays the emotion; the emotion is now waiting to spill out. You suddenly don't feel your legs anymore & collapse where you stand. You lay your head down on the asphalt drive. Someone has pulled the plug from your belly button & all the air rushes out of you. None of this can be real.

A battered, old pickup truck, the kind only driven in farm country where you're not breaking down in heavy congestion, the kind of truck that would get lost lumbering across the Bay Bridge, drives over grass, flattening clover & parking near the other cars where drivers who arrived earlier in the day did the same. [When we leave, the cars will leave tracks on the grass; the grass will remember us, that we came here today. Then the sun & wind will happen, days will pass, grass will grow & you will never know that we parked there.] No one would have guessed that Willie's family, so at home in Marin, originally came from the Valley—Modesto. Family from all over are turning out for this. An aunt you have never met answers the door for you & you step inside. Young nephews & nieces are sprawled on the floor playing a game of Mousetrap by Parker Bros. Sitting in a barcalounger is a compat, someone you recognize, so at least you are not here alone. He is peering at Disneyland scenes through an ancient Viewmaster with 3D stereophonic vision. Other compats sit on the sofa, poring through the plastic pages of family albums, grooving on photographs of someone else's family, studying the smiles in the pictures & wondering what the people in them are all about while wondering what it was like growing up with them. [The pictures tell it all.] You walk through every room, surveying the scene, shaking hands with people you are meeting for the first time & hugging those you have met already. You walk outside & greet compats & family members in lawn chairs & picnic tables—the ones in the shade beside the pool. The family has set up a buffet atop a ping-pong table covered with a tissue tablecloth. You change into your swimming suit & bounce high on the diving board & jump in the pool & stay underwater for as long as your breath will hold. The sky above the water's surface looks purple.

Part II

File under water

Chapter 19: Palaver over pentagons & pyramids

Our house in San Francisco on Font Street near State is close enough to the Pacific Ocean that when everyone is talking at once, if you lean back & make yourself quiet in those split-second moments between the words & sentences of the others, you can hear water. We call it the Joshua Tree partly for the jangly, spiritual U2 album of the same name but also for the lonesome desert tree growing out in the American southwest. *In nameless streets we walk alone, beds of nails & hearts of stone.* We call it the Joshua Tree, though, mostly because we like the name.

Entering through the front door, you see a huge steel desk, standard-issue government surplus, strong enough to withstand a nuclear blast despite the vaporization of its contents. Next you see green. Hanging ferns & houseplants humanize the Joshua Tree, taking the edge off of the dusty mounds of newspapers, magazines & government documents lingering in piles in the front room. Mostly the newspapers & magazines include articles that track stories of interest to Eleanor Cookee—if only someone would take the time to sort through them. The government documents are mostly US Fish & Wildlife biological assessments of endangered species, detailing the appropriate activities that can take place on federal

& state lands where specific animal populations are dwindling. When people have time, they pore through the docs, trying to find locations where activities are taking place—ranging from logging to dune buggy day tripping—that violate the all-too-often unenforced Endangered Species Act. Then we can inform Eleanor Cookee's lawyer friends & they can threaten to file suit. [No one reads the biological assessments anymore. Eleanor Cookee has collected far too many of them for anyone to make a dent. People check them out, then never bring them back. They lose them on buses & underneath dorm room beds.]

Suddenly, the room isn't so bad, especially with California sunlight & fresh air coming through the front window —for always somewhere at the Joshua Tree a window is left open. You find your way to the living room where there is a table around which we sit. When people fill the room, a din surrounds you. In this room, when the time comes to let it loose, let it fly, everyone takes a turn. People blurt out everything on their minds & confusion abounds; this blurting is what we are all about—it's an atmosphere for conversation: *Bicycles & solar energy, waves & the sea, bells & pomegranates, trainwhistle stops & spontaneous human interruptions.*

We unfortunately mire ourselves at times in the how-can-we-make-something-happen-without-ever-leaving-this-room approach to wingnut gigs, kicking out all the ideas. In field work, you only want to go with people you trust. You want to breathe in the same rhythm as the people around you. This room is different—everyone is here, but no one is in sync. Around here, it is less about trust than it is about pure banter. People don't even know each other's names!

There must be rooms like this all over the country. We're a think tank without the corporate or government trappings. It's beautiful in its way: a group defining its direction, a group defining itself, then redefining everything before the last person is out the door.

See Jokerman. See Jokerman run. Then find that there's nothing there. We are a hoax, really. You can't see us through the glass. You can't see us because we are made of air. We resolve to dissolve. You may have heard us once: We are capable of making noise—a soft rumbling you probably thought was something else. In a group like this where the path we choose is usually beyond ridiculous, we follow our beyond ridiculous instincts & love them. Even amid all this reckless talk, we go forward—untroubled & unworried—never mindful of what we have to lose, though fully aware of what the world is losing & knowing we have nothing left to lose. Ideas bandy about with reckless abandon.

Sometimes through the noisy haze , everyone speaking at once, voices overlapping, the air turns human.

1990—Here we are. We achieve harmony. Water shines through the light we make. Come listen: *All this murmur of an Egypt prank—what's it all about?*

How does this look? A sign for the Presto Pyramid Construction Company is held up for everyone to see by Eleanor Cookee, the paint just now dry past dripping. *It's called Presto Pyramid Construction. The others can tell you more about it than I can.*

Keep in mind we bend toward laughter, always.

We're becoming pyramid builders, just for laughs.

Heavy!

Great, I flunked wood shop.

The idea is, wouldn't it be funny, yet poignant, to build an Egyptian-style pyramid on federal land, the land that belongs to the American people? Wouldn't you think it just a riot to see a pyramid—I mean, a gargantuan pyramid —built right there, by us?

Where do you mean exactly?

In a forest somewhere—out in the wild—maybe near Hazel Dell, Washington, or Walla Walla.

I'm sorry. I don't find that funny at all—just the opposite. I'm from Yakima.

We can't do it. Think of land use, best environmental practices. Remember we are supposed to be anti-development. Building a pyramid, especially one Egyptian size, goes against everything we believe in. Think of the catastrophic impact on the ecosystem, the displaced wildlife, the soil erosion.

Maybe we could minimize those negative impacts by building it out someplace where it's flat & barren, somewhere in the doglands maybe. I'm thinking Nevada or Utah, maybe somewhere near those nuclear test sites where the kids all have leukemia & the dogs have no hair.

Even there, you have desert plant & wildlife that just aren't copacetic to the building of pyramids. The most rugged of terrain will support the most delicate of ecosystems.

Just how big of a pyramid are we talking about?

No one knows exactly.

I have an idea. Let's build a pyramid in Washington, DC, as a monument to the environmental movement. Washington is overdeveloped already as it is—swampland all paved over. A new pyramid would hardly hurt & not to mention, who would notice? Washington abounds in monuments already. We can put together a new American monument from ancient Egyptian blueprints.

We can remodel the Pentagon as a pyramid.

Now that's an idea I like.

Are you drunk? It's ridiculous. We can dream about it all day, it won't happen. We can find better ways to spend our time.

Hey, I like the idea. During Vietnam, thousands of protest kids circled the Pentagon & attempted to levitate it through chanting. The point is the building never came unglued from the ground & the war lasted several more years. But the idea has certain charm to it. We should remodel the Pentagon as a pyramid.

You know, the Pentagon isn't even in DC. It's across the river in Virginia—as if that makes any difference.

It makes a difference to me.

Do you realize how silly all this sounds?

Hey! Some of our best ideas are our most ridiculous.

I wish I knew more about how this pyramid-building process works before I decide anything. I mean, we are going to vote on this?

It's simple, really. With one arm, I can lift 40, maybe 60 pounds, but with both arms, I can lift 160, 180, maybe even 200 pounds. Picture life without dump trucks & tractors. Picture architecture designed to last an eternity. It's the force of two arms working together. Now imagine two arms of 50,000 people all at once surrounding the Pentagon building. We can really move some rock. With a lever long enough, we can move the world.

How do we make 50,000 of us?

Foot Apples explained that to you? That we need 50,000 people?

No. I just made it up. I've tried prying an explanation out of him & don't understand a word of it.

What's up with Foot Apples anyway?

You're asking the wrong person.

I mean, who is Foot Apples? I keep hearing that name.

His real name is Anthony Burchetta. Foot Apples is the nickname we've given him—don't ask me why. I mean, Foot Apples is a pretty silly nickname for someone as serious as Anthony Burchetta. He's working on a master's degree in Egyptian Studies at State. He speaks Middle Egyptian fluently.

I bet that comes in handy.

He was working on his thesis & found a new way of reading hieroglyphics. He uncovered what he calls a second layer of meaning that rides alongside the standard interpretation of the hieroglyphic texts. He says he now understands how pyramid building works & that it's not difficult—easy as pie. Even we could do it, he says.

The problem is that Foot Apples is a linguist with poor verbal skills. Not to mention, his handwriting is so bad that hieroglyphics are easier to read. The problem with Foot Apples is that he can't explain his new method of translation to anyone & don't even bother asking him how pyramid building works.

Yes, that is a problem.

He says that the ideas don't translate into English very well. But still he's trying.

I see. So la prank egyptienne *is all talk at this point.*

Not at all. We're going through with it just the same, whether we understand it or not.

Don't we get to vote?

Pardon me for interrupting, but I'm still back when we were talking about pulling off this prank at the Pentagon, you know. What bigger threat has there been to the environment, not just of the United States, but of the world as a whole, than the one constituted by the Pentagon? The Pentagon is old & ugly. I just read an article where it said that the roof is leaking, the paint is peeling, the walls are cracking, the building itself is sinking into the swamp beneath it. I mean, they could have left it a greenspace & forgotten about war; they had a chance. The world would be better off for it. Now they're spending a fortune to fix up the damn thing. We can do the remodeling for them for free. Imagine a pyramid lifting up into the Virginia sky!

This is a joke, right?

With us, what isn't?

Maybe we could put a hole in the wall. We can put a dink in the bathroom wall & let the defense brass take a whiz in the wind.

We could paint the Pentagon so that it looks like a pyramid.

That will surely fool everyone.

I can't imagine that they would let us actually touch the building. I mean, it's the Pentagon. It's the holiest cathedral of the US Military. It's guarded by soldiers. Most peacetime soldiers have never had a kill—why should we offer ourselves up?

Wow! Think of it—a pyramid in DC. What will people call it?

The Pentagon.

But it won't be a pentagon—it will be a pyramid.

Changing its name might cause confusion.

But keeping the name might cause confusion.

Since when do names matter anyway? Like I'm so sure.

If this has a chance of working, or even if there is just a chance of this failing brilliantly, it will be worth the risk, because it's so damn funny. It's the perfect wingnut gig.

I hope this works, because I hate running around chasing futility. We can find a better way to spend our time this summer.

Do you know what I like about the Pyramid-Pentagon prank? It's the ultimate show in not taking ourselves too seriously. Willie Shoman would have liked this idea.

[Now why do you go & do that? Just mention Willie's name in this crowd & you draw a collective sigh from everyone. I am still getting over the idea that we're going anywhere without him. It's not like he is ever far from our minds. It's not like enough time has passed for us to let go of grieving. We have not reached the point where his name can come up in casual conversation without someone turning pale & asking to leave the room. That's frequently how things go around here—someone mentions Willie Shoman & we lose our train of thought.]

Chapter 20: The living pursuit of all things Egyptian

Hey! Let's make like Egyptians & build ourselves a merry, little pyramid! We'll make something of ourselves.

Yes! Cool!

All this Foot Apples talk starts on a Friday night in the dining center across from the Mary Ward Hall student dormitories with a joke. Please realize ahead of time that this is a joke that loses everything in the retelling. Foot Apples & Eleanor Cookee have just met. There aren't enough tables in the dining center that night so people are squeezing together; people who have never met each other before are sitting at the same table. Most nights, the person who asks people to call him Dean (but whose real name is Anthony J. Burchetta & who is called Foot Apples by people in Jokerman after they meet him) eats alone. Such was & is his way.

Tonight, though, he ends up eating at a table with Eleanor Cookee, who never lets a person keep quiet. Eleanor herself never says much; her talent is that she can make people talk, even when they have nothing to say. So Eleanor Cookee takes an interest in hearing about Dean Burchetta's major in Egyptian studies. Dean Burchetta senses Eleanor's genuine interest. He relaxes & decides to tell her a joke about Egypt that he has made up—a joke that has been brewing inside of him for months now, a joke that he thinks is the best way he knows of communicating to others everything he is about, a joke that sums it all up, a joke that he thinks is funny as hell, if only you understand where he's coming from. Once he tells her *about* the joke, she, in turn, asks to *hear* it. She even looks forward to hearing it.

So Foot Apples tells Eleanor Cookee his joke: He gears up to avoid mis-speaking, then considers not telling it. What if she doesn't laugh? Then he decides to tell it anyway. He stalls & laughs at himself before even telling it. He half stands up, as if to pretend he's going to walk away & leave her hanging. Then he bears down & tells it. He says, *Did you hear the Great Pyramid was built in a day?* [He can hardly stand it—the seeming infinity between the build up & the punch line.]

Eleanor Cookee says, *No, I never heard that.*

Then comes the sparkling punch: *Rome, on the other hand, took much longer.*

That's it. That's the whole joke—uncorked, poured & quaffed.

Eleanor Cookee doesn't get it; she stares blankly at Anthony J. Dean Burchetta. *I mean, it sounded like a joke—what happened?* Jokes like this destroy her faith in her ability to get jokes. What poor Eleanor doesn't realize here is that the joke—if you want to dignify it by calling it a joke—lacked something—namely anything worthy of laughter. It's a joke without a butt, without bite, without edge, without much going for it at all. Yet this does not explain why Eleanor is not laughing. Eleanor Cookee is someone who concentrates deeply while listening to other people. Her energy comes from being around others & listening to them. She would love nothing more than for people to pay her the same degree of attention, but she knows better than to expect it. Knowing that Foot Apples is intelligent, Eleanor Cookee now senses that the joke is on her—exposing her as unintelligent—& that if she were smarter, she would have laughed. Eleanor is not someone who laughs just because others are laughing. Rather than pretend that she finds something funny, she digs deeper, asking question after question, determined to get to the bottom of the matter, as she is known to do when believing herself the butt of a joke.

Foot Apples, whom none of us believe has many friends & is unaccustomed to any kind of attention, is glad to answer all of Eleanor's questions to the best of his ability. What eventually comes to light is that through his research of Egyptian texts, Foot Apples has discovered the truth of how the Great Pyramid was built & that it was built not in twenty-three or thirty or ninety-nine years like many scholars believe, but in significantly less time.

How significant?

Don't think in terms of years. It took much less than that—maybe weeks, maybe days. They built it, too, without wheels & machines.

The pyramid was built in days?

Maybe even in just one day. If not a day, then really quickly—a blip on the map of human history, a blip on the map of a human lifetime.

She asks him what the secret is & he says that that is difficult for him to explain & he is still in the process of understanding it himself. He says that he needs to work on the texts more & then he can tell her.

Looking back, that's the real punch the one that has us all in stitches.

Chapter 21

In cafés all over the City, people are reading dog-eared & coffee-stained copies of Budge's *Egyptian Grammar*, a particularly difficult & spotty text according to Foot Apples. Library copies of Budge & Gardiner are quickly checked out or stolen & people at bookstores tell you when you ask that the texts are on back order—but if you try back on Tuesday.

If you look these days, you'll see people reading Budge on the streetcar lines M, L & K on a regular basis. Egypt is all the rage at City College & State, schools where everyone commutes. Overnight, San Francisco State University becomes Polaris for the reading of ancient Egyptian literature. We're making waves underground—it's all the talk. Something big is going down—everyone knows it. A change is in the works & we are at the cusp.

The talk, too, reaches halls of the university & the Classics faculty. It turns out they ride buses & streetcars, like the rest of us & they are wondering why every other person seems reading Budge on buses all of a sudden. [*Last year it was* Catch-22—*this year Budge? What on earth is going on?*] As sexy as hieroglyphics are, hardly anyone deeply studies them, learns to read them, or makes them a scholarly pursuit. But none among the faculty who hear the buzz, stop & listen & actually think & deeply consider the implications. After all, they know Egypt; Egypt is their life's work. What these students say they are pursuing is light years from what they know—eons. [*It may not be as romantic as we like, but Herodotus gives us the best explanation as to how the pyramids were built— by 100,000 workers over thirty years. The first ten years were spent in planning & building the substructure to allow the construction to take place. The suggestion of there being any other way is far too ridiculous to dignify with any further inquiry. There is no other way—stones were picked up & moved by vast legions of people. They built ramps; they dragged the stones. At night, they took baths & drank beer. We have all the evidence. It's an amusing thought, though, to think there was another way—I'm glad you shared it with me. Perhaps space aliens built them, in honor of Elvis. A few years ago, the students held a strike protesting something or other & now this. What will these kids think up next?*]

1799—Napoleon comes. He sees. He brings scientists: a crew of 500 savants to accompany his soldiers. Believing there is no glory in his little corner of Europe alone, Napoleon heads east. On his Egyptian tour, Bonaparte finds himself simultaneously gaining & losing ground. Though his soldiers win the Battle of the Pyramids, he suffers some of the worst setbacks in the twenty-nine years of his life: The British sink his fleet at Aboukir, his troops lose a battle on land at Acre & the plague strikes down even more of his forces.

Yet there is more to glory than empire building. On the expedition, he brings along civilians—biologists, mineralogists, linguists, mathematicians, chemists & other scholars—to study Egypt. By 1828, the savants compile a twenty-volume *Description de l'Egypte* & in so doing, Egyptology is born. [The re-emergence of Ancient Greek ideas about truth, beauty, justice, etc., sparks the Renaissance; Europeans suddenly find themselves applying what is antique to who they are today. The reemergence of Egyptian art, religion & language inspires no renaissance. Instead it results in collections of curios, gallery displays, out-of-this-world theories revolving around pharaohs & pyramids & the occasional Department of Egyptian Studies at universities like San Francisco State.

At first, Ancient Egyptian was a dead letter. Greeks, circa 500 AD, gave the birds, stick figures, squiggles & other shapes a name, hieroglyphs, meaning literally, sacred carving. The Greeks believed that in their randomness, hieroglyphs honor the gods & pharaohs of the Egyptian tradition. The word hieroglyphs is the Greek way of saying they have no idea what Egyptian writing means or whom to ask—for by that time the Egyptian people were lost, too.

More than a thousand years later, by the time of Napoleon's arrival, the Egyptian language is still lost. Even the Maluks who ride their horses & flash their sabers & wear turbans & silk pantaloons & challenge Napoleon's professional army in defense of Egypt do not descend from the Ancient Egyptians & the language they speak is not Egyptian; rather it's a form of Arabic with what might be an Egyptian accent.

Murmurs abound that there is more to hieroglyphics than what meets the eye. A gathering of savants takes a long look at the Egyptian desert, wondering about her secrets. The official duties of the savants include finding out whether the raw materials needed for making gunpowder are available in Egypt, whether windmills are practical, whether beer can be brewed without hops & other tasks deemed vital to the success of the military expedition. Duty aside, their real interest is discovery.

In Rosetta, they turn over one gray slab of basalt in particular & discover writing on it—inscriptions. Bang! Nothing. The turning over of the stone is followed with no lights, without sparkle, no razzmatazz, no sinister voices booming from heaven—the Earth below stays put.

The savants see that the slab includes three levels of inscription— Greek, hieroglyphic & Coptic. They see, too, that the stone is the key to unraveling the mystery of Egyptian language. How can they tell? The last line of the Greek text, which they can readily translate, says that the three inscriptions contain the same message—a praise of Ptolemy.

In the years prior to the stone's recovery, the unraveling of hieroglyphics had become a cottage industry, sentiment being that the hieroglyphs were more than pretty pictures arranged orderly in rows, that at one time, the hieroglyphs comprised a spoken language. The bandwagon was overflowing with linguists—both scholars & amateurs—racing to claim credit for deciphering Egyptian language. Some went as far as to claim they had discovered a key to translation & ascribed whatever meaning to the language they desired, often bending the Egyptians to make them the forerunners of the Christian age.

1822—Working from a handwritten copy of the Rosetta Stone inscriptions on the stone, Jean Francois Champollion seeks a key to demystify ancient Egyptian language. The unraveling begins when he finds a grouping of hieroglyphic letters he believes spells the name, *P-T-O-L-*

E-M-Y. From there he inserts the *l, e, o* & *t* into another grouping of letters, which he then surmises spells out the name, *C-L-E-O-P-A-T-R-A.* With more letters at his disposal, he decryptifies the name of *A-L-E-X-A-N-D-E-R.* Before his eyes, an alphabet unfolds. Egyptian language is suddenly closer to ours in form than anyone had previously imagined.

How had the nature of the language become so thoroughly forgotten? By asking that, you are forgetting that Ancient Egypt is deeply shrouded in the mysterious & that people forget things. Then, as if from pulling one loose thread, Champollion completely unravels the ancient, wool sweater. The knots of Egyptian language untangle & fall on the floor—a pile of yarn.

After Champollion, any guess as to the meaning of Egyptian language that didn't incorporate the process developed by Champollion was suddenly discredited, seen as a hoax. So conclusive was Champollion & so powerful was the authority bestowed upon his discovery. Most serious linguists gave up the quest for a system of translation & began the dauntless task of applying Champollion's key to the seemingly endless record of Egyptian texts. The key, though, befuddles one linguist, an Oxford scholar named S. Martin Day.

Day at first believed that Champollion's key was a conspiracy & was amazed that it seemed to work; that by applying it to hieroglyphic texts, one could translate Egyptian into English. To Day, Champollion's key was a typically European way of projecting European cultural expectations onto others & then finding themselves there. What's more, Day went so far as to believe that the meaning read into Egyptian language through Champollion's key was possibly a matter of coincidence: You spell out the name *C-L-E-O-P-A-T-R-A* & the word will forever spell Cleopatra—any question of its meaning is solved. You make yourself believe there is only one way; but why stop there? Why not continue uncovering new layers of meaning & why not keep going & going?

S. Martin Day continues his work, inventing a process of reading hieroglyphics apart from Champollion's key—a process that does not easily translate into English. Eventually, Day leads himself to believe that the meaning uncovered through Champollion's key is built into the language in order to disguise what else is there, to keep people from looking over the same language twice, to foil grave robbers. Champollion's key is a way of disguising the code & keeping people from even recognizing it as code. The real meaning—if it can be called meaning & if it can be called real—remains buried below the surface. The layer of meaning Day wishes to uncover is so distantly removed from speech, writing & other forms of communication that when Foot Apples comes along near the end of the twentieth century, he has trouble grasping it completely.

His name is Anthony J. Burchetta, although he wants people to call him Dean. How do you shorten Anthony & arrive at Dean? We cannot tell you. We do not know.

We mull over pages of hieroglyphic texts without translation. We make of it what we can; we recognize people kneeling, snakes, hawks, canaries, squiggly lines & dots & a round object with feet shown in the act of walking. We ask Dean what the object is. He meets us with a disdainful silence & averts meeting our eyes, his demeanor meaning, *if you want to know what it is you are looking at, decipher it for yourselves. Go to the books.*

We are too slack for that. Let's just look at it. What it looks like to us is an apple with a foot—a foot apple. Perhaps large herds of these foot apples used to roam the Nile Valley & all got together one day & built the pyramids. This, of course, ignores that we don't even know if apples grow, or ever grew, in Egypt—such are the limits of our knowledge. Because we can't bring ourselves to call Anthony J. Burchetta, Dean, we call him Foot Apples instead. The name sticks.

This new way of reading, do you believe the same principles apply to English—hey, Foot Apples?

Nope.

Why's that?

Because compared to Egyptian, English sucks. Foot Apples walks away, leaving the rest of us to wonder what he means.

How does English suck? Lucky for us, we all have done enough college to take a phrase, like *English sucks* & turn it into a full-blown analytical essay. Working together, this is what we write:

A language like Latin was made for poetry & ideas.

English was made for selling things to one another.

English structures our thought.

English is our limiting factor.

English is why we don't build pyramids.

English is for game show hosts & people who sell used cars & other assorted hucksters of the world. It's for disk jockeys. It's for Regis & Kathy Lee.

English is why we build superhighways & nuclear reactors & why we drill for oil at the bottom of the ocean & why everyone seems to have forgotten about the sun.

It explains everything. It means nothing.

Before Foot Apples brings his S. Martin Day spiel to us, he takes it to San Francisco State University's Egyptian Studies faculty. He approaches them with a proposal to write a thesis reconstructing Day's method of hieroglyphic translation.

Reading S. Martin Day gives Dean insights he has never had before, opens up new possibilities, illuminates paths he had suspected were there but had not managed to arrive at by himself & helps him resolve some of the difficulties he himself has had in his transliteration exercises. It's perfect.

The faculty believes, however, that the path Day was pursuing will lead only toward nothing, for nothing could be more obvious than the fact that the Rosetta Stone solved the riddle of the hieroglyphs. The thesis Dean proposes, in their minds, constitutes needless backtracking—glorifying a hoax & not even from a historical angle. *Now history, there's an angle. If only young Dean had any interest in history—but he doesn't.* To the professors, all they can make of Day's process is that it requires staring at the page for a long time. They will not give it the time to study it deeply. They have grants to write.

Dean's professors consider him a student hardly distinguished from his fellows. His papers they find sloppy, half-baked, unfinished & ultimately misdirected. Dean seems smart & unquestionably believes himself brilliant. Perhaps his biggest deficit is that he lacks fundamental writing ability. Certainly, something is lacking in the articulation of the information lilting about in his head.

What's more, Dean has no interest in visiting Egypt. Even when the funding is in place & all he needs to do is fill out the paperwork, Dean has no desire to go. Perhaps his writing skills are poor to the degree that he cannot even fill out the government forms. There comes a point in Egyptian studies when people no longer find you credible if you haven't visited Egypt. It's not like you can go to Arizona & pretend real hard. [*So much of what Egypt is about you will never find in books; nothing beats seeing it firsthand. Yet, there is always so much more you can never know.*]

Foot Apples, against the grain, believes Egypt is finite, knowable & that he can work with the language & reach a point where he understands it entirely—a point where he has nothing more to do—exhausting Egypt completely.

Interlude: A passage in which Cy sees the Light from outside his dorm-room window

1988—Joel, a resident of Mary Ward Hall—the merry ward—lives on the same floor as Cy & Eleanor Cookee & the on weekends puts on his favorite brown T-shirt, closes his dormroom door, turns down the lights & turns up the Steely Dan. He remains that way most of the weekend, groovin on the Dan through the night while sleeping away the day. No one is sure when he eats, when he relieves his bladder & bowels, when he studies for class—we are not even sure he does any of those things. [Years later, we run across Joel. He's into Scientology now.] The reason we mention Joel here is because when Cy—which is short for Cypress, like the tree—experiences the Unexplainable Light outside his dorm room window late one Thursday night, it is the type of thing we might have expected to hear about from Joel. The Light itself may have been designated for Joel's eyes, only Cy catches it instead.

Eleanor Cookee's phone rings in her dorm room single—it is past 3 A.M.—yet she doesn't answer it. She's not there to hear it. After several rings, the answering machine clicks on, then quickly clicks off as the caller decides not to leave a message but rather to call again. Within seconds, the phone again rings until the machine again picks up & the process repeats. Sleepy dorm residents from across the hall angrily throw shoes at her door; the phone rings on.

Calling frantically from a few rooms down the hall is Cy, who has just seen something & must tell someone. If Eleanor answers, Cy doesn't know what he is going to say. *Wow!* is what he is going to say. Then, he is going to say calmly, *Eleanor Cookee, this is Cy.* He will tell her no, he is not high & hope that she believes him when he tells her about the Unexplainable Light outside his window. Then he prays Eleanor

Cookee, will ask him some questions, because he doesn't have the language in him to describe what he's seen.

Still lying in bed, freshly awakened by the Unexplainable Light, Cy wonders. *What was it? I can't remember. Why can I not remember?* He had been in the throes of a deep sleep & now all he can do is think & rub his eyes & try to get Eleanor Cookee on the phone, so he can tell her about it. He wonders what it was: A vision? A scratch on the eye? A reaction to something he ate? When he tries to remember the details of what he saw, the memories become fuzzy. He is losing them by the minute. How will he keep this with him? In the dark, he scribbles down what happened on a pad by his bed, but in the morning he will not be able to read a word of it. He needs to tell someone about the Unexplainable Light.

Where can Eleanor Cookee be that she is not answering her phone?

Not long before Cy sees the Unexplainable Light, Eleanor Cookee, a restless insomniac, stares at the patterns in her ceiling before deciding to take a walk around the empty campus in the dark, along the walkways between buildings & replays conversations in her mind that she has had, as well as conversations she might one day have. She wonders, too, why she is still living in the dorms during her senior year, why she never chose to move into the Joshua Tree with the others when the rent there was free. She sees nothing out of the ordinary. She might have been on the other side of campus when the Light went down.

Interlude: A passage in which Squirrel discovers Eleanor Cookee trying not to breathe & encourages her to take up the habit

I wouldn't think of telling anyone else this, but I've been thinking about what I should be saving toward my retirement. In two years, I will be twenty-three & I haven't saved anything yet. I know that the earlier you start saving, the more you have later. I just wonder why no one else seems worried about it. I worry that all of a sudden I will be thirty or forty & won't have saved. Do you think I'm out of my tree? Am I being shallow? Jude's not thinking about retirement & see how attractive she is, her body's thinness & gentle slopes. She feels good in her clothes & her clothes feel good on her. How is it that Jude can get by without thinking about retirement while thinking about it consumes me? TS is in love with Jude, I know he is. Don't let anyone know it bothers me. I can't sleep.

Squirrel listens to Eleanor Cookee's whispered rant patiently, knowing all the while that the solution will involve movement. Now Eleanor is finished & Squirrel can begin.

Pick up your arms, Eleanor Cookee, Squirrel commands. *Now let them go.*

I can't let go of my arms, not just like that.

Try again. New approach: Make a fist as tight as you can—now let it go. Feel how good letting it go feels? It takes practice, but you can let anything go.

Even when my checking account is overdrawn?

Ignoring Eleanor's last statement (because Eleanor is serious when she says it), Squirrel carries on: *Feel the top of your head—the tip-top—where you can thump loudly with your thumb, where you can hear yourself knocking but not feel anything. If you let yourself feel what is happening there, you feel yourself radiating heat. Don't forget to breathe.*

Suddenly, Squirrel realizes this is exactly what Eleanor is doing—the source of her stiffness & sleeplessness: *You are forgetting to breathe; you're holding your breath; you're not breathing. It's as if you were afraid of the rest of us hearing you breathe. No one minds if you breathe. No wonder you're all wrapped up. Breathing is important to human beings & other mammals, you know. We like oxygen.* Then adopting a hoity-toity British accent & two inches, up on tiptoes, she says, *Oxygen has been very good to us.* Now she's back to her normal voice. *Breathe, Eleanor Cookee—loud & obnoxious. Snarl when you breathe: Arrrrr! No one cares, no one is even noticing us over here. Do you think people will laugh if they hear you breathe? Loud & obnoxious as you can be. It's just you, breathing. No one cares. On the count of three.*

Chapter 22: The nervous wreck

We can find traces of Eleanor Cookee in all of us—last vestiges. We see them in their full-blown state more clearly in her than we do in ourselves. Whether we like it or not, we always leave traces. We leave the place where we sleep as clean as we found it & still you can find our tracks. Places remember. Traces—footprints & tracks—are reminders that someone (or something) has traveled this path before us. Sometimes, we watch from an eyehole in the shrubs as others follow the tracks left by us.

With Eleanor Cookee, we feel we have lived her life before her. We have already sprung all the traps she lays for herself. We always see her in hindsight. It's like watching someone through one-way glass as they relive the moments you wish you could have back—your past moments that when you think about them now, you cringe.

This passage revolves around Eleanor Cookee. She is always taking on so much: umpteen class credits & the Jokerman organizational work that no one else wants to do. Now along comes this Egyptian prank. What exactly is the first step in taking this gig forward? Of what use are protest signs? Of what use are the chains we use to lock ourselves to gates & bulldozers? Of what use is a clandestine operation when it's so ridiculous that the only reason to hold it secret is to keep from embarrassing ourselves? It's not like organizing a tree sit where the first step is finding a stand of old growth trees earmarked for a timber sale & you send off some of the others to go out & see what's there.

There is other news carrying significant impact into our lives; all this Egyptian talk is blinding us to our immediate world. Now that Willie has died, his grandmother, who owns the Font Street house, writes Eleanor Cookee a letter saying she wants to turn it into a true rental. She thinks we should pay rent. Who can blame her? She knows us & likes us, but we are not related. If we don't want to pay the rent, we will have to move out & set up house elsewhere. She's giving us until when the school year ends in May, so we have time to decide what we want to do.

Taking on rent to keep the Joshua Tree is just adding one more responsibility at a time when the group is becoming more & more divided. It's hard to begin paying rent for a place that you are used to having for free. We spend so much time away as it is that it hardly makes sense to keep a home these days. We travel light—now even more so. But it was always nice to know we had a home. These days, Jude & TS are both acting funny. Jude is finishing her master's degree at Stanford this spring. How is she managing to graduate in just four years? Don't master's degrees usually take at least five? Plus, molecular biology can't be easy. Endless gigging has cost the rest of us semesters in the progress toward degrees, but Jude graduates right on time. Now Jude is itching to do something. She just wants to get on with it & everything is moving so slowly. She's too quiet to say anything, but I can sense it in her. The way she goes, she leaves the rest of us behind. Who can keep up with her? Then there's TS who isn't himself these days. He just isn't getting enough sleep. There's something not right in the way he falls asleep all the time—a disorder, though no one else thinks so, because falling asleep is, after all, normal. Everyone sleeps; it's just these days (& nights) TS sleeps all the time. We're beginning to unbe, break apart & loosen ourselves from ourselves. I *can feel it. I wish it didn't matter so much to me. But it's only Jude & TS; I don't feel the same commitment to the others.* [Eleanor is lying to herself—Cy & Squirrel—she loves them all. She would do anything for any one of them. Her energy comes from other people.]

Then softly out of the blue, Eleanor Cookee's mother sends her a care package. Among the contents are Hershey's Kisses; store coupons; Elvis Presley postage stamps; earth friendly glycerin soap; a recipe for humus;

a picture of the family dog, a border collie named Fido Fiasco & a check for twenty-five dollars to help cover the phone bill—you know, usual college student stuff. Also included are a couple of envelopes—ancient—one containing carbon copies of two letters from Eleanor's stepfather & mother addressed to Eleanor's real father in upstate New York & a letter from Eleanor's real father sent to her stepfather & mother. The thirteen-cent postage & postmarks from September of 1976 put the letters into a frame of time—Eleanor's childhood.

Can Eleanor remember September 1976? Not really. It blends in too well with all of the other months of her childhood. She was a kid & all the days seem the same. It was the Bicentennial, but she hardly has any memories of it—maybe the song "With Your Love" by Jefferson Starship on the radio but not much else.

Years later, in 1980, when Eleanor was twelve, her real father, a man named Cliff Madison living in New Jersey, contracted throat cancer. Cliff had four sons, who were born over five years by his second wife, one boy quickly following another—since the divorce from Eleanor's mother when Eleanor was eleven months old.

One of the sons was the first to notice the cancer. On a Sunday morning while Cliff Madison was shaving, Jimmy, the youngest, asked, *Hey, dad, what's that on your neck?* Cliff turned his head to see himself in the mirror more—*aww, shit!* How had he been carrying that lump right there on his neck without noticing it sooner? Did it hit him overnight?

The cancer spread & within a year, overtook him. [Willie dying of cancer disturbs Eleanor greatly, although she shows it less than some of the others.]

Sometimes, you make decisions that when looking back years later, you don't know why you made them. Eleanor's mother had thought it best not to tell Eleanor, who had not seen her father since she was three, about the cancer until after Cliff's death. The decision had seemed right at the time, though not so much now: *I thought he was too much of a son of a bitch to die.*

Eleanor is taken out of school for four days to fly to New Jersey to attend the funeral. She had wanted to see her father for as long as she could remember & had been looking forward to growing up so she could go & visit & become reacquainted with him. Then, suddenly, they tell her when she gets home from school that he has passed away. She had not seen much of him as a little girl due to her mother's lingering hard feelings toward him & now so quickly, he was gone without any kind of goodbye. She wanted a message from him, a clue letting her know he loved her, a goodbye especially meant for her.

While at her father's house, where she was staying with his new family, they went through his things. [A letter? A photograph? Some clue or another?] Cliff's second wife, Rosemary, wanted to find something for Eleanor. She considered forging a letter to the girl supposedly from her father saying how her father loved her. In the end, though, Rosemary succumbed to her belief that adults should always treat children with honesty. *Honey, I wish I could find something to show you how your father loved you.*

Cliff always traveled light—hardly keeping any mementos from his life—& then getting rid of even more in the months before dying. *I'm sorry, Eleanor. I can't find anything for you. I wish I could.*

The four boys, each of them younger than Eleanor who is twelve, can't believe their eyes when Eleanor appears in their home a day before their father's funeral. There she is—their father's looks & image formed on a girl's face. The boys are learning they have an older sister at a time when they still believe that girls are only good for teasing. To them, their father didn't seem like a man who could *make* a girl, even if he wanted. The truth, though, is that a girl came first.

[The oldest goes so far as to wonder what other secrets the family is keeping from them.]

The boys give their newfound sister some photographs, which she takes home with her. Of course each photograph shows Cliff full of life in a way that Eleanor had never known him: playing Nerf football with his sons; red cheeked, brushing his teeth in his bathrobe on Christmas morning; taxiing a small airplane down a runway—always smiling, always breathing. How can cancer come & take someone away from life like that?

She never tells anyone, but Eleanor Cookee holds herself responsible for her father's cancer. She can't figure how, but she knows it must have come from her. She knows it isn't logical, but it is just something she feels. [Where does cancer come from anyway? Why does it come? Where else could it have come from?]

After the funeral, Eleanor returns to her family in western Michigan who now seem to her strangers as much as the family she just met. Her mother feels awful that she had never given Ellie a chance to know her real father before he died. In hindsight, it seems as if it would have been simple—at the time, it seemed impossible. Eleanor's mother sees the photographs Cliff's family had given Eleanor & wishes she could give her more. Eleanor's mother, too, had thrown out everything from her first marriage, wanting to erase it from her heart & mind & start over.

A decade passes & Eleanor's mother finds two letters while sorting out a desk drawer where the letters were stashed in the event of a legal challenge that never materialized. A day after finding them, she sends the two letters to Ellie who is away at school in San Francisco. Eleanor removes the letters slowly from the envelopes & begins to read. The first envelope without an address on it contains the carbon copies of two letters, one written by her stepfather & a second written by her mother:

September 21, 1976

Dear Cliff,
Hello. You & I have never met, but I have enjoyed watching your daughter, Eleanor, or Ellie as we call her, as she becomes quite the young person. She has had some good teachers at West End Elementary & wants to go to college & become a teacher herself. She's one of the stars of her soccer team & I had the pleasure of watching her kick two goals in a game last Saturday morning. She's a terrific kid.

I am writing to you today with a sensitive matter at hand & by my desire to do what I believe is the right thing. In all fairness to Ellie, I would like to adopt her. I already have been like a father to her & want to take this to the logical next step. I would like to give Ellie my last name & take full legal responsibility for her well-being. This hopefully will make things easier for her in the years ahead, especially now that she is readying herself for junior high. Of course, we will not let her forget that you are her biological father & that you care for her.

I am sending you paperwork that requires your signature in order to set the adoption process in motion. Please sign the papers before a notary & send them back to the address written in the upper left-hand corner of the envelope. Thank you, Cliff.

Sincerely,

[The signature that follows the letter is written out beautifully.]

Dr. Jerry Cookee

RICHARD MELO

[The beautiful signature is surprising, considering that Eleanor's stepfather is a physician. He included his title, *Dr.*, with his name not in any attempt to impress Cliff, or to pander his respectability. He includes his title merely out of habit.]

On the day he writes this letter, his office's wastepaper basket is full of crumpled up rough drafts. When Eleanor's mother reads what Dr. Jerry has written, she insists on writing a letter of her own & including it with his. The second carbon copy letter, written by Eleanor's mother, is more direct to the point at hand:

Dear Cliff,

Let's expedite matters. Sign the papers. Send them back. Do it soon, Cliff. We want to get this over with.

Claire

They fold together the combined letters & put them in one envelope & mail them. They keep the carbon copies & store them in the desk drawer in case the situation becomes complicated on Cliff Madison's end, in case more lawyers become involved. A ridiculous waiting period follows; the two of them are uncertain how Cliff would respond, uncertain what it is he is thinking. Will he laugh & throw the letters into the fire? *The man can be a real shit. I would put nothing past him.* Eleven days later—a relatively quick turnaround everything considered—a letter from Cliff arrives. It reads:

Dear Claire & Dr. Jerry:

I was glad to hear in your letter that Eleanor is doing well. There is a great amount of love here for her, even though it may not seem that way by the way things have turned out. I have missed seeing her grow into the fine young person you have described & am glad to know she is living in the warm & happy home you are providing for her. I will always love her, as she will always be my daughter.

I have signed all the papers you have sent me. Let me know if there is anything else I can do to help you speed along the adoption process.

Yours,
Cliff

Now here it is. For so long Eleanor had wanted a sign that yes, her father loved her; she had wanted it so badly but thought she would never have it. Then she let it go & made herself forget about it, but it

123

hadn't forgotten about her. Not knowing that her father loved her had made it so hard to smile.

[*I will always love her, as she will always be my daughter*, her father writes (though indirectly) to her. Remembering him always turns her back into a little girl, the age she was when he died.

Well, Daddy, just so you know, I am still your daughter.]

Funny how looking back Eleanor Cookee remembers hardly anything about the time when her stepfather, Dr. Jerry Cookee, adopted her. She starts a new school year with a new last name & though it takes a while to get used to, the transition is simple & complete & leaves no lasting impression on her.

Her mother & Dr. Jerry had done their talking & made all the arrangements without her knowing, at night when she was in her room asleep. Even reading the letters doesn't jar her memory. The days & minutes of childhood really do blend together.
She again says to herself the words, quoting her father, *I will always love her, as she will always be my daughter.*

Eleanor Cookee nurtures a heart-wrenching crush on TS that she isn't telling anybody about. Everybody knows, though—how could we miss it? We see it in the way she smiles when someone mentions his name. We see it in the way she trusts him. Then again, we all trust him; TS has honesty written all over him. We see it in the way she can't pull herself away from him. We see it in the way she describes him as having qualities none of the rest of us can see.

She thinks of him & dreams of him while exercising & while dieting & she doesn't even look like herself these days. She looks more like someone who is holding her breath & can't wait to breathe again.

Eleanor, please, just be yourself—be comfortable.

[Let's go to Oregon for the summer. We can live out of a van if we have to; we can live out of tents. We can work out all the particulars of the pyramid prank—if there even is such a thing. We can organize another West Coast Tree Sit Week. We can learn more about ourselves this way. We can reinvent ourselves, because we have to when the Joshua

Tree isn't ours anymore. We're losing it. Jokerman, what will become of you?]

Eerily, the planets line up at that moment just so. As she finishes reading the three letters, who do you think walks below her open second-story window?

TS is walking to his bus stop fresh from night class. Passing by the dorms, he sees Eleanor Cookee through her window. He stands underneath it & tries to get her attention without yelling. Softly he calls, *Ellie!* (Funny how no one but TS calls her that around here. In every situation, people call her Eleanor Cookee as if not to confuse her with all the other Eleanors of the world, of which, in these times & of all the people we know, there are none.)

Sweet, wonderful timing it is that it is TS calling to her—TS, whom she loves so much.

Can you come up & see me? She calls down to him.

TS looks over in the direction of the bus stop as if to say he needs to go. Then he again looks up at her.

A moment later, TS is sitting beside Eleanor Cookee on her bed & she explains the story to him. He assures her that she did not cause her father's cancer. Then he reads the letters. She can hardly hold back tears while he reads. She had let no tears fall while reading the letters to herself.

A muted *wow* [*Wow* never comes across as well as a printed word as it does spoken. In typeface, *wow* looks sarcastic. TS says *wow* without any shade of sarcasm; he says *wow* in his own TS way.]

Now he's going & leaves without kissing her. The thought never crosses his mind, but it certainly crosses hers. Now she loves him even more. *He listens to me; he listens to me better than anyone.* They aren't supposed to kiss—not now—not tonight but maybe sometime.

In high school, Eleanor Cookee used to write poems. Lying on her bed summer nights with the window open, she wrote poetry to get her mind off of boys. Since then she has learned to apply her energy elsewhere. Tonight feels like one of those nights when she used to write poems & God knows, there's a boy she needs to get her mind off of.

The only writing Eleanor Cookee had ever shown us is in the genre of protest signs. Eleanor Cookee becomes a student & practitioner of the grassroots organizing of movements & wants so much to pass on the knowledge she gains through the hard knocks of her own experience. She has written out her version of the techniques of protest sign writing & hung them on the bulletin board in the foyer of the Joshua Tree. The sad irony to Eleanor Cookee's *Guide for Making Spiffy Protest Signs* is that when protest time rolls around, people say they are busy & she ends up making all the signs herself.

Now here she is again, lying on her bed with the window open & in a poem-writing mood, but she cannot write one. That's not who she is anymore. Who she is now is a person who writes slogans for protest signs.

Eleanor Cookee's brief yet helpful Guide for Making Spiffy Protest Signs:

1. Signs should present one thought simply, clearly & legibly. Avoid rhetoric. Large drawings do wonders for a sign's presentation.

2. Before making the signs, brainstorm what ideas should go on them & reach agreement among the group. It is often effective to have no more than two or three messages repeated several times.

3. Use cardboard or other firm backing & waterproof lettering. Waterproof magic markers & crayons work terrific. Remember that red, orange, yellow & light blue do not show up well on TV.

4. If rain is a possibility—in the Pacific Northwest, it almost always will be—waterproof your signs with plastic wrap or bags.

5. Put care into making signs. A few well-made ones will have more positive impact than many sloppy ones. A soft, smart touch in lettering, spacing & size will make all the difference in the world in the value of the sign.

Since writing a poem is out of the question, she might as well do what she knows how to do: make a protest sign. The slogan she wants to give the sign is her father's message to her: *I will always love her, as she will always be my daughter.* As much as the words mean to her, they are too sappy for a protest sign. People will think she's around the bend if she writes that. People will think she's writing about her own daughter & everyone knows Eleanor Cookee is childless & twenty-one.

The words, *keep following gentle impulses*, pop into her head & that's more like it. That's what she wants to share. She pulls out a blank sign from behind the door, finds her paint & brush & sketches out the words first lightly in pencil & slants each letter in her own personal italic: *Keep following gentle impulses.*

Following gentle impulses is the way to live.

Gentle impulses are the bus that drives everybody back home at the end of the night.

Gentle impulses are everywhere, in everything.

Gentle impulses are God waiting to happen.

Gentle impulses are how Eleanor Cookee knows her father loved her.

Keep following gentle impulses is what you mean when you tell a person, *Peace*.

Gentle impulses are what TS is about.

One day soon, gentle impulses will follow you.

They are more than TS's theme song. Gentle impulses are what we all could learn from him.

Aren't gentle impulses what Willie Shoman was telling us about before he died, though not in so many words?

When you find yourself in a jam, you can find your way out by following gentle impulses.

Gentle impulses will right the course.

Trust them; keep them with you.

Follow softly. The lead is within.

Just recently, Eleanor had noticed how stiff she is; Squirrel helps her by showing her how to breathe. This protest sign is her first breath. Through gentle impulses, Eleanor Cookee, who had frustrated herself time & again in attempting to define the troupe in cascading mountains of words, realizes that the only way other people can understand what it is we are about is through this—protest sign poetry & following gentle impulses.

Chapter 23: A passage in which the overstory reaches zero

1990—Yellow beer—watery, carbonated & corporately American—is the thing that Barry Weathers & Wendy drink at night in taverns amid local people as the two of them rollick all over the West. Yellow beer makes us all Americans—or so the beer companies would like to have you think—whether or not you choose to drink it.

For Barry Weathers and Wendy, drinking yellow beer in a backcountry watering hole in Oregon's Blue Mountains is a put-on. In the morning (or whenever it is they wake up), the two of them will disappear into the woods not five miles from the local tavern they had closed down the night before. They will blaze their way up the mountain & drill & screw spikes into ancient trees that Eleanor Cookee has marked on her map as scheduled for cutting next year as part of a Forest Service plan to reduce the overstory around here to zero.

From high above the forests of the Pacific Northwest—from the tops of mountains, from airplanes, from tagalong rides with birds—you peer down over the green canopy & see an unbroken layer of trees. The branches of one tree reach out to where they touch the branches of the next tree over & this happens hundreds of thousands of times over in a national forest. The part of the tree that penetrates the sky—the part that tickles the clouds—is the overstory. It is a perch for birds who don't realize how lucky they are.

In the Northwest, no one swings from tree to tree. On the taller trees, the trunks are thick, but the flimsy pine branches cannot support the weight of swinging mammals, with their heavy legs & all. Firs & cedars are not good climbing trees, either—dead branches hazard your ascent & even live branches can break free. We hear, though, that these trees make excellent lumber. Is it any wonder monkeys never made it here? Monkeys had to find ways to arrive in the Pacific Northwest other than evolution. [Yeah, we like walked here.]

Overstory: Untouched is just as it sounds; the wild left wild.

Overstory: Zero is just as it sounds: the elimination of canopy, the clearcutting of trees from an area, the ground scraped bare except for stumps & instant seedlings genetically designed to grow faster than regular Douglas firs, so that the timber companies may re-harvest the area again even sooner than ever before possible.

Overstory: Zero is starting again & guessing wrong.

Overstory veils the ground. Without it, earth is naked. Cutting growth away is the same as flaying Earth's skin.

A legion of mite technocrats—pesky as wood ticks; startling in their lack of vision, their absence of foresight; little cogs in the big, bright green pleasure machine—see trees as jobs, see trees as their jobs. They are driven by the mantra, *We can always replant*.

Rich communities of plants & animals develop only after the forest is several centuries old; you cannot buy a virgin forest with reforestation.

In a clearcut, rain erodes the slopes lain bare of topsoil so that new seedlings never grow; silt clouds rivers & streams, pushing the salmon & other native fish to the brink of extinction. Downstream urban centers flood as rainwater, which once trickled downhill, now gleans off, causing rivers to rise to levels higher than ever in recorded history.

Timber companies are driven by profit. They go as far as to steal trees that the law proclaims belong to no one but the ground upon which they grow. Timber theft runs rampant. Timber companies steal ancient trees when no one is looking; they get more board feet that way. [*Later we only find the stump & we count the annual rings.*]

It originates in the when-we-fall-we-take-it-all style approach to forest management—nuts & bolts, nuts & bolts, nuts & bolts. Green cathedrals are measured in terms of the board feet they can produce.

The US Forest Service won't stop timber companies. They're in cahoots with them & the Forest Service wants to keep wood cheap & available; the price will be marked up elsewhere.

No one will stand in the merciless vandals' way—unless we do.

We have gone to spiking only old growth trees. In the past, we were less discriminate. We once found in the Kalmiopsis a stump to a tree that had been standing over 400 years & cut a few days earlier. It was in the way of a planned logging road intended to pass within six inches of the boundary to one of the most pristine wilderness areas in the lower forty-eight. We peer into the stump, into its gentle waves of closely spaced, annual rings that huddle more closely together toward the outside. We are looking into history—a history that holds still & lets life happen to it.

You can take a tree & leave the forest; you can take the forest & leave nothing.

The alternative to Overstory: Zero is careful, thoughtful logging. You take some trees while leaving most of them & you leave the oldest ones alone. Rather than cutting all the ones you want & bulldozing the rest, sterilizing the environment & robbing it forever of its genetic diversity—its past glory before God—you go gently.

That's what you can do.

We can live & vanish & hardly leave a trace.

Those who came before us did.

We can always get by with less; we are smart that way.

We can always find a way.

The story here, though, is about nothing more than drinking yellow beer at night amid the local people in the Blue Mountains. This is something Willie Shoman & Jude back in the day would never do. Jude &

Willie would go to extreme lengths in making sure they would never be caught. They would buy food & gas as far away from the trees as possible & brew their own coffee at camp.

They would know what they're doing. They were caught just once & only when Willie Shoman badly turned an ankle. Never see us, never notice us, never catch us & we'll all coexist peacefully. Barry Weathers & Wendy play out their lives more recklessly, drinking yellow beer in taverns at night amid local people who begin to wonder about them.

Do you think those are two of them those forest agitators, Dolores?

They don't know; they can't tell. Barry Weather & Wendy keep changing before their eyes. A reputation precedes Barry & Wendy's arrival— a reputation established by groups other than ours—stirring hatred & fear. Barry & Wendy are easy to identify, even with Barry's long hair tucked underneath his Chicago Cubs baseball hat & his earring left in the Subaru.

Why else in the world would these two show up here tonight?

Barry & Wendy like playing the role of the outsider. They like it best when people notice how out of place they are & talk about them. They even play the outsider with us, never letting themselves fully become part of our troupe, never taking on any of the responsibility & showing up whenever they want. They come knocking at the door; we know them & let them in.

We cannot say that we trust them; we cannot say that we don't trust them.

Oh, they would not do anything to bring us down or lead us into danger, unless they catch us up in their recklessness.

The way Barry & Wen see it , just being there is a put-on.

The truth is as simple as it seems: *Yes, we are forest agitators here to defend a few two-hundred-year-old trees that no one has any business cutting, trees that the law forbids cutting. We are citizens enforcing the law—reinforcing the law. Who does the forest belong to anyway? We are here with the law on our side.*

These trees are what make us all Americans, not the yellow beer. The trees belong to a great, unbroken chain of being to which we are all connected. When trees touch other trees, branches brushing against each other in the wind, they become complete. Trees all get together to shade the ground from hard, falling rain & the garish sun. The organism is no longer the tree—it is the forest itself.

Two local folks, divorcees, though never married to one another, send a round of beers over to Barry & Wendy's table. This is what Barry & Wen had been waiting for—contact. Now comes playtime. Making themselves out as strangers jes passin' through, Barry & Wendy amble on over amicably, *hello, hello, hello, hello*, introducing themselves as Chuck & Delilah. The local people exchange pleasant greetings. *You from around these parts? No*, Barry answers in a deadpan, then a sigh.

From his pocket, Barry produces a crumbled piece of paper. Printed on it is a black & white photograph, a Xerox copy of a suspect, the photo looking as if it had come down off a post office wall, which, indeed, it had.

We are looking for this man.

Ain't seen him. What did he do?

Let's just say we have an interest in locating him. Barry folds the paper & returns it to his pocket.

The silence hangs heavily. The local people are dying from curiosity. They want more.

We might be able to help you if you tell us what he did.

Sometimes Barry & Wendy act more drunk than they are & begin to let information spill that they act as if it is not prudent of them to share, but since these people are good, good local people with good & trustworthy faces, they reveal everything.

The man in the picture, his name is Claude Dallas, a French Canadian. He's wanted for the murder of two U.S. marshals.

He's a grizzly trapper, a poacher of the meanest sort.

We can forgive him for poaching, but for the murder of two good ol' boys he's wanted; those marshals had families who love them.

The local people listen intently to every word, then ask: *You have reason to believe he's somewhere around here?*

No one else can locate him. That is why we are here. We are looking everywhere, tracking down every lead.

What's your part in this?

If we find him, if we can haul him in, we take home the reward money.

Now if these two local people looked at Barry Weathers & only at Barry Weathers, they would buy none of it. They would call everything bullshit & wonder why these two are really here & why are they speaking in German accents. Barry radiates a kind of energy that if you pay attention to, you can tell he's a fake. Wendy, though, has the kind of face you can't help believing, the kind of stare that draws you in & will not let go. Inside her piercing gaze, you find yourself believing whatever it is about her she wants you to believe—this despite Barry's transparent acting.

The local people shudder at the thought that someone of Claude Dallas's bullying kind might be lurking in their town. The photo didn't look all too familiar—a face they would describe in no other way than as belonging to a mean s.o.b., but the more they look at it, the more familiar it becomes, until they reach the point that they swear they've seen him around & plenty.

What matters is that Claude Dallas is real. The photograph & the listing of his offense, Barry & Wendy had stolen from a post office wall—oh, the cliché of it. Claude Dallas is an outlaw of the murderous kind, someone who had killed one U.S. marshal who approached him merely to verify that his traplines were licensed. After killing the first marshal, Claude Dallas had enough nerve not to run; he left the body aboveground for wolves to eat. A second U.S. marshal arrives a day later to investigate the disappearance of the first, but Claude Dallas again drew an eagle as the marshal approached & shot him, too. This time, though, Claude Dallas ran.

Where did he run?

Into the forest. Into caves.

He was already living in a hand-built cabin at the forest's edge; the pornographic magazines they find when they search the place are his most basic contact with the outside world.

Now he can be living anywhere.

Has he been chased?

We cannot say.

Is he still at large?

If we didn't think so, do you think we would be here?

What does all this mean?

I have no idea & they all break into nervous laughter.

Rumors fly that the new Forest Patrol, established by the DEA & whose mission it is to comb wild lands in search of clandestine marijuana cultivation as well as bring about arrests, will also be on the lookout for tree spikers, truck disablers, & tractor juryriggeurs. More than likely they will have something more on the ball than your everyday Forest Service law enforcement officer. They will strategize all day new ways of trapping us & catching us. This new-well trained corps of former gymnasts & sprinters will be outfitted in North Face gear & will go about their business believing they are in service to their country. There's talk of throwing us out of trees. They'll climb up after us, force us into a harness & throw us out. That remains to be seen. News to the world: We can run faster & outsmart them in a chase.

Going nowhere are the old school Forest Service Law Enforcement branch officers who for years have wanted to kick our little asses. News to the world: We can run faster & outsmart them in a chase.

Going nowhere are the loggers themselves who want to break every bone in our bodies. News to the world: We can run faster & outsmart them in a chase. Even if we are caught from time to time, if we play it right, it can be fun.

We can stay one step ahead of them all.

We fear only Claude Dallas because he's mean & random, filled with a sense of I-don't-know-what.

Claude Dallas is so large that he can grab you from behind & take you with him. Carrying you would hardly slow him down.

He hardly needs shotguns & traps, he can take what he wants with his bare hands.

Communicating with him is nearly impossible, he being French Canadian & largely uneducated, not to mention extremely antisocial.

What do you do if Claude Dallas sees you first?

You just hope he doesn't.

When you see Claude Dallas, run.

We know we can run faster than Claude Dallas, but he can bully his way more easily through obstacles, fallen trees, his bullishness more than making up for lost time.

As we go, we refuse to take Claude Dallas too seriously. We do, however, acknowledge the Claude Dallas factor; the unforeseen & the unforeseeable; Murphy's Law rewritten to foil ourselves; the thing for which you can neither account nor prepare; the stone left unturned; the move you wish you could have back; the variable outside our control, because that's the way life is.

Claude Dallas is the unthinkable suddenly come to meet you—bang, you're dead.

Claude Dallas is the opposite of a gentle impulse.

Beware the Claude Dallas factor. It doesn't even need to be the real Claude Dallas.

Chapter 24: Outfoxing

Barry Weathers, born in 1968, like so many of us, grew up in Chicago, amid the legend of the Fox. When Barry Weathers first started coming around these parts, hanging around the Joshua Tree, it was as if there was nothing else he wanted to talk about: *the Fox this the Fox that.*

The Fox was an eco-saboteur from the early 1970s so shrouded in mysterioso that no one had ever seen his face. There were no composite sketches, which led people (especially wild-minded children like Barry Weathers) to believe that the Fox was a costumed superhero in the best Superman & Green Lantern ain't-got-nuthin-on-me sense. In the Fox's crowning moment, he used a firehose to pump raw sewage through the building ventilation system into a board of directors meeting of a company responsible for the leaching of PCBs into the Illinois groundwater & took no responsibility for it. The Fox vanished completely by the time they discovered what had happened, that what happened wasn't an accident, that someone dowsed them on purpose.

From what the Chicago police & media gathered, the Fox worked alone & only around Chicago & always left a card at the scene that said nothing more than *Compliments of the Fox*. Unlike Superman & Green Lantern, the Fox had a sense of humor.

The Chicago media had a field day with the Fox before his appearances suddenly ceased in 1973. After that the Fox was seemingly forgotten by all except Barry Weathers who includes accounts of the Fox's adventures among his earliest memories, the kind of memory that pushes him along in the direction he travels in today.

Sleek, uncatchable, never identified, the Fox left no trace of himself & made a huge impression on a young Barry Weathers. In high school, during the time when the Fox emerged as Barry's personal obsession, Barry mounted a search for the Fox, talking mostly to reporters, hearing mostly rehashed stories of the Fox's adventures & how thoroughly the Fox had covered his tracks. While in college, with an increased resourcefulness, Barry sometimes considered returning to Chicago, visiting his family & reviving his search for the Fox, knowing this time his chances of finding the hero would be much better. But Barry had lost the drive, it no longer meant that much to him, especially now as he saw himself carrying on the Fox's work all along the west coast. The Fox of his childhood whom he merely imagined, Barry thinks of himself as having become.

The image of Jokerman we have seen used most frequently in newspapers is that of Barry Weathers, his palm raised & fingers folded under. It's a photograph taken by Eleanor Cookee & sent to the media each time she issues a new press release. Barry's gesture appears a sign of strength & defiance, when actually Barry was doing nothing more than demonstrating how he signals a right turn when riding his bicycle & that's when Eleanor snapped his picture.

Barry thinks that wearing his hair long gives him an edge. Everyone can tell he's soft.

Barry isn't angry, although he might like to think so. None of us are angry.

Yes, there are people & we know them & they believe that if you are not outraged you don't know what's going on. The problem with that is if you go around outraged your blood pressure soars, you hold in your sneezes, anger festers inside of you, you knock out nasty letters-to-the-editor about everything. You grow a tumor where there wasn't one & *living just ain't no fun at all*. The key to unlocking it all is letting

RICHARD MELO

go, or as Eleanor Cookee wishes to remind everyone: *Keep following gentle impulses*.

Interlude: Molly Ringwald's gone wrestling

While Barry Weathers is turning the legend of the Fox into his own plans for the future it is the middle 1980s. The rest of us are busy being who we were at the time, hanging out with the kid who knew all the words to "It's the End of the World as We Know It (& I Feel Fine)" & you yourself were using words like *awesome & fantastic & hey!* Then suddenly, giving no thought to dark clouds & chilly winters of the Ronald Reagan years, you find yourself perpetually falling in love with the red-haired girl from *Sixteen Candles*. For the first time since we last saw our home movies, we are seeing a face on the screen that we know is ours. Molly is one of us. Molly Ringwald makes us want to jump, dance & make movies. In the middle 1980s, during an era when kids dance like robots, we are all ghosts in the machine & Molly Ringwald is as popular as the Beatles.

Chapter 25: Animals soon will roam the streets of your town in slacks & dress shirts

Media pranks hold an allure & no one takes them more seriously than Barry Weathers & Wendy who watch television when there is nothing else to do. They are easily the most theatrical of the bunch of us. While Jude & Willie Shoman will often go to great lengths to pass through their daily lives unnoticed, unrecognized & unremembered, Barry & Wendy more exhibitionistic, belonging to the hey-go-mad-look-at-me crowd who dye their hair blue & wear tattoos & schedule appearances on daytime talk shows. Sometimes, we think they're around because they think the life we are living would make an excellent movie. If there ever were one made & Hollywood should cast it, they would of course, star as themselves. They spend much of 1989 trying to book themselves on a national daytime talk show to share their many ecotage adventures & for months they are greeted with no interest from the stable of American daytime talk show producers.

Chapter 26: ANDY

1990: Rejected, Barry & Wendy try again to land themselves a gig on a daytime talk show, this time with a comic twist. They will pose as Christian fundamentalist animal rights activists, a group of young people who believe that Jesus holds the souls of animals as dear as He holds the souls of people. Keeping that in mind, they ask believers to clothe the animals. They hoot & holler: *It's indecent the way animals are running around in their nakedness like that—dogs, cats, horses, pigs & goats—every last one.*

Stretching themselves out, bending their faces into something they are not, talkin' crazy things—this is what gets them noticed by show producers.

Barry & Wendy call themselves ANDY, short for Animals Need Dressing. They added the *y* to the end of it because it sounded better that way. ANDY sounds sexy yet simple, a name ready-made for television. They draw a logo, which they screen onto T-shirts & business cards. Wendy makes drawings of a variety of household & domestic animals—dogs, cats, horses, pigs & goats—wearing clothing & happily.

Suddenly Wendy & Barry are on TV asking people to have the shame & decency to clothe Rover & Kitty. On the air they wear their ANDY T-shirts over their everyday clothes. They hold their mouths differently; they wear expressions on their faces that spell intolerance.

The inspiration to commandeer daytime television originates in another incident. At first Barry & Wendy want to appear on a talk show pitching animal rights.

We support Amnesty for Animals.

We believe in granting political asylum to kittens rescued from animal research facilities.

That's their spin.

After rescuing several kittens from an animal research facility in Palo Alto, they go about the process of finding each of the kittens homes. Then authorities appear at the door of the house where Barry & Wen are staying. The cops demand the kittens so they can take them back to the animal research center. In an over-my-dead-body attempt to save the kittens, Barry and Wendy hold their ground. The police wrestle them to the ground, subduing them with mace & sleeper holds & lock the two of them in jail while the kittens are returned to the hallowed name of science. Less than a month later, Wendy & Barry go on the road & sabotage a labrador retriever farm in Astoria, Oregon where dogs are raised to become research subjects. They bring with them hand-sized sledge hammers to smash glass, computer screens, coffee makers whatever is within the radius of their swing. They pour sand & water into fuel tanks. Wendy & Barry smash & smash without fear, having severed the power lines that feed the security system before anything else. They are moved fiercely by a sense of vengeance, thinking all the while of the lost kittens while suppressing their most burning desire: to set free the seventy-five howling dogs in the adjacent kennel building. Seventy-five dogs would roam the streets of Astoria & the outskirts of the town. Maybe some of the dogs would make it all right & find homes or adapt to street life, to life in the wild, but then it rains so much here that many of them would die of exposure. Others would die of starvation. Others might drown in the Columbia; they might drown in the ocean. So you smash the place to pieces, then you leave the dogs behind. You would like to set the place on fire but you might injure the dogs. So instead you smash & smash. You find yourself in the throes of decisions that will not feel good no matter what you do. You do what you can & hope for the best for the dogs.

This is what Wendy & Barry want to bring to daytime television, but the shows' producers aren't biting. Some of the troupe begin to wonder why it matters so much to Barry & Wendy to play on television; TV matters so little to the rest of us.

People love seeing animals on TV; there must be a way!

Yes, there is a way, a Christian way at that. They tweak their message with a Christian spin & suddenly the producers from a daytime show called [*we are not about to say*] are on the phone making travel arrangements to send Barry & Wen to travel to Chicago for taping of the show.

Back at the Joshua Tree we gather around Eleanor Cookee's television. For us, it is as if we are going to watch the Beatles on the *Ed Sullivan Show*.

My God, look at Wendy, her mouth seems so severe, a little slit. She is not at all herself.

This is a riot!

We listen closely, hanging on every word Wendy & Barry share with the live studio audience.

The Rapture can go down at any moment, are your pets ready? Not without clothing, they aren't. Wouldn't it break your heart to pieces if your animals didn't get to go with you?

The studio audience looks at Barry & Wendy as if they're around the bend, even by the slim standards of daytime talk TV.

Stop the exploitation of their unclothed bodies! Mercy, Lord Jesus! Rights to all Christian animals!

Too many American animals are going about unclothed, vile in their nakedness. The animals aren't choosing to sin. Rather we are choosing for them to sin by not providing them clothing.

We are an industrialized nation, the best there is in the whole world. We can do better.

Animals need to wear trousers at least—for covering their privates.

The women need to wear tops as well, to go along with cute little matching skirts.

After a commercial break, Wen & Barry take questions from the audience.

Q: How would you treat animals living in the wild?

Oh, we think they should be clothed as well, but we are not unreasonable people. We understand the impracticality of clothing all the quote-unquote outdoor animals. Remember that wolves, weasels & rats are going to hell anyway. Any one of them who desires may enter human society, accept the teachings of Jesus Christ our Lord & wear clothing.

Q: What about birds?

We are not so much offended by birds; their genitalia are hidden.

I don't think birds even have genitalia; I mean, we have never seen any.

By this time the audience is catching on to Wendy & Barry's spiel, believing that they are Barry & Wendy's real beliefs, while disagreeing with them sharply.

It shames me to see genitalia of any kind, Barry rants.

An audience member yells out: *If you don't like it, then why don't you just look away!*

This barb inspires a round of applause from the live audience.

The camera cuts to Wendy. She bites the air, sneeringly defiant of the anonymous audience member who spoke against them. Wendy is way, way, way, way, way, way, way, way, way, way, way, way, way, way, way, way, way, way, way, way, way, way, way, way, way, way, way, way, way, way, way, way, way, way, way, way, way, way, way, way, way, way, way, way, way, way, way, way, way, way, way, way, way, way over the top. We all love her.

We watch Barry & Wendy as the camera lingers on them while the show's theme music plays in the empty seconds before a commercial break. It's as if we can tell from 2,000 miles away exactly what they are thinking:

We are the villains in this landscape, the oddity, the statistical anomaly.

Chapter 27: In which the tables turn on Barry Weathers & Wendy

1990—Later, while going through the motions of drinking yellow beer with local people before disappearing into the nearby forest to spike trees & smash traps, Barry & Wendy meet a woman who introduces herself as Nancy. She listens more attentively to them than any other person they have ever come across in their tour of North American backcountry watering holes. The thing is Nancy is not interested in anything they are saying about Claude Dallas, their usual spiel to local people; she recognizes bullshit when she hears it. Nancy knows exactly who they are & what they are doing there. What's more, she is glad they are there. She understands how important it is that they are there. The night ends, Nancy having bought them all the yellow beer they could drink & they part ways, Barry & Wendy never knowing who Nancy is & ultimately what she means to their place in the shape & spin. We only know about Nancy (whose real name is not Nancy) because after the troupe begins to garner more & more media attention she writes a letter to Eleanor Cookee describing her visit with Barry & Wendy (who had introduced themselves to her as Chuck & Delilah). She also writes in the letter many of the high points of her life story, about a time when she was trying to do the work that all of us do all by herself, though she is less bent on the preservation of forests as on the stopping of corporate polluters.

So much madness in the world, she writes, *so little time.*

Included in her letter is a card. It reads, *Compliments of the Fox.*

When the letter arrives, Wendy & Barry are gone. We have not seen them in ages, nor do we know where they are. We have yet to have the opportunity to share the letter with them. Most interesting to Eleanor Cookee is the reason that the woman offers for giving up her life as the Fox:

I became a mother.

She writes:

> *After my children were born, saving the world didn't matter as much to me as what I could give my twins. Saving the world takes time & while the world needs saving (badly), I have faith in the young to follow through & do what they can.*

> *It was tough giving up the cause I had wholeheartedly believed in, but the decision of what I needed to do was obvious to me. I still support the cause of bucking up against polluters & loggers & all multinational corporations, for that matter—but for the last several years, I have been finding less flashy ways to fight them, working out of my home, writing letters & articles, often with my children working with me. I know the song is banal, but it does contain some truth & I will quote it anyway & say, I believe that children are our future.*

Chapter 28: University libraries & the madbomber tradition

Libraries are an exercise in American freedom; libraries grant Americans the freedom to read, so that when you practice your freedom of speech, you don't sound like an idiot. The best part about public libraries is that somewhere along the line, someone forgot to make them a profit deal. We are in love with the libraries of the United States. They are places where books are free for the reading; you can even take a few home & read them there. They are places where you pay only if you bring books back late; what matters most is bringing the book back, so someone else can read them. With few, dear exceptions, books aren't for keeping anyway. You keep what's inside of them, whatever has meaning for you. The book itself you pass on to someone else to read. You lighten your bookshelves. Bookshelves & the books that fill them are deadweight that loads you down every time you move.

Metropolitan libraries, many of which are grand old buildings recently retrofitted to meet earthquake safety standards, are becoming less a place for research & more a place to check out books by John Grisham. The heart of matters you'll find at a university library.

The J. Paul Leonard Library at San Francisco State University has been used over the years for countless subversive purposes. Yes, leave it to ol' San Francisco, one of America's great hotbeds of New Left, revolutionary thinking, to trot out yet another subversive generation right on the heels of another. [As we fade, along will come the bicycle activists.]

Where better than the student library of the city's public university for subversives to find books to help them hone their craft? Students, faculty, alumni, the public at large & madbombers alike use the library's services. It comes as no surprise that books that describe how to build incendiary devices are often checked out. Even more amazing is that these recipe books for social anarchy are returned before the due date.

Books in the library do not discriminate. Bomb what you will—the ROTC Center at the University of Wisconsin or a neighborhood Planned Parenthood site in Boston, Massachusetts, the books themselves will treat you the same. Books are not self-conscious. Books can talk but cannot talk back & what would they say if they could?

[*Don't try to touch me with words.*]

When society finally reaches the point where people stop worrying obsessively about the big one dropping, they now have all these little ones going off all around us. [Package bombs containing nails in them, the idea of nails piercing unsuspecting flesh, that's not what we are about.] Those who stand too close quickly learn about kingdom come. Smithereens are all the same; smithereens, like libraries & books, do not discriminate.

American libraries are in violation of the First Amendment. How strange it is that libraries enforce a prohibition against speech! The reason is clear; talking aloud impedes the reading of others, but what about sitting? If the person sitting next to you is full of restless energy, turning pages loudly, rustling papers, doesn't that spill over? If he or she is up & down in his or her seat or chair, isn't that enough to smash your concentration to tiny bits? Isn't that person no less a violator than the incessant chatterer two tables over?

Still, just the thought of a place where people aren't allowed to speak to each other!

People in libraries go ahead & talk anyway. We stand united in our rebellion against library silence.

Libraries make the patrons nervous & the least concern of the library workers is the madbomber sitting in the next cubicle over taking notes on the pros & cons of different fuse detonation systems. The patrons themselves are oblivious to the notion that there may be a madbomber reading among them.

People fidget, they scratch, they shudder at the thought of where they are; there are too many books & not enough air. They peek over the tops of the books they are reading. What falls outside the edges is always more interesting than what is inside the book. They stare off into space. They just can't sit still among the library's two million volumes on a day like this, considering how nice the weather is. It's rained so much this year & we're all so glad to have the sun back. Some stare out a window at the lawn outside the student union building where people are playing Frisbee. Others stare at others who appear to be reading but who secretly, around the sides of their books, are staring at others. It is a great unbroken web of staring & not much reading is getting done. The only person still reading is the madbomber on the third floor. The library itself becomes a hoax, fostering a generation not engaged in reading, but in staring. *Hey, we are all undergraduates on this bus.*

In a corner, TS is sitting up perfectly straight, though having fallen deeply asleep, cradling St. Bonaventura's *The Mind's Road to God* open in his arms.

The most industrious in the immediate surroundings is Cypress. He is writing a six-to-ten page history paper, its topic: Effective 60s-era Protest against the War in Vietnam. Cy wants to write about something that didn't happen & say it happened. Cy is funny that way. That is the kind of writing Cy likes. Essentially, Cy wants to write a paper proclaiming that the Pentagon did levitate, the problem being that even if he were able to prove that the Pentagon levitated in the arms of 60,000 protesters in autumn of 1967, how could he explain why the war lasted another eight years? You would think that levitating the Pentagon would make people stop & listen.

Then Cy finds a footnote concerning Norman Hartman & the Pentagon. A footnote is all he finds, but it directs him to another source which, in turn, directs him to yet another. A Quaker named Norman Hartman doused himself in gasoline, then set himself on fire outside the Pentagon in 1967, under the window of the secretary of defense. For Cy, who never reads footnotes, why this one caught his eye is beyond him. Now that he's read it, he will never forget it. He will take the footnote

& flesh it out; Norman Hartman will become the thesis statement of a paper he is writing.

Chapter 29

1967—High on Pentagon Hill in the District of Columbia there lies a shotgun shack. From that tiny wood fortress, rotting after years in the sun & elements, the United States administers its war/defense policy. Holed up inside, how is it, Robert McNamara, that you ever heard of Vietnam in the first place? Whatever gave you the idea that Vietnam is the enemy?

There is more potential upside to running moonshine out of the shack than trying to administer yet another in a never-ending series of American wars. There is more potential upside to letting the shack slip down the slope & sink into the swamp.

What will it take, Robert McNamara, to show you that reality is something other than it appears to you? Who can impress the hardwood hammock & trees to unfix their earthbound roots & rise in rebellion against you? Will these boulders & stones have to come to life? [They just might.] Why can't you hear these people?

For Robert McNamara, a Harvard scholar who served briefly as the youngest president in the history of Ford Motor Co. before heeding JFK's call to service & giving up his plum job & salary to head out on the New Frontier, everything breaks down to simple mathematics. This is how it works: After a certain number of bombing sorties over a certain number of days the end result is in the bag & always send in more troops to cut your losses. Everything is darkness & light, lives are measured in terms of nuts & bolts, widgets. You expend some & you make some gains. You expend more & make greater gains. You expend even more, so that those who have been sent to die will not have died in vain.

Missing from the Defense Department's accounting of the enemy is the tenacity of the Vietnamese, who run away from their villages as American bombs are raining down upon them. They run away, naked, on foot, even on fire—the Americans having sprayed napalm & poured gasoline over straw huts before setting them ablaze. You can say that the DoD's calculations account for some of the villagers running away. You can even say the numbers account for how fast they can run.

They run faster. They run to places where no one can find them.

McNamara is what Eisenhower had warned Americans about, Mac belonging to the movement that ushers war & peace into the office place, oblivious that every office in America, in the world for that matter, is at least one step behind the times. Life has a way of happening with or without offices, most frequently outside of offices. Always there is a paper delay, a float period before life is validated, its paperwork filled out. The problem is that the world doesn't like falling into place in this way. The world wants its wildness.

One of the first tricks in selling to the American people that the Soviets, Chinese, Cubans & Vietcong are the enemy is to make it sound as if Communism hurts. Under the big C, God is absent; humor is absent; your freedom becomes lost under absolute government control; you lose your capacity to say anything you like—you have to wait in line for hours to buy a loaf of bread. Nikita Khruschev doesn't help matters, pounding his heel into the ground at the United Nations, saying, *I will crush you* & promising that American grandchildren will grow up under a Communist sun & Americans are quick to forget that all that matters is growing up under the sun, period. How does Communist sunlight feel on your arms? How does Communist water taste? Do Communist countries fluorinate?

Mass protests come & go; they ain't the Birnam Woods.

The protest kids pass one at a time, yelling out the name of dead soldiers; they ain't the Birnam Woods.

They give talk about levitating the Pentagon; that ain't the Birnam Woods.

McNamara, you are so right on; Birnam Woods, roots unfixed from the ground, will not rise & meet you high on Pentagon Hill. Norman Hartman, though, will.

1967—Norman Hartman, a family man & Quaker, feels deep concern after hearing the news out of Southeast Asia. He is someone who cannot sit still after seeing photographs in *Life* magazine of a Buddhist monk, sitting in the lotus position, in flames, protesting the American presence in his country. Norman Hartman is a human being who takes his life into his own hands in protest of the Vietnam War. On an unseasonably warm November afternoon, he strolls across the Pentagon's outer walkways with his baby daughter, Emily, in his arms. He stops under Robert McNamara's office window just after lunch; how he knew it was McNamara's window is anyone's best guess, the Pentagon operates under a cloak of secrecy. He places his daughter gently onto the lawn. He sits down several feet away from her and assumes the lotus position. He pours a jar of gasoline over himself & strikes a match.

The match's first spark engulfs Norman Hartman.

There is yelling. A bystander, tears pouring from her eyes, whisks Emily into her arms & turns her back, shielding the child from the flames rising off her father's body & reaching out in the breeze. A DC police officer, a balloon tied around his foot, lumbers over hurriedly & attempts to douse the flames with his jacket. The flames pop the balloon. When the flames are snuffed the officer musters the courage to check the man's vital signs. An ambulance is called, but by the time it arrives Norman Hartman is dead. It is protest theatre obviously, craftily played out for the eyes of the secretary of defense, but where is he? Robert McNamara sees everything from his office window.

What could I have done to save him? Throw my typewriter through the glass & run to help? Dial the operator? No, I must be careful not to let myself fall into what's happening outside. For an instant, McNamara realizes the scope of what he has seen; the scenario he had never imagined; the unforeseen & the unforeseeable; the unthinkable suddenly come to meet you; the variable outside your control; the Birnam Woods have come.

[You go to the library, hold a book open before you & stare at its pages; its pages stare back at you. When you've read enough, you pass the book to the person on your left. After a predetermined amount of time has passed & a predetermined number of books have been read, you answer enough test questions correctly, you spill enough words onto sheets of paper & make it look like an essay & they hand you a degree.

Education? Education! Whatever!]

[*I'm drunk, lying on the floor of the Joshua Tree, my head spinning. I turn around to see the cause of the commotion. In the meantime, the bed spins, I'm still spinning.*]

Cy keeps on the course, chasing down the research paper about Robert McNamara & Norman Hartman, plotting out the paper he intends to write, noting that the self-immolation marks the beginning of a string of events that eventually lead to McNamara's resignation. What Cy wants to write is that Norman Hartman made the most of his moment, his sacrifice signaling the beginning of the end, the first time someone had stepped up & spoke out against the war & made a direct effect. He gave the world a budge, but how many Norman Hartmans would it have taken to end the war forthrightly? Twenty-one simultaneous suicides by fire on the Pentagon lawn? Twenty-one hundred? [Cy goes on & on & on & on & knows that there will come a day when he will no longer be a student.]

[Moments after McNamara descends the Pentagon steps one last time, following his resignation, his spirit returns in a new role under a new face & new name, but don't let it fool you. A legion of mite McNamaras begin making a name for themselves in federal forest management, but that is another paper entirely.]

On another planet in another time, TS cannot read. This has less to do with the failure of the school system as it does with blood sugar. He used to be able to read; as a kid, he loved reading. It happens to him sometime after he becomes an English major—halfway through *The Brothers Karamazov,* that he discovers he can read no more than a few pages before falling asleep. As he dozes off, he makes promises to himself that the next day he will get a fresh start & read double what he would normally assign to himself. Then the next day, it's the same thing all over again & he falls even farther behind. Before he knows it, he can measure how far behind he is in his literature classes in terms of linear feet; if he stacks the books on the ground, the pile will stretch past his ankles. By the semester's end, if he doesn't wake up, he will be up to his knees. Late in the semester, he decides to switch & become a Laughing major. Laughter—it's new, it's interdisciplinary. It subverts the serious, it calls the non-serious *sublime*. It finds what it finds ridiculous to an absolute degree. Its lessons lessen in the best, Lewis Carroll sense. His becoming a Laughing major is a benign way of saying that he is dropping out of school.

Chapter 30: Tran Nguyen

1990—TS now minds an Outer Sunset liquor store off 48th Avenue on a Friday night. Two of his Jokerman compats stop in on a Friday night, randomly, for *Wow*, they say when they see who's working behind the counter, *we didn't know you work here. We're just stopping to buy all-cool.*

Something, though, seems out of the ordinary.

It's all right, TS, they assure him. *We're twenty-one. You won't lose your job or go to jail for selling liquor to us.*

That's not it, though.

One of the two Joker compats, Clumsy Carp, asks TS if he can use the bathroom. TS points back through a door, which Carp stumbles toward across the room, tripping on air. In the back passage of the store, a place that neither customers nor delivery people ever see, there hangs on the wall a red flag with a bright yellow star in the middle. Sure, the flag looks familiar to Carp as he passes, but he doesn't recognize it as a symbol of the Vietcong. It's all fabric to Carp; all the flags of the world signify nothing. This flag, though, represents the enemy of the American people from the not so distant past. If Carp were nosy enough to peek inside the defunct ice-cream freezer propped against the other wall, he will find a cache of hand grenades & Soviet & American-made guns. If he would happen to rifle through the contents of a manila envelope on the bottom of an out-of-circulation comic book rack, he would find the schematic for an interesting electronic device. Carp is not nosy & knows nothing about reading schematics. All Carp wants is to drain his bladder, buy alcohol, say goodbye to TS & go. Minutes later, a fifth of whiskey in hand, Carp & his compat are out the door.

No one can remember the last time TS had any money. He gets by on nothing. We remember the long stretch when he was looking for a job & how shy he was & how everyone seemed to like him, but no one hired him. So TS gave up & the next thing he knew, this job came looking for him.

At the liquor store near where he lives at the moment in the Outer Sunset, the owner TS gets a job. Tran & his wife, Anh Le, who live in the apartment above the store, are the only two people who ever work there. Lately, Anh Le has been ill & less able to tend the store as she has in the past. Would TS have said no, even if he weren't looking for a job? TS would work for Tran for free.

There are times, too, when Tran needs to take his wife to doctor's appointments; during these times, he needs someone to watch the store for him. Tran does not know many Americans, nor does he feel welcome in San Francisco's Vietnamese-American community. Back in Vietnam, he sat on a different side of the fence than the other Vietnamese living in the Sunset. While the others had escaped their war-torn homeland & the regime of Ho Chi Minh, Tran had embraced Ho's vision. He came to America not in order to escape Vietnam, but to cause trouble. Americans had been making trouble on his soil, dropping bombs on people, burning villages. Now it's Tran's turn to return the favor.

The Americans whom Tran had run across back in Vietnam intrigued him. More than anything, he learned that Americans are predictable. They always choose the route on the map that shows the shortest distance between two points. They cannot tell their friends from their enemies & it is easy to gain their trust. They never suspect Asian people of being able to outsmart them, to outwit them, which they often will do. Americans act crazy; they place themselves in the line of fire to carry a dead comrade off the battlefield & in the end, double their losses.

Tran tells TS a story about an American officer who mined an open field in the zone of battle so that he could sit defiantly smack dab in the middle of it on a Sunday afternoon, drinking beer & playing rock 'n' roll on a transistor radio, as if to say, *Come & get me, you communist fuckers.* Little did the officer know that while he suns & plays rock, Tran is raiding his camp & stealing his stash of American cigarettes. Tran is full of stories about stealing cigarettes from dumb Americans. At first, it's a game to him. Then he becomes desperate; he has to keep stealing cigarettes or give up smoking them.

Tran also likes telling TS that during his first three years in America, he experienced an awakening. It was as if Americans are better people when they all weren't out to kill him. They are vain, dumb & enormously wasteful—benign, though always interesting. Americans love their advertising, their Marlboro Man & their Union 76. They are for the most part good natured, though, much like people from his country; people probably are friendly everywhere.

In a way, Tran is telling TS that he likes him.

Tran also likes the delivery truck drivers who bring beer & Pepsi Cola to his store. They share a smoke break & laugh together. [If only Tran had known how subversive TS is, standing watch while his friends drive spikes into trees & sink whaling boats!]

When Tran first came to America, it was with a plan to steal an atomic bomb. The plan seemed reasonable; Americans are dumb; he can outsmart them all. Then, once he arrived, he finds Americans are much more serious about matters such as atomic bombs than he would ever have thought back in Vietnam. *Getting your hands on blueprints for building a bomb is not impossible—getting your hands on enough plutonium to do the trick is another matter altogether.*

In America, you can't just break into someone's tent & steal plutonium. Still, he believes he could do it if he ever sets his mind to it. *It's just that in America, there are so many distractions, Disneyland, advertisements, cigarettes on every corner.* What's more, in America, Tran doesn't blend in as well with the countryside as he was able to in Vietnam. At least he speaks English well, better than people think he can. When he finally acclimates himself to the American way, sets up shop, he cannot remember why he wants to steal an atomic bomb in the first place. Tran mellows.

More than anyone, Tran's wife has had a calming influence over him. Coming to America in the early 1970s, Tran & Anh Le experienced all the heartache that immigrants endure. Tran, though, liked the place. He liked it because he came here with her. Initially, she didn't want to come to America. After a while, though, she liked it as much as he does.

Living in America doesn't change Tran's communist convictions, although he lies about his beliefs to the Immigration & Naturalization Service, nor does he tell them about his plan to steal an atomic bomb. He still wants to topple the corporate system, but spilling blood isn't worth it. As far as he knows, all people out there have other people who love them as much as he loves Anh Le.

A year before Anh Le becomes ill, Tran has a mild heart attack. If Tran owns a gimmick, it is fearlessness; he is the one always putting himself in harm's way. He doesn't fear his own death. Tran is fearless in all except his fear of his wife dying. He only fears that she will be the one who dies first. He never thought about it much, because it never seemed like much of a possibility, until she becomes ill.

When Anh Le finally succumbs to breast cancer, he has her cremated & takes her remains with him back to the Philippines & from there, to Vietnam.

It never was her idea to come here in the first place.

His will & spirit leave him.

There is nothing for him to do now but close up the shop & go home, to go & carry on with the rebuilding of his country, the rebuilding of temples, schools & hospitals.

They're gone & as little as it matters to TS in the shape & spin, he is without a job again.

Chapter 31: Chilly waves rolling off the Pacific

1990—School's out, track season is over & Jude is graduating from Stanford with her master's degree in molecular biology. What she wants to do next, she doesn't know. A doctorate? Train for the Olympics? [Which Olympics? The mountains are preferable.] In the meantime, she wants to spend time at the Joshua Tree, helping to put our house in order. The Tree, though, is in transition. A few months after Willie dies, his grandmother decides she doesn't want to let us have the house rent-free anymore, it's a valuable piece of real estate. Suddenly, we are faced with paying $950 a month, which is relatively inexpensive in SF, or moving out. We choose the latter, as we have no revenue. We begin packing government documents into boxes & delivering the boxes to the recycling depot. Losing the house, we will always have a Joshua Tree of the mind; the Joshua Tree is wherever we are when we all arrive together; it's wherever we are when we all go home.

Jude, helping pack up at the Joshua Tree, pores over stacks of government documents & finds something mixed into a pile, an undergraduate history class essay entitled, *Effective 60s Anti-War Protest: Norman Hartman on the Pentagon Lawn*, Cy's finished paper. [Cy had received a

B+. The professor wrote across the top, *Too much dramatic license.*]
Now, if Cy's paper is in a pile of other 300-level history papers, you can
easily gloss over it & find one more interesting to read. But when you
stumble across an essay with an interesting title such as this in a pile of
government-issue biological assessments, it stands out.

Read me, it whispers.

Something is happening to Jude these days—change & growth, a sense
that other than to change & grow there is nothing for her to do. Jude,
like TS, had once loved to read, but now that she has her degree & is
holding off on going back for more degrees, not to mention steering
clear of the track coaches who want her to train for Barcelona or
Atlanta, she has become bored by books & libraries. While Cy reads on
& believes he is learning something about Norman Hartman & Robert
McNamara from the words on the page, Jude is contemplating a different path. The part of the Norman Hartman story that touches her is the
story of the baby daughter, Emily, left a witness to her father's self-
immolation & suicide, an unwitting accomplice. *Where is Emily now?
How is she doing now?* She is only a couple years older than Jude. They
both lost fathers to the two different sides of Vietnam. As the thought
enters her head, Jude knows what she wants to learn & what she wants
to do. The question she is asks will find a way to answer itself.

Jude saves her voice for when she has something to say. She avoids chat-
tering incoherently from one free association to the next like the rest of
us. She comes from a conservation (rather than a conversation) sensibil-
ity. She will, though, chime in & say something riotously funny.
Everyone, ranging from the forever jovial to the brooding glum, all
break up when Jude spins a wry comment into the face of all serious-
ness & while tears are rolling down people's cheeks, she, too, will join in,
slouching & holding the back of her wrist over her mouth to hide it
while she laughs. There is something that happens to her eyes, when she
laughs, even while her mouth is hidden her eyes are laughing for her.
Laughter is part of her natural air, though a part of her not everyone has
a chance to see. Jude becomes self-conscious when she laughs. It is the
only time she ever seems self-conscious.

Consider the energy it takes to stir oceans of water, to hammer away at
sea cliffs, to press the water against the shore; this is the same energy
that moves Jude. She is orange fire dispersing in blue. She is wavelike.
Her energy crests, then becomes soft before reaching the shore.

Eleanor Cookee sometimes calls her Ethereal Girl, as if suggesting there is a side of Jude that is pure superhero—airy & wavelike , with super strength & speed. Eleanor Cookee is the only one who calls Jude that. Eleanor Cookee works hard to sell our personalities. The press she lures to Jokerman wingnut gigs arrive & ask, *Where is the hippie superhero girl we have come to see?*

Up in the tree; Jude is always up in the tree.

Jude is superherolike in the sense that she seems to have a secret identity; we all know there is a side of her we never see.

The more time we spend with her, the more we realize how little we know her.

She may be someone else when she's not busy being herself.

We might not know her at all.

We know she was named for a Beatles song. We know that her brother, a soldier like his father, died in a blast in Lebanon early in the days of Ronald Reagan & that his body now lies in peace at Arlington & that her father's name is on a wall on the other side of the Reflecting Pool. We know she was a champion middle distance runner at Puyallup High School up north in Washington state & that she never lost a race. We know that she was one of the best runners in the nation during her four years of eligibility at Stanford but that she attended Stanford not for athletics, but rather on a full-ride academic scholarship, because she fared even better on the SAT than at the state invitational track meet. During her Stanford track career, Jude was all about taking winning in stride, taking losing in stride, for there were races she lost at Stanford, taking everything in stride, always doing her best, knowing what matters most is keeping running. We know she finished her master's degree in molecular biology four years after her high school graduation while leading a daring double life as an *ecotage provocateur*: sinking Icelandic whaling ships one summer, risking her hide in the shotgun scope of hunters in British Columbia one winter & all the treespiking & juryrigging she did in between.

[We know nothing about molecular biology, except that Willie Shoman explains to us once that in essence, Jude is engaged in the study of life in its smallest units & even though the units are small, she can see the life in them & that when the units are that small, all life looks almost the same. He also tells us that Jude's approach to molecular biology is as if it were a liberal art, poetry & that lately, he himself had been thinking of DNA & its aspects & wondering if single cells dream.]

Jude & Willie were the troupe's finest performers, its soul & vision, the ones who knew enough to write a book about what we are all about, only that Jude & Willie never wrote anything down. They did not consider their actions to have violence in them, they physically hurt no one, they picked their moments.

Their relationship was sexless as far as anyone knows. Jude & Willie might have laughed at the very thought of having sex with each other. To them, sex didn't matter. They had nothing against sex, they just didn't view sex in the same light as the rest of us.

[In time, your hormones get the best of you. Glands secrete; your body listens. Your body seethes with wild progenitive energy. Hormones shape your desires; hormones fool you into thinking these impulses are actually needs.]

Then along comes TS, who joins Jude & Willie's circle. Then Willie dies & Jude & TS go alone. Jude & TS are different from Jude & Willie Shoman. TS loves Jude; it's plain to see. Though they are the same age, TS seems the younger of the two. He is always a half step behind her. He's the one who seems to be experiencing the world as if for the first time. He seems altogether free of his childhood, as if his childhood were a dream he woke up from unable to remember, as if his childhood were something he is still waiting to happen.

We know Jude travels without a plan & never gets lost. Somehow she's always prepared, she always takes care & she always has her shit together in the way we all wish we had our shit together. She brings what she needs & never looks back.

Then one day she disappears.

1990—When Jude disappears, leaving no trace, not even telling TS anything about where she is going, we are surprised, but we understand. No one can call it unexpected. We sense in Jude that something is going to happen. It does. She leaves.

As a runner, Jude has a pure stride. It's a hitch in the stride, an impurity in the play between the arms & the body & the legs & the ground, that invariably slows down everybody else & Jude crosses the finish line alone. Not only can Jude run faster than anybody else, she makes it seem effortless. She can run with her mouth closed, while others all around her gasp for air. Her college coaches cannot understand how she could push herself for so many years, then walk away from it as if it were nothing. If she had a history of injuries, they would understand, but she is healthy & on the verge of entering her athletic prime.

Her mind is made up; she just walks away. She's still running, she's just not competing. She has no reason to push herself beyond what's comfortable. She feels no competitive urges. She ran & raced only for the sake of running & racing & these no longer hold a place for her in the shape & spin. She is moving on.

A lingering image we have of the years we spent together at the Joshua Tree, partly because of its regularity, is of Eleanor Cookee walking through the halls, opening every door, freely interrupting every party she runs across. It is as if we are following her, seeing her from behind. Her shoulder blades are as expressive as a human face. She is out to get to the bottom of it, believing there is a conspiracy against her to leave her the last to know, as if she is the only one who doesn't get the joke, or even worse, the joke is on her.

Anyone see Jude? She asks once & again.

No one has.

She last questions at TS, figuring he is the most likely to know. He doesn't; it's news to him. His reaction, though, betrays no surprise; he knows he will see her again. It's no big deal.

Maybe the two of them don't have a connection after all, Eleanor Cookee wonders.

Eleanor Cookee wants to find Jude, not because she has a favor to ask, or to ask a question about the seven lawsuits that Eleanor Cookee might be able to bring about thanks to Jude's research, or to ask if she is sleeping with TS, for Eleanor Cookee already knows she isn't. Eleanor

Cookee only wants to find Jude to show her a magazine article, because it features Jude more than any of the others.

Chapter 32: Clipping from a tree-in

[This passage was written by a journalist whose name goes without saying.]

A door of all things! A junk yard door!

Old and stripped of its finish, it seems out of place here in the middle of a backwoods Oregon virgin forest. The door ascends up, hoisted on a thin ropeline into an ancient Douglas fir, its slow, smooth motion regulated by a man with what appears to be an oversized fishing reel attached to a belt around his waist. A clicking of the reel accompanies the door's ascension.

The door flies up into the tree. Eventually, it reaches a thick layer of branches sixty feet above the ground. From that height, a human arm, its body hidden in branches, reaches out and seizes the door, drawing it toward the tree's trunk.

A round of applause follows, perhaps prematurely, from a crowd of fifty or so who have gathered around the foot of the tree, each of them craning their necks upward.

The crowd has gathered not merely for the sport of hoisting old doors into even older trees. These people have a definite purpose in mind. They nervously check their watches, knowing that if the authorities arrive and pull the door back down before it is disconnected from the ropeline and braced into place, everything changes. No one is in the mood to resort to the backup plan.

Once the door is resting firmly in place, the crowd breathes a collective sigh of relief. The rope disconnected, now the human in the tree, who, as I overhear, is a woman, comes down only at the moment of her own choosing.

However, the woman's work is not yet finished. Having scaled the tree with rock-climbing equipment, she works diligently the next twenty minutes, securing the door to the tree, creating for herself a platform that will bear her weight for the next several days or longer, while she engages in an act of protest against the logging of old-growth forests called a tree-in.

How does it work? For as long as the woman remains in the tree, loggers cannot cut it. Nor can they log the trees in its immediate vicinity. Nor can they work in peace and with utter disregard to environmental decency while protesters are milling around and photographers are poking cameras in their faces. Nor can they drag her down from the tree without risking injury to her or to themselves. Nor are union loggers crazy about the idea of chasing people out of trees, even when injury isn't a factor.

Kalmiopsis is a name the tree-in's organizers are convinced will forever haunt them. Visit here (and you better hurry) and the name may well forever haunt you, too.

The Kalmiopsis Wilderness lies in southwestern Oregon's majestic Siskiyou National Forest. Abounding in canyons too rugged for even a trail, it is one of the most impenetrable and least explored mountain regions in the lower forty-eight—American Shangri-La. It is forest primeval; paleobotanists theorize that Earth's first trees evolved from this region. Over volcanic terrain with a unique geology and mix of soils in a climate that produces two-hundred inches of rainfall per year, plants that do not grow anywhere else in the world thrive here. The region's isolation creates ideal stomping grounds for a variety of people-shy animal species—the black bear, cougar, and osprey, among others. The northern section of the wilderness area houses a vast old growth forest where pristine streams feed into the fisheries of the Illinois and Rogue rivers.

Kalmiopsis is a throwback to what life here was like in the distant past of a million years, a billion years. Kalmiopsis shows us what the world wants to be like, a rare place where they have not heard of us, nor are they expecting our call.

That's on the verge of changing. While the Kalmiopsis itself is protected, its surrounding lands in the Siskiyou National Forest are not. A planned logging road will come within six inches of the Kalmiopsis Wilderness Boundary.

Members of the press corps bring cameras and notebooks to document the protest. The event's organizers tell the journalists right away that they will not try to justify the reasons behind the day's tree-in, that they would prefer to let the Kalmiopsis speak for itself. They will talk about anything else, the weather, college, babies, just don't ask them about this. They prefer not to resort to the rhetoric of the moment. It's a game and some journalists leave, deciding instead to visit the mill offices and hear the other side of the story.

Biting her tongue is killing the event's primary organizer. I never learned her name as I was introduced to her after I stopped asking them questions. She's the one in charge of enforcing the group's silence. She's also the one who most wants to talk so she can rattle off statistics and reasons to justify why they're here and what they're doing. She says nothing other than "We are here to protect the Kalmiopsis for the sake of the Kalmiopsis. Listen—" and then she is silent while the Kalmiopsis is not.

Playing devil's advocate and possibly crossing their boundaries, I remind the primary organizer that the clear cut zone falls clear of the Kalmiopsis Wilderness Boundary, even if only by six inches.

She has been waiting for this. She produces an empty backpack, which she hands to me. The pack has two holes in it, the result of a single bullet passing through it. The backpack's wearer was inside the protected Kalmiopsis wilderness a few months earlier when the bullet struck his

RICHARD MELO

pack. The twenty-year-old was spiking protected old growth trees when spotted by an unidentified shooter. The tree-in's organizers will say no more about the occurrence than that the backpack's wearer survived unharmed. The point of the backpack is that when the bullet passed through the pack, it missed the wearer's spinal cord—by six inches. Had the wearer twisted at the moment when the shot was fired, the bullet would have penetrated his heart.

In parts like these, six inches matter. Out here, everyone is playing for keeps.

Forty minutes later, the woman in the tree whose, groundling compatriots tell me is named Jude is perched upon the door, relaxing. No one can see her, the door having eclipsed her from our view, though everyone knows she's there. The authorities still haven't arrived, as if to say that these young people can climb all the trees they want, and we shall cut them down anyway, tomorrow, on schedule. Why should we break away from Sunday dinner with our family just because some woman has climbed a tree?

During the 1960s, doors were a metaphor for the New Consciousness; opening the doors of perception was what youth subculture was about. Open the door and reality bends before you. That was the idea, at least. This door, firmly entrenched in the now unfolding 1990s, is different. This door doesn't symbolize anything. It has a practical purpose. Lifted into a four-hundred-year-old Douglas fir, this is a real door. You can't tell if it's open or shut; it's braced in a tree.

The other remaining members of the press want an interview with the mysterious woman in the tree. They have an idea: Send a cellular phone up to her and conduct a phone interview.

The tree-in's organizers, who lay the groundwork for the woman's sustenance, allowing for her vigil in the tree to happen, have never seen a cellular phone before. They gather around it and curiously study it. When the question is whether to send the phone up the tree to Jude, they pooh-pooh the idea, suggesting that as much as they are amused by the phone, Jude probably won't be.

The media continue to insist on sending the phone up to her, but because of the tree's location, in a mountain pass, the satellites cannot connect and the phone doesn't work.

The environmentalists breathe a sigh of relief, and it is apparent that even asking the woman to use one is treading beyond the woman's comfort zone.

The pulley system brings a bucket of food, containers for her urine and excrement and a Polaroid camera, the organizers & members of the press thinking that if they can't get her on the phone, the least they can do is have her take a picture of herself for us.

The organizers of the event want Jude to hold the camera at arm's length, aim it at her face, snap a picture of herself, then send the photo and camera back down. The photograph will then be distributed among us. Although I have never met her or spoken with her, from what I know, I can imagine what she might say. "Why do you want a picture of me? This is not about me. This is about the Kalmiopsis."

We in journalism are given the charge of documenting the important events of our time on a daily basis. We have a tendency to overphotograph everything, as if by taking more pictures than we can possibly use or need, we effectively eliminate the chance of losing the story.

We watch as the Polaroid picture turns from grey, slowly transforming into a color print. No matter how often you take Polaroids, it's always a surprise to see what develops. The photograph shows a beautiful woman in her mid-twenties with straight, reddish hair cropped at the shoulder. She is healthy, intelligent, serious about what she is doing. Her skin tugs tightly at her face, no baby fat, nothing extra on her. Hers is not a face in outrage. Hers is not a face passing judgment on the rest of us. Hers is not even a face asking for our sympathy. The woman is not self-conscious. She directs her vision toward the future. She will not stand to let the misdirected forces of the past continue. She will not wait while the future she wants no part of happens around her.

The hours and days she will spend in this tree are a small sacrifice. This is the way her life chooses to unfold. Sacrifice implies consciously giving something up. This is not sacrifice. "This is not about me. This is about the Kalmiopsis."

Speaking as a veteran of twenty-five years in the media, and having traveled all over the United States and world to cover many of the significant events of our contemporary history, I can tell you with unwavering certainty that this Polaroid photograph is one of the most telling and enduring images I have seen. The photograph and the experience of seeing it, here in the wild, I will always remember.

Hanging out with these young people, I realize I am not young any-more. The torch was passed on to this generation while I was sleeping. I had not heard the name Kalmiopsis before coming here. I was aware of issues involving American forests, but they seemed of a lower tier than the issues of my day—Free Speech, Civil Rights, Vietnam, and more recently, the Women's Movement and No Nukes. Suddenly, here in the middle of Oregon backwoods, I realize that this matters as much as if not more than any of those other struggles.

What's more, the members of the press corps who are sticking around aren't getting it. The revolution, this time around, will not be televised. The revolution will happen out here, beyond the reach of their satellites.

So what do you do, still having a story to write, a deadline to meet? You sit around with the event's organizers, breaking your silence, asking more questions about Jude, while staring at her picture. Questions about Jude are fair game; they are not rhetoric.

I write down their answers and my impressions in my notebook. The next thing I know, the nameless primary organizer is at my ear, hoping I will write down everything she says: "It's simple, really. We are all interconnected. We are as much an extension of this tree as it is an extension of us. Cutting these trees is like cutting the fingers off your hand. Although maybe you won't notice right away, someday you will miss your fingers.

"We are here for climate, oxygen, erosion control. A year from now a small town downstream from here will experience flooding directly related to the logging that takes place tomorrow.

"There I go—rhetoric again. I promised myself and the others I wouldn't go into rhetoric. We only came here today to save this tree. But you know, trees run on different clocks than people. Humans hustle and bustle about, cramming as much life into a lifetime as possible. Trees live long, growing slowly and in accordance with the sun and season. Trees move, although slowly. Trees are not predators; they only pursue the sun. All the forest needs is to be left alone, but try telling that to corporate timber execs who believe the only good tree is one that has been pulpified into paper and printed with green ink and a portrait of a president who more than likely owned slaves."

Their stance on rhetoric softened, my questions flow more freely. They fire back answers in free associations. What, if anything, would you like to tell the folks back home?

"We have nothing to give back—except maybe a message to be kind to others & clean up after yourselves."

"Our hope is to leave this planet so clean, you will never know we were here."

Do you believe in God? I ask.

"Yes."

Why's that?

"Because we need someone to thank for all this. I am big on saying thank you."

"Because there is so much symmetry in nature, we acknowledge not a creator but the process itself."

What do you want to see in the future? What do you expect will happen to you in your life?

"We'll have to wait and see. I rent my apartment on a month-to-month lease."

Will you own a house someday?

"No."

Do you believe in home ownership?

"Do I have to?"

Will you marry?

"Marry you?"

At this, everyone laughs. I come right back: No, no, no, no, no—do you believe in marriage as an institution?

"I'm happy just like this. I'm happy enough as I am."

"People have wildly divergent views on marriage these days. I might marry someone whose expectations of marriage are like mine."

Will you have children?

"No."

Never?

"Probably."

Why's that?

"Kids are great, but the thought of having my own has never crossed my mind. Having kids is too much for other people to do."

Do any of you imagine you'll have children?

"No way."

"Not me."

"Nope."

With this last response, I realize I am on to something. Attitudes were different when I was young. During the Vietnam protests of our youth, our generation was about staying alive. Love and procreation fit right in, the progenitive engines driving us right along. As John Lennon said, the 60s happened because it was a great way to meet girls, but staying alive mattered more. We didn't feel like dying. Procreation mattered. It felt good. It was right on.

The tree-in protesters are the fruit of our procreation. They were beautiful hippie children, born during the apocalypse of 1968. Their parents had enough faith in love to bring them into the world. Now the children are old enough to rear children of their own, and they say they want no part of it; they have nothing they want to prove. Have they seen enough of the world in their short lives to know better?

What effect will this thinking have on birth numbers? *Close down the schools, honey, we don't have the children to fill them.*

The way to cover this story is to stay with it; afford it commitment; break the deadline and promise the editor something big, sometime later. I ask more questions, this time directed toward the entire group.

No children? Why is that? I ask.

"The population brings too much to bear on Earth's resources."

"The last thing the world needs is another mouth to feed and saying things it doesn't mean."

"The last thing America needs is another consumer. Making babies is the same as conspicuous consumption. You might as well drive a Cadillac."

"I plan to live simply and live well, childless."

"If we want a child, we'll adopt someone else's."

"I am not so thrilled about my genes that I need to go out and make a baby of my own."

What would you say if everyone in your generation held the same view?

"More power to us."

"We're fooling ourselves to think we can stay on top of it."

"This is not about us. This is about Kalmiopsis."

[*Do you remember that reporter? You would think he became best friends with us, but I can't remember him at all.*

I remember him, he had a crush on Jude.

Oh, brother.

Did we say those things? I can't remember.

Yes, I said much of it, I was thinking of Willie Shoman's mother & remembering.]

Part III

Life is strange.

The willie-nillies.

The heebie-jeebies.

Chapter 33: Journey to the heart of Pacific Wonderland

June 1990—Her Egyptian ring is magic, sparkling when she speaks. So magic, it draws you in for a closer look. You squint, you hold her hand close to your eyes, so you can see the ring in detail. You hold your breath, so she won't feel you breathe on her arm, because that would be unseemly & *yikes! Since when have I started using words like unseemly?*

Engraved along the band of the ring are serpents, feathers, cats in pharaoh headdress & false beards. The stone itself, set in the middle, has a bluish hue.

Then she speaks again, saying something no one catches—an utterance & nothing more. She might have said boo for all anyone knows.

Now you close your eyes & an afterimage of the ring's light remains & you still don't know what she said. All you remember is the sound & the ring's light as it fills your eyes—soft, diffused, blue.

As our bus rattles about, prattling, night begins its descent over Interstate-5 in northern California. Night falls & we are now shaking through in a creaky, ghost-ridden 1963 Volkswagen bus dubbed lovingly by us the FunTime. We fly bumpily along over land in between fifty-four & fifty-six miles-an-hour, sometimes seeming faster. The nuts & bolts in the engine struggle to hold together, knocking about, a knocking that in every moment reminds us we are always *this close* to the wheels falling off, leaving us to walk the rest of the way.

Before the trip, Eleanor Cookee told everyone that we are going on a secret journey. It was her way of generating excitement for our purpose, considering that everyone is already in on the secret. Anyone not in on the secret probably couldn't care less about us & what we are doing & is probably happily resting at home right now. *A secret journey—all right, let's go! We'll turn the world around while the rest of you are busy holding still.*

Squirrel closes the book she is reading, *Dune*, & pulls her notebook out of her backpack. It's too dark to read, but she can still make her scrawl. *We are doing things that don't have a name yet—or rather, we are doing things that don't have names anymore*, she writes, regarding what Eleanor Cookee considers *our secret journey*, although everyone else is now calling it the Pentagon Pyramid Prank.

Where you find trees bending & conversations dimming is a state called Oregon. It is our destiny to join each other in a spectacular experience & it is Daphne's destiny to join us as we ease forward from day into night & back again into day. She joins us amid all this talk of a secret journey when all she wants is to visit her friend in Seattle. She's only bumming a ride. The sparkling Egyptian ring belongs to her.

Daphne wears a hippie vest & a white T-shirt. Her arms are as skinny as they seem from a distance; her arms are as skinny as the rest of her. A bone holds up her long chestnut-colored hair. (*It's not a bone, really, but a piece of wood carved to look all bonelike & somehow Catholic.*) She's a senior at State, majoring in journalism, though considering a change; she wants to switch to art. She's asking herself what she would like out of college, what she wants out of life. She knows journalism isn't the answer. Journalism only rudely butts in to ask questions. *I mean, it's like you know what art is & at the same time you like don't. Do you know what I mean?* She might like to make the switch & see what happens. Daphne grew up in Orange County & her family had a swimming pool, as if that explains everything, or even anything.

[*We all have enough college credits to know college can be a stimulating experience as long as you steer clear of the courses that will eventually help you find a job*, Squirrel writes in her notebook, as it comes to her.]

The ride feels less like rolling along as it does lurching forward; we lurch along sometimes as fast as fifty-seven miles-an-hour. It goes without saying that it is the softest lurching we have ever felt. A lurching so easy, it lulls you sleepward. Go ask TS—oh, no, you don't, he's asleep already.

Cy knows Daphne, though vaguely. They had two classes together at State as freshman: Chemistry 101 & 102. Back then, they never knew one another's names. In hindsight, he has no idea how that could have happened. The sun now having set & darkness filling the ship's cabin, simultaneously he can't see her & he can't take his eyes off of her. He's beheld by her outline—the lines holding her in. Stray light defines her outer edges, while she herself becomes darkness. She becomes her own shadow.

Daphne poises herself to say something to add to the many swirling conversations. Then she remembers the gaudy, glowing ring & holds herself back. The Egyptian ring has made her self-conscious, glowing the way it does. Because of it, she's now keeping quiet. Then from out of the blue, she lets fly a raging sneeze, the sneeze itself bursting the ring in a sudden flash of light. Our eyes follow a million tiny sparkles, each resembling microscopic electric flower petals, illuminating all the colors of the prism as they settle through the air, lingering before her. The sparkles reflect off her face & her expression tells us everything we will ever need to know about embarrassment in front of strangers & were afraid to ask.

According to Foot Apples, the sparkling ring itself is (if it's anything) *gaudy, souvenir crap—tarnished & antique but hardly ancient in the sense that the Old Kingdom pyramids are ancient.* Two friends of Foot Apples's mother found it at an estate sale in Stockton, California in a box next to children's clothes amid so many charm bracelets & pieces of costume jewelry, all of it tangled together. Then this Egyptian ring popped out of the bundle; they could tell it was Egyptian by the serpents, feathers, cats in false beards & pharaoh headdress engraved along the band. The stone, though, seemed real & the band seemed gold & the ring didn't cost them two dollars & for all they knew it was a treasure thousands of years old & worth a fortune. Egypt is oh-so exotic! Such a mysterious place! They couldn't wait to show the ring to Anthony Burchetta. He'll know its value, he's studying Ancient Egypt at college. He can read the writing on the ring.

Foot Apples looked over the ring & couldn't tell them much. After all, he's a linguist, not a jeweler. *The hieroglyphics on the side do not say anything, the ring probably isn't even Egyptian.* When he told them he did not believe the ring was valuable, they decided on the spot to give the ring to him. What other use do they have for it? It only cost them two dollars & the spirit of giving feels so good & he's so smart.

Really though, Foot Apples doesn't know if the ring holds value or not. For all he knows, it could have once belonged to Cleopatra. Finding out would be easy, finding out means asking anyone else, perhaps a fellow Egyptian studies major. Because he doesn't know, he cannot bring himself to throw the ring away. The least he can do is keep the spirit of giving alive & pass the ring along to somebody else. He passes it around the other five riders aboard the FunTime just as they are shoving off early in the afternoon. People take a look, then pass it on to the next person. *Whoever wants it keeps it; the ring is not such a terrible thing, really.*

Without trying the ring on his own finger, Cy passes the ring on to Daphne. He doesn't want her to see his hands, he keeps his fingers tucked in. His nails still have dirt under them from a gig last year. He doesn't want her to think he doesn't wash his hands. Unlike many of the others, Cy wants people to think he's clean. [It was Kalmiopsis, the stand off. To show his defiance, Cy handcuffed himself to a gate installed to protect the heavy equipment from the calculated wrenching of his wingnut tribe. For as long as he remained cuffed there, the heavy equipment could not pass through—no road could get built. Pissed off, a bulldozer operator dropped a three-yard scoop of misting forest soil on top of him, the soft soil raining down & burying him. Cy's compatriots looked on in horror at the sight of Cy buried alive, the last thing any of them wanted to see happen to a fellow human. The soil itself was neither cold nor heavy & gave Cy a sense of what it might be like to be a freshly planted seed. Cy wondered what would sprout from him. He enjoyed his sudden burial & when the day was over, despite the goading of the others, he decided not to press charges against the bulldozer operator for aggravated assault. In turn, the site foreman chose not to press charges against Cy for criminal trespass. *The next day, construction begins. We lose again.*] [*The dirt beneath Cy's nails,* Squirrel writes in her notebook, because she was there & she remembers, *is living proof that you can come back from the seeming, steaming grave, but it leaves its traces on you.*]

Daphne takes the ring, tries it on & it fits her finger perfectly—yes, you could say in a screwball Cinderella sense. Within minutes, for no one who had worn the ring before had worn it longer than a few seconds, the ring begins to sparkle when she speaks. It only needed time to warm up to her body heat. *Stellar! The ring is way cool!* We all now know the ring is magic. In its way, it affirms our pyramid dream is on its way to reality. The sparkling Egyptian ring is just something else to remind us that Eleanor Cookee is right on, we are embarking on a secret journey. We have no idea where we are going or what we are doing, but we know we can do anything.

Here's the secret itinerary: First we pass through Portland, then head onward to points east, diving deeply into the Columbia River Gorge to a place in central Oregon near a town called Antelope, to a ranch called Big Muddy where rests the remains of an ancient city, though hardly ancient in the sense that the Old Kingdom pyramids are ancient—*all right, so it's a city that was built as recently as the early 1980s by the followers of the Bhagwan Shree Rajneesh, but it's already seen its twilight.* The plan: To spend time working out the particulars of the Pentagon Pyramid Prank in the middle of nowhere, where no one can find us & bother us & laugh at us, because we know what we're doing is beyond ridiculous. It's going well so far.

[*A tree holds darkness on the inside, yet every annual ring holds the memory of 365 days' light. Light leaves a dark trace of itself.* This is an unfinished thought, inspired somehow or other by *Dune*, that Squirrel writes down in her notebook.]

Squirrel shakes TS in an effort to wake him. Rather than awaken, he sways back & forth while remaining upright, eventually falling to his ease with his head lying on her shoulder. *Poor TS, spring semester took everything out of you, not to mention that you lived half the year sharing a room with Kanga's smelly ferret & the coughing heat pipes & then you slept the rest of the year in a sleeping bag on other people's floors.* She picks up some pages from a newspaper nestled between them. TS had worked on a crossword puzzle during the afternoon. She looks at the puzzle & finds it amazing that TS has filled all the blank squares with letters & words, while at the same time none of his words jibe with the clues given. It's as if he solved a crossword puzzle altogether different from the one in the paper, given the correct answers to an entirely different set of clues & everything fits just right. No, Squirrel is not above laughing, TS solves the puzzle as only TS can & she laughs quietly, consciously not letting her shoulder move & awaken TS.

[The engine's lull puts you to sleep. We all nod off.] *Sometimes in dreams I am living someone else's childhood & I can't tell whose & I don't know why. Meet me at the edge of the reflecting pool, past the eyeholes in the willow shrubs. Into this light, out of that shadow, we poke, we go. The blackberry vines prickle our legs. We will go & eat the apples now.*

Next thing Squirrel knows, she, too, is asleep & dreaming. She dreams of working as a woman's assistant in a 1968-flavored mod house with white plastic furniture shaped like human bodies. The dreamside Squirrel stares out a window into the night, waiting for her boss's client to arrive. Wind rustles in the leaves. The woman's client, Squirrel knows, will turn out to be Jackie Onassis & Squirrel remembers the phone conversation when her boss suggests to Jackie O, who is feeling low, that maybe the best thing for her would be to take off her clothes & come over. So now Squirrel is watching out the window for Jackie O to arrive & wondering if she will be naked when she comes. What she remembers most about the dream is wondering what Jackie O will look like naked. When Jackie O does come, she arrives wearing cotton work out clothes. Awake later & telling the rest of us about her dream, Squirrel theorizes that it originated in her anxiety about not having a job that summer.

Eleanor Cookee, riding up front, seems upset about something—maybe TS sleeping against Squirrel's shoulder. Then again, upset is Eleanor Cookee's natural air, the way she always seems. She would be upset with her boyfriend, if she had one. She would be upset with her mother, if she were here. Instead she's upset over nothing. *Why the long face, Ellie? Everything seems as if it is going well for us these days; the Pentagon Pyramid Prank has not yet reached the phase where pessimism sets in, where we give up. We have done more than our fair share of giving up in the last few years. Kalmiopsis always comes to mind. Too often, giving up seems unavoidable.*

Maybe Eleanor Cookee is in a preemptive mood, worrying about things yet to come, worrying because she can't help it. One look at her & you can almost hear the struggle inside of her, the voices that cannot agree.

We still don't understand why she's upset.

Maybe she's worried because green fish made of light swim outside the bus.

You only say that only because you are asleep & dreaming.

No, really—look for yourself.

Staring outside the passenger-side window of the FunTime, she quietly loses herself. Eleanor Cookee, how can we help you?

I am letting my tears fall. I know better than that. Trees bend.

Chapter 34: Do you dream in color?

First, you sleep; you lie still at night; you relax; you close your eyes. Sleep comes for you. All of it is voluntary. The urge to sleep is a gentle impulse come to find you. The nature of the sleep contract is this: You like sleep & sleep likes you. If you refuse sleep long enough, you first become cranky & then sleep begins to feel involuntary—toothpicks can hold the eyes open only so long. You begin to dream while awake & pose a danger to yourself & those around you.

What if we went gently toward all things the way we do sleep? We would go around like TS & get along with each other & give to one another & forgive each other our trespasses. We would all take it easy & realize that life's disasters, including those from which we can never recover, have their place in the shape & spin.

Two of us, not long after the FunTime ride, begin learning about life through the act of sleeping next to one another, lulled by our culture into thinking that the physical act preceding sleep matters most. Between the two of us, it becomes a come-what-may counting of experience, learning what happens while the other one sleeps, while the other one dreams.

Throughout history, billions of pairs have slept together in the same bed. Question: What new can these two sleeping together in late 1990 hope to learn? Answer: Everything they let themselves.

What is she dreaming about? he wonders.

I wish he would just fall asleep, she dreams.

He's a warm sleeper, never snoring, but breathing loudly in long, slowly drawn breaths, while in her dreams, she can fly & see the world from a bird's perspective. He wakes convinced that when she appears in his dream he simultaneously appears in hers, only when they awaken in the morning, they always forget the dreamside rendezvous that passed between them. She's the one who believes that dreams are recoverable through deep relaxation & breathing.

Dreams are as much about forgetting as they are about dreaming, he says.

If you let yourself, you will remember your dreams, she explains to him, knocking on his head as if it were a door. *Like anything, dream recovery takes practice.*

Chapter 35: Oblivion & obligation

Taxing its engine, the FunTime works hard in low gear, the gear that makes an engine human, as it rolls up & over the Siskiyous. The mountains will last another two-hundred miles, practically to Eugene.

The FunTime is Cactus's scene & he wants the show to go off peaceful easy, without an ever-lovin hitch, nuthin thinkin, electricity comes from other planets. Cactus, whom we have never known by any other name, is our driver on this trip. He is a survivor of many Vietnam-era New Left misadventures, a man unlike the rest of us, well past his college days. His age is indeterminate, the number of years Cactus carries on his back probably approaching fifty. His skin smells like eucalyptus & the battered old T-shirt he wears says, Welcome the Rolling Stones. This rig, the FunTime, is itself a maritime wonder, a '63 Volkswagen bus with barnacles on her side after spending fifteen years parked below the San Francisco Bay. By twilight during our most recent past, while someone else had briefly taken the wheel, Cactus poked his head up through a hatch in the roof to experience fifty-three miles per hour of wind blowing the skin on his face backward, his long, greyish hair flapping all over. He sounded his barbaric yawp to the interstate, sun & sky.

His hair tangling, frazzled & bugs sticking to his face, he comes back down after a long moment: *It's flying*, he says. *Jet fighters flying into* [He strikes a hippie poet pose, taking a moment to conjure magically his last word] *oblivion*.

Old-time Jokesmith Cactus—for there is no denying around us Cactus seems (& even worse, feels) old, has given up everything except drinking cola from cans. Many of his former activities had become habits worth breaking. *Get obsessed & then let go*, he likes to say. It becomes his personal rallying cry, even though none of us know what it means, or how it relates to habits. Cactus now prefers Shasta Cola, thoughtfully avoiding the huge multinational soft drink conglomerations. He crushes the cans with his skinny, swollen fingers when the pop is gone & keeps them in a canvas bag to recycle.

Cactus is a grinning, happy version of his former self, a madman about his past, though he follows no illusion that he's going back. He's the family fuckup, the drifter barely getting by. He lives with nothing hanging over his head, no credit cards, no mortgages, no outstanding warrants & no children, for yes, Cactus was always careful. He knows there are no children, although he has lost track of every person he has ever had sex with. [*It just happens like that, you lose people. Every time seemed like we were going to be together forever, but when you are always glovin your love, like I was, you lose a certain aspect of the foreverness in your togetherness.*] [He again strikes his hippie poet pose, which he might have developed at City Lights or while practicing yoga.]

Later: *You okay to keep driving, Cactus?*

He shakes himself awake.

Something in Ol' Cactus doesn't seem all right. Cactus used to have a dog. The dog, a dependent, a responsibility, a friend—as Cactus himself says, was the closest to family he says he will ever know. Holler was an American dog, a melting pot of breeds, peaceful & smart, a Left-leaning dog who would have voted if they had let him. Cactus had found him one day, the dog running alongside the highway in Arkansas. *That dog needs a ride*, was all he could think & he stopped. Later, when times were no longer what they used to be, the two of them were given rides from people sympathizing not with the man but with the dog. For instance, there was the couple in the BMW in the rain, bless them—people who would never think of offering a ride to such a dusty person, especially a sweaty, stinkin' Joe such as Cactus. *That dog, though, has places to go & you might as well give his person a ride, too.*

When Holler disappeared, it wasn't clean. It was preceded by a recurring dream, a dream that felt like someone else's that Cactus had somehow intercepted while flying too low over the treetops at night. It looked like a dream belonging to Cactus only because he was in it. Along a crowded Santa Monica beach, he is riding a fat-tired yellow Schwinn by the seawall. He makes a sharp turn & nearly rolls into an old man who's muttering to himself something British. Police descend from everywhere, but not to bust Cactus for nearly running the old man down, nor for any past indiscretion. Nor are they appearing from nowhere to help the old man who has stumbled over his own feet & is lying broken on the sidewalk. The police are discussing what they want to do respecting the present crisis, having been tipped anonymously that land mines litter the beach—it's a Middle Eastern terrorist plot to destroy south California sunshine Pacific Ocean blue. How can you warn people that when they walk down into the ocean for a dip, when they roll over to sun the other side, when they walk across the sand, even on tiptoes, back to their cars, that they may blast themselves to kingdom come? Fortunately, at that moment, the people on the beach happen to be holding strangely still. It won't last. At any moment, someone will throw a Frisbee & someone else will run & catch it. All is silence & smolder, then, *whoa!* Out there on the beach—movement, a dog running. Look again more closely. Cactus, it's your ol' boy, Holler, rocketing across the beach to greet you. *Holler, heel. Stop, buddy.* The dog has no sense of the danger. Sometimes in the dream, Cactus is unable to move. Other times, he springs forward, racing onto the beach to save his dog, ready to outrun any explosion before it can catch up with him. He never knows what happens next. No happy ending, no bloody ending, no ending at all; the dream just stops moving forward & Cactus wakes up. Then Holler turned up missing in real life & the dream stays with Cactus, haunting him, worsening him for the wear, carving deep rings under his eyes. The dream plays in Cactus's head while he sleeps as if by a cruel joke.

Holler disappears the way Willie Shoman already has—though, unlike Willie, without an explanation or goodbyes. The dog disappears like Jude will someday, like TS will someday.

Cactus losing his dog like that just didn't seem possible. Was he stolen? Was he run over? Who would do such a thing? Cactus hadn't pissed off anyone in twenty years, although that doesn't mean some nasty person wasn't out to get him. Maybe that was when the secrets from Cactus's past finally caught up with him, as if taken the form of Mayor Daley on a Harley alongside the Karma police. Maybe it was the conspiracy, the evil right-wing consortium that claimed the lives of Huey Newton,

Abbie Hoffman & Jerry Rubin & made Jane Fonda leave Tom Hayden for Ted Turner.

Daphne listens as Cy whispers something to her while they are riding together in the FunTime's middle seat. She responds by nudging him, a deliberate move of her elbow against him. It's still dark—she still wears the Egyptian ring, now stuck on her finger, congealed & because of that she won't say anything.

Cy looks around at the others. Squirrel & TS are asleep; Eleanor is awake, though silent, her eyes closed, crying again, quietly, so no one will notice; Cactus is driving & Foot Apples—who can tell what he's up to? He slumps in the back seat to the side of Squirrel & TS, his head pressed against the window. He stares at the painted lines along the highway, thinking about how the road changes while the line always looks the same. Something about Foot Apples staring out the backseat window of a moving VW bus at night seems eternal. He holds no starting place, nor any stopping point. He's just a person forever mesmerized by the yellow line outside the right lane of Interstate-5 north as it weaves inward & out again.

Since the others are all either asleep or oblivious, Cy whispers to Daphne again. *Do you think you'll miss the 80s?* It's a loaded question, a ploy, he wants to see the ring sparkle. The 80s are at the moment shriveling in the rearview mirror.

She's not playing the game, whispering back, *Like, I'm sure*. Her other hand covers the ring to mute its glow. Nonetheless, its sparkle is bright enough to sneak through from between her fingers, causing both she & Cy to hold back giggles—they do not want to draw attention to themselves.

Cy wants more, he wants to see the ring full throttle: *Just recite something from memory—a nursery rhyme, the Pledge of Allegiance, the Lord's prayer—*

Then, quickly, as if to get it over with, Daphne whispers the chorus of a pop song by the Divinyls that's all over the radio & stuck in her head at the moment. Cy, for the first time, sees the ring's sparkle clearly. He sees that the sparkle is not random, that it forms patterns that quickly reset into new patterns. It is as if the sparkle is a code & something about the code seems familiar—how can he possibly be making sense of this?

[Everything in Daphne's world is *like* this or *like* that. Her use of like doesn't make her seem unintelligent; her use of *like* is definitely premeditated. She sees the world made up of similes, less for what it is than for what it resembles. Using *like* all the time is her way of saying, *Like, don't take everything I say too seriously, don't take anything I say like too seriously, like don't take anything I say seriously at all.*]

Then Cy falls, not literally. When he thinks back later, he's not sure what happened, he's just glad it did. Words recreate the experience—perhaps the closest he can muster is *illu*, the prefix to both *illumination* and *illusion*, and although he cannot trace *illu*'s origin, he knows it relates to light. It starts with the ring's sparkle & constellations rise & set—*you lose yourself in them oh, so completely.* Maybe it's because the other's dreams are spilling over into him even though he's awake. It makes sense because when he thinks back it reminds him slightly of *Dune* & that's the book Squirrel is reading & maybe she dreams about it, too. [*Squirrel lives for sci-fi & fantasy. We like her so much we're funny that way.*] [*My God, Cy . . . put yourself back together from the pieces on the floor. Find yourself. Look into her eyes, she's full of stars. Now you are there, floating randomly through space, drifting, wanting desperately to break away, to study the constellations from books & then return to her eyes & reorient yourself, recoup your place in the world once & for all. But look closer now & see that the stars in her eyes are from a perspective other than here on Earth. Could this be the southern hemisphere? A perspective far more remote? Arrakis, desert planet*—Dune?] Cy knows just enough about the heavens to know that he's seeing stars from somewhere he's never seen them before. Finding out where he is could take more studying than he even knows how to do. *So this is the secret journey—it's bound to her.* All of it had been building up & now was happening—a rupture, a rapture without the Christian trappings. He would never again be himself. He would be someone just like his old self, only different. He's recycled. He's no longer *Cy* short for *Cypress*. He's now *Cy* short for *Cyclone*. [*You can feel it, can't you, Cy? You're falling, though not yet fallen, & there are vines. Inside you turn a million atoms of soft blue.*]

Mysterious how the FunTime's motor up & quit. First, someone smelled the smoke. Someone else heard what sounded like a muffled explosion. Someone else looked out the back & saw a dark cloud tailing us in the night, a billowing of our own generation, a sinister internal combustion cloud that would not let us escape from it, a cloud we were towing, a cloud signaling that the motor's life was running out. Engine out, the FunTime keeps rolling & rolling.

How far have we coasted since the motor died?

A mile or two, maybe. Her sails catch wind & she keeps going.

But the FunTime has no sails, she's a friggin Volkswagen bus.

Some charm in the FunTime's nature, though, keeps her wheels turning long after the gas has run out. *But it's not that we ran out of gas, something in the engine blew.*

Suddenly, we're stranded & Eleanor Cookee is openly in tears. She has said so little during the trip & worries so much over everything that we begin to worry about her. *It's all right, Eleanor, we were planning on stopping for the night somewhere anyway. The FunTime picked a spot for us, that's all. Sometimes that happens.*

She's crying not because of the stranding but because TS won't wake up. He looks dead. You can't see him breathing. TS is not dead. No one dies in our world—*all right, except for Willie Shoman, but he got cancer. TS is alive. He's just dog tired, that's all.*

Chapter 36: 1973

Look there, it's Cactus in 1973, younger & more vibrant, just a trace recognizable under all that thick, freaked-out hair. He's driving the same bus, the storied FunTime, shuttling fugitive members of the Black Panther Party & their oh, so armed & stoned bodyguards up through Nevada as they emerge from hiding in Mexico, keeping themselves under night's cover on their way back to the Bay Area. This is Cactus's life in its full rage.

We know where Cactus is, but where are we? We are at the place where our families live, making ourselves out as children. We are five. We are childhood smiles & infinite silliness. There we go, picking raspberries, eating the best & throwing the rest at each other; having fun with root beer floats & remote control boats; watching the birth of kittens & wishing to see the runaway dog who never came home. Turn the corner, here we go: bouncing ourselves high on trampolines; dancing because we just can't help it; bringing looks of mortification to the faces of adults in the supermarket produce section as we brazenly sing songs from *Hair* in our sweet, angelic voices; finding an abandoned school bus underneath a mountain of prickly blackberry vines & turning it into a fort; stealing plums from a neighbor's tree; digging for buried treasure in the same neighbor's backyard; not knowing our left from our right; building a contraption for watching the total eclipse of the sun; watching for UFOs off the back porch late at night; not wanting to go back inside where our parents are yelling at one another. Life is an Easter egg hunt, running home from school & sleeping late on Saturdays. We only wish our parents would keep down the shouting & love each other the way they used to when everybody was happy—when we were little, like in the picture albums that help us to remember. Sometimes life happens this way, folks—themes recur. The radio plays the same song over & over until it is forever stuck in your head. You can choose either to like it or else turn off the radio.

Word was that the FBI was moving in, for the FBI has an uncanny knack for knowing more than they're supposed to know about the people they're spying on. Likewise, the people who the FBI are spying on have an equally uncanny knack for knowing the FBI is watching them. The Panthers & Cactus desperately needed the bus to disappear. The bus constituted evidence of illegal flight from justice & God knows what other misdeeds & crimes against the American people. No, Cactus could not just drive it away—not to Canada, not back to Mexico, nowhere. Nor could they just paint it & sand away all the vehicle identification numbers. This was what the FBI will suspect them to do. *They will know what we're doing. We know they will know.*

No one can feel safe unless the bus disappears without a trace.

Lucky how at this time in their history, the Panthers own a helicopter. Ordinarily, they used it to transport Huey Newton from the roof of his Lake Merritt condominium to his college classes in Santa Cruz. Under the cover of night, they chain the bus to the helicopter & tow it through the air & drop it into the water somewhere in between the Bay Bridge & Alcatraz. Aboard the chopper, Cactus watches it plunge, as does the Panther pilot. The bus floats & bobs before sinking. They hover & circle, the pilot cursing the damn bus for not sinking right away; Volkswagens are famous for their ability to float. Moments pass & the bus begins its slow descent into the Bay. The Panthers believe themselves free of the bus forever, which is just as well to them—finding a new set of wheels is easy. This says nothing for the love Cactus feels for his vehicle; the bus is like his flesh & blood; the bus is what Holler the Dog will become to him later. Cactus likes the idea of storing the Volkswagen beneath the Bay's surface, letting it rest there until the heat is off, because he knows that it is the one place where no one would ever fuck with it.

Cactus never sees the sinking as permanent. In his eyes, the bus is merely garaged in Davey Jones's U-Park, where it will not be forgotten, where it will not remain forever. The Bay Area has plenty of underwater parking for those with the courage to stomach the elements, plus much less car traffic & fewer break-ins than anywhere above water. A shark might nibble your limbs as you swim but will leave your radio alone.

Interlude: In wildness lies the preservation of the world

Twist a feather & she will return.

Chapter 37: the family fuckup, the drifter barely getting by

1963—Cactus's parents, who were prosperous in the 1950s, gave the Volkswagen to him new, as a gift honoring his graduation from the University of Michigan with a major in business. Next thing Cactus knew, he was driving out to California, following voices calling him over the radio—the Beach Boys. He surfs that summer in Malibu, where at twenty-two, he is already one of the oldest cats on the scene. His parents expect him to find a job or go to graduate school. Before he knows it, he is estranged from his parents. The years become a hazy blur: 1964,1965, 1966, 1967, 1968, 1981. He remembers the places he lived over passages of time: Springfield, Oregon; Saskatchewan; Oakland; Santa Fe; La Jolla; Monterrey, Mexico. Somewhere along the way he learns a trade: painting the insides of people's houses. It's something he can do whenever he needs to stop & breathe & earn enough to keep a roof over his head during those times when sleeping under the stars or in the bus loses its sense of wonder, or it rains like hell.

1987—No one really remembers how he hooked up with us. When he went out searching for his dog, rather than find Holler, he found us. He sniffed out the Pentagon Pyramid Prank & wanted a part. He was at the levitation attempt at the Pentagon in 1967; we ask him his opinion of it. The levitation is a mystery that Eleanor Cookee wants solved.

Cactus has this to say: *Not only did it levitate, it soared.*

How can you say that? If the Pentagon, as you say, soars in 1967, the world wears a different face than the one we see before us. Janis, Jimi & Mama Cass grow old gracefully. The Beatles reunite, the four of them alive & eager to let go of past differences & keep topping themselves. RFK is elected president in 1968 & MLK in 1976. People realize that the new Nixon is the same as the old Nixon & refrain from paying him any mind, no matter how many dirty tricks he plays. Ronald Reagan wins election as dogcatcher in San Diego & aspires to no higher office. The revolution takes effect, peacefully, because that's truly the way everyone wants it.

The bus resting below the San Francisco Bay, Cactus enlists the assistance of an ocean-faring diver/salvage team specializing in the recovery of sunken treasure to help him recover it. To sweeten the deal, he tells the team that he left something in the bus all those years ago—a chest strapped beneath the middle seat containing loot in the form of greenbacks. The trawler team does not care about the bus & its radical history or Cactus's sentimental attachment to it. People overhear Cactus stammer that the chest contains fifty-thousand; fifty grand is always the number tossed about.

Had anyone deeply considered it, they would have wondered why Cactus would have let the bus sink with that much cash in it. Perhaps naively, we believe that he let fifty-thousand go down with the bus so that he could later convince people to help him hoist it out of the Bay. *Let me keep the bus. The contents of the chest, with the exception of a few small personal items, are yours. The loot will be yours; everything of value will be yours, if you want it.*

The promise of monetary reward is enough inspiration to get the team a-sailin' on a Saturday morning. People turn out in droves to help, to take part in retrieving the loot the bus holds. The prospect of treasure hunting thrills us; undersea mysterioso drapes the bus in its watery parking space. Divers explain to Cactus & the other Jokerman compats on the mission that it might take several days to locate the bus & bring her to surface. Cactus, though, disagrees wildly, believing that the bus is instantly recoverable & an early start that is all we need. *Wait & see, wait & see, wait & see*, he keeps reassuring everyone.

The team begins to think that Cactus is around the bend.

His original suggestion is that they let him gear up & dive into the Bay at the place in the water where he believes the bus is parked. Deep underwater, he will find the bus & drive her along the sandy Bay floor & onto Treasure Island, stealthily past the Navy installation housed there, then onto the Bay Bridge & from there into the City & on to SFSU & the Joshua Tree where he will meet up with everybody. How funny everyone let that remark slip, as if Cactus is joking, as if even this is nothing worth taking seriously. They think he's around the bend & steam forward across the Bay.

On the water, Cactus leads the ship & crew quickly to the right spot, as if he recognizes the piece of water the bus is hidden beneath, guided by landmarks no one else can see & the voices of seagulls. Divers find the wreck & attach chains to her. She is unlodged from her spot beneath the Bay, reeled in & dropped by crane onto the ship's deck, barnacled & dripping seawater from seaweed strings. There follows a stinging antic-ipation, breath baiting, toward the opening of the small seafarer's chest as it is unstrapped from the vehicle's middle seat where it has been hid-den all these years. The trawler crew, Willie Shoman, Jude, Eleanor Cookee, among others stare at the chest while Cactus tries a key. It turns & the latch pops up, but the hinges are rusted & the chest refuses to open. Cactus forces the lid open with his swollen-knuckled, nervous fingers. He opens it so only he can see. He quickly surveys the contents & meets our eyes. Then it's as if he becomes an actor from a traveling troupe per-forming melodrama. He lets roar a booming stage voice & vigorously proclaims, *Let the eyes behold!* One item at a time, Cactus shows every-one the wild array, the loot, holding each piece at arm's length so we can see. Then he himself inspects every last piece, holding each close to his eye & squinting, for he is not wearing his reading glasses. He shows a wide range of emotions at the nostalgia every item conjures. It is all stuff he's glad to see again, stuff he has nearly forgotten about. He pass-es each item around: A dog-chewed baseball; a packet of rubber bands; a book of matches; a pad of carbon paper; wildflower seeds in sun-faded packages; phone numbers without names, scrawled on pieces of scrap paper; a sample-size plastic bottle of Woolite; a buffalo nickel; a foot-long lock of frizzy hair held together with a yellowing ring of scotch tape; JFK postage stamps; a package of sunflower seeds with sprouts growing out of them; a dried-up bottle of Liquid Paper; assorted guitar picks; lost pieces to different jigsaw puzzles; string; chalk; a blue Flair pen; *Growing Up at Thirty-Seven*; a broken Duncan glow-in-the-dark yo-yo; an electric toothbrush still in the manufacturer's box [*a gift from Mom perhaps? So sweet!*]; a golden locket, open it & find inside a button-size picture of a blissed-out hippie chick, circa 1969; issues of *Silver Surfer, Blue Beetle* & *Ghost Rider* comic books; a cereal-box toy submarine; store-brand baking soda; a can of black shoe polish; Bactine; marbles; an unlabeled reel of 16-mm film, that when examined more closely, contains a Dippy Dawg cartoon; pipe cleaners; a ripped-out page from a random, roadside phone book; a deck of pinochle cards; an issue of Ramparts from 1971 with the photos cut out; *Soul on Ice* in paperback; boxes of powder fabric dye; eight-track tapes of albums by It's a Beautiful Day, Yellow Balloon & The Growing Concern; a postcard from Greece. The chest contains stuff Cactus had collected through the years, stuff too good to lose. Most of it is yellow, some of it damp as traces of seawater had managed to seep inside the chest. In all, it is the kind of stuff that always belongs to somebody else, the kept treasures that mean nothing to anybody except the person who saves them. For Cactus, it's as if nothing else in the last fifteen years were worth keeping. Hell, we all might enjoy watching the Dippy Dawg cartoon. We could show it on the rusty walls of the bus, as soon as night falls, if only anyone had thought to bring along a movie projector. It is a real zoo collection—it ain't fifty grand. If you want to place a fair-market dollar value on it, it is all worth zero. At a time like this, who would possibly dare to say anything & break the gape-jawed silence? *I have a drawer like that at home*, Eleanor Cookee says, after Cactus finishes showing everyone every last thing.

The men & women of the salvage crew hide their eyes, unsure whether they are embarrassed or pissed off. One of them says *Jesus* under her breath. *The cash, brother?* asks another, the others in the crew instantly echoing his sentiments. *The cash, yes, where's the cash?*

Voila! Cactus rattles the chest & removes one last item hidden behind a trap door in the chest that no one would have ever suspected being there. He reveals a manila envelope, gray & mottled & coming apart every in conceivable way. Inside are tatters of paper, soggy, besmeared, hardly recognizable as paper money. He squeezes the water out of clumps of it & hands it to a few of the most vocal members of the salvage team individually.

Something is funny about that money. Money doesn't fall apart like that when it's wet; its ink never bleeds.

Cactus confirms the fears. *Ever see counterfeit money before?*

No one has. Everyone there is on the up & up as far as counterfeit money is concerned. [Show us boltcutters & monkey wrenches & suddenly, we're not so innocent.]

People, hear me out: It takes bread to bankroll a revolution. We were all about publishing manifestoes & justice for the common man. I can't say we knew much about printing money. Hell, look at this. A wad crumbles in his hand. Hell, we weren't even capitalists. He pays out a portion of the wad to each of the divers. I'd save this, if I were you, it's going to be a museum piece someday.

It's a museum piece already, old man, someone says.

So that's what we're looking at here, counterfeit money, wet & crumbling. Now it makes sense. Cactus's people were as anxious for this money to disappear as they were the bus itself. In addition to Black Panthers, Cactus had associates who were revolutionaries & counterfeiters. The FBI was moving in on all of them.

Then Cactus opens the driver's side door of the bus, water & seaweed spilling onto his feet. He climbs on board & inserts a key into the hole where the ignition would be if it had not rusted out. The engine doesn't turn over. *Just a little moisture in the carburetor, that's all. She'll get up & running in no time*, he says, waving us off. Then, after repeated turnings of the key & no life breathing from the engine, comes the stellar punch, *Do you think I can trouble you for a ride out to North Beach?*

Suddenly, it happens. It becomes apparent, what all this is. Cactus gets it. He isn't around the bend. He just refuses to make more of this than what it is. The only thing he takes seriously is his own unseriousness. That's the show he puts on for us.

At that moment, we get it, too. No matter how small the first laughs are aboard ship, people know they will be laughing about this later—about the old man thinking he could drive away a Volkswagen bus that has spent the last thirteen years at the bottom of the San Francisco Bay, then later asking for a ride back to the City. The scene breaks open, turns riotous. Perhaps the loot is this, the laughter that follows the day's work. Take away a story & a laugh & it's not so bad when you spend all you have until next Friday's paycheck on beer tonight.

What has become of the days when you could pay your way anywhere in the world with a song, a shaggy mutt who performs funny tricks, a good riddle, any laughing matter? A trick for a treat—it's the bartering system dogs use, all dogs have a sense of humor & speak with southern accents or Irish brogues. We have much to learn from them.

Let us now return to a time when you could walk around with a monkey on your shoulder—a macaque in a funny suit & hat & as long as the two of you are out together in the open, you will never need to worry about finding your dinner. It's never too late to learn card tricks & street magic.

Yes, with a monkey on the shoulder named Gumshoe, I want to live in a streetside marketplace world where you pay for eggs with posies—always a surprise—some magic beans for your cow. Talkin, talkin, talkin; you work & you talk. Joking is always welcome here, it's what people do, it's what you sell. Grinning toothless. Happy, yes. A pain in me goiter—happy, yes.

Yes!

Your hips gyrate: Suddenly, funny little dances transpire, arms & legs flying akimbo in rhythm alongside people you don't even know, touching each other on the arms, neither unafraid of incidental touches nor titillated by them.

Out driving several weeks later, the bus's windows rolled down, Cactus is overcome by the feeling that he is getting away with something. Turn a corner, stop at a light, a police officer stands beside a parked car writing a ticket. Cactus can't resist making conversation. *Hey*, he calls. *See this here rig?*

She looks over.

Then he tells her, *This rig used to transport political fugitives on flight back in '73. Case never did get solved—no arrests made, no evidence found. In theory, the FBI is still looking for it—this bus, right here.*

Smacking her gum, she replies, *Like I care.*

A month after the bus's recovery, Cactus has the FunTime running & street legal, zipping up & over San Francisco hills, high overlooking the Mission, rolling down from Twin Peaks into the Sunset along Portola, sweeping up Potrero Hill & later down Lombard. The horn honking, blinker blinking—the FunTime resurrects itself as an internal combustion shipwreck on wheels. Cactus has replaced all of the glass. The heavily rusted & bent out of shape sections of frame, he sanded over & painted, replacing rusted-away sections with fiberglass—the new FunTime is half Volkswagen, half surfboard. The bus remains misshapen, but is roadworthy no less & *seaworthy, to boot*, Cactus laughs. In restoring the Volkswagen, Cactus left patches of barnacles all along the outer walls. *Let's paint a mural on her flanks over the barnacles, they look like mountain ranges. Let's paint an image of Earth as seen from space on the side of the bus.* In the past, we always used nondescript vehicles—you know, along the lines of Willie Shoman's mustard-yellow Ford truck replete with Gem Top & NRA bumper sticker. These days, a muralsided Volkswagen bus suits us fine. We are not hiding anymore, we are not planning anything illegal other than our whoopty-whoo at the Pentagon, which is understandably illegal in the highest degree, at least, without proper permits.

Hiding nothing, we understand that this is our most ridiculous pursuit ever, but I don't believe we've crossed the line where the authorities reckon us a force they must stop. If they've caught wind of us at all, I'm sure they've gotten a big kick out of it & perceive no threat, because they would never want to fill out all the paperwork detailing intentions & activities as bent as ours.

Chapter 38: Amid bugs that sing thee electric

We are aware of the hazards being stranded on farmland: sprinkler systems, crop dusting, losing ourselves on the property of a trigger-happy farmer who's out in his fields several hours before the first light of dawn. Cactus, rather than wait for morning when he can see what he is doing, tinkers with the engine by the light of a flashlight held in his teeth, trying to find & correct whatever is causing the nasty black cloud that trailed us shortly before the FunTime lost power.

Leaning against the FunTime, Cy & Daphne talk, though quietly. The ring seems less obnoxious out in open spaces. Cy talks & Daphne listens, reacts, then responds. She plays off what he's saying, grooving on him, making him sound interesting, at least to himself.

Like, what you are saying is, the sun & moon are the same size.

No, but the seem that way during an eclipse.

But if you like watch an eclipse, you will go blind & then all you'll have is the memory of the sun & moon & like no real frame of reference.

All this time, we considered Cy unintelligible & along comes someone who understands him, someone who talks the same jazz. Daphne might even dig on his account of the Light that one night that hovered outside his dorm room window when he gets around to telling her about it.

DNA is pretty, the loops on the end of the strand. This is the image running through Cy's head. After a lull in their bus-side conversation, Cy begins mumbling incoherently to Daphne about DNA when suddenly, he realizes that what's inspiring this train of thought is her DNA. Just then, she yawns.

Your DNA is pretty, he tells her, seemingly at random.

Her eyes rivet over—*what?*

But I'm sure you hear that all the time.

Here comes the brush off, mostly because she's sleepy, *Yeah, all the time.* For the moment, she will not look at him.

Now he yawns, the power of suggestion taking effect. Then he continues, *The component parts that comprise you, the energy that gives you color & form, all your codes—your very DNA is pretty.*

So do you tell that to all the women you meet?

No, you're the first.

Been saving up that line a while, have you?

It's not a line, it's a double helix. You have pretty DNA. The ring flashes the code. I am reacting to it. I am telling you.

He lifts her hand close to his face to look at it closely despite the dark. He looks at her wrist, arm & elbow. He takes her pulse.

Just then it quickens.

Do you know much about genetics? she asks, pulling her arm away.

No, but I have a cousin named Rita.

You are so weird! Daphne cannot stand the thought of someone flirting with her, especially when she can't help flirting right back. She likes the things he is saying, random as they are & with such little substance behind them. *He seems so spontaneous, he flirts without thinking. I wonder, is he like this with everyone?*

I like you, he thinks & if she were able to read minds she would know. If he could read minds, he would know that what's most important to her right now is finding a way to slip the ring off because, not only is it annoying, it's also become congealed to her finger. Since he cannot read minds, he sometimes likes to make up what he thinks people might be thinking. He would like to think that what she's thinking is, *I like you, too.* While that's not verbatim the thought she is having, a slight variation runs across her mind.

He likes me, she thinks.

Chapter 39: Oregon without tears, Oregon without rain

Morning ascends & the FunTime starts right up, revving healthily in spite of good Cactus's tinkering, as if she needed nothing more than a good night's rest to get her motor going again. It turns out the FunTime likes to sleep as much as the rest of us. [*The question is, does she dream?* Willie Shoman from beyond beyond wants to know.] To think: Some of us worried that she needed a new engine, that fixing her up would ground us for a day or longer, that we were stuck here in farmland, where poisons & pesticides stick to your clothes & coat your insides when you breathe. [Then your breathing stops.]

Cactus lifts the engine compartment door. Dandelions are growing from the crevices of the engine. They don't seem to mind the vibration & they like the heat. Cactus throws some water on them to keep them happy. Every day he opens the engine compartment door to see the dandelions & every day he gives them a sprinkle. Air-cooled Volkswagen engines are never supposed to need water. Air-cooled Volkswagen engines that have dandelions growing from every available crevice need water daily. Its time underwater has made the FunTime mysteriously fertile. Look closely & find there's more there than just the dandelions, there are wildflowers indigenous to all the places the FunTime has passed through. Seeds attach themselves to the FunTime's body as we fly down the road, embedding themselves in the barnacles on her flanks.

If we didn't know better, we would say the vehicle was powered by the seeds themselves & the energy they process from the rain, wind & sun. We rarely stop for gas & the FunTime sips rather than guzzles. We would be interested to see what would happen if we ran out of gas. Would water work in her fuel tank? Would rainfall & sunlight power us along? Maybe we broke down last night for lack of photosynthesis. [*I doubt we would travel fast on sprout power alone. Plants never hurry, their energy comes gradually when compared to the hustle-bustle of the human world. But isn't it true we have all the time in the world? School's out, we don't have jobs, our house is no longer ours.*]

Cactus drives up & down the farm road, honking at everyone to gather, to return to the mother ship. *Reboard!* We are on our way again. *Rejoice!* Soon, sun will flood the area with intense light & heat. The air from movement will keep us cool & light.

When we cross into Oregon, the climate changes as soon as we cross the border. The rain sweeps away highways & if the tires slip, there's always the danger of the rig veering off the road & plopping into the Willamette. Oregon is a place where straight lines go wavy. Bring a paddle in case your rig runs out of gas. The Oregon sky of legend is so waterlogged that if you jump, you float—you can tread sky. Portland is the rainsurfing capital of the world & you don't need fins. It's a place where dogs who have the hang of it paddle across the sky & can accidentally kick you in the head while chasing a thrown ball & always watch out for yellow rain.

In the restroom of the roadside gas station in Medford, the soap from the dispenser is white & granular—the kind of soap we remember from elementary school. It does not turn into lather, it does not turn into foam. Rather, it maintains its grainy texture even when wet. Daphne & Cy twist the ring back & forth on her finger, pulling gently, trying to get it off. It's not going anywhere & the soap, Cy's idea, makes everything worse. She runs her hand under cold water & tries again; she relaxes. The ring slips off & she drops it into her vest pocket. The two of them exit the restroom & join the others for the final leg of their journey to Portland.

Chapter 40: Who do you wish were here?

We are the Jokerman 8 on this trip. It's the name we give ourselves despite there being only seven of us on board the FunTime. We are somehow incomplete. Our eighth is missing. It's Jude. She disappeared just when the plans to go to Oregon rolled forward. On her heels, we also disappeared, leaving behind the empty Joshua Tree. It's not like we didn't try to leave a forwarding address, just no one took our forwarding address seriously. No one believed we were going where we said we were going & doing what we were setting out to do. So Eleanor Cookee began to call it a secret journey. By calling it that, she no longer felt she needed to tell everyone about it.

In May, Cy had completed his six-page, double-spaced undergraduate history paper showing how he believed Norman Hartman's self-immolation triggered the events that ultimately brought about the end of the war in Vietnam—he even turned it in on time. Typing away at 4:30 A.M. the morning before it was due, he tacked on an elegant ending, a tribute to Norman Hartman that honored the level of commitment & courage the man held within him as he approached a cause in which he deeply believed. Cy himself pledged to keep the flames of Norman

Hartman close to him—he intended for the *flames of Hartman will never die* to become his personal rallying cry.

Things change. The semester ended & Cy began new projects. The Norman Hartman paper was graded, the grade converted into semester units & entered into his transcripts. The transcripts were applied toward his degree—a bachelor of the arts in American History that he has since left unfinished. Within weeks of the semester's end, Cy had forgotten about Norman Hartman, forgotten the rallying cry & even went so far as to forget the graded copy of his paper at the Joshua Tree where it became mixed up in with a stack of biological assessments & other government documents.

This is where Jude found it. When she read the paper, she hardly noticed that Cy received a B+ for his effort, or the elegant ending tribute. Just as it was a footnote, a throwaway afterthought, that led Cy to his study of Norman Hartman in the first place, it was a single sentence that caught Jude's eye, a sentence from which Jude will not be able to escape until she rises from her chair & travels cross country, a sentence that inspires her to up & leave without a goodbye. It is the sentence in which Cy writes that on the day of Norman Hartman's self-immolation, the man was not alone. He brought along his baby daughter, Emily.

Chapter 41: The fastest girls are not supposed to beat the fastest boys—that's why we race them separately

1971—Jude's mother, newly widowed, decides that now for once, from this moment & ever after, she will live. Funny how rather than go out & meet people & splurge on herself & stay up late & live like a teenager all over again, she first goes to Sears & buys a transistor radio—a small portable that she keeps on with the volume low, tuned to an AM station, while she raises two children & works her way through college. The radio will keep her in tune with the world as she works. She never gives serious thought to bringing a new man into her life, into their lives. There will be time for that when she wants it. Funny how she doesn't want it. Even as time passes, she still doesn't want it; close personal relationships with members of the opposite sex are overrated. All she needs right now is to keep the radio on & oh, a bachelor's degree & master's degree & a doctorate. Besides, a new, close interpersonal relationship will keep her from what matters most: providing a good life for her two precious children.

1973—Through photographs on the mantle & refrigerator, the father who will always remain missing in action is more present than the mother always working. The photographs become a steady influence on Jude's older brother who is already set in his way. He wants to grow up & become a soldier. His hair will never grow out—he will always wear a buzz cut. He will always have a serious look in his eye. [Referring to him as a young killing machine can make the boy blush.]

As a child, Jude turns in another direction. At five, she is a no-nonsense glossy-eyed dreamer, a little girl turned hippie, droopy eyed with long, straight red hair; beads & clogs; bellbottom pants with butterfly patches. A peace symbol hangs on her bedroom wall next to a poster proclaiming, *War is harmful to children & other living things.*

In a sense, Jude spends her first years taking care of herself, while her mother studies all night with the radio on & her brother plays with his G.I. Joe dolls. Jude's primary contact with other people comes on Monday & Wednesday nights when her mother takes classes & two older girls, Vickie & Christine, babysit & play Elton John, David Bowie & the Beatles's Blue & Red albums on the portable record player they bring over. They think Jude is the coolest little kid ever.

1975—Now in the second grade, Jude sees boys racing against one another in gym class & to her, it looks as if they are moving in slow motion. She is not judging the boys negatively, their slowness does not change the way she sees them as kids, as people. In no time, the gym teachers, Mr. Cahill & Miss Hudson, label Jude their *little miss speed demon.* She is faster than any of her classmates—it isn't even close. They keep letting her race against faster & older children, the young champions from elementary school's track team, just to see what will happen. She beats them all, even the school's fastest fifth-grade boys. By the time she earns the Presidential Physical Fitness award for her school & wins first place at the regional Junior Olympics, she has outgrown her hippie-little-kid phase. The gym teachers & track coaches tag Jude as a child with a killer instinct, as a competitor who hates to lose, believing that she desperately wants to prove herself. They have Jude all wrong. She doesn't care about beating others. Her velocity comes to her because her motion is fluid & because she doesn't care about beating others.

Chapter 42: Chinmeyr's here

1990—This is the place where we go next. Eleanor Cookee knows the strings to pull, whom to ask for keys. The city is sitting here on the Big Muddy Ranch just outside of Antelope, Oregon as it has since they left, abandoned these past five years. It's a city nonetheless & the streets & buildings are accustomed to people with funny ideas. When Oregonians remember the Rajneesh & his followers, they recall the vivid images: the Bhagwan's fleet of Rolls-Royces; the red clothing; the talk of wild, free love; the importing of homeless people in an effort to sway Wasco County elections; the food poisoning of a salad bar in the Dalles; the attempted murders; the plot to assassinate Oregon's attorney general; the work in Ma Prem Sheela's secret laboratory to reproduce & propagate the AIDS virus, which they then planned to use to infect their enemies. These are not run-of-the-mill images in these parts. The people who liked Rajneesh & his sannyasin followers, who believed they were victims of religious persecution, who disagreed with the manner in which they were treated by the State of Oregon & the United States, in the end gave in to popular sentiments: They were led by people of spotty character.

We mark our territory in an abandoned city, a ghost town vibrant but without electricity & water. We have no plans for the next week other than to work out the particulars of the Pentagon Pyramid Prank in hopes of taking the show to Washington this fall. A canyon, desert, hills in every direction—such innocuous seeming land, this is. Yet at the same time it is big enough to foster another bizarre Oregon roadside attraction. We discover some good places to hike, only there's no shade & we are becoming conscious of the sun. *Snakes are a maybe? Snakes are a yes.* The city is built of wood, two-by-four & wafer-board construction, flat roofs. The architecture reflects a vaguely eastern style, though also similar to a West Coast small town downtown. Mainly what you see is the shoddy construction. They built the city themselves in the early 1980s. They built it in a hurry. They were not builders. They were intellectuals, doctors & business professionals. Funny how the windows aren't even boarded up. Some are, but not all of them. In ways, it's as if the place is anticipating our arrival. The buildings wear their sunshine smiles & Sunday best. The strangest part is seeing empty streets. While a forest or desert or any free & wild space is in its splendor without other people, an empty city such as this one just seems out of place.

1981—Bhagwan Shree Rajneesh comes to America because he believes America is the place where he can build paradise. Unfortunately, United States zoning laws prohibit the construction of paradise. America in the 1980s is zoned for superhighways, strip malls, clear cuts, nuclear power plants & Burger Kings—not paradise. [*When you mix asphalt with cement, it's even stronger & lasts longer. If you find a way to mix in plastic, you invent a surface that might last forever.*]

In arrogant disrespect of American zoning laws, Rajneesh, along with the sannyasins, considers many promising sites to build their shiny new city. They consider Arizona, New Mexico & southern Colorado. Many sites hold promise, but they will not jump to a rash decision. The sannyasins are for the most part an educated bunch, many hold advanced degrees & some hold doctorates in psychology. All together, they will find Bhagwan a home, an American paradise. The final decision, however, belongs to the Bhagwan's personal secretary, right arm & voice during his three-&-a-half year vow of silence, Ma Prem Sheela. During the Bhagwan's silence, he speaks to no one but Sheela & his doctor, the same doctor who, as an aside, Sheela will eventually attempt to murder. Sheela makes one trip to central Oregon & knows that Big Muddy must & will be the place. She lets the others keep looking, but she knows in her heart the search is over. She pays cash on the spot to close the deal, paying more than the land is worth. On her first night there, Sheela spends the evening out, drinking heavily with some of the locals at a tavern in the nearby town of Antelope. She drinks as if she were one of the locals &

babbles incomprehensibly. One ranch hand understands her to say that Big Muddy will be the place where—*hiccup!*—where she will meet Chinmeyr again. The locals find Sheela a strange person, but they like her, oh, yes & they have no idea that Chinmeyr is the name of Sheela's first husband who had died years earlier from Hodgkin's disease.

I was just thinking, Rog. My father bought a piece of desert once. He rode his horse atop a ravine & looked down on it. The land was his & that's all it was. He would pound his fist on the ground & know he couldn't bust it.

What do you think they want the land for? Raise cattle?

Beats me. The geologists come in & say the land has no mineral value. You can't get water here. There aren't enough people living out this way to start a business. There isn't even a reason this place is here other than to make space, to hold the opposite ends of the country together.

Maybe if you come from far enough away, this place might seem pretty.

Hey, I'm from here! This place always seems pretty to me.

1990—Now it's our turn to tread here. We arrive ten years later, in a joking spirit. We walk to the cliff's edge as it stretches out before us. From high above, we look down into the gorge. There's not much to say about the place. We are merely borrowing it. We are practicing our pyramid-building skills on it. We will be on our way shortly.

Up here, the silence will drive you over the edge if no one says anything. Someone say something, please.

He's here, I can feel it.

Who's here?

Chinmeyr.

A long, thoughtful pause. *I thought you were going to say Willie Shoman.*

Chapter 43: It's been pretty simple so far

STAGE 1—Pyramids are cool. They are sleek, breathtaking, without ornament, built through engineering that seems like magic.

Pyramid building takes sun, water & air. Pyramid building takes a whisper.

Pyramids are monuments to people working together. Working alone, it would take a person a million years, if not more & still it would be difficult. You need one person to pull & another to push at the very least. A person working alone could never do it, even if given a million years, a billion years—a single soul could never get it done without help. A single soul would sooner or later give up & find something else to do—like wash the car.

Given all the time in the world, what is the smallest number of people who could build a pyramid on the scale of the Great Pyramid?

Twenty? How about twenty plus one, twenty-one.

Twenty-one people & everybody knows everybody.

Twenty-one people & we can put it all together.

Twenty-one people. Oddly enough, that's the number of Jokerman who show up here.

The Egyptians moved seventy-ton stones. For us, that would be more than three tons per person.

We need a stone-moving machine, a contraption, an apparatus.

No, no, no—the Egyptians weren't machine-oriented people, they used no gizmos nor wheels. Machines are the wrong approach.

Standing around like this all day & talking about it will never get it done. Or will it?

It might—who knows? Maybe when we fall asleep, the pyramids will build themselves.

We thumb through pages of hieroglyphic text without translation, making of it what we can. We recognize people kneeling, snakes, hawks, canaries, squiggly lines & dots, a round object with feet—it looks like an apple.

STAGE 2—*Okay, okay, okay—what you are saying is maybe the stones sprouted legs & walked into place, herded by cats wearing diamond-studded collars, pharaoh headdress & false beard.*

Yes, I've like seen it pictured in stone relief.

Maybe the Egyptians were maniacal & glued herds of fruit flies to the giant stones & the flies did the rest of the work.

It's a nice theory, but what it hinges on is whether or not the Egyptians had glue strong enough to make the flies stick.

STAGE 3—*No, but really, maybe it was a sudden change of weather that built the pyramids—wind & rain like you've never seen whipped the stones into place.*

STAGE 4—All of the old-school building theories assume that the construction involves a picking up & moving, picking up & moving, picking up & moving. Now we're finding there is perhaps—no, *definitely*—a simpler way.

So you say that you want to build a li'l pyramid? What is your number one obstacle? Simple, gravity, the heaviness of the pieces, the energy required to move them into place, the energy required to cut them so that they fit together perfectly.

So you say because the pyramid builders of Egypt lived in an age before ours, we assume they knew less than we know? The pyramids are lingering proof they knew more. They knew how to build pyramids. This is not to say our civilization is incapable of building pyramids, but can we do so without ripping a hole in the ozone layer?

STAGE 5—The outlaws of physics are making out like bandits. We wish to share their company.

STAGE 6—Maybe they built a giant mold & poured in the stone. It set like Jell-O. Maybe they built the pyramids from the top down, so they were able to stop anytime they wanted. Maybe they built the pyramids underwater. Plate tectonics moved them to where they are now. Maybe they built the pyramids one night on a wild drunken spree of masonry. You should have seen the looks on their faces in the garish morning when the sun woke them & they saw what they had done. They dunno how they dunnit, but they was so glad they did.

[*Look at those, my love, do you suppose we did that?*

Yes, I remember well. That's not all I remember about last night.]

STAGE 7—A few days after raising the pyramids, no one could remember anything—the process was lost. Suddenly, their backs & arms weren't so sore anymore & these three massive pyramids stood before them. They found themselves wondering just how they did such a thing. In turn, they never told their sons & daughters what the trick was. Because of that, we have 4,000 years of speculation & no straightforward pyramid construction plan. Until Foot Apples comes along, that is.

Chapter 44: To itself

We sleep heartily here. The moon, a pyramid dream, vermin, bats, serpents, a cover up. *It's not a tomb, really!*

Chapter 45: Under

The next morning, we roll ourselves out of bed, wipe the sleep from our eyes & stumble two spaces forward into the sun-ripened day.

Why don't we just admit that the pyramids were built by people who worked hard & had incredible talent for cutting, lifting & aligning stone? They worked from the blueprints of a talented architect. When they finished, they laughed together & drank beer.

Maybe we should read the books rather than keep guessing what's inside of them.

Foot Apples awake yet?

No one's seen him.

TS stands. He can't remember where he was standing because he wasn't standing there long & he isn't standing there anymore. The more he thinks about it, he might have been lying down. He remembers now that it was nowhere. Sea foam surrounds his ankles & then suddenly, the undertow rips him straight down. His arms over his head, he slides downward, as if through a tunnel, sucked down deep into the water. Finally, he lands in an underwater place & he is up to his eyes in dolphins. They swarm, they touch noses with him, they seem to like him. Among them, he sees laughing jellyheads, dancing trilobites. The water bubbles with laughter & singing & the funnylooking one roving over the bottom & peers up at him with two eyes on the same side of its face. *Oh & Jude's* there, too, breathing underwater & swimming over without using her arms. As a child, TS never learned to swim, but down here, that doesn't seem to matter. Swimming here is as easy as breathing. *Hi, Jude—it's good seeing you again.*

Jude's off again & a dolphin, the one with the silliest grin, swims by in pharaoh headdress & false beard & instantly, TS gets it all at once. *It's all a joke*, he thinks to himself. *Everything Egypt—everything everything.*

Then another dolphin, this one more earnest in countenance, swims over to him. TS cannot tell if the dolphin is male or female, he doesn't know the difference. *I wanted to give my soul to you,* the dolphin says to TS & he wonders what just happened. *I wanted to give my soul to you,* the dolphin says again & remarkably TS can make sense of the dolphin sounds. *I wanted to give my soul to you.* It is an interesting statement in a grammatical sense in its use of the perfect tense, placing the desire in the past. The past is the verb tense you never can fully trust as it relies so much on memory.

When he awakens in his tent, amid crickets, moonlight & air—earth beneath him & not just any earth, but solid Oregon earth , TS cannot remember what just happened, although he doesn't think he was asleep. If Jude were here, she would know.

Interlude: A quick & dirty method to finding people, circa 1990

Step 1—Gather all you know about the person. In this case, we believe the name of the person we are seeking is Emily Hartman, although that might have changed if she is married or if her mother remarried or if she chose to change it herself. She is older than Jude by no more than a year or two. We do not know her birthday. We believe she lived in the eastern United States during her early life, within a day's drive of Washington, DC. That's more than twenty years ago & she could live anywhere now. Oh & her father was a Quaker.

Step 2—Now apply your known information to the listings in available public directories of residential phone numbers. In some states, you may also access people through their vehicle registration & tax assessments. With a social security number, you can run a credit check on a people & learn their spending habits or nonhabits. You can learn whether they have a criminal background. With the knowledge of a person's birthdate, birthplace & mother's maiden name, you can, on paper, become the person, abducting the person's identity for a crime spree or anything else you desire. You can make guesses to break a person's passwords or secret codes. We suggest trying the name of the family dog.

Step 3—If all else fails, you can comb the streets, asking people questions, feeding them twenty-dollar bills one after another like they do on cop shows. If you ruffle through a person's garbage, you can gather all kinds of information; at the very least, you'll learn whether or not she recycles. Get a temp job doing data entry at a person's bank & become privy to her financial wheelings & dealings. You can invade a person's privacy & she will never know it's you. You, though, will know it's you.

This is the Quick & Dirty Method to Finding Anyone in America.

Nothing about Jude is quick & dirty.

In searching for Emily Hartman, Jude goes a much simpler, more personal route. First, she goes home & visits her mother. Then she goes to the University of Washington library & pores through phone books from all over the country. Then she makes a list of the potential Hartman families she would like to contact. She ranks the list according to her hunches. Too shy to call the families whose numbers she finds, she chooses the ones her hunches tell her are most likely & she decides to head east & start her search there.

She boards a Greyhound bus & begins her odyssey to the East Coast. She is not going for the gold medal, not for a college degree, not to save the world. She relaxes & stops trying so hard, breathes, closes her eyes & falls asleep, slumping against the window.

Chapter 46: In which Jude gets a haircut

1990—A hair salon pops up where you least expect to find one—nestled in the middle of a nowhere pine forest near Rockville, Maryland—hidden down a winding woodsy driveway outside of town. It's the last place you would think of going for a haircut, perm, or manicure. It's the place Jude goes to find out why she's come here. A wooden sign out front announces the name of the establishment: *HAIR TODAY*. Then another, smaller sign, this one in the shop window, drawls, *WALK-INS WELCOME*. [Jude is literally a walk-in. Considering the out-of-the-way location of Hair Today, most clients drive. It's just like Jude to find a way to walk.] Yet another sign, this one even smaller & hanging in the door glass, pips to all who read it: *YES, WE'RE OPEN—COME ON IN!*

What else can Jude do than go inside?

Jude pushes the glass door open, suddenly slipping into the middle of a conversation about this & that, Jodie Foster & Martin Sheen—a story in *People* magazine, a neighbor boy gone off to college, the colic dog on the other side of the fence who bawls every time it rains, Nancy Reagan & her astrology. *Oh, do you remember that?*

The woman in charge, Jude gathers, is the widow of Norman Hartman, the mother of Emily. The other woman, her client, is wearing curlers in her hair & seated in one of those chairs you find in styling salons & barber shops with one pedal that when pumped will raise you up; the other pedal lets the chair exhale & ease back down. It's the kind of fun chair that makes you wish you were a kid playing on it with other kids. Emily's mother escorts the client over to a hair dryer, a monstrous upside-down salad bowl kind of contraption. No one else is here in Hair Today & Emily's mother has time to cut Jude's hair.

Just a trim, Jude says.

Emily's mother gives Jude a look of recognition, though for her life, she cannot remember where she knows him from & *this one doesn't even need a haircut*, she thinks. *Have I cut your hair before?* Emily's mother asks.

I don't think so.

After wrapping a tissue around Jude's neck & covering her in a smock, Emily's mother leads Jude to the shampoo station. Jude leans her head back into the basin & she can feel warm water cascading from the spigot, then comes the shampoo. It's the kind of soap that causes a healthy tingling in the scalp, herbal. Jude can feel the woman's fingers as they massage her head. She can hear the song playing on the country western station as it repeats its chorus.

Emily's mother dries Jude's hair with a towel & leads her back to the chair where she will sit while her hair is cut. Jude looks into the mirror at her face & falls into a moment of stark recognition. Her wet hair holds tightly to her head—this is the first time in ages she has looked intently into a mirror, seen herself this closely. Jude notices how her jowls stick out from her face, how they make her seem sharp. Do people see her as sharp? For so long, she has given no thought to what other people think. She remembers how she had been a pudgy child. That changed when she started running, *bye-bye, baby fat*. It was as if her metabolism knew she was going to be runner & was waiting for her to discover it. Then she became lean. Her coaches & mother encouraged her to use discipline in her diet & that much was easy. Now she's wondering what she may have missed by keeping herself so thin. [Fat is fun, fat is the fun she missed, the ice cream slumber parties—*oh!* & she missed out on going to pizza with the team after a soccer game.]

[*Jude is, like, so gone.*

I'm glad she is. She's twenty-two & already done everything—except live.

She's never even had a boyfriend—unless you count TS.

TS doesn't count. They were together but not together. Like, do you know what I mean?]

Jude takes her eyes off her image in the mirror & takes her eyes off Emily's mother. She notices the photograph taped to the mirror's edge. Pictured: a sunny day, a young woman, the woman's daughter—Emily. A sudden mixture of happiness & confusion overcomes Jude all at once. A softening moves through her tear ducts.

Did I say something? Honey, I didn't mean to make you cry. What did I say?

Jude cannot speak, she had been holding back her tears, but now that they have come, they won't let her say anything.

What's the matter, Sweetie?

Jude can't get a word out, just the sound of the letter *m*. The woman hugs her. It's all right, Sweetie. [The woman wonders what's wrong. *Who is this girl who walks in off the street & breaks into tears?*] The more Jude tries to speak, the more difficult it becomes. Why is the woman's name so difficult to say?

Mrs. Hartman—?

Emily's mother, the older woman, her face falls. [*No one knows me by that name anymore.*]

Jude gathers herself & says, *That's your daughter in the photograph?* Jude phrases the question matter-of-factly.

Suddenly, everything becomes clear to the woman. Her first response is fluster & anger, though in no way directed toward Jude. Her face turns red. *Goddamn the man for never saying anything.* Then follows love & compassion *for this poor creature who has come to seek me out, even though I have nothing to do with her when it all boils down. You are his flesh & blood, not mine.* [*I knew you were out there, I dreamed you were out there—my daughter's half-sister. Let me look at you. Yes, I can see—I can see the him in you. The rest must be her, but then I never knew her. I just saw her that one time on the back of your father's motorcycle—just before the two of them rode off together. She was so young, not quite grown into the person she was going to be. I want to say none of this matters anymore, but I still feel it.*]

The client, meanwhile, has fallen asleep, her head encumbered under the dryer, has fallen forward under the dryer's soothing hum.

Girl, I am glad you've come—I understand why you're here, the woman tells Jude. *Your half-sister is the one who you really want to meet.*

Nothing stops the flow of Jude's tears more quickly than this confusion. [*Why I'm here? I haven't told her anything. Half sister?*]

So have you talked to your father anytime lately? the woman asks. *Say the last twenty years or so? That's about the last I seen him.*

No, my father's dead. He died in Vietnam.

Nothing jibes, something isn't right.

Then everything clicks for both of them at once—neither is whom the other thinks she is.

[*Norman Hartman didn't die in Vietnam.*]

[*Norman Hartman is not my father.*]

Jude, who is usually so careful, so thorough & scientific, found the mother of the wrong Emily Hartman, daughter of Norman. Sometimes in America families have the same name. After Jude explains to Mrs. Hartman how she came to be here & the story of the other Norman Hartman (from the Pentagon) & the other daughter (the Emily who survived her father's blaze) & the Quaker connection, then it's Mrs. Hartman's turn.

The reason that we put on Emily's birth certificate that she was a Quaker was that we knew that Quakers were conscientious objectors to war & we thought that we were having a boy. When she turned out to be a girl, we said, okay, what if by the time she's eighteen, the draft includes young women? *We wanted to give her a choice in the matter. Funny how idealistic we were & how it turns out we had nothing to worry about & Emily now goes to the Presbyterian church. Norman & I were both against the war in Vietnam, but Honey, there is no way my Norman Hartman set himself on*

*fire as an act of protest. Norman Hartman took off on his motorcycle with
his seventeen-year-old girlfriend & headed out to California, leaving me to
raise his one-year-old daughter by myself. The only times I've heard from
him since then are when he's needed money.*

Laughter, hugs, goodbyes—Mrs. Hartman asks Jude to drop her a line
when it's all over, she wants to know how the story turns out, wants to
know about the other Norman & Emily Hartman.

[Do I know anything? Is any of this real? Is it really there?]

Interlude: Did the New World want to be discovered?

When time comes to discover the New World, Columbus wanted to be
first & claimed he was first but the Norse beat him by hundreds of years.
The Norse didn't care if they were first, but they were beat by thousands of years by Asiatic people who walked to the Americas over a
land bridge where the Aleutian Islands now are, or so the popular theory goes. When the Asiatic people turned around & wanted to go back,
they couldn't find their way home, all they could find was water. So
they stayed. They filled out two continents while avoiding population
density. Long before human beings arrived, dolphins would take a long
look at North America & sigh. North America, at the time, was a
wilderness teeming with wildlife, fertile & diverse—so many thousands
of birds fly overhead during their migration that they eclipse all but tiny
slits of sky from your view. But North America was without monkeys
of its own. Monkeys want to be funny. Monkeys drum up trouble.
Monkeys leave a path of destruction in their wake, clothing scattered
along the floor & worse. [The clever baby hides a snake next to his
mother while she sleeps. When she awakens, does she find baby's little
prank funny? *I don't think so!*] Dolphins sigh because they know monkeys will one day find their way here.

Chapter 47: Bicycling is flourishing on American backroads

On a hot Wednesday morning during a week when all the days blur themselves together, you stare at a wavy road horizon watching it ebb & flow, knowing you are in for another hot one. Then over the horizon pops a bicycle helmet followed instantly by the appearance of the rider himself, seeming to emerge as if from the road itself—the eyes play tricks. Before you recognize that the physical manifestation you are witnessing is a cyclist—the rider sees you & waves your way. *Hey, that ain't any ol' rider—that's Spokes!*

Spokes! A member of the original Jokerman 6, Spokes! whose idea it was to call the group Jokerman! Spokes, who was there when Eleanor first started finding gigs to do, from long before TS's time!

Even though he is now off the bike & walking & talking & giving dusty, sweaty hugs & high fives to everyone, there's a jigger in Spokes's step. His legs still think they're pedaling—they have become so used to the ride. There's no way he will be able to catch up with everybody completely; he's been gone too long & missed too much.

Moments off the bike, Spokes feels himself a distant outsider, but he's glad he found us & he's glad to see Eleanor Cookee again. A few years older than the rest of us, Spokes actually graduated from college, something that we seem to have forgotten about for ourselves. He was groomed by his family to go to law school, but instead climbed on a bicycle & began riding. His bicycle has been turning over seemingly infinite American spaces ever since. Now he's one step older & never going back. Spokes can't regret choosing to ride rather than to burn out. Burning out would mean that he would hate every day in which he has to participate in his own life & at least riding is cardiovascular. He doesn't understand the first thing about pentagons & pyramids & why everyone is taking them so seriously. He realizes how out of touch he is. He has done nothing other than ride his bike for the last eighteen months. He's gone as far south as Panama & is considering going south again, this time even farther.

Everything has changed since he left the fold—even the *I am Elvis* tattoo on his right arm. The tattoo dates back to another time in his life. He was drunk one night in North Beach & decided he wanted it. Three years later, the tattoo is still with him, much more so than his arm, which has lost almost all of its body fat after so much endless riding. *[I remember the night I came back to the dorms drunk with that tattoo, I tried sleeping it off, lying on Eleanor Cookee's bed while she stayed up all night studying. The bed was a merry go round. I would spot Eleanor Cookee at her desk sometimes while I spun & damn, the skin on my arm hurt.]*

Jude, bless her, wherever she is, is a person who never looks back. She is firmly grounded, self-complete; Spokes is different, all he ever does is look back. Looking back is in the nature of the ride, you ride all day hoping to outdistance it all. You look back because if you don't whatever is gaining on you might run you off the road. You ride faster & avoid stopping.

How long you been goin', Spokes? Eleanor Cookee asks.

Eighteen months, this last time out. This is my own personal graduate program, what I am doing in lieu of law school. I will keep going until my trust fund runs out. Then I'll do something else—probably won't do much falling out of trees again.

Spokes's trust fund—this was the stigma that had always had set him apart from the rest of us, something always hanging over his head. Spokes has money. He is never going to have to work. All he has to do is avoid extravagance & he can live forever. While the rest of us are held back because we don't have money & we have to work in order to eat & make rent, Spokes is always free to move the next step forward. He keeps moving & leaves the rest of us behind.

He had fallen from a tree once & although he wasn't hurt, he never wanted to go back up & when he decided to leave, this was the reason he gave—the experience that caused him to burn out. We always understood that Spokes left us not because of the fall, but because his girlfriend left him. She ran off with a Kennedy vacationing in San Francisco. She had that run-off-with-a-vacationing-Kennedy look about her—you know, a turned-up nose, dainty hands, perfect skin & a taste for expensive clothing. She ran off the instant a vacationing Kennedy presented himself. Spokes is tall enough, thin enough & deep-voiced enough to attract the kind of woman who would run off with a Kennedy, but he wasn't Kennedy enough to keep her. Though, if you asked him, he would tell you that her leaving didn't matter much to him. She was never his type.

Even before his girlfriend left, Spokes had fallen in love with Eleanor Cookee. Even now, he knows in his heart she is the only woman for him. While he rides, he remembers the night when he was drunk & freshly tattooed & nothing passed between them. She studied & he spun. He hides his feelings for her because he senses, or rather, because he knows, she doesn't feel the same.

What do you do when it rains? she asks him.

Keep riding, or find shelter, Spokes tells her. *Rain always seems worse that it is when you are warm indoors & looking through a window.*

Twice, Spokes stopped at a town—found himself a place to live, bought some clothing at the Salvation Army & got himself work as a day labor-er, wearin a shiteatin grin & hopin it don't stick. This is another part of his American adventure. It gives him a break from riding, to keep from burning out on this, too.

[I ride in my sleep. I dream about it. My legs feel like they're still going. When you ride all day the body never stops. While you sleep it simultaneously grows & thins out, it reshapes, it applies the day's fitness to you.]

I am traveling light, Ellie (Spokes is the only one, other than TS, who calls her Ellie. No one else thinks to call her that; no one else could get away with it). *I got it all right here in my saddlebags. All I own are bike parts &*

binoculars & a radio & my Gore-Tex rain gear. He gave up everything for the ride, even his record collection. He doesn't mention the bank card in his pocket that will let him withdraw any amount he needs.

Eleanor Cookee notices, too, the saddlebags under his eyes. *You look tired, Ryder.*

It was a push to get here. I am glad I did, though. Hi, Ellie, it's good seeing you again.

The next morning, Spokes is ready to shove off. When he goes, he leaves two wavy lines along the dirt road, we can see the path by which he left. He leaves his tracks uncovered. He takes everything with him.

Chapter 48: The blue disperses, broadcasting back upon itself

Oceans rise, we can't say why—it's part of life's ebb & flow. Tidal waters sweep away whatever grows along the shore. They pull you out into the undertow. Next the water submerges the shore itself. The water reaches out as if to embrace, then doesn't let go. Waves smother you, if you let them. Oceans rose three-hundred feet over the years during an 11,000-year period ending sixty centuries ago. Along seashores were cities, incredibly elaborate, highly stylized that, for whatever reason, refused to retreat from the ever-rising water & were swept away to sea. It is beyond us to imagine a society of people who do not flee from the rising waters of time. [Yet they rebuilt San Francisco after 1906 & again in 1989.] It seems the people could have sought higher ground rather than stay where they were when the flooding began, when ocean waves were rolling through their bedrooms & kitchens. Were they convinced the water would to soon back off, or did they not care? Maybe they knew something we are incapable of understanding. [*I imagine they will keep rebuilding California no matter the size of the next earthquake. It's no different, really. Only we understand that what keeps Californians staying put is ultimately a profit motive, along with the sunshine & the surf.*]

[Grains of sand make friends. They sleep next to someone new each night. Here come the waves.]

We wonder if Egyptians, or anyone else back in the day, discovered a means of human flight. They clearly had the wherewithal to build pyramids. If they were anything like us, more than likely they also had the desire to fly. If you can build pyramids, why not fly? How much more difficult can flying be? It would be easier to say they flew if there were any evidence—any recovered flight craft wreckage, any lingering pollution. Birds in the sky never think twice about flying. It's the only life they know. Flying comes as naturally to them as breathing. We can never fly like birds because we are too self-conscious about it. Leave it to America to advance the cause of building flying machines out of steel. American engineers have got themselves into thinking there is no way other than steel & internal combustion. Steel doesn't want to fly, steel likes Earth. Steel returns home as soon as it can. Planes crash because steel wants to find its way home.

Let's build flying machines from nothing more than air & our bodies.

Wouldn't it feel good to have the wind hold you, your body pushed against it, ebb & flow, ebb & fly. You can do it all without fuel & unlike hang-gliding, you keep going—a long, meaningful trip between one place & another, over hill & dale, just you, your food & water, tent & sleeping bag.

Wouldn't it feel good to fly by the wind, by the strength of your body. You fly a long distance to visit your parents. You touch down on beaches, the flat part just at the edge of the water. You touch down on hillside meadows on the way though the passes of mountains.

Young birds see you & think, *There goes one huge, ugly bird.*

440 BC—Bearded Herodotus sails down to Egypt in a wooden vessel resplendent with brightly colored sails. Upon seeing the pyramids & Sphinx located upon the Giza Plateau, he asks some of the locals just how these ancient structures, particularly the most magnificent of the four pyramids, had come to be there. Herodotus, for all his good nature, had sailed much of the known world. (The known world, at that time, constituted what Herodotus knew, at least in the Greek mind.) He has never seen anything quite like them, certainly not in Greece & not on any of the islands in between. The locals tell him that 100,000 slaves

built the Great Pyramid in thirty years. Ten to build an infrastructure & twenty for actual construction & that it was a monument to the Pharaoh Khufu. Herodotus takes this information with him when he returns to Greece to write his *Histories*. The problem is that the people Herodotus asked were not the pyramid builders themselves, nor were they descendants of the builders. The people who Herodotus befriended understood how the pyramids were built about as well as we do. Their best guess is as good as ours. No matter how you add the numbers, the building of the pyramids seems miraculous—all those people & all that work. Even more miraculous is that the farmers grew enough food to feed the work corps. Even more miraculous is that despite the paucity of the trees, Giza Plateau supplied all the wood they needed to build scaffolds, levers & rollers. Even more miraculous is that hardly left a trace. Sites believed to be quarries have been found, as well as deposits of rubble. They are nothing like you would expect from projects this large. What remains of the pyramid building process are the pyramids themselves.

1990—Then along comes TS, wonder of wonders, usually so silent, but he has given this thought—his idea comes bursting out of him: *Maybe the pyramids were built by dolphins.*

The room stops. *Say what?*

If you go & build the Great Pyramid, what do you do with yourself afterward? If you can build a pyramid, you can do anything & if you can do anything, why not go back to the water?

He raises his hand, makes a parting gesture & walks away without further explanation.

A silence falls that no one breaks. We look around the room at each other. Because of the silence, no one knows what anyone else is thinking. Those who think TS has gone around the bend will think others in the room are thinking the same. Those who wonder if it's possible, to a degree, wonder if the others are wondering the same.

The compats talk it over. Some leave, because the idea of it is ridiculous beyond their comfort zone. Those who remain are still processing TS's statement, searching for meaning. According to Darwin, some land-roaming air-breathing mammals returned to the water, evolving into dolphins, whales, sea lions, etc. What we cannot understand is why. Was this a conscious decision on the mammals' part? Perhaps they were hominid & if so, why not Egyptian? We evolve too slowly to notice. This is evolution's way of hiding itself. We find traces, last vestiges, the five finger bones in a dolphin's fin. What we lose we strangely remember, the way an amputee can still feel his legs long after they are gone.

[The weirdest part is that Squirrel sometimes still feels her tail.]

So what I am taking him to say is that after the pyramid builders finish, they take to the water. It makes sense. In the water, swimming is the same as flying. They walk out into the waves without any thought of turning back, treading at first. The choice they give themselves is to evolve or drown. They choose evolution. Their arms become fins; their legs stick together; their skin turns bluish-grey; their noses become snouts. The hardest part of evolution to understand is why everything takes millions of years to happen. Species rarely have time for that. I think TS has a point.

I have no idea how evolution works. All I know is something happens & we're here.

Where is Jude when you need her? She could make sense of this.

Maybe Darwin was wrong. Maybe evolution doesn't need thousands & millions of years. Maybe evolution enjoys occasional bursts of spontaneity as much as the rest of us.

When TS first suggested that the same Egyptians who built the pyramids took the secret of pyramid building with them to sea, I thought he was trying to be funny. I'm guilty—I laughed. But suddenly, I have a feeling in my stomach, as if someone had pulled a cork out of my belly button & the air is rushing out. I guess I would say the truth is, I don't know which direction is up anymore.

No matter what, it doesn't help us build a pyramid.

A rumor flies: *Yes, we're having fun,* conspirators whisper into cloaked ears. Then something else is passed along. The message is enough to raise the eyebrow of the hearer: *The pyramids built themselves.*

The stones sprouted feet & walked into place.

Oh, no. Oh, yes.

The truth is, mates, we haven't the foggiest notion how to build pyramids. Foot Apples studies much & knows, but says little. We had asked him if he could show us what he was doing. *It's all in the language study,* Foot Apples says. *People can't learn a new & complex language overnight. Building the pyramid will be the easy part. Learning a language takes time.*

Show us each one small piece of the puzzle, Foot Apples. Give us each a few words to learn, a facet of the grammar—between us, we can understand it all.

No, you couldn't.

Chapter 49: Outer Banks

The phone book serving Hatteras, Ocracoke, Nassawaddox & outlying areas in the Outer Banks of North Carolina is thin. In the sparse volume, one name, Midgett, appears over & over, occupying page after page. The Midgett name carries over into the yellow pages, too—Midgett Floral, Midgett Hardware, Midgett Travel, Midgett This & That. The Outer Banks have more Midgetts than Smiths & Joneses!

Jude finds only one Hartman listed, a Norman. The phone & address are still listed under the dead man's name, more than twenty years after the fact. That assumes the name in the book doesn't belong to a son, or a father, or yet another someone else named Norman Hartman.

1948—A hurricane comes along & sweeps through long narrow barrier islands off the coast of North Carolina & washes the world away. The ocean rises to higher levels than anyone has ever seen, dating back to when folks named Midgett first landed here & began keeping records. Rolling waves sweep seaside houses off of their stilts & foundations. Some residents begin believing that the water will never recede, that their homes now belong to the Atlantic once & for all, that they will now have to learn to swim or find new places to live.

When the water recedes, as it eventually does in life's ebb & flow, people find their houses in new locations—the waves leave them several hundred feet from where their mothers & fathers built them. The Atlantic knows nothing about the sanctity of property lines, of fences & good neighbors, of Robert Frost.

Even now, as Jude walks past forty years later, you can see phantom stone walkways that lead to nothing, that lead to where the houses used to be. The homes remain in their new spots, which is better than losing them completely & a change in view does a soul good.

1990—Along the stone road in Nassawaddox, on the route to the address listed for Norman Hartman, amid so few houses & all of them with so much space in between, Jude walks & passes houses that have fences that look great for hurdling. [Jude never was a hurdler. From childhood, she specialized in sprints, middle distance & long jump.] Jude has traveled so far & come so close & all she can think of are track meets & playing with childhood friends. She might as well be thirteen years old. She might as well be seven. She might as well be six. She will arrive at the Norman Hartman family house as a five-year-old girl wearing a yellow summer dress & pig tails. She will knock on the door & when the mommy answers, ask, *Can Emily come play?* [Inside the fences are yards where the families are attempting to grow lawns, as they have for years, but where they can grow nothing more than splotchy patches of yellow-green grass. The soil simply has too much sand in it for the lawns. Yet many Nassawaddox families, many of whom are named Midgett, send their sons & daughters out on a summer morning to mow the sand in the yard. The sand, in turn, chokes the lawnmower's engine—the motor grinds & won't turn over. The mowing this morning ends before the job is finished. Jude walks past the abandoned mowers on her way to find the house.]

Standing on the porch of the Hartman family house, Jude gathers herself. Rather than knock, she stares into the door, its wood grain & walnut finish, the distorted annual rings that continue to count the years from before the door became a door, not to forget the dime-size circle of light shining from inside the house through the peephole, showing her that inside the shades are open, that inside people are living. Then the pinpoint of light is eclipsed—someone is standing on the door's other side, peering through the peephole at her—sizing her up as much as is possible from the wide angle of the peephole lens. The someone standing on the other side of the door wonders who Jude is.

The door swings open. A man standing on the other side looks Jude over. He does not recognize her, but he seems to know why she's come. He gestures as if to suggest to her that she be the first to speak.

Jude doesn't know what to say. Does she ask for Emily? How can she? What if there is no Emily here? What if she has found yet another someone else named Norman Hartman? What if her second attempt is empty?

Realizing that Jude is unable to say anything, the man speaks first. *When I answer the door & the person on the other side doesn't know what to say, I have a realization that this person must be a veteran, a writer, or a theatre lover. We receive more than our fair share of each. Sometimes solicitors & Jehovah's Witnesses knock on the door, but they know what they want & have no problem saying their piece. The Vietnam Vets who show up here usually have read about my father someplace & feel a strange connection to him. It's not often you find a Vietnam protester with the courage to sacrifice his own life & that's how they perceive my dad. My father's story moves them; grown men come here to cry. My father was more than just a peacenik with an army haircut—he was a peacenik who they can relate to—a peacenik who proves to them how fucked up the world really was back then. The writers who come here are usually younger & shy, which is the reason they are writers & not actors & if they were older, they would be veterans, whether or not they were ever in uniform. The writers have heard my father's story somewhere & come here with the belief that they can turn our life into a beautiful poem, because, they reckon, it already is. When the time comes, they will try to sell their piece, reduce us to magazine fodder. The theatre lovers who come here want nothing other than to peek their heads into our doorway & see what lives inside. They want the family dirt. They have heard our story & they feel like they know us without knowing us. They want to see for themselves what has become of us. They take pictures while they are here & when they leave, they take a souvenir, any little thing they can get their hands on. A week later, we notice something missing—my father's letter opener. It's a strange desire in people, wanting to instantly insert themselves into an historical moment well after it's happened.*

Jude has yet to say anything, even to introduce herself. She can't believe she found the Hartmans [& Emily?] & it seems as if they were expecting her; it doesn't seem real. All she wants is to explain that she is not a *the-*

ater lover or anything else, that all she wants to do is meet Emily. She can't say anything.

So he carries on instead. *My guess is that you don't see yourself fitting into any one of those three groups, am I right?*

Jude shrugs. She knows she's not a writer, she can't be sure about the other two. She begins to say something.

He cuts her off. I have something you will want to see. The man directs Jude inside the house & to a sofa in the front room by the window. The man introduces himself as Charlie Hartman & calls Jude *Jude* even though she can't remember introducing herself to him. He hands her a bulky, oversized photo album. Jude opens up the book to the first page & looks at photographs, as old as the invention of photography & protected under sheets of plastic. Jude turns pages quickly, passing by the ancestors who, Charlie Hartman is trying to explain to her, descend from Paul Revere & how important those ties are toward understanding everything that has happened since. She arrives finally, near the end of the book, at news clippings from the day & week after Norman Hartman set himself on fire on the lawn of the Pentagon—a story from *Life*, an article in *Time*. While she looks at the pages, he stands behind the sofa—behind where she's sitting—looking down at the album in her lap. She can sense him through the back of her neck. She pretends not to notice.

One way of looking at it is that my father is a hero, a martyr in the purest sense—I don't know. You can also think of him as a suicide who left his family behind. It's not like my father didn't suffer from depression, you know. How can we ever forget that our father's suicide didn't cause the war to stop? He could have lived & the war would have turned out just the same. Not only did he leave behind my mother, sister & I, he left us knowing that his death not only didn't end the war, but that ultimately it was hardly noticed & quickly forgotten. Then every once in a while, someone like you remembers or hears about what happened & the next thing we know, someone is outside knocking on the door.

The way Charlie Hartman carries on reminds Jude of Willie Shoman. He seems as if he is talking to himself—only that he is in the presence of another person. Jude feels a sense of urgency to respond to him in some way. Finally she speaks. *I didn't have a father, either. He died over Laos when I was three.*

He lets go a sigh & thinks to himself, *Jude, I had you pegged as a writer when you showed up here. Maybe you're a veteran after all.*

Jude senses that someone else is in the room. Peeking around a corner is an old woman wearing a child's grin. The woman extends her neck farther around the corner to get a better look at the visitor. Seeing that someone has caught her peeking, the woman disappears again behind the wall.

That's my mother, he says. He wants to leave it at that.

Jude keeps her eyes toward the corner, half expecting the woman to reappear, wanting the woman to reappear. Jude identifies much more closely with her than she does with the man—she is more comfortable with her. The woman is closer to the reason why she came here in the first place.

Before Charlie Hartman can get another word out, a second interruption occurs. The front door explodes open & a young woman bursts inside, carrying in her arms a broken bicycle, the front tire having gone flat in the middle of her ride. She lets go of the bike & it slams against the wall. She tromps off into another room without saying a word.

At first, Charlie Hartman acts nonchalant, as if nothing happened. Then he looks as if he is on the verge of telling Jude more about his father & the family history. Then he looks at the bike lying on the floor. Then he looks embarrassed, raining his hand in the air to obscure Jude's view of his face. Now he, too, storms out, in the same direction the young woman has just gone. Jude sits quietly on the sofa as the man & woman yell at each other two rooms over, each blaming the other for recent atrocities, though Jude gathers no sense of what they are yelling about.

All Jude can think is *that's Emily* & rest easily knowing that she's found her.

The man, Charlie Hartman, charges back into the living room & gives Jude a look, as if to say, *What are you still doing here?* He takes a set of keys from the mantle & stomps again, this time out the front door. Jude hears a car start, then speed away.

Left alone in the Hartman family house—Jude was not expecting this. Neither the mother nor the young woman know who Jude is or even that she is still here. Jude just sits calmly on the sofa, the bulky photo album still spread open across her lap. She considers leaving, then decides against it. She wonders if staying means she's a theatre lover.

Now she's on her feet, walking along the perimeter of the room, looking closely at the framed black & white photographs hanging at eye level along the walls. She pauses at each one. She hadn't noticed them before.

Norman Hartman had been a photographer. He took dozens of photographs of his young family that capture the time in which they were taken, the 1960s. The photos are lifelike & jumping with black & white artistry. Norman Hartman does not appear in the photos; he is too busy operating the camera, you see the world through his eyes. The only time you see Norman Hartman himself is in a single photograph. His reflection is caught in the bathroom mirror, his face half obscured by the camera incidentally appearing inside a trapezoid toward the edge of the frame. From his distorted image, you can see that he was tall & that he wore black-rimmed glasses that hid nearly all of his face. That's all. There's nothing more of Norman.

Then she notices in the photos where the furniture is placed in the house. Nothing has changed since when the pictures were taken. The house is astonishingly the same as the time when Norman sat in his chair.

Though invisible, Norman Hartman still casts his spirit over the family's house, almost as if he has to run to the store for a couple of pints of milk & will be right back—*hold supper, please*. The house is kept like a museum, a living memorial, or maybe they've never bothered to change anything since he has been gone. The house is in the spirit it was in 1967, in complete disregard of 1977 & 1987 & 1997 & 2007 & beyond; you can almost smell the tobacco from the father's pipe from under the smell of baking bread.

Everything changes & one day the house, too, will change. Let the house speak for itself, unspin its many secrets. Jude looks intently at the many photographs of the happy family, of Emily. [The house bears a resemblance to the house where Jude lived while growing up in the Pacific Northwest. There, on every mantle & shelf, were photos of the family with her father appearing in each of them, as if by sleight of hand or trickery. Just who was it taking the picture? Her father was the type of person who would always manage to talk someone into taking the family's picture for them. Then he dies & years pass & slowly all those old pictures come down off the wall, replaced by photos of Jude & her brother. Her mother never seems to appear in any—her mother doesn't have the same talent for finding someone to take their picture for them.

Even on vacation, her head is busy working at school. Then Jude's brother dies & more & more the pictures on the wall are just of Jude.]

Jude hears a door open. The mother again—she peeks around the same corner as earlier, playfully, seemingly believing she is a child, feeling as if she is a child. When you look at her, you can see the young girl locked inside the old woman's body peeking out. Just over her head, you see the photographs you have just pored over, but now they take on deeper meaning. The woman in the photos is young & strong, a mother & wife, dauntless & ready for anything the world throws her way. Her strength & energy haven't left her; they are still bottled inside the tiny package that comprises the woman. She now flits away just as quietly as she had come. [It was in a defiant spirit of *I am leaving & never, never coming back* with which the brother had left, though he will probably return within a few hours. You hardly know Charlie Hartman & you do not know Norman Hartman at all, yet you know the two are not the same.]

Jude steps softly through the house, stopping finally at a closed bedroom door that radiates the energy of the person leaning against it on the other side. Jude stands still & hears a quick breath, a clearing of tears.

Jude knocks, twice, lightly. The door gives no response other than the weight easing against it. She pushes the door open.

Emily is sitting up on her bed, her arms wrapping around her knees, her body wrapping up into itself. Jude knows better to think that these tears are because of her father's suicide—she was only a baby. What happens next maybe Jude learned from the hair stylist Mrs. Hartman who she had met two days earlier, or maybe it's the emergence of a natural instinct. What we know is that Jude doesn't think about it; she is running without thinking; she is playing her jazz solo.

Jude sits beside Emily, moves her hand behind her neck (so warm, the heat from being outdoors, the heat from coming inside) & draws Emily's head into her shoulder. Emily lets her tears fall. Despite all the tears from previous days & hours, there are yet more inside of her. Everything Emily has been keeping inside herself, Jude feels falling on her shoulder.

Jude holds Emily. The two of them remain together like that.

Who are you? Emily finally asks after several moments.

Is Jude being herself or the person she was going to be? Mother, sister, friend—maybe this is why Emily is asking who she is, not out of curiosity regarding Jude's identity, but how she can come in so many ways at once. Jude isn't changing, we just never knew her as well as we thought we did. What makes Jude *Jude* is that at times like these, when we have so many questions to ask about life & our place in the endless spinning, Jude is the least likely to ask questions, to analyze, to wonder what on earth she is doing.

[Jude finally answers the question.]

I'm Jude.

[The answer is good enough.]

The Carolina coast owns a blueness unlike anything you'll see out west & up ahead is a black & white candy-striped lighthouse. Off the shore is a bank of dark clouds—they don't mean anything, *we can still go.* You walk against the wind's resistance along the shoreline. You ride the ferry to Okracoke & back, not so much to go anyplace as to just go out on the water. You go for the boat ride. The two of them enjoy the other's company & the silence when they can't hear themselves above the wind whipping in their ears. Eventually, they will talk, Emily will tell Jude everything about herself.

At night, what you hear in the house is the ticking of a grandfather clock. In another room, a cuckoo clock announces the quarter hour. There are so many clocks throughout the house, you can hear a steady ticking wherever you are, in a house where time remains unchanged— a house fading, dust embedded, the glimmering newness all gone. Jude sleeps on a couch.

The brother comes in late, drunk. Jude can tell it's him, because although she hardly knows him, she already can recognize the space in his step. She pretends to sleep. In the near dark, he looks down upon the sofa, sees her lying there. He's surprised, since he expected her to be gone by now. He looks down upon her, she can smell his breath. Does he know she's awake? He is not familiar with the way she sleeps & can't tell. He mumbles, but she can't hear what he's saying. He turns & walks to his room for the night.

Later that night, there is another ticking inside the house. Behind a closed door in the next room over from where Jude is sleeping, a clock has gone out of control, ticking wildly. [It's just the brother, typing away at a rickety IBM Selectric.]

The next morning, Jude wakes up & Emily wakes up—*what now?* You repair bikes in Norman Hartman's garage where the walls are covered by tools for all occasions, for working with wood, for fixing the car, tools hanging on the walls, worn. They look as if they've never been used since Norman passed on. [Off in the corner is a chest held closed by a padlock belonging to the brother. Emily often wonders what is inside of it.] [Is it ticking?]

What do the two of you do now? You spend time in the garden cultivating tomatoes; you shovel on generous heaps of compost & hope they grow because the soil here is sand. You throw a Frisbee to one another. You play soccer in the park with a number of children as their parents watch from benches along the sidelines. You ride bikes & become friends. You talk about your lives. The time blends together. Emily has had boyfriends. Jude hasn't. Emily shows her pictures of the boys she has loved, the boys who loved her, too. She even misses some of them— she even misses all of them, except for the last one, who never really was her boyfriend anyway. It all happened so fast. Emily's boyfriends, the close ones she can count on her two hands & without counting her thumbs. These are the ones she loved, though she can't remember now whether she loved them & then they became close, or if they became close & then she loved them. She loves none of them now, but loves the memory of every one. *If I had the chance to do it all over again, I would keep the memories of all of them, except for the last one. The last one caused problems.* [*I can't remember who I was then. Where did my recklessness come from? I had been keeping it inside of me. I don't need it.*] You sit outside at a café in the historic downtown of Nassawaddox & drink iced tea. You attend meetings of a neighborhood shoreline conservation association of which Emily is a member.

Mostly you keep yourselves quiet, spending your time together as if you were by yourself, yet still glad the other is with you. It's a time for fresh air & not doing much of anything & staring at the Atlantic & wondering how the horizon could form such a straight line. It's a time for quiet & for healing—for Jude, too, who may not have known she had open wounds inside her. You feel the healing power of the sun—not all its rays are deadly.

That night, a Saturday, they stay up late, a slumber party for two, sprawling sleeping bags—lights out & flashlights in Emily's bedroom. Emily spills to Jude the stories closest to her. [Jude doesn't say much. She acknowledges what Emily is saying, but does not judge, does not give advice. She just listens. She prefers listening to talking. She needs to relax before she can tell her own story. When she finally relaxes enough to talk about herself, talking doesn't matter anymore & the two of them are falling asleep.]

[Nothing to do, nothing to worry over—rest easily, Jude. The others are out there saving the world so tonight you don't have to—relax. The world will keep on spinning until it's spun.]

The next night, Jude is asleep again on the sofa. The brother is awake in the next room, again at the IBM Selectric, typing out his memoirs, his thoughts & life. He doesn't type everything. He pauses. He says to himself, *Fuck it all—the lunacy & the laughter, the sorrow & the sorrow & why the fuck do I take everything so seriously?* He knows that there must be more to life than marrying some Midgett. Now he wonders, he remembers three days earlier when Jude arrived. He remembers the instant he opened the door, saying to himself, *This is the woman I am going to marry.* He quickly realizes that it will not come true. Still he can't get it off his mind. [*I hide myself well, I would like to think. Most people who know me would never dream that I could engineer such romantic thoughts, that I'm a sentimentalist.*] Why is she still here? Since arriving, she has hardly spoken to him. He can't help himself. By day, he shoots her glances that say *I love you—marry me.* The glances express everything his life is about—the lunacy & the laughter, the sorrow & the sorrow— more than will ever spill out through the typewriter keys. [She quickly turns away, she doesn't want to know. She doesn't feel the same.] He retracts his glances, it's too late. *Oh, brother!*

Through the closed doors between rooms, Charlie Hartman senses all of his sister's sadness, blaming himself—these walls are thin. *Before Jude came, at night I would I hear Emily sobbing & talking to the bathroom walls. I would worry & know there is nothing I could say or do. She blames me because I made the appointment—I made her keep it, I drove her there, I even paid for it. When she came back from college this last time, I remember looking at her, thinking her eyes seem strange. Then I knew why, it was the him now in her. Had he only used a condom we could have flushed the him down the toilet. Now it's too late. She's haunted, I'm haunted. We're all haunted except him & he doesn't even know. When I sleep, I have dreams of the bruising old boyfriend arriving in a black Bronco 4 x 4 with monster wheels. He has a shotgun & a fifth of whiskey flowing in his blood & he's probably mean & crazy enough to be deadly even when he's gunless & sober. I always thought he would come back, but the truth is he wants nothing to do with her, not now. To him, she's all used up. It's easy for her to blame me—I'm an easy target. Who else can she blame? She's forgetting I was looking out for her. Maybe she is ready to have a child, but, please, not this child, not a child conceived like this. This way Emily forgets. We all forget. Not now & not in a week or even a year, but over time. Somewhere deep inside of her, she'll be glad that I supported her at that time when she had so many conflicting emotions to consider that she couldn't think straight. Right now, I just want her to forgive me.*

This is the house where the husband & father knew the right thing & did it. The same house has now fallen into a less knowing state & our mother has forgotten everything. It's become a house incapable of knowing what to do. Except my mother, Elizabeth, who flits. Except my sister, Emily, who grieves. Except Jude who arrives unexpectedly & will soon go just as suddenly—but we are so happy & surprised she has come to us, she is our angel. We need to know what to do so we can go on living. [I need to know what to do so I can go on living. I can't go on living this way.]

You probably think my mother's around the bend & that I have a drinking problem. Up until now, I had it under control. I hardly know what I am doing anymore. I had stopped, I was feeling none of its side effects, thinking quitting was going to be easy. Then suddenly, I'm on my fifth scotch without realizing that I had even finished my first.

Please don't judge us, Jude.

My father had a touch of the rebel spirit in him. He became a Quaker, a conscientious objector; he turned his back on his family that came before him. He would have become a beatnik, a Buddhist, a jazz musician, if any of those incarnations had been part of his world. Becoming a Quaker was his way of expressing his spirit, for allowing himself to turn his eyes inward, for inspiring his desire for peace. Then we lost him. He was peaceful but not happy. The war depressed him, he became suicidal. Maybe he just didn't want to be a father. He just wanted to park himself in a place where he could hurt himself & make it seem heroic. He wanted to kill himself & for the world to forgive him for it.

I wish I believed in ghosts.

I wish I could show him that I have a touch of the rebel spirit in me, too. In the garage, you might have wondered what it is I am keeping in the chest under lock & key. Emily thinks I am building mail bombs. I keep the chest locked to keep her guessing. The chest is empty. I don't have it in me to build bombs—maybe I do, in spirit. I can't seem to finish anything, most of all, my memoirs & I don't know how I would ever get around to building a bomb. Even if I did build one, I wouldn't have any idea who to send it to. I suppose I could send them to people who deserve them, the new legions of Robert McNamaras in the world, but even they have families who will survive them; the families will idolize them & call them a martyr & it will reinforce every bastard idea they ever stood for.

No, the rebel spirit I have in me I am taking out on my ancestors. The Paul Revere blood that mattered so much to my ancestors stops with me. I am not having any children. I will not even marry. They worked all their lives, generation after generation, to preserve the Paul Revere bloodline. I will stop it in its tracks. That will be the one sacrifice I make.

Days pass, they grow shorter. Emily prepares to go back to college in Maine. Jude & Emily have talked enough—it's time to go. They will see each other again; they will find ways. Emily will visit California. The same wind that drew Jude here is changing directions, sending her back. She misses running & remembers how she always made time in the day to run & all the creativity that it took. She enjoys remembering the times when she would go running just before midnight to keep alive her streak of consecutive days. What Jude ultimately learns about herself is that, more than anything else, that's what she does. She runs.

Chapter 50: Night slips & falls

With sleep flowing through it, the body owns a certain heaviness. Nowhere near the ocean, you can hear the waves rolling in. Next, you are up to your eyes in sea water—this despite two-hundred miles separating us from the deep, blue Pacific. What are you going to do when the waves sneak up on you, so quietly & unexpectedly.

Daphne dreams of blurred words. She awakens, thinking she reads too much.

Another drifts & dreams of a place where it slopes, where the whole world is steep. People are planting crops along the slope. They have no trouble handling the steepness. They can scamper across the slope with ease. The farmer pushes his plow. They are a people with no single word for slope. They call the slope by several different names, each name unique to a particular facet of the slope, each of those facets invisible to me.

I dream of following a cave down to an underground city in the Columbia gorge. I see monuments & buildings made entirely of silver & gold, chests upon chests, overflowing with jewels & coins. They always say there's no gold in the Pacific Northwest. It's a lie. They brought all of it here, until they closed this city up & forgot about it.

[*Please let's all keep our dreams to ourselves. Your dreams are keeping me awake at night.*]

[One of them cannot sleep & roams. *Why am I always the last to leave, the one who turns out all of the lights? Why is it I cannot function outside of a close personal relationship? The thing is, I am never in one. I only come close, only on occasion. I am losing TS, we are all losing TS. He's losing his interest in us. I used to think he had a crush on Jude. He pays more never-mind to her than anyone else. Now I've seen them together enough to know they love each other—the way siblings do. Jude, the older sister, shows him how to do things, to tie his shoes, to take care of himself.*]

I have been dreaming of dolphins to a soundtrack of Police songs, since way before anyone else was talking about them. Maybe the pyramids exist only in someone else's dream & we're caught up in it. Everything in our world flashes before us: Jokerman, Cactus & the FunTime, Aunt Frances, her apple pie & smiling white dog, the grocery store where the rich people shop & the price they charge for a sourdough roll, the kids next door with a swimming pool & wishing you were friends with them, so you could swim, too.

Dream brightly. Headlights behind us, they are as bright as anyone's ever seen. Look away & have nothing but afterimage in your eyes. Eyes closed, you still see the headlights, forever stamped onto the inside of your eyelids, no way of getting around it. Approaching from behind, a 4 x 4, wheels oversized, bright halogen lamps on the roll bar, its body painted black, its windows darkly tinted—it's gaining on us. *Staring at the other's face but I will not touch you, you're tainted. Oh, my God, your skin is soft, I love your face—but oh, it burns. Is this the torch that was passed along to us? It's a legacy for which we are on the receiving end, the torch that scorches. [Her name is the Pandora of my skin, here come the waves.] It burns in the places most sensitive. They say the burn will never go away. It will go away sometimes, then return. I want to kill myself.*

A child & me? I'm old enough to be her brother. Her home looms in the distance, at the bottom of the hill. You can see the chimney smoke from the dying fire, the windows white with blinds. Her parents are sleeping past Sunday sunrise. They will waken soon to brew coffee & read the paper, but they won't read about us. The wind is whipping in our ears. We had changed the clocks so they wouldn't know the time when they see she is gone. But they discover what we've done & change the locks so she cannot return without knocking. Rather than knock & face her father's music, for he is a musician, we walk away. We climb the hill. She's wearing a parka too big for her. Her hands cold, they disappear inside the sleeves. Me? I'm without a jacket, eternal dummy, I left it at home. My hands are numb, freezing. She takes my hands & holds them inside her hands—inside her sleeves. We are joined at the wrist, Siamesed at the sleeve, facing the other's face. She turns her head away, looks at the ground, looks at the tree, looks at the sleeves, looks at anything other than my eyes. She looks so good to me, the world spins, we spin together on this crazy carousel & we are together on this ride. The wind blows. Seagulls scream kiss her, kiss her!

Chapter 51: Sometimes you fall apart, sometimes you fade away

I think we've called him Foot Apples once too often. Gone are the binders of photocopied papyri. Gone are his own sketchbooks, filled with his drawings & notes. Gone is his funny Ancient Egyptian dialect. Gone is his uptight way.

So you know, the way Foot Apples freaks out is to read detective novels. For all the time he spent engaged in reading, no one had seen him read anything in the English language before. Now he reads one mystery story after another, leaving the Pentagon Pyramid Prank up in the air. After reading another Agatha Christie, he wants to talk to us about it & the last thing we want to hear about all day is Hercule Poirot & Inspector Fordney. He asks around if anyone can recommend some good Ellery Queen.

Before, when the secrets of pyramid dynamics were swirling around inside him, we couldn't get him to say a word. By the time Foot Apples knows what pyramid building is all about, he also knows what we are all about—our vanity & sunburn & all the stupid things we say & everything else that rides alongside us. By that time, he wants nothing further to do with us other than to talk about mystery novels.

I cannot say, becomes Footapples's all-purpose answer to every question we ask him. [We are spelling *Footapples* now as one word. We no longer need the space within the word. If we could overlap all of the letters into a single space & make a Chinese character out of it, we would. That's not what we need to do. We need to build a pyramid.]

Did we carry our teasing too far? Footapples had finally translated a bothersome passage & when the words hit him like a 2,000-pound brick, he figured it out. Now it is all over for us, our Egyptian dreams. He decides he doesn't want to trade in Egyptian anymore. He closes his books & puts them away in his bag. He picks up one of the detective novels he finds lying in cardboard boxes around the abandoned commune & he starts to read.

We do not let go that easily, bugging Footapples to tell us what he has found out. *This is the way we are spending our summer—we want to build a pyramid.*

He scribbles some words on a piece of scratch paper, hands it to us & asks that we not read it until we are out of his presence. Of course, it is this simple; all you need is a piece of scratch paper to pass along the secret, not an engineering manual. All you need are a few choice words. We read the message Footapples has written. *I want people to know my name is Anthony J. Burchetta, but I would prefer to be called Dean.*

Are we disappointed? Yes. Could we call it unexpected? No.

Now Cactus is saying he knows how to build a pyramid, that he knew how all along & was just joshing us. Standing behind him atop a stray slab of concrete, he says that it has something to do with putting our hands up into the sky.

Frustrated, we will try anything.

Daphne's got the tambourine shivers. That tambourine's sound is spellbinding, sparkling percussive, forming its note with a touch of rage—a somewhat frazzled, messy note, its rhythm unclean. Nice thing: The tambourine isn't the violin, which takes so long to learn to play. A single note & a beat are all you need to write songs on the tambourine. The tambourine is not a neat freak; its laundry, both clean & dirty, is scattered across the floor along with so many magazines & newspapers dating from months ago. [The tambourine sounds like a box of dishes rolling down stairs.]

We have got to get our hands into the sky, people! Cactus bellows & there is something to it.

[He told us that once already & we would have remembered if not for losing ourselves beneath that fuckin' tambourine.] [*What on Earth are you going to do with this? Is this useful in any way? I want to go home now.*] When listening to Cactus becomes tiresome, we find new ways of having fun. We do sky pushups. You lie on your back & do pushups. You press against sky. Sky has no weight. Sky gives no resistance. You push away from you nothing more than the weight of your arms.

A fall backward, you conk your head on the cold ground. Your eyes reopen, your head resonating in a ringing clarity. A stark realization happens while you're lying there. This Egypt prank—we're in over our heads, Baby Blue.

Chapter 52: The night sky plotted

Squirrel's hair, she wears in tight, natural curls & a severe, short pony-tail. Her hands are small; she's left-handed. If she doesn't tell you she was a ballet dancer, you might guess she is anyway, or guess wrong & think her a gymnast. She has an in-shape quality about her—no body fat on her & her limbs own a certain looseness. She can twist her legs over her head & frequently will. She flies; she goes. Her feet flutter like hummingbird wings. She pirouettes across the floor. One minute she's talking to you, the next she's on pointe or into a plie, or on the other side of the room. We have seen her slip & fall; she falls gracefully all the way down. She has practiced movement more than the rest of us & it comes to her as second nature. She can never step outside of graceful move-ment. Squirrel is self-complete, though she misses dancing—missing dancing is what is burning inside of her. She comes to join us by the road of ballet. After having danced since the age of four, both feet give out during her sophomore year of high school, the pain killing her, keeping her off of the floor. Returning to dancing after two foot opera-tions that keep her feet in casts for over a year, she finds her strength is gone, some of her flexibility is gone & the pain is always there. She does her best to overcome the pain, pushing herself as hard as she can; but some days she can't even walk. She keeps going back, but her body will not move the way it knows how to move. She lies crumpled on the floor. The other dancers pass her by. They will dance. Squirrel won't. She can go back in a limited capacity, try out for musicals, but rather than do that she gives it up completely & plays out the role as an environmental prankster along with the rest of us, partly because she just can't sing.

Squirrel's nickname is given to her long before she meets us. It's because of her button nose. She enjoys the dismantling of tractors & the disabling of heavy equipment at the sites of wilderness road construction immensely. No one's better than Squirrel at sneaking around & eluding security guards, at moving on tiptoes, in & out of shadows, blending together with darkness & light, peeking through an eyehole in the brush. Squirrel would make an excellent outlaw, knocking over banks & armored cars—too sleek & quick to catch. Her ballet training gives her concentration, physical grace & nerve. Her knees don't hurt when she runs & she can run faster than most of us.

At night, they sit, the awake ones, around a campfire near a thicket of streamside willow & talk about sleep. The ranch air, meanwhile, is thick with dreams. Tonight is the kind of night where the light of the stars is all you need. You have no need for fire. The atmosphere at night glows. You can climb a tall tree & dive down into the Milky Way. You take a quick inventory of everything you know. [*She lies sleeping before me all night, her chest rising & falling with every breath. A jar of electricity, holes poked in the lid, tips over when you bump the table. Stone floats in air; birds are singing in the orchard. The world is bursting with flowers.*]

Squirrel, whose shoulders are the smallest among us, now takes it upon herself to find a way to keep us from giving up. She's still awake, prowling about the grounds in the pitch-black night, her eyes adjusted, so she can see where she's going, see what she's doing. Wherever the rest of us are, we fall asleep. Then we jar awake at the sound of hammering. *Are people going ahead & thinking of building a pyramid anyway—thinking they can get away with it at night while everyone sleeps?* No, it's just Squirrel, hammering a stake into the ground. Silencing distant coyotes, each strike reverberates through the canyon. After the sound finds you once, it finds you again & again & then fades.

Why hammer at this hour? Why hammer, period?

In the morning, the array of stakes Squirrel had hammered into the ground through the night seems to be of haphazard design. Anyone is free to ask her what she was doing, what the stakes mean, but through the morning as the sun warms up the rocks, Squirrel sleeps & by the time she wakens in the late afternoon, the curiosity fades & no one asks. Then at sunset, she goes out again & this time, TS joins her. They lie on their backs, staring up at space, pointing out to one another what they see, piecing together an idea of the night sky. It is clear now that what Squirrel is doing has to do with stars. It is clear now that Squirrel's hammer, which always seems to strike & ring out at the moment when we finally doze off, also has to do with stars. We wish we could all stay awake & watch stars. [*I can watch a sleeping baby for hours; I can watch waves pounding a shore for hours; I can watch a campfire for hours; I can listen to wolves or coyotes for hours. Staring up at a billion stars, though, one minute I'm overwhelmed by how tiny we are in the universe & the next minute, I'm asleep. The first step to long, contemplative starwatching is lying down. Lying down puts me to sleep. It's the same thing as watching nothing.*]

This is how the ancients did it—staying up all night, keeping one another awake through conversation & then sleeping through the next day's sun. They chart the stars over years & generations & centuries & for all we know, millennia. They gather everything they need to form a sophisticated astronomy, more than we will ever give them credit for inventing. Squirrel & TS note where pinpoints of light rise & set on the horizon. They note the ones that do not set, remembering everything they can from Astronomy 101 & 102, discussing Polaris, the hub around which the universe appears to turn & the controversy surrounding Sirius A & B. They laugh & become better starwatchers with every passing hour, loudly hammering in new stakes always as soon as the rest of us fall asleep.

The morning after the third night of Squirrel's all-night starwatch, it becomes clear what is happening. Squirrel, with TS helping out, is planning to build a pyramid. Squirrel decides for herself that this time she will not give up. In the past, she has been forced to & she hates it. She wears determination on her face. She needs TS & TS is glad to help. If we ever knew one thing about pyramid building, it's that it takes at least two people—one to push & another to pull.

Let's gather & regroup.

We would not belong to a movement if we did not have a capacity for joining in: *We will build this pyramid, the twenty-three of us, the key ingredient is fervor. Fervor is love expressed with a stern look on your face & sweat dripping . . .*

Interlude: Shall we turn the air blue?

While the others work out the particulars & an early morning raincloud passes overhead, Cy & Daphne steal away in the FunTime on a trip to the Dalles to rent sledge hammers & chisels & the largest wheelbarrow *we can get our hands on*. It becomes a downpour & the windshield wipers hardly work, they are worn out from previous rains. Still they sway back & forth across the windshield in beat to the song on the radio while trees blur by along the side of the road. Daphne & Cy stare straight ahead, mostly silent, though sometimes making small talk. This is Daphne's first trip to Oregon. The rain breaks.

On the return trip, on the other side of the Columbia River, they cannot believe their eyes—it's Stonehenge. They cross the bridge & visit the replica, a Columbia Gorge roadside attraction. This particular Stonehenge has nothing to do with the summer solstice & is made from concrete, not cut stone. *The builders took the easy way out.* Still, the site abounds in eeriness. Out of the FunTime, they walk the perimeter of the structure, they touch the stone. They lie down upon the sacrificial altar, head beside head & stare up at the momentarily blue sky & the clouds that sail across it as fast as any they have ever seen. The concrete is wet & cold & the wind is wet & cold, but they are protected. As they lie, images & ideas move through their heads in sync with the clouds. Later, in the journal they are keeping together & in which you cannot tell their handwriting apart, they will jot down their thoughts on where they are in this moment. The wind picks up.

Sometimes it feels like ocean air, the steady east wind. Mostly, though, the wind is dry, you feel your skin cracking under it. The wind shapes the hardwood trees. They grow diagonally, their roots clawing the ground, holding on for dear life. We imagine there used to be more trees around here, but their roots lost grip & they wound up blowing away. They took the form of high-speed projectiles, flying just below the range of radar, landing forty miles away from where they started.

Lava flows in underground rivers along a chain of Cascade volcanoes, some of which are not entirely dormant. Steam & warm springs flow from fissures in some places, reminding the people who live here that Earth is made largely of fire, that Earth is not yet finished with itself. We can close our eyes & pretend this is Iceland.

The government built the Bonneville Dam in mid-century to harness the Columbia's River's potential as hydroelectric energy. They installed fish ladders & a hatchery to preserve salmon from being squished in the dam's huge turbines. Millions of salmon get squished anyway—to the point where now there are hardly any left. Please Portlanders—turn off your lights—it's the least you can do.

Far upstream on the Washington side are the Tri-Cities & the site of the Hanford Nuclear Reservation. Hanford is the beat up ol' Ford on cinder blocks of nuclear reactors, the scene of a Chernobyl-like mishap or two (ones that people never heard about), a laughingstock for nuclear scientists. No wonder the wind has a metallic taste to it. You hope that your hair doesn't fall out & that your children are born with five fingers on each hand.

The wind is seen as junk in the Gorge, blowing without ebb—a reason to buy Chap Stick & not much else. You send skyward the kite you have no hope of seeing again. Then someone discovers the wind is fun. Let the windsurfing games begin. Suddenly, people are harnessing the wind for recreational use. Suddenly, Hood River becomes a tourist attraction. Windsurfing becomes a full-blown cottage industry, a windfall harvest.

There are signs that more people are going to come. Look no further than the expansion of I-84 to replace the old Crown Point Highway, the opening of a Wal-Mart or two. These are tangible signs of sprawl. If you are still & quiet, with the wind rattling in your ears, off in the distance you can hear faintly a galloping horse whose rider proclaims, The people are coming! The people are coming!

The wind still tastes like metal.

Chapter 53: Fun!

The square is lain on the ground & the next step is cutting stone. *Hammers fall, sparks fly.* The step after that is moving the finished stone onto the site. *Drink some water; this is going to take some effort.* We are using, as our units of measurement, the length of Squirrel's foot & the distance between TS's armpit & the tip of his middle finger when his arm is outstretched. We discuss the pyramid-building process among ourselves. All we can do is agree & argue, always ultimately deferring to Squirrel, as this pyramid is hers. She is leading us; we are all just helping. We hammer away at rocks, carving out slabs we figure must weigh as much as six-hundred pounds. They are unmanageable if not unbudgeable by a single person. We create more & more rubble, finally arriving at a single slab we can all agree upon: cubic, rectangular, angled. Moving the first one takes longer than anyone could ever imagine. We sleep. We drag the stone across the ground, pausing often along the route to rest. [*Don't forget we want to cut the stones so that they lean inward so that the pyramid is always collapsing inward upon itself. Here, I'll show you what I mean.*]

We move the slabs in concert, the moving going more easily the more people we have. Tipsy Tulip & Tom go away & then return having built a sled from some scrap wood lying in a pile behind one of the buildings. After hoisting the heaviest rocks onto the sled, they move more easily onto the site. Dumping buckets of water in the sled's path makes the pull even easier, but carrying the water in buckets, too, is sweaty, grueling work.

Back at our makeshift quarry, Squirrel wants every stone cut perfectly. She shows us the proper chiseling technique as if she has done this all of her life. The lower courses require larger stones; the larger the stone, the more margin of error we have in breaking them. The smaller stones that will make up the higher reaches of the pyramid need much more exact breaking. By the time we begin cutting the smaller stones, we are experienced enough to break & angle the stones smoothly.

Try cracking it with the grain.

It's not easy because the grain forms in waves through the stone—look how it knots up.

You cannot hurry the breaking of the pieces or nothing will go right. When you find a way to be perfect, it becomes Zen.

Let's try a lever system—a quickly built platform, a long plank, a teeter-totter effect, roll it into place. Hello, it works, though not very well.

An argument breaks out when it appears that the pyramid is going up less than perfect, that one of its sides will be heavier than the others. *We will have to start over, but this time we will know what we're doing.* Rebuilding what we have, though, doesn't take long—all we do is remove some ill-fitting stones while reusing most of them. We can break the ill-fitting stones into smaller pieces & use them on upper courses. *The higher we go, the lighter they are.!*

No one notices when Cactus goes away until he returns, this time with huge baskets of apples. *You scored good apples, Cactus. Hey, try Cactus's all-new apple miracle diet. [I've been dreaming of apples: A stairwell, I'm running upstairs, turning corner after corner, hurrying—run, run, run. Then, coming down upon me, rolling red apples. They crash over me, as if they were bursting out a closet door. I ride them down the stairs, bouncing on top of them, bruising them. I wake up before I learn what happens next.]*

After this, we will have no more plans to hatch. Gathering is good—gathering ourselves & the stones. We built this without nature, without science, without Footapples. All was wrought by nothing other than Squirrel's will.

Chapter 54: A passage in which Cy & Daphne make light of the situation

The two of them find a round, spacious room of glass, light & hardwood floors, a round room with 360 degrees of windows & light. They spend the day dusting it, wiping clean the windows, preparing it as if it were a room in a fancy hotel. There is a large bed, too big a bed, the two of them have more than enough room to be together. They fall down upon it & bounce; the white sheets roll out of the bed in waves. Suddenly, they are locked in an embrace & neither is letting go. They kiss with such vigor that they sometimes miss the other's lips. Their shirts fall off & their chests press together & they strip the rest of the way, their pulses racing. They go, rubbing pelvises together so that their pubic hair rubs against the other's—a tingling stirs below the waist, but also behind the neck, proof that all nerve centers are interconnected. Wild moments pass—they know what it's like to be together without yet having had the experience. Then his penis moves as if by a will of its own. He doesn't move his hips, nor does she move hers—he finds her with speed & grace & enters, quite well accepted here & oh, it feels so good, too good to move, one move might spoil it, one move & both of them will come. *Let's save it for a few more minutes at least. I just want to look at you.* They look at each other's eyes, surprised—*wow! This is what it's like to be with you. I've wondered about this. Let's not take this too far. Condom, condom— it's not too late. [Condom, condom!]*

He goes to his backpack to fetch one. When he returns, she has one, too—unwrapped & ready. He uses hers, rolling it over himself, saving his for another time. You cannot call this unpremeditated.

Again, his penis, this time latex-wrapped, makes its darting move, finding her vagina without any assistance from the rest of their bodies, a trick neither one of them has seen before. Both imagine it's just their bodies wanting each other, their bodies desiring to join each other. Accompanying entry is sound, not unlike the messy tambourine shivers, though neither hear it. Instead they see it—tiny glistening sparkles as if from a sneeze & the light shining into the room that hits them just right.

One can look at this as just sex. Both of them have had sex before; sex generally feels good. This feels better. *If our bodies fit together so well, does that tell us anything about the rest of us? I desire you in a way like I have never felt desire in my life. This is soft & nice, I like when it's soft & nice.* In the past, she would have thought that this feeling were scary. She won't let herself have any second thoughts, not now. No, this is safe for her to enjoy & he's enjoying it, too. Gone is the desperate feeling he used to experience when he was a teenager, incredulous at where he was & what he was doing. They both like it. They have found more than sex in this. They already feel a sense of gentle needing for each other.

It's finally fair to say we like each other. We couldn't call this unexpected, not after the way we've been going about.

I think you're keen. [Keen? Oh, brother, where did that come from? Did I really say that?]

Now we'll be together forever.

Let's not say that now, not yet.

I was making it all right on my own, but there was something lacking.

It was the way you looked at me that first time that caught me. When I like stopped to think about it, I hated the way you looked at me. I only liked it when I let myself go. I let myself go with you. I'm trusting you.

I'm glad you did & I am glad you do.

I'm not promising anything.

We fit together well. I like when it's soft like that. We aren't about sex.

What on earth are we going to do?

About what?

About everything.

Let's just hold each other.

I want to know about your family, everything about them. Is there cancer?

Let's fall asleep & save that for another time.

All right, but tomorrow I want you to tell me about your family.

Chapter 55: Squirrel explains the relations of the pyramid to satellites

By the way, Squirrel, I have been meaning to ask you [*Yes?*] which stars are the ones you used to align the pyramid & what is their mythological & technological significance.

You really would like to know?

Yes.

Well, I have always considered all of that bullshit, so this pyramid is aligned to nothing, except for where I wanted it to lie. I like astronomy just fine, but the reason I stayed up those nights & hammered stakes into the ground was to get out my aggression & frustration. So there, does that answer your question?

Chapter 56: Gloria!

Suddenly, it's finished. I wouldn't say that it looks at all shabby, either. It was as if we knew what we were doing, after all. But gone are any plans to take this road show to the Pentagon. I think if we saw the Pentagon now, we would break up laughing at what we wanted to do & Eleanor Cookee has it all set up for us to move back to California, but not before marching in a demonstration on the state capitol. We're glad we did it, though. We learn more about ourselves this way. Squirrel's pyramid is a tribute to sleeping & standing up & breathing. Squirrel still says dancing is harder work.

While building the pyramid, Eleanor Cookee at times would disappear; we thought she was taking a moment here & there to escape the heat, gather herself. Really, though, she was on the phone, first learning of an old-growth timber sale on state land in Tillamook County near Oregon's Pacific Ocean beach access & then designing a march in Salem in protest against it. She had been sleeping well here at first but was now spending her nights painting signs & making lists for herself of details she needed to cover.

A march in August on a Saturday? Will legislators take notice? Usually we avoid the hot summer months because tempers might flare and there is an increased risk of violence that follows.

By this time, Eleanor Cookee is efficient & thorough at organizing events such as these. She arranges speakers & gives us a prepared spiel for what she wants us to say if we are approached by media.

We have little else to do. We go; we march.

Chapter 57: I painted my teeth blue for a forest policy rally

Imagine seeing a movie—projected not on the kind of screen you might find in a commercial movie theatre, or even a school—but rather on a makeshift screen, a powder-blue bedsheet hanging from the door. You would just watch the movie on the wall if it weren't for the wallpaper & its pink & green floral print. It's hot, the fan in the window blows waves in the sheet. You could fix it, but you don't mind it that much. The distortion is welcome here. It's a home movie. In the movie, you witness a minor disturbance in the shape & spin. It's so subtle you can pinch yourself & make yourself think it never happened. In the lower right-hand corner of the frame, you watch an arousal of leaves while everything else in the picture remains the same. The street trees remain & the parked cars at the curbside don't budge. You have time, so you memorize the letters & numbers on the license plates. No movement follows, though perhaps there is music—a wordless song, varmint harmonies & dissonance & accompaniment from nowhere that come after a distant blast—the kind of sound only dogs would notice. What with airplanes & trucks, illegal fireworks, homeowners who shoot at moles & fornicating cats in the backyards, a parent screaming at a child, who else would notice? But the street trees remain & the parked cars at the curbside don't budge & the U.S. mailbox & the window glass record no change. *Dig the stillness, dig the slowness.* It's not like we are having an earthquake that everybody feels. Instead, it's just the leaves well stocked on the trees, the leaves on the ground, susceptible to wind, swirling. That's all.

Part IV

Synchronicity.

We all know each other.

Chapter 58: The Seldom scene

Turn, the door opens. *See-prise!*

Hey, like you've never seen us before, but we feel like we know you. We, like, know your son, TS. Do you call him TS at home or are we the only ones who call him that?

I don't know how much you know about his extracurricular activities but we all belong to a radical environmental group. We are radical, revolutionary slash evolutionary, you know? [It like sounds weird when I say that.]

I don't know how much you know about us. I know I haven't said a word to my parents—God!

You see, there was like this march in Salem—we are here because we're in trouble. Though don't worry, like, no one was hurt, at least, we don't think anyone was hurt.

Carl stands in the doorjamb, beaming, welcoming them to his home. He has no idea who they are or what they're saying—he's not even looking at them or listening to them. What their sudden appearance means to him is that his son, whom he loves very much, will be coming home soon.

Three years had passed since Molly & Carl Seldom had seen their boy. Once TS left for college in San Francisco, they stopped hearing from him. He was busy. [He was asleep.] The periodic postcards from him were their only communication; he never called & they didn't know a number to reach him. When they wrote to him at the return address on the postcard, the letters always came back, because TS was already living someplace else. The summer before last, TS sent his parents a postcard from Iceland of all places. The picture side showed an Icelandic fjord with a tourist bureau slogan written under it. Its message: *Visit Iceland, Where the Summer Sun Never Sets.* It was pleasant enough. On the back of the card, TS, who was never one to write lengthy messages anywhere & in particular not on the back of a postcard, scrawled a short message to his parents:

I'm in Iceland.
Everything is going good.
I just wanted you to know I love you.
After reading this postcard, please burn it.
I'll explain what I'm doing after I come home.

Regards,
Theo

The problem was that after sending the postcard, TS never did come home. He never even called, nor did he ever tell them about what happened in Iceland, not so much because he wanted to hide his involvement in a double boat sinking, but rather that to him, it was no big deal—he thinks nothing of it. He would rather eat eggs & toast with marmalade. The card from Iceland was sinister, particularly the part asking them to burn it. They didn't know where or whom to call, or why he was in Iceland, or anything. They sat on pins & needles waiting for him to come home & *explain away the danger* to them & tell them that it's over. Days would pass, then weeks & although they still did not know his whereabouts, their overt worrying over him subsided, gradually nestling itself instead in her unwaking consciousness. In short, Molly could no longer sleep. She would pace the halls of the house at night, emptying buckets of rainwater that dripped from leaks in the roof. She would even empty the buckets on nights when it was not raining. Then, two months later, another postcard from TS arrived from San Francisco where he was starting another semester of school & looking for a place to live. He gave no mention of Iceland or why he asked them to burn the last postcard. Their worry was foolish. They are just glad to know he's okay.

Together, we move in synchronicity—parallel lines that join along the horizon's edge & sing "Til We Meet Again." The same idea occurs to everyone at once. We have spent so much time together over the past few years, dogpiled into the Joshua Tree, that now we all think alike & when we find ourselves in the shit, we find the same way out.

Let's discuss this calmly. We need a place to go—we can only run so far before stopping. Just where do TS's parents live again? The FBI, local police & who knows who else are after us—the janitorial staff at the state capitol building. Where else can we go?

The natural place for us to hide would be the woods, but we don't have our gear on us.

Me? I'm scared of dogs & who's to say we're any match for dogs in a man-hunt situation? I never thought this could happen.

Let's stay urban. We're best off mingling among people, blending in.

Didn't TS grow up in Oregon? Let's find his parents' house & gather ourselves.

No one can say Molly & Carl Seldom are expecting us to arrive at their door, expecting us to knock & ask to come in. Before the night is over, thirty-one of us will arrive, a tired, hungry mob. The atmosphere becomes circuslike. We are used to it. We bring it with us wherever we go. TS's parents are enjoying themselves. Our sudden presence thrills them. Molly cooks for everyone. That's new to her, yet the house yields enough food. She makes spaghetti, salad & garlic bread. No one goes without.

TS is among the last of us to arrive at his house, the home where he grew up. When he walks up to the house alongside his Joshua Tree compats, he experiences sudden disorientation. *Yes,* he can remember the floor plan, *yes,* & where to find the silverware & *yes,* glasses, the stairs that lead to the attic where Uncle Richard lives, the bay window with the view of the hill out back, the apple trees & the broken-down windmill, the stone memorial under which Andy Kaufman is buried, *yes.* But most of the memories that fall on him like hail are from his early youth, as if hardly anything has happened between then & now.

How did he lose all the time between?

TS, feeling himself more an outsider than any of the others who are now here for the first time & who are basking in the pastel feelings of hiding out together in a family home, enters the kitchen & stops. His mother comes to greet him, hugs him & kisses him on the cheek. His father's handshake pulls him in, turning into an embrace. Both of his parents holding him tightly close to them, he stares off at the wall & wonders what is happening to him. *Where am I? Who are these people? These people are my parents?*

Daphne & Cy escape Salem together then find themselves at a roadside gas station, asking for a ride from a friendly stranger & going to Portland. They take a public bus to within forty-five miles of TS's parents house. They find another ride by asking around at a truck stop. They arrive the latest of anyone, for almost everyone else rode out in cars of their own. They explore the grounds alone together, hours after Carl gave tours to everyone else.

A faded wood-carved sign out front that has survived a few Oregon winters—which we imagine can be worse than even nuclear winters & much more rainy—announces the name of the place: *Earthshippe Seldom—the Family Home.* We want to ask Carl about that & the windmills out back, about the solar panels on the spiraling LaMancha-style roof of the house.

Cy & Daphne banter. They wake us up, walking by, with their chatter. How these two found each other seems like a miracle to us now. In a way, the rest of us feel like people in the margin of the adventure Cy & Daphne are experiencing. On this trip they are taking together, Daphne & Cy collect wherever they go, though keeping nothing in the physical sense.

[*Nothing beats traveling light, just ask Spokes.*]

They keep what memory selects, holding on to whatever will be useful later on. Their hands are not altogether empty. They carry a small notebook that they pass between each other, sometimes writing words, sometimes drawing pictures—Daphne is an artist.

While the rest of us worry about the FBI arriving & making life difficult, Cy & Daphne are nonchalant about the ordeal. *So what if we go to jail, we will find plenty to talk about & if they separate us, we'll spend our days writing long letters to one another.*

When the entire throng settles in for the night, Uncle Richard seems agitated, anxious. He keeps to himself, away from the others. It isn't long, though, before Kelly & Tracy, knowing nothing about Uncle Richard, not even knowing there is an Uncle Richard in the attic, are sitting at the piano playing songs from Side 2 of *Abbey Road*. Slowly, Uncle Richard emerges from his seclusion. He comes down the stairs & steps into the room. He stands beside the piano to feel its vibrations, vibrations that make him feel drunk, drunk because his fascination with the Beatles has never waned. Next thing he knows, he's talking. He finds a group of people who are not only friendly but willing & eager to listen to his stories about *Paul McCartney's death in a car accident in 1966 & his subsequent replacement by an impostor, the Bastard Paul.* In conversation, whenever anyone begins to allude to the Beatles breaking up, when anyone begins to allude that a Beatle other than Paul McCartney has died, Uncle Richard raises a hand as if to ask for silence. He doesn't want to hear about it. *Vicious rumors, no need to discuss them & spread them even more, others do not need to hear them. The new record will be out soon & that will silence the rumor mongers.* [You can believe the Beatles never broke up. You can believe the four of them are living. When the record spins & the needle falls into its groove, the Beatles are alive, together & real. The music rises above the world & rather than leaving us behind, it takes us with it.]

We love him, God bless him, Carl tells us after Uncle Richard has gone to sleep for the night, *but my brother is living in a world all his own.* Carl turns off the light & shows us stragglers to the nooks where we are going to sleep. He leaves a radio on for us. [Living in a world all his own is not far from what Carl Seldom himself is doing.]

Chapter 59: House in order

The TV news reports an incident of domestic terrorism at the state capitol—the bombing of a first-floor public bathroom in the middle of a demonstration protesting the state's timber policy. Now the tag domestic terrorism will be forever attached to us; people will remember the Jokerman name & that we blew up a government bathroom & nothing else.

We are innocent of everything. Take a deep breath, stop taking the news so seriously & go on living.

It's kind of fun being on the run from the FBI. I just wish we had had time to think of disguises & evacuation plans.

The best news is that no one was hurt. We are all accounted for, aren't we?

If the authorities figure out we're here, then we're all as good as arrested. All they need to do is tail one of us back here to lead them to all of us—all of us except Barry Weathers & Wendy. They disappeared.

Cactus has gone missing, too. Maybe he thinks we will want to sink the bus again.

By coming here, at least we can get our stories straight.

Our stories are straight. We didn't do anything.

The FBI will surround the house in helicopters & there will be snipers in trees. They'll toss nerve gas through the windows, cops will follow, red & blue revolving lights shining in the trees.

My guess is that we were set up—timber industry stooges setting us up to make us & the entire conservation movement look bad. I wouldn't be surprised if the FBI was in on it from go, because this is so not us. We might sink a whaling ship here & there, but we would never set off a bomb in a bathroom.

This means people will need to find a new place for shitting while the old one is under repair—that's all.

Someone might have been hurt. Someone might have been killed.
Didn't a security guard die when you scuttled those ships in Iceland?

What are you talking about?

Everyone, be serious; hold still. The news is on.

Chapter 60: Escape momentum & the after-baby blues

Pull a photo album down off a shelf; we're curious to see what life was like while TS was growing up. [His haircut hasn't changed since he first started growing hair on his head.] Now here comes an agit for a n'er believer—

The more you think, the less random you are.

The more you talk, the less it turns out to be you.

The more you read, the less you know.

The less you know, the better off you are.

The better off you are upsets the balance of all things.

Do we contradict ourselves? Fine, then—we contain multitudes in the best Walt Whitman sense.

All that remains are wholesome foods & exercise; talking less & listening more & being in love with people & the world around you; feeling the throbs & pangs; flowing & ebbing at every turn; gently pulsating & maybe going home to visit the folks for a change & the old school up the hill from the family house now seems so small. The time is now to enjoy what you enjoy: Games of Risk & Twister; television; Andy Kaufman gone wrestling; eating chocolate cake in the bath; staying up late on Saturday to watch *Sinister Cinema*; an old LP with Vince Guaraldi playing *Cast Your Fate to the Wind*; the green chenille blanket that covers you only up to your knees.

I'm glad to spend it with you.

The sadness & guilt that Molly Seldom had felt in earlier times slowly disperses into the soft blue. For so long, Molly feared that her baby was never going to speak. That fear was nothing compared to the fear that follows it, that her baby will never be close to her. This second fear, she experiences alone, as Carl does not understand it, nor does he have the capacity to understand it, not until later, not until he stands in the door jamb listening to two perfect-stranger hippie kids jabbering away at him. In this moment, Carl realizes how much he loves his son, how close he feels to his son, how much he misses his son & how glad he will be to see him again. To Carl, the sudden appearance of hippie kids is a sign that Theo is on his way home to see them again—not that there is a concrete logical connection. Carl knows his son is on his way home to see them because of a deeply rooted desire to see him again. Sometimes you do get what you want. Sometimes God is listening. Sometimes karma remembers. What you want will happen to you at the moment when you are finally ready for it to happen.

1968—Pentagons are levitating & child is on the way & Carl Seldom feels an urgency to react. He convinces Molly that they need to move to Oregon & off they go, scampering up the West Coast. They take a mortgage & move into a two-story home outside of Rill on a lot alongside five acres of apple trees. Then suddenly comes the struggle of Theo's birth. The doctor suggests to Carl shortly after the birth, while Molly is still under anesthetic, that they give his wife a tubal ligation to prevent her from having any more children. Future pregnancies pose risks to the child & the mother & the child just delivered may be quote-unquote *damaged goods*. [*You came closer to losing this one than you may realize.*] Carl agrees but wants to ask his wife before he signs the paper to allow the procedure. Carl shakes Molly's shoulders & she awakens in a groggy anesthetic haze. He asks her. She answers, *Yeah, sure.* To Carl, she seems clear & awake when she says it; it seems that that she understands the consequences & wants it, too.

Days later, Molly cannot even remember him asking.

[*He called Baby damaged goods?*

Yes.

What kind of a doctor is this?]

Thus Theo Seldom is an only child who is reluctant to speak & Molly is living forever after with a decision she cannot remember making.

1973—After breakfast on Sunday, Molly returns to bed, not to sleep, but rather to lie there while in the next room Baby sleeps. For while a child, TS is always sleeping & after breakfast on Sundays, Molly is always in bed. These days, she spends much of her time there, her after-baby blues lasting into their fifth year. Nothing Carl can do can make the home happy—still he wants it & tries. The *Sunday Oregonian* is the diversion that occasionally allows Carl to sidestep his life's more troubling issues & focuses him instead on the troubling issues facing the entire world. Just as an article years earlier in *Time* magazine about a levitation attempt at the Pentagon forever changes him, again a news article sets his thoughts in motion. This time it's about OPEC. He reads enough to understand it to mean, *a sudden shortage in the flow of oil to the United States of America & the other industrialized nations of the world.* The article suggests the price per barrel of oil will skyrocket. Already there are long gas lines at the two stations in Rill; this is what those long lines are about—OPEC. The cartel can charge any price it wants & that's the price we will have to pay.

A blinding succession of lightning-white flashes go off before his eyes. Carl sees visions of what OPEC means—no cars, no planes, no garbage service, no food on the table, no Olympia Beer truck to drive, for that is his work. He sees Earth standing still—a nightmare, an apocalypse, a Great Depression that will shut down the country for business through the 80s & 90s—no oil. He tenses up. The skin on the back of his neck curls, unfurls, turns red. His pulse quickens, his abdomen tightens, a rush of adrenaline lifts the hair up on his head. How will he & his family make it through this present crisis? Then he becomes lucid; more flashes follow, a new round of visions, though when asked about them later, Carl cannot remember exactly what these visions contain. He remembers vaguely—rain, air, sun—the last of what's free in the world. If there were only a way to harness energy from them, to help his family become self-sufficient. He cannot remember the specifics because of the way the visions have evolved over time. The fully-realized visions replace any overly simplistic rough sketches that initially pop into his head. It takes years for him to flesh out these visions. All he remembers now is that the initial visions included rain, air & sun.

In taking his first steps, Carl dreams out the idea of installing solar panels on the roof to supply heat & hot water & of a mammoth windmill ascending above the apple trees out back to supply the family's electricity. He dreams of driving past lines at the gas station & knowing that his truck runs purely on solar hydrogen that he produces at home from rain water collected in buckets. He can use energy from the sun & wind to break down water into its elemental parts: hydrogen & oxygen. The hydrogen he would force into steel canisters for use as a fuel; the oxygen, he would let loose into the atmosphere for any wild creature to breathe who wants it. The family would sell apples at the farmer's market in hopes of making enough money for wine & meat. They would trade apples for grapes & make wine themselves. To live in a perfect world such as this, all it takes is gumption.

1975—When Uncle Richard returns to the Seldom Family House after a three-year-long, mysterious holiday, driving a beaten, old Plymouth Duster, he parks in front of a house dramatically altered from the one he had left years earlier. The changes to the house itself aren't what immediately catch his eye. Rather, he zeroes in on the tall windmill rising above the apple trees behind the house & its four smaller companions. Like spinning plastic flowers, the five windmill kits groove in the wind. He rubs his eyes thinking that will make them go away & opens them to see the windmills still there. This is Uncle Richard, remember; he gazes fondly at the windmills without seeing them as windmills at all. Instead he sees the Rolling Stones, without sound, mouthing the words to their greatest hits.

1973—Carl pays for the five windmills with his Bank of Americard & they seem to work fine; the wind is almost always strong enough to keep the blades spinning. The next step is to rig it to an electrical generator to supply electricity to the family home. The windmill will allow the Seldoms to take advantage of an obscure Oregon law that says that if an electricity ratepayer can generate enough power to make the meter run backward, then the utility must compensate said ratepayer for the energy's full market value. Sooner or later, the windmills will pay for themselves & rather than pay a power bill, the electric company will write Carl Seldom a check every month. If everyone installed windmills like Carl Seldom's, Portland General Electric would become insolvent. PGE would have to pay its customers out of its own pockets. All its employees would need to find new jobs. [*It's all right, we were never that in love with the power biz anyway.*] The Trojan nuclear power plant would shut its doors forever. The Bonneville hydroelectric dam would be rendered useless; the Columbia River would return to its natural flow & fish runs would return to the way they were hundreds years ago. Now if Carl can only figure out how to rig the windmill to make electricity. [If others could see the windmills as Uncle Richard sees them, the windmills could easily pay for themselves—all you would need to do is charge admission.]

Carl builds the solar panels himself with glass slabs in wood frames. He laces a pattern of water hoses to resemble a Celtic tapestry that will heat up under the sun's energy. The hot water will pump through the house for bathing & cooking & keeping a pleasant room temperature.

Heating a solar house has as much to do with water moving through a closed system as it does the sun. We will make changes to fill our house with light; we will fill our house with air. Water is compliant. Water is our friend. It flows through pipes with ease. It allows people to harness it. It holds onto heat until air cools it down. The trick is to take advantage of the heat while it lasts. Blow air over hoses & pipes full of solar-heated water & you can heat your home. You can use the same hot water in the shower & washing machine. I bet we can draw heat out of the sun even on our colder days. OPEC holds no sway over the sun; let the clouds decide my price to pay to heat my home. Goodbye, evil cartel—you will never hold my family hostage again!

Building the solar panels takes longer than Carl had given himself & he is running out of time to install them on the roof before the rains begin, so he hurries. He tears off the old roof to build a new one that will orient toward the south where the sun's rays are most direct. To get the orientation correct, the new roof will swirl upward, none of its angles will be square—a twisting skyward of wood, then a tapering off & the roof will now stretch out like hands opening to catch the southern sun in them. He is running out of time. He is running out of money.

Driving past the neighbors where they stand in their yard & hose down their lawns, Carl can see their glares. No one needs to tell him—he can hear what they're thinking:

Imagine that—a solar house smack dab in the middle of Oregon.

That house is solar? I just thought it was funny lookin'.

He must be out of his goddamn mind. People ought to know better than to go & build a solar house in Oregon.

Just where do you expect the sun to come from? This isn't exactly Phoenix, Arizona, you know.

How do you expect to stretch five minutes of sun into a year's worth of heat?

This idea has California written all over it. Crazy Californians go & think Oregon is just another name for California.

Carl feels no need to respond. His neighbors are not the ones to whom he answers. The house will do all his talking for him. [The neighbors next door watch as a delivery truck brings Carl Seldom three metal canisters the size of Volkswagens. He explains to them that they are the receptacles he will use for storing solar hydrogen. They, however, understand him to mean he is building a hydrogen bomb. They put their homes on the market & move to Madras.]

In tearing off the roof, Carl also disconnects the TV antenna. Molly turns on the TV anyway in hopes of getting good enough reception so that Baby can watch *Sesame Street* & sure enough, the public broadcast station comes in clear, without white noise or snow. Then suddenly, Baby's show is preempted for a test of the Emergency Broadcast System— a high-pitched tone that lasts for sixty seconds & causes Andy Kaufman to howl to like a wild animal, his nose pointing skyward & his mouth forming a perfect O. The tone ceases, the station airs a special news report [*Shhhh, quiet!*]: *An American space station orbiting the sun has veered sharply off course before vanishing completely. Communications with the crew of the space station have been lost & cannot be reestablished. According to NASA sources, the fate of the crew is in question.* [Static interferes with the signal, Carl whacks the side of the set. The TV fades out, then fades back in.] *All we can do is send out our prayers to the crew & their families & hope for good news during the next forty-eight hours.* [Static again disturbs the reception & no amount of whacking on the side of the set makes it any better. When the static fades several minutes later, the station is off the air, broadcasting nothing more than a test pattern.]

[You panic.]

Carl nearly falls over. He frantically phones the TV station who deny broadcasting any such report or even going off the air & then hang up on him. Carl then calls the FCC, the agency who coordinates tests of the Emergency Broadcast System & they too deny any ripple in the system that day, & when Carl describes the report he had heard, the person from the FCC laughs at him & tells him to give up the booze.

That night, TS has hiccups & cannot sleep. He lies in his bed under the open sky, for the roof above his room is open. He stares up at a billion stars & watches for satellites. Or even better, maybe he will be the one who spots the astronaut crew stranded in space. No one tells TS that August is the season for meteor showers. No one tells him anything about meteors. That night it rains shooting stars over his room's open ceiling. He knows what they are. They are people. They are the crew, soaring through space to new destinations.

Do you breathe in space? Do you need to breathe?

Do you need food or water?

Do you get older?

Do you piss?

Do you become your own planet?

In a spaceship orbiting the sun, is the difference between day & night all in the direction you turn your head?

[Earth abounds in gravity. Earth is the friction that burns you alive on reentry. You can't even get close to Earth without gravity sucking you in.] *Will you attract your own moon?*

[If nature abhors a vacuum, why is space an infinite vacuum?] *If space is a vacuum, where is the floor?*

The lost astronauts watch each other from vast distances & drift apart. To them, Earth will forever seem the size of the full moon that used to wake you up at night, shining through your bedroom window. They will draw themselves closer, while simultaneously drifting farther away.

The next morning, the newspaper reports nothing & Carl covers the exposed second story of the house with tarps & tires thinking that it might rain any time & knowing he cannot work fast enough to install a new roof before the next shower.

Chapter 61: Rainy days without end

1973—Some days it rains more than others. Some days it would rain inside the house more than others. [*Uh-oh.*] It's as if on some rainy days, the house with the hastily installed swirling upward wood-construction roof chooses to remain sealed. On other rainy days, the flood gates open. Out come the buckets & bowls & we fall asleep at night to the steady plinking. Torrents of rain began to fall in November & lasted through the winter. It would begin with a puddle on the upstairs carpet for which the dog was blamed & sent outside to sleep. Molly was the first to feel the water dripping on the back of her neck as she sopped up the puddle. The dog was forgiven & let back inside. Theo would fall asleep that night to the steady sound of water dripping into a tin bucket in the next room. He would hear commotion through the night as his parents fetched more & more buckets, coffee cans & pans to place beneath new leaks.

Carl, tomorrow you need to seal this house as tight as a drum.

A sealed house is a house that cannot breathe. Take care not to caulk too much—the air we breathe comes through the cracks in the window frame. [But unless the roof is sealed, rain will fall indoors & your family will come *this close* to leaving you.]

By day, Carl would climb his ladder onto the roof in the wind & rain, hammering down pieces of wood & tarpaper & stapling down plastic, which in turn would blow away in the windy night. When the wind subsides, the rain begins again. Through the night, all of them would awaken having to pour out buckets on the verge of overflowing. Every time it rains inside the house, Molly becomes homesick. *Oh, we miss California. We miss a roof that works.*

The next day, in Uncle Richard's empty attic bedroom, for these are the years when he is mysteriously absent, Molly gathers overflowing buckets of water that have seeped in from cracks in the roof. Outside the window she watches her husband walking in circles on the lawn in his rain gear. He does not walk in perfect circles; he takes a few steps one way, then changes direction & ends up back in the place where he started. In the past, she has seen the dog walk in circles before lying down. She has seen Baby go in circles while learning to walk. She can even remember herself walking in circles, waiting impatiently for a bus in San Francisco on days when she was late for work. Carl has other things to do today other than walk in circles, *like doing something about these leaks*, though she knows nothing will get finished. She has other things to do today than watch him walk in circles. So she opens the attic closet door, looking for more water damage. The closet itself is surprisingly dry, except for one cardboard box that has taken the brunt of a streaming leak. She lifts the box to move it to a drier place but it so soggy that it falls apart in her arms, dropping its waterlogged contents all over the floor. It was a box containing Carl's letters & papers, mostly from before they were married. Most of it can be thrown away & he would never know. She begins by peeling some of the envelopes away from the clump. To her surprise, many of the letters are still in the envelope, they have never even been opened, although the rainwater has softened the glue so that the envelopes now fall apart. Then she discovers them, a cache of unopened letters to Carl in official-looking envelopes from the U.S. Army, the draft board in San Francisco. She remembers vaguely when they arrived—1966, 1967. She thought he had opened them & answered them.

She knows what those letters mean. When he received them, Carl was a student & could have qualified for a student draft deferment. All he had to do was answer the letters. All it would have taken was a few minutes & a five-cent stamp. Then, he was married with a child on the way & even if he weren't married with a child on the way, odds were with him that he would draw a high lottery number & avoid the draft altogether. All he had to do was answer the goddamn letters. Why was this so difficult? It seems easy enough—you open the envelopes, read the contents & write back. You write back saying that you have reasons to justify not being drafted. They even include an envelope for you to use. Instead, he just stashed the letters away. The more urgent the mail, the better the hiding place he found to keep it. *This is so Carl Seldom!*

Even though he never replied to these letters, they were never far from his mind. All that talk about his dreams of moving to Oregon where the child could run through fields with geese was bullshit. In truth, Carl himself was the one running—from Uncle Sam. She thinks of the consequences, the move to Oregon where it now rains indoors, the child who took forever before learning to speak & who now treats her with utter indifference. She returns to the window where she fully expects to see him still walking in circles, but he has gone back inside the house to get out of the rain.

No one should have to endure a house that leaks for three seasons. No one should have to endure a tubal ligation without asking for one. No one should have to endure raising a child detached from you no matter how much you reach out to him. Molly is far away from a place where she can live with this.

Oregon is still under the law of the United States of America. Draft resisters are colonizing British Columbia. Stalling in Oregon is falling short. *Next time, Carl, if you go, go all the way, please. But oh, no, that's not what you are about.*

One more breath & her anger subsides. For years, she could hardly get out of bed, Carl & the doctor fooling her into thinking she can't have babies anymore—she has more babies inside her that want to come out. She could have had more babies, perfect babies & the second & third & fourth would have made the first one better. Then Molly decides she can stay in bed & mourn her losses or she can get out of bed & celebrate everything she has, everything God has given her in this world: baking bread, daffodils & Baby. Replying to his mail is beyond Carl. Opening his eyes & seeing what there is in the world is beyond Carl. Molly gets out of bed.

1973, 1974, 1975, 1976, 1977, 1978, 1979, 1980, 1981—Carl does everything he can to repair the roof, but for nine seasons it rains ferociously inside the house, numerous steady drizzling leaks kerplunking into buckets that need emptying every few hours. Every summer, Carl makes an effort to fix the roof while never sealing it completely. The summer of 1980 is no different. Thinking the roof repaired, Carl sprays water on it from the garden hose, but no garden hose can deliver enough water to duplicate the conditions caused by Oregon downpours. Then in winter, it rains inside again. Come summer, Carl fixes the roof again & it's *wait & see, wait & see, wait & see* when winter comes. Then in January of 1981, the indoor rain stops & not for any measure taken by Carl. The house becomes tired of the leaks that span winter after winter. The wood has two choices: Rot or swell; the wood chooses to swell. The paths the water follows through the house's seams are suddenly choked off. It's now dry & warm inside. Strangely enough, a warm, dry winter is just what the family needs to rekindle its spirits & to set the relationships on the road to peace.

Interlude: Clumsy Carp

Clumsy Carp never realizes that TS's parents live in Oregon. He ventures north, hitchhiking I-5 to Puyallup, Washington, where he finds Jude's mother. He knew she was from someplace near Seattle, a place with a silly name. When he caught up with us again later, he had this to say about his visit: *Jude won trophies. Trophies are all over the house; it's embarrassing.* Not that Jude's mother was overly proud of Jude's accomplishments. They just bring them out when family comes to visit & forget to put them away. She wasn't running for the trophies or for the recognition. What was moving her? Quiet people are never easy to understand. If you only knew Jude by visiting her mother's house, you would think Jude was all about track & field & academics. She has won trophies for academics, too.

Chapter 62: Afterthought

Jude thinks about her time at the Hartman Family house so often, it's as if she never left. When looking back, she would see the image of Mrs. Hartman peeking around the corner & she would remember a conversation she had with the brother, one in which he would emphasize over & over that *life is for the living.* He would tell Jude of packing his mother's suitcase & taking her on a road trip to Michigan where the two of them drop in unexpectedly on a doctor's doorstep, but he wouldn't see them. He insists on getting to know his patients, becoming familiar with their conditions before beginning to *treat* them. *How can any sort of intimacy make his business any easier?*

Life is for the living & worth taking into our hands, the brother would keep saying.

So the brother & his mother will return to Nassawaddox to several frantic messages on the answering machine from Emily who is away at college in Maine & wondering where they could have gone. Charlie will tell his sister that he had taken their mother to Niagara Falls for a restful getaway, though to Emily, this will not ring true. She would never suspect what had actually happened & Charlie will never tell her. Her mother will never tell her, either, because it all happened too recently for her to remember. Charlie too will forget, only to remember late at night in a cloud of scotch. He drinks to remember & will tell Jude on the one night when she stays awake & listens to him as he murmurs & babbles as if to absolve himself of his attempt at sin, though he would be the first to tell you he is not at all religious.

Chapter 63: We disperse & broadcast back upon ourselves

We grow tired of waiting for an FBI who never shows, so we disperse, trickling away from Earthshippe Seldom & going home. Pulling up the rear are Daphne & Cy. Daphne leaves first. Cy runs as fast as he can, catching up to her then catching his breath. They had said goodbye, but there was something else he wanted to say. *I can't help it Daphne, I'm around the bend in love with you.*

Cy- [infinity falls between two syllables] *-clone*.
Just what is it her look is saying? [*Don't be.*] [?]

It sounds like you need to convince yourself? She says.

No. I'm convinced—trust me.

Please realize I was raised never to trust anyone who says trust me.

The more you put me off, the deeper I feel for you.

The more I put you off, the less I want to see you anymore.

Why is this so difficult for you?

Why is it so easy for you?

I feel it, that's why. I wouldn't say it if I didn't feel it. Would you rather that I not say it?

No, say it, if you feel it. Just make sure. Don't lose yourself in it. It's just—if I don't say it back, don't think that I'm not feeling it, too.

Really?

Yes. But don't, like, go getting any funny ideas.

Funny ideas are all I have & I love you anyway.

I like when you say it, I want you to say it. Just don't lose yourself in it.

Like, what if I told you, I am lost & gone already?

Like, what if I told you, don't be? Like, let's just cherish the crush part. That's what this is, after all, a mutual crush.

Mutual? All right, I'm ready. I am cherishing it now & will shut up.

Now no matter what happens let's cherish the crush part.

Chapter 64: Fixing a slope where the rain gets in

1975—Janice & David arrive, moving into the house across the road vacated by the neighbors who feared Carl was building a hydrogen bomb. They set up a nursery with a greenhouse & grow sunflowers & plants native to Oregon & more specifically, the plants of the Pacific Northwest coastal region, plants grown from seeds they collect while hiking—they are careful never to take too many. Carl does not like Janice & David at first. He suspects that the two of them smoke marijuana & cannot bring himself to approve of such things. He suspects that marijuana plants are growing in their basement under grow lights that coat the ground outside their home with a spacey lavender that shines brightly at night.

1981—One rain-drenched February night, the murderous, unmistakable sound of a Volkswagen Bug pulling away from the house across the road wakes up Carl Seldom, Molly, Uncle Richard, Andy Kaufman (who barks) & TS (who doesn't make a sound). The adults look out the window & see David's tail lights disappearing over the hill. No one sees him again after that. Part of the slope is gone, too, a Doug fir washed into the stream, everything sliding away—did it make a sound? When the slope slips, Janice knows the relationship is over. David must know, too, because he speeds off & though no one knows, Janice suspects he drove & kept driving before eventually arriving in New England where his childhood sweetheart lived, the one he always called his soul mate. This made Janice feel like shit, not so much because she wasn't David's soul mate, but rather because she wished she could find a soul mate of her own & *good riddance, anyway*.

The next morning, Carl picking up the Sunday paper out front, notices that the VW had not returned while he was sleeping. He walks over to see that everything is all right at Janice's & notices the missing slope. *Did David do that?* Carl Seldom wonders, bestowing on David some kind of supernatural power, as if he took out his anger psychically on the poor slope moments before speeding away. *David & Janice were into herbs— who knows what could have happened?*

Janice has enough money to make payments on the mortgage, cover her heating oil & electricity bills & buy herself food & wine—does she need anything more? She takes no lavish trips & buys no expensive durable goods. She keeps herself busy reading magazines & newspapers & dime novels (that seem to cost more than a dime) & smoking cigarettes. She sells sunflowers & nursery plants she cultivates herself in the greenhouse alongside her house & her sheep dog named Talbert gives her almost all the companionship she needs.

Carl & Molly Seldom never take trips, either. Over the holidays, Janice comes over & spends time with Molly, Carl & the family. Though these occasions are few & staggered over the course of the year, Janice begins growing closer to the Seldoms, becoming a part of the family & when an aging Andy Kaufman (whom they thought was past her puppy-rearing years) gives birth to shaggy white litter, it is immediately apparent that Talbert is the father.

Janice's house is full of brightly colored bric-a-brac caricatures of the sun & the moon & tropical houseplants hanging. The place has a living feel, warm & human. More light comes in from the windows than seems possible; on cloudy days it is brighter in here than out in the open. Candles are placed all over because at night she prefers to keep electric light to a minimum. (The grow lights in the basement were snuffed not long after David split.) Yet despite having carved out the life she wants, perhaps she is lonely living in the old house by herself—who's to say?

How else can one explain why she is the only one who can take dear Uncle Richard & look past his rough outer shell & find a person living inside. Yet it isn't loneliness that coos her into noticing him. She knows all along about Uncle Richard & his Beatles fixation, as well as his other personal defects. When she hears that he had been arrested along Portland's waterfront riverwall during NeighborFair for insisting to passersby that he was the real & long suspected dead Paul McCartney & that the other Paul McCartney was actually an impostor, she laughs. No one else laughs, no one else thinks it's funny & even if others did laugh, no one laughs like Janice. At lunch, Janice thinks about it again & laughs. Her laughter is not the derisive kind; hers is the laughter of human kindness. In Uncle Richard's case, it is the laughter of the one person in the man's life who actually *understands* him & accepts him for who he is & what he's become. How else can you describe what Janice is feeling, drinking tea & thinking of Uncle Richard in terms of compassion, caring & dare we say, love?

1991—Several summers after losing the slope, blackberries are taking over the stream bank behind Janice's house, as if they are creeping up out of the stream itself. Every year she cuts them back, but they grow faster than she can keep up with them. *The dirge of Oregon*, she calls blackberries & finally decides, ten years after the slipping of the slope, to rid her life of the blackberries once & for all. *Blackberries are an obnoxious exotic that take over your lot if you let them; they will take your life if you let them.* Janice stops letting them. She asks Uncle Richard to assist her. On cool mornings before hot summer days, the two of them put on their rubber boots & attack the blackberries, hacking them with machetes, clipping them with clippers & carrying the severed vines to a burn pile far away from the slope. The thorns on the vines rip through their pants & bloody their legs. Where they lay the ground bare, they plant stakes made of live willow, cottonwood & alder shoots that will help keep the slope from slipping again in heavy rains & in time, grow into a dense thicket of trees.

Let me reward you, Sweet Richard, for all the help you've given me. Later, during the pink twilight of that sweet early summer evening, with its California wine & bread & cool breeze, Uncle Richard sits in a rocker on the porch of her house, eating muenster cheese & Triscuits, digging the stillness, digging the slowness.

Richard, Sweet, I have something in my eye, a speck of dust. Will you help me with it please? she asks as she stands over him, pulling him out of his rocker so that the two are standing face to face. Her eyes, open wide, focus on his. His eyes, meanwhile, dart from right to left, avoiding her gaze.

I don't see any dust in your eye. It's too dark, anyway. I can't see anything. He strains to pull away. She cusps his two arms, looking up him directly. He tries again to pull away, but doesn't want to seem rude.

Keep looking, I know you'll find it.

He to turn away again & keep outside her eyes.

Don't look away—it's still in there. It's still bothering me.

Uncle Richard looks & sighs: *It's no use, Janice. It's too dark.*

Keep looking, she tells him firmly.

Uncle Richard looks again closely, opening his eyes, looking into hers. Then it finally occurs to Richard that it isn't a speck of dust in her eye that Janice wants him to find. What she wants him to find, he finally discovers—gloriously. What a charming portrait all of this makes! He focuses his two eyes into her smiling two eyes. Their eyes meet, he laughs at himself & *Hullo*, Uncle Richard says.

Janice & Uncle Richard are married two months shy of 1993, while TS is away. Don't think that now because he is married that Uncle Richard changes too drastically. He keeps his odd fascination with the Beatles, above all else never admitting that Fabs have broken up & mercy goodness never admitting that any of the four have died. Janice, however, does expose Uncle Richard to Joni Mitchell & Neil Young & restores some of his social graces. He bathes more often & she cuts his scraggly hair so that the world may see his eyes.

Interlude: The resonating sound we heard

1991—It just occurred to me, something that happened a year ago that everyone remembers & no one talks about. I can't explain why I am only now thinking of it. UFO weather back at the Rajneesh ghost town. Then, while hard at work building Squirrel's pyramid in the beating sun, we hear the sound, deeply resonating as if a single note plucked from a homemade, washtub bass. Birds fly; other animals hold still. We hear the sound not only through our ears, but at the bottom of our stomach. We drop what we're doing, we wonder what the sound is & it's over. Everyone resumes—the birds return. [Sometimes the eyes play tricks & the ears are the red-headed stepchild in a vision-centric world.]

Chapter 65: Sweetness follows

If Jude were less stunned she might have wondered why the trap she found was so deep onto the trail, so far from any road. She has often found traps & always juryrigs them useless. In all her trap-busting experience, she has never come across a dead animal caught in one. Less than a moment earlier, she was following wolf tracks, excited that at least one wolf still roams these parts, that there may be hope. Wolves are supposedly extinct in Northern California, yet she finds tracks & follows them. Then she finds the wolf dead in the trap's steel jaws.

What happens next we don't know what to call. Eleanor Cookee calls it an accident. Can we fairly call it an accident? All we know is Jude never comes back to us.

Hiking a stretch of the Pacific Crest trail for no other reason than the experience of it, Jude isn't being careless. You can say she should not have been out there alone, that someone else should have been with her, but if someone else had been there, it might have happened to two people. Besides, TS is only a few hundred feet away, boiling water for coffee. The wolf appears to have been dead for several days & there is no sign of the trapper. Jude frees the wolf from the trap, carries its body over her shoulders, walks off the main trail a good distance from where she made the discovery & lays the wolf's body down on the ground where she intends to bury it. First though, she will return to where she found the wolf & cover her tracks, in case the trapper returns.

The trapper, though, is already following her tracks. She turns a corner around a tree, believing she is alone & there he is.

It happens with such abruptness. TS hears the noise—other hikers along the Pacific Crest trail hear the noise. The noise is unmistakable. Birds, in trees, who have never heard a noise like it in their lives, fly away.

When TS finds Jude's body, lying there on the trail as if she were asleep, he kneels beside her. He lowers his head & eyes. He stays like that, in silence, for a long moment. The world will keep spinning no matter what he does right now & the world couldn't be farther from his mind. He wraps her up in his sleeping bag, leaves everything else & carries her down the mountain.

On the trek back down, other hikers see TS & realize instantly what has happened. They, too, had heard the noise. After all, sound travels. No one can believe it.

Accidents happen involving hikers. This was not an accident.

One hiker collapses when seeing the way TS is carrying the sleeping bag, then revives an instant later thinking it is all a dream. More hikers approach; they heard the noise from miles away & the road is even farther. The entourage continues adding more until there are at last fifteen of them, shaken & descending again into civilization.

What follows are helicopters & dogs & police holding TS for endless questioning, telling him repeatedly that it was probably a hunting accident, though everyone knows better than that. TS slows police at first by saying, *I don't know what happened* rather than saying, *Someone killed my friend.* The police never for even a moment suspect TS, but they still don't let him go. They want to pry more information out of him. The problem is he only knows as much, or less, than they do. Meanwhile, the trapper remains at large, hiding & laughing, having even retrieved the wolf's carcass—knowing that they will never catch him. The police inform Jude's mother before they release the name of the victim to the media. TS, still holed up in Maryville, answers the same questions with the same answers over & over, unable to call anyone. Eleanor Cookee learns about Jude's death from television. Squirrel, Cy & Daphne learn about it when Eleanor Cookee calls them. No one believes it.

Where do you go? What do you do now? Without Willie, we moved forward as if an amputee. Still we were lucid & found a way to function. We could still feel our missing left arm. Willie walked with a stutter in his step; he was somehow vulnerable. Jude, unselfconsciously, never had the same vulnerability. Willie's death somehow fit into the shape & spin. We were able to understand Willie's death. In a way, Willie dying was about peace. Jude dying is just the opposite. Without both Willie & Jude, we stop being a living, breathing person altogether—the desire is gone. Everything is easy. We do nothing anymore.

Then TS vanishes—he has to vanish. It's as if there is no other choice for him. The work we started is never complete, but we have exhausted ourselves from it & lost two of our friends in the process. All we are left to do is miss Jude deeply & wonder why she goes, while starkly realizing we will never get over this.

Part V

Jefferson, I think we're lost

Chapter 66: In which we are rolling down the hill

Everyone avoids Eleanor Cookee these days because just enough time has passed since Jude died that they think she's setting up a gig. The idea of doing a gig is troubling to us at the moment. No one wants to go. The sense of reluctance is overwhelming. The Oregon state capitol bombing rattled everyone's nerves, but after what happened to Jude, we cannot see ourselves going back & doing anything more, not right now, maybe not ever. We are moving on & in different directions. We are taking up permanent residence inside ourselves. The last thing on Eleanor Cookee's mind, however, is organizing a gig; she has no plans whatsoever. Yet she comes to people's doors & when they see her through the peephole, they decide not to answer. You have to give Eleanor Cookee credit for her persistence. She knows you're home & keeps knocking. She will keep knocking until you answer. You will not be able to leave without her seeing you. *Maybe if I disguise my voice, she won't know it's me & will go away.* [She recognizes you anyway; your disguised voice sounds too much like your own.] She is still knocking & you are still not answering.

Why are you doing this to me? She says to the door that won't open. [She already blames herself enough for what happened to Jude.] *I am not setting up a gig, just so you know. I am only here to find TS.*

TS? What about TS?

Interlude: The Pacific Ocean & waves, part 2

When TS disappears, he walks away & keeps walking. Then he finds himself at the Pacific Ocean, the shore of northern California where there is no escaping mysterioso—*mysterioso* is one of the words the Pacific whispers. You look upon the waves rolling toward you; sunlight from above penetrates them; soft grey-green light shines through them. Cymbals are rolling crescendo. The ocean calls out the word *us*, long & drawn out: *Ussss*. You never hear the beginning of the *usssss*, because you arrive too late. Nor will you ever hear the end of the *usssss*, because you will leave too soon.

Ussss, the ocean says & nothing of them tonight. [*Us* is not a doer, *us* is a receiver of an action. It's what the ocean calls out & how can you interpret it in any way other than *join?*]

The undertow pulls sharply at TS's ankle, the waves wish to meet him. He takes two steps forward, stumbles, stands again. He keeps going without stepping back. What has TS come to see? [The soul of the body that ascends from the depths of the sea.] The Pacific is not calling TS to swim tonight, rather it calls him to sleep. He falls asleep on the sand in a cove made by a piece of giant driftwood just large enough for him to take shelter. People pass by after watching the sunset on the beach & cover him in their beach blanket; it seems he needs it more than they do & sharing with this poor sleeping boy seems like the right thing to do. They can feel the night wind picking up.

Chapter 67

1991—Phones ring all over the place—it's a call for Eleanor Cookee. It's her place & they are her phones. The buzz is that someone else from another scene is setting up a gig. They are contacting her to rouse some volunteer action. A secret plan is unfolding across the Bay in Berkeley. *Yes, we're in, we will bring as many bodies as we can put together. Just let us know the whens & the wheres & the what-else-we-can-do's of the matter.*

Planting the seeds for the gig is a likeminded group, a troupe with thoughts & feelings similar to ours but who act out on the urban side of things—the Animal Liberation Collective. While we ourselves seem more at the moment about ebb than flow, the urban side is flourishing. The secret plan is for a gig to delay the building of a new animal research facility on the University of California campus, to cause cost overruns, so that, as a best case scenario, the university regents will decide to scrap the plans altogether—the ol' letting bygones become bygone, by golly. The university's plans are even more sinister than they sound. Underground, windowless, acoustically sealed so that the out-side world will never hear the screaming of dogs & monkeys as they await pain to be inflicted upon them in the name of scientific research—people will not know what is happening in there.

The contractors hired to construct the building move a behemoth crane onto the site. *Why* is a mystery—why on earth do they need such a tall piece of machinery to build an underground fortress? Perhaps their plans are more diabolical then we suspect. Perhaps they plan to erect a pyramid out of the blue, perhaps Footapples is on the company's payroll. The crane gives us an object to focus upon in our plan. Cranes cost a fortune to rent. We will occupy the crane & shut down the project. It's an urban tree sit, really, the crane occupation. The idea is that we remain up there for days on end. This will force them to stop.

Guards stand a twenty-four-hour vigil at the crane, meaning we will have to plan around them. No problem: Doggo DeSilva is on our side. He's a person who can climb anything; scale steep inclines & sheer walls; leap from rooftop to rooftop; topple billboards, if he takes up the notion. His gear includes ropes, suction cups & rock climbing gear that have never seen action on actual rock formations—Doggo is a city boy. He is the piece that completes the puzzle.

Doggo DeSilva's life as *a climber of things* begins when he is a teenage graffiti artist, specializing in painting the words *Trust Jesus* in the most unlikely but highly visible of places. The message then undergoes a transformation, changing to *U.S. out of El Salvador*. The message changes again, a few years later, this time to *Silence = Death*. Then Doggo decides that *the best message is no message*. Rather than painting over billboards, he begins toppling them, quickly, sawing almost all the way through the support beams with a handsaw & attaching ropes to the top of the billboard, then pulling the ugly thing over, knocking the corporate system back upon itself. Tired of repairing fallen signs, the Ackerley Billboard Co. replaces all of the wood supports at the base of their billboards with steel. Unable to topple billboards any longer without heavy machinery & without calling excessive attention to himself, Doggo returns to painting graffiti messages across them. He again paints his ol' standby, *Trust Jesus.* [Doggo was arrested once, though not for anything political. Doggo went bungee jumping off the Golden Gate Bridge & the authorities were less than thrilled. They held him & then released him. They never knew that he was the one responsible for countless crimes against humanity—his acts of vandalism to the billboards of the East Bay.]

The night of the gig is quickly upon us. Guards stand vigil, chain link fencing keeps street people & all others away from the crane & other construction equipment. We spread out—in cars, on foot—blending in with the people of the street, milling about in flamboyant nonchalance. It's a warm California night, the kind people mill in, though also the kind that can make you anxious, the way any urban environment like this can make you anxious.

[*Cities ride in jungle screams, distant sirens howling & buses right below the window. We miss our days in the wild & daydream about going back,* Squirrel writes in her notebook at the scene while no one is looking.]

Doggo quickly ascends the crane. Guards yell *shit!* & give chase. Doggo moves too quickly, hauling ass, scaling the crane beyond the reach of the closest guards. When Doggo climbs, he climbs for dear life & goes quickly. How were we to know there were so many guards? Two guards climb after him, keeping chase, but what will they do if they catch him? One guard manages to grab Doggo's leg, but Doggo kicks him in the face with his free leg while supporting his weight with his arms. The guard topples backward & nearly falls off the crane before catching himself. This quickly stops being funny.

Sirens follow—police, the word *shit* shouted over & over. The crane is sectioned off, yellow plastic tape proclaims, *Police Line, Do Not Cross*— no one may come close to the crane. News helicopters swarm, flying close to the ground. A ruckus seethes all over the Berkeley campus. Something is going down, cloaked whisperers beckon to others. The homeless of People's Park become restless; students wake up; the protest tradition in this town is a main reason why people wanted to come to school here. *Someone go wake up Mario Savio.*

The police hold people back. *These kids think this is all fun & games.*

The police turn their backs & yell *shit!* again.

Squirrel notices something on the ground lying fifty feet from the crane—Doggo's pack. Nestled high enough on the crane so that guards & police cannot reach him without killing themselves & him, Doggo realizes that he left his pack on the ground. *Shit!* he mutters to himself. He becomes mournful. Suddenly, it appears he is facing a hunger strike he never bargained for. He was all knotted up earlier & didn't eat & now he's hungry & wants his cigarettes. Now here is Doggo, who never hikes or goes camping, who is not a survival hound, knowing not much else about the wild than it's something he passes through on the interstate in between major urban centers. Here he is, not so much occupying the crane as stranded atop it. There had been the expectation that the crane's occupation would last several days, but he knows now that it will end once he suffers a nicotine fit.

Then *flash!* one of the protesters sneaks through, makes a break for the crane & scales it in a single movement. She scurries up the crane—beyond the lunging reach of a dozen of Berkeley's finest. It's Squirrel, the one Joker compat Eleanor Cookee could convince to join in the gig, hauling Doggo DeSilva's backpack up to him. She is weighted down even more heavily because she's bringing food & water for herself, too & her notebook—she's not going through all of the trouble of climbing the crane if she's not going to stay a while. How she managed to carry two packs & elude a force of alert & irate cops adds to Squirrel's legend.

What I'd do right now for a nice taste of Indian curry, Doggo thinks at that moment. From the top of the crane he can see the Indian restaurant he likes. Doggo DeSilva wonders how people who know him can confuse adrenaline with talent. His entire time alone on the crane he is saying to himself, *Never again, never again, never again.* He is scared shitless.

Suddenly, Squirrel is upon him. He heard the commotion but never saw her coming. *Hi, Doggo. I brought your stuff*, she says.

On the ground, Eleanor Cookee plays the role of spokesperson. *This isn't a standoff. There's nothing to negotiate here. I mean, if the university wants to make concessions, we'll gladly accept them. The idea here is to occupy the crane for as many hours as our climbers can stand—each day pushing the cost in lost construction time skyward. Do you know how much it costs to rent a crane?*

The reporter asks her, *Don't the climbers fear the repercussions, for example, jail time? Being sued? Losing everything they have?*

These people are running on nothing but guts & the knowledge that when they come back down, they have a team top-dog lawyers waiting to make their case for them. What matters to our climbers is making it so that the construction of this animal research center does not take place. When this so-called standoff ends, if the university wishes to prosecute, we will happily move this to the courts. We have nothing to lose & even if there is jail time, that's nothing compared to what the animals would be going through. Nor is it anything compared to the hell the university would go through when everyone learns about what's going on.

Just then someone off-camera hands Eleanor Cookee a box with kittens in it. She opens the box & gently picks up a kitten to hold, explaining to the camera all the while that these kittens were liberated from an animal research facility in San Jose earlier that very evening. *We have a San Francisco phone number. Call & if you're looking, we will give you a free kitten, as long as you promise to love her. Regents of the University of California need not call. I mean, really.*

The reporter lets Eleanor Cookee run the show. In the reporter's earpiece, the show's producers are telling her that Eleanor Cookee makes great television—*Keep it going.*

How many kittens have you rescued tonight? the reporter asks.

Forty, so far. [That's it—on television, giving away kittens, Eleanor Cookee becomes an instant media darling & how good she looks smiling on camera. She has lost weight & the media falls in love with her. She makes good TV. She attracts viewers. She makes it easy for them to sell advertising. The next day, she appears on a live TV talk show as an in-studio guest. Even though the show is breaking for a commercial, the cameras remain on her as she sits in her chair beside the host who is busily chatting with other members of the crew. She appears on a monitor you can see from the back wall of studio. Eleanor is keeping quiet, to herself, looking down at her shoes, sorting her thoughts. She is someone else when she is not on TV. Seconds pass & they are again on air & suddenly, her energy returns. She becomes real.]

Now Eleanor Cookee is on *60 Minutes* & Mike Wallace, who everyone has warned her about, drops a bombshell. He informs Eleanor that the true motive for the building was to serve as a cloning research center & that the animals were the unwitting test subjects. Eleanor Cookee's face falls; this is the first she's heard of it. She says nothing, her face tells the story. She readies herself to reply, breathes in & the first words that come of her are *I don't know what to say.* She then carries on, swept away by the moment. [*All eyes on you, Eleanor. We are watching you handle yourself with style & grace. Eleanor, have you been wasting your breath in the woods where no one will listen to you? There are people out there wishing you were on their side & some of them you would rather not know who they are. Tonight, you sink your whaling boats, Eleanor Cookee. We love you.*]

Half of the home audience thinks she's a kook. The other half listens closely. There come in people's lives moments when people want to stop living like they do, when they decide to recycle or become vegetarian.

Listening to Eleanor Cookee on *60 Minutes* talking about cloning research is one of them.]

Interlude: Gee, are we really wasting another year?

1993—Toward the end of everything, a certified letter arrives in Eleanor Cookee's post office box.

Dear Ms. Cookee:

After careful review by the Disneyland public relations office, we regret to inform you that you may not use Disneyland and/or any of its trademarked characters in the group autobiography/work of fiction/whatever the hell it is you are presently intent on publishing. While the work does not depict Disneyland in a markedly negative light, it does not cast the park in a markedly favorable light, either. We suggest that you contact one of the many other theme parks in the Los Angeles area & set the scenes from your story there. Our legal department is receiving a copy of this letter & will closely monitor the publication of your work to ensure that all images & depiction of Disneyland & all of its associated trademarks are removed from the text. Good luck to you & thank you for letting us read your story.

Sincerely,

Maria Lovesong-Underwear,
Public Relations Lead

Eleanor shows the Maria Lovesong-Underwear letter to a lawyer she knows, the same lawyer who is always hitting on her although he is old enough to be her father. He reads it & laughs aloud. He cannot believe the folks from Disney even sent it to her. He tells us that, legally, Disney does not have a leg to stand on; we can set as much of our story as we wish to take place there. He also encourages us to use the letter writer's real name—*Maria Lovesong-Underwear*—as he gets a big kick out of it & says everyone will think it's a name we made up because there is no way someone named *Maria Lovesong-Underwear* could be so uptight as to write a letter like that.

Still, Eleanor Cookee doesn't want to give the Disney folks any more *free publicity* than she has to. She decides that in the next passage, the park's name will be spelled with a random asterisk (because she thinks asterisks are the ugliest symbol she can make) implanted within it as a gesture of protest against the park & everything for which it stands. The next time you see the name, it will be impaled.

Chapter 68: Touching down in Swimming Pool Land

1993—A wild ride takes Daphne & Cy to Disneyl*nd, the "Happiest Place on Earth" in Anaheim, CA, USA, where the summer sky is the color of the beer we never drink. Something happens when you pass through the turnstiles of Dis*eyland. First you see a knoll featuring the face of Mickey Mouse made from purple flowers. Then you see *them*, in all shapes, sizes, colors, ages & from all political, economic, religious & social persuasions—people taking pictures of each other. They are taking pictures of cartoon characters come to life with skin & fur made from foam rubber & plastic. They are taking pictures of babies & rides in the distance, world-famous landmarks that absolutely lack authenticity— the wood, cement & chicken wire Matterhorn. You remove your camera from its case & join them. Shutters snap, reflected light from the sun adheres itself to the media inside the camera; the camera hums while the film advances. When the pictures are developed, you see the people you love (maybe your children) locked in an embrace the shape of a smile with perfect strangers dressed as animals—Pluto, Donald Duck, Chip & Dale & any of a number of Disney characters. The smiles captured in the photo show nothing of the hundred-degree temperature, the long lines for rides, the terrible food & other miseries associated with a summer day's visit to the park. These are the photographs you will cherish always. [We have visited happier places that brag about it less.]

Then you notice something else. In the margins of the picture, just over Captain Hook's shoulder, along the edges, sometimes half cut off in the margin, you see other people. These are people who you do not know from Adam, people you do not know from Mickey. They clutter your picture. They are often on the move from one part of the park to another. They are often engaged in the act of taking their own pictures. Their faces often show sunburn & impatience. They do not see you; they are not posing for you. They are far less interesting to you than the people you love & the perfect strangers dressed as animals. You do not remember seeing these people at all, yet you must have because they are walking within a few feet of you in your pictures. At Disneyl*nd, once inside, you cannot help it—the shutters go off all at once. [*Look closely, at those two, the ones nearly cut off along the edge. The young woman there is shielding the sun from her eyes, looking for someone off in that direction. The young man with binoculars, he's looking into another crowd in the opposite direction. Why the binoculars? I bet they lost their child!*]

In the history of D*sneyland, thousands of visitors have lost track of their children only to find them again, usually within minutes of losing them. Daphne & Cy are a different story. They have lost a parent. Daphne's father walked out on her family twelve years ago. Today the two of them will find him—that's the plan—they know he's here. Will Cy recognize him even if he finds him? He has only seen his picture briefly once on the wall of his office cubicle in Boston.

Five days earlier, Daphne & Cy quit their jobs—his idea. They climbed aboard a Greyhound to journey together to Boston, Massachusetts on a bend to find Daphne's father. Riding Greyhound is an uncomfortable mode of transportation when you are traveling coast to coast—the lack of stretching, the lack of exercise, the lack of sound sleep, the lack of good coffee. People riding aboard Greyhound stuff themselves on junk food. If you are not eating junk food yourself, someone else is spilling it all over you. The recycled air, squeezed through a spigot above your seat next to the reading light, causes your throat to hurt. All the while you wish you could just get there faster, though you would rather walk. The saving grace of the trip is that Daphne & Cy are making the ride together. Maybe they are becoming closer, or maybe not. On this trip, sitting next to each other & the constant close proximity between the two of them only makes the ride seem longer.

Two weeks earlier, Daphne tells Cy she wants more time to herself, but she doesn't know how to ask for it without making it sound like she wants something other than what she wants. *You know what I mean?* Then what if she changes her mind as soon as she asks? Why does she need to explain herself to him? Why on Earth does she owe him an explanation for how she feels? Why does she owe anyone an explanation? Why does she even owe herself an explanation? *Who the fuck cares?* Suddenly, nothing is working between them & finally, after long days with every word becoming a fight, Cy leaves, not because he wants to leave, but rather because it seems to him that his being around is making her miserable, making her feel suffocated & besides that, she asks him to leave & there is nothing he can say that will change her mind.

Lights out that night in her second-story apartment, she watches as he rides away on his bicycle. His shoulders are expressive; they show her how broken he is over this—how badly he wishes he weren't riding away into the cold, how he really has no other place to go tonight. [Cy is supposed to live in a six-bedroom flat in the Mission with seven roommates. Since he's been sleeping over all the time at Daphne's, he doesn't go to his own place often. Likewise, Daphne has one roommate in her Outer Sunset two-bedroom apartment who spends most nights at her boyfriend's place. A few weeks earlier, Cy had returned to his home & found that a new person had moved into his bedroom, which makes sense since he was never there. Since then, other roommates have moved out & new ones have moved in. It's now to the point that he has never met anyone presently living at the flat, nor do any of them know him. To make matters worse, he has lost his key & can't bring himself to wake up house full of strangers to plead with them to let him sleep there.]

He loves me. Thinking that makes Daphne sad. *What is happening to me?* Through the night, her sleep is thin as a veil. She half expects the phone to ring; maybe she dreams that the phone rings; she half wants the phone to ring; she's half dying for the phone to ring & for it to be him & for him to tell her he loves her because she likes when he says it, even though she doesn't always say it back & she will only say it when she feels it & she hasn't been feeling it lately—lately, all she's been feeling is numb. She wonders why he's not calling. Maybe he was hurt in an accident—*no*. He's not calling because she asked him not to call. He's respecting her wishes. Not calling her tonight is the way he's saying, *I love you.* Then something happens. Darkness from outside her bedroom window flows into her room, it covers the walls & hides everything. Vision becomes a sense denied. It becomes so dark that she cannot tell if her eyes are open or closed. It becomes so dark that she cannot tell if she is awake or sleeping. [Cy is just now drifting to sleep in

Eleanor Cookee's bed. He had hoped Eleanor would let him sleep on her couch, but as it turns out, she is out of town & though he has lost his own house key, he knows where she hides hers & she always tells him it's all right for him to use her apartment anytime he needs. Tonight, he needs, so he sleeps alone in her bed. He stares at the phone wanting to call Daphne, but resisting. Not calling her is Zen. It brings him closer to letting go & closer to her than ever before.]

Daphne awakens from a deep sleep at 8 A.M., the darkness in her room now dissolved into bright sunlight that pours in with soft edges through her open window. She is lucid & energetic, replete in a feeling of being well rested. She takes a hot shower, washes her face, combs her hair, eats cereal, reads her roommate's magazine, then calls Cy at Eleanor Cookee's where she senses she can find him.

At Eleanor Cookee's, the VCR in the bedroom whirs & ghigs into action even though the TV is not on. Before leaving town, Eleanor Cookee preprogrammed the machine to record herself on television. She is on television often & wants to watch herself later since she will miss the chance of watching herself live. The VCR wakes Cy up, but before he can fall asleep again, the phone rings. That's what Eleanor's phone does—rings. People call for her, she belongs to a telephone-ringing culture. Cy can let the machine pick up the call or answer it himself. He decides to answer.

It's Daphne—his pulse races. He wanted her to call so badly that he thought she would never even think of calling him. The more you want something to happen, the less chance it ever will. Yet here she is on the phone. She asks him to come over; she wants to talk.

He rides his bicycle over hills as the fog rolls in, but he escapes it all & arrives at her door in perfect sunshine. They embrace. She can feel from the embrace that, *Yes, he loves me.* Through his arms & body, a warm energy flows into her. He can feel from the embrace that they are not yet all the way back together, nor will they ever be quite the same as they were before.

We go walking & I tell Cy I am not ready for what is happening—the love & the trust, the constant closeness. He says he understands, but I know it's not what he wants to hear. I can't help wanting what I want & needing what I need. I have never treated him in the way that he deserves & cannot understand why he always comes back to me.

[*If you want to leave me & find someone else, I understand. You deserve better.*]

[*Close your eyes & hold still. You will know why I come back.*]

[*Why can't I accept that you love me & leave it at that?*]

I tell Cy how the night before I fell asleep staring hard at the ceiling, watching the car lights slide along the dark walls & ceiling, waiting for the phone to ring. I tell him how it suddenly became very dark & I fell into a deep sleep. He knows what this has to do with. I told him about it once, about my father—not so much how much I miss him or love him. I just have some unfinished business with him.

[*She tells me the story once, how her dad had abandoned her family on the Wednesday before Thanksgiving when she was in the fourth grade, leaving behind his wife & four children & taking with him the family Volvo. She tells me how he told his children as they were playing outside that warm November afternoon in Riverside that from now on, you kids won't have ol' Daddy to kick around anymore, as if any of the children were ever kicking him around—as if Daphne's mother were kicking him around, as if the people at work or at church were kicking him around, as if anyone in his life were ever kicking him around, as if he was Nixon. But the kids believed they were responsible, because they were at an age when they still believed everything their father told them. She tells me how all the family ever did was love & rely on him the way that families do with their daddies; how after he left he stopped in Indiana to pick up a woman he knew, one of Daphne's mother's friends from college & from there drove to Boston where he found a new job & started a new life & a new family; how when her older sister Johanna had invited him to her wedding, all he could do was write back on a sheet of notepaper on his office letterhead with the words,* I respectfully decline *& how Daphne saved that paper in her mementos, for whatever reason; how now she hates Thanksgiving & now she hates Boston. She thinks about him often & rarely says anything. I remember every detail; it's as if I was there myself. I can even see the construction paper turkey art projects the kids made by tracing the outline of her hand & never had the chance to show him.*]

What was wrong with the family my father already had? Every day we remember that he walked out on us & every day we know he hasn't come back. Do you know how long it takes to understand that no one was kicking him around & that we had on our hands one fucked up daddy? Then I meet you, Cy & you tell me that you love me & I want to love you back, but certain things you do remind me of him. I haven't let go of this yet, not really. Sometimes when I see you out of the corner of my eye, I see him. When I hear your voice on the phone, I think I am hearing him. When I watch you shave,

I am a little girl again. It's not like the two of you are alike in any way other than you both have penises, but sometimes that's all it takes. Deep down, I feel I can trust you but can't let myself go all the way. I think you will make me believe that you love me & I will fall in love with you & then you will go away. You will go away to someplace like Boston.

When Cy used to find himself in situations like this, he would fill the air with his voice, not letting Daphne get a word in edgewise, not letting her say anything & directing the conversation back toward himself.

Something is changing inside of him, growing. He remains silent, listening to her, replying only when she asks him to. He remembers a message Eleanor Cookee had written across a protest sign hanging on the wall at the old Joshua Tree: *Keep following gentle impulses.* He's following them now.

I say we go to Boston & see your father, Cy mentions off-handedly, but seriously.

To her, it's not an option.

I'm serious, let's go to Boston.

He hardly knows what he's saying. Perhaps she needs to go see her father in Boston, but is it not presumptuous to say *we*? Is he not injecting himself into something deeply personal to her? No, he needs to go, too—they are in this together.

Let's both go to Boston. He says it again. Let's go on furlough & visit Boston for a while & see him.

She cannot believe what he's suggesting, it's the last thing she wants to do. Her father is the last person on Earth she wants to see. He makes it sound is as if he is dragging her there for her own good, so she can begin getting over & letting go. [*Yes, this has to do with me & yes, it has to do with him also. He wants to be a part of my life. I'm letting him.*]

So they climb aboard a Greyhound together & ride for four days from San Francisco to Boston—having quit their temp jobs, sold back their college books, sold their compact disks & clothes & bringing all the money in their savings accounts with them. They have no other clue to her father's whereabouts than the blunt RSVP he had written on company letterhead to Daphne's sister Johanna when she invited him to her wedding.

I can see the him in you, one of her father's co-workers tells Daphne after she & Cy arrive on a Monday morning at her father's office & ask to see him. Daphne explains that he is her father; she is his daughter. *You missed him, though, he is on vacation this week. He has taken the family cross country to Disneyl*nd.*

Disn*yland? Disneyla*d! This is so just like him, right in the backyard of where he used to live with his old family, the family he left with hardly a word. He's going there without a word to them. They will never know how close he is; he will never contact them again. Yes, of course, that's where he would go. Disneyl*nd is his weakness, his Kryptonite. He loves Disneylan*.

Cy's parents are long past second-guessing their son's motives; nothing about their son makes sense. Though if he & his friend say they need plane tickets to fly from Boston to Southern California, the least they can do is give them the money & God knows why he's in Boston. They know he wouldn't ask if he didn't need it. Whatever this is about, Cy needs to do it & they will help him.

Cy's parents order the plane tickets over the phone & Cy & Daphne are free to fly. They touch down at John Wayne & board a shuttle to Anaheim, heading directly to the park where lies the Happiest Place on Earth. Daphne knows her way around these parts; she grew up in Orange County. When she was in high school, she & her friends went to the park all the time. On a better day, she actually knows how to enjoy herself there.

[*The key is not to think too much about the rest of the world while you're here. Kick back. Relax. Go with the flow. Enjoy the faces of the children when they meet Donald Duck for the first time. This is the world, like it or not. It's all right to let go.*]

[*I am not ready to accept that. This place disgusts me. It's all about conspicuous consumption. The place runs on energy generated by the souls of dead animals. I am glad we're here, though because we will find him.*]

The people at her father's office had been so cooperative. They showed the two of them his workspace, his cubicle where he has photos of his new children taped to the monitor. His co-workers give Daphne his flight & hotel information in hopes that she can find him. They have no idea what his feelings are toward his California family. He never mentions that family to them. They have no idea the extent to which he has abandoned them. He never gives much thought to that family at all. Clutching her father's vacation itinerary in her hand, she rides alongside Cy in the air-conditioned shuttle. Next stop: the park. *Do you really want to do this?*

So around Dis*eyland, we walk, Daphne stressing over finding her father & me, I can only see the idealization of everything we hold in opposition—the rampant consumerism, everything disposable, nothing renewable, a place where you can go on a day when you don't have to work & spend all the money you've earned or will earn plus interest. People walking around with Di*neyland smiles are missing out on what it's all about. Life is free. Here, it's not. This is nature all dressed up with nowhere to go. The excess of Disneyl*nd reminds Cy of something. What it reminds him of he cannot articulate to himself, it's just that after everything they've been through, everything they have seen, for them to wind up now at D*sneyland suggests that we are near the end. [What's ending? I don't know. Not our lives ending; we will live always. Not these relationships ending; we will always be together. Not our ideals slipping; our ideals are what compose us right down to the DNA. It's just a feeling that as a horse, we have run our course.]

Disneyla*d. Too many people, too little a chance of finding him! Too much sun, not enough water! Let's go back to his motel & wait for him there. They ride back on another shuttle, Daphne tense & Cy rubbing her shoulders. On the bottom of the stairs near the Coca-Cola machine, they sit in the shade & wait for him. The time is drawing near when she will have to see him again. This is where he's staying; he has to come back here. They watch obnoxious children splash each other in the motel swimming pool. He won't be easy to identify. Every passing stranger begins to look like him. She half wants to leave right now. Forty minutes pass, a shuttle from the park arrives & there he is. Finding him is that easy. Cy knows he's the one only when Daphne quietly, almost to herself, says, *It's him.*

Her father is stunned to hear an adult person call out the word *daddy* in his direction. At first, he doesn't seem to know who she is, although he can tell he's supposed to know her. Then he recognizes her just in time to pretend he knew who she was all along. He pretends, but can't get over himself. Does he remember her name? His face is fallen, he's a fugitive longtime on the run & now the law has finally caught up to him. He shoos his wife & two small children up the stairs. Neither Daphne nor Cy had noticed the wife & children when they originally walked up; even now they can't remember their faces.

Cy stands several feet away, huddling against the wall, thinking about its masonry & knowing he can do better; give him the bricks & mortar & he will erect a wall unlike any you have ever seen before. He turns his back to Daphne & her father while they talk. Then the two of them jovially raise their voices, beginning to say their pleasant, spirited good-byes—they even laugh. As well as he thinks he knows her & how little he thinks her father knows her, the two of them still have a way of communicating that he cannot understand at all, a wavelength all their own. When Cy turns around, Daphne's father is writing out a check. *Unreal,* Cy thinks. *Reparation for war crimes, I guess.*

Daphne & Cy walk away, neither looking back.

See this, Cy? He, like, wrote me a check for $700.

Why?

I don't know. I have no problem taking it. Now I can pay your parents back for our plane tickets.

They keep walking. They walk faster. She breaks into a run, not a breakneck or desperate run, not a Jude & Willie mad dash from gunfire with their names on it, but a light, quick run. He keeps pace with her.

Why are we running? Cy wants to know.

Don't say anything, just, like, keep running.

On the street, a public bus is pulling away from its stop. The driver sees the two of them running & pulls over, thinking they are running for the bus; why on Earth would anyone run like that without a reason?

Daphne boards the bus, Cy following. It's full. They head to the back where empty seats are available. They find seats in the middle, right next to each other. They hold uncomfortably still, staring straight ahead, not touching each other in any way, catching their breath. They have no idea where the bus is heading. The other passengers, the ones who think they know where the bus is going, because they ride it every day, turn around in their seats to look at Cy & Daphne, half staring & half ignoring. Daphne & Cy, meanwhile, relax & carry on staring straight ahead .

Seen from behind as it pulls away, the bus ascends directly into the sun.

Chapter 69: The soft left

1992—Leave it to Eleanor Cookee to ascend rapidly into the Greenpeace braintrust; Greenpeace is in love with her. She goes straight to the top. They give her an office in New York City. Many of the sticky thickets that the Greenpeace organization finds itself in, Eleanor Cookee knows how to solve & what's more, she adeptly handles the media. She creates sympathy for the Movement. She raises funds & for that Greenpeace loves her most.

Within months of relocating to New York, Eleanor follows a gentle impulse & becomes pregnant. She will not tell anyone who the father is, only that she & he have agreed that the baby is hers (meaning *not* his) & if he is going to be a part of the child's life, that is something the two of them will work it out later. Ask her now & she will tell you that the child is not an accident, that this pregnancy *is* deliberate & she has never been happier than this. The child is hers. Having the child is what matters most. The child is what she wants.

When she tells her new New York acquaintances she's pregnant, they say *I'm sorry*. But the whole idea that we are a generation so wrapped up

in ourselves that we are beyond mothering & fathering a new generation—she wants none of that; she wants the baby.

This is what I want, why are you sorry?

Getting over TS might take time. She promises herself not to miss him,
not to worry about him, but she can't help it anyway.

[*TS, wherever you are, I still can't get my mind off of you.*]

1991—TS won't know where he's going until he gets there. When he
arrives, it suddenly makes sense. Looking like a battered old bird, he
finds himself on the doorstep of Jude's mother's home in Puyallup,
Washington.

She answers the door & greets him warmly. *Of course, I know who you
are—you're TS.* As quiet as Jude always was around the troupe, she
had told her mother everything about all of us. Though Jude's mother is surprised when TS arrives, she is happy to see him & when it
becomes clear to her that he has nowhere else to go, she hopes that he
will stay awhile.

That night he sleeps in Jude's bed, the bed she grew up sleeping in, a
bed still strangely warm, as if Jude had been there just moments before
he crawls into it.

TS settles in. Jude's mother hardly notices he's there but does notice the
little things he does around the house—changing light bulbs, fixing
sinks that drip. She never wonders how he became so disconnected
from his own parents, why he doesn't go live with them. She never
wonders why he's not living with his friends. She has lived almost her
entire adult life disconnected from her friends & family; TS seems as
natural to her as anyone.

[Jude's mother still keeps a radio on, an old habit. The AM station plays
a song by the Beatles while TS is within earshot. He walks over the
radio & cranes his neck to listen closely. This song is what his childhood
was like.]

Then ten days into his stay, just when all the days are beginning to
blend together & seem the same & warp & weft, TS suddenly decides,
Tomorrow I leave.

That night, a knock comes through the door. He checks through the peephole.

Standing on the other side is a young woman who will introduce herself as Emily Hartman. Emily had come looking for Jude. She had gone to San Francisco first where she learned what had happened. Distraught, she then wanted to find TS, but he too had run off.

She finds him purely by intuition. When Emily & Jude had talked about old boyfriends, since Jude had never had a boyfriend, she talked about TS. It turns out that everyone who knew Jude knew TS as well; they would know him before meeting him. Jude was quiet. When she did talk to people, though, she told them about TS.

When they meet, Emily gives TS the news that she had traveled cross-country to tell Jude—news that might not matter to TS as he has never met Emily before. *My mother died*, she tells him.

That night TS & Emily Hartman sleep beside one another in Jude's bed even though they have just now met. Both wear clothes & nothing physical passes between them. In the morning, TS awakens early & goes, again unsure of his destination. She goes, too, unaware of hers. Their paths diverge.

Maybe TS is going home to see his parents again, to live easily with them. [Sure, it's Oregon, but this year, bad back & all, his father is putting in a swimming pool.] Maybe TS is going to San Francisco where his friends are. He moves slowly, walking along Highway 101, alongside the Pacific Ocean. He sleeps in a makeshift tent made from garbage bags.

He has run out of places to go.

Chapter 70: Fly the Co-op

1991—Traveling south & now midway through Oregon, TS wanders away from a diner along Highway 20 & ventures into the forest, wandering aimlessly, lost before he even leaves the road, unprepared for any of life's dangers. Less than a mile into the woods, he finds himself in a clearing—a clear cut. Seedling Douglas firs are planted but none are taller than his boots & none of this matters.

He verges on slipping further.

Then he hears a buzzing behind him. Chainsaws high in ghost trees above him are cutting away. Then he turns & sees it, a human being riding a bicycle with wings. It flies low over him, the flyer waving down at him, then flying away. What do you do? You follow the direction of the flying bike.

It's a winged mammal machine, a flycycle. It's small & collapses down even smaller for the times when you are not flying & need to haul it with you.

The wider the wingspan, the slower you go but the less energy you need while pedaling. Likewise, when you shrink down the wingspan, you go faster & have more maneuverability, but your legs burn. The flywheel system stores pedaling energy. The same gravity that pulls it back down to Earth pushes it back into the air again. Its gyroscope effect keeps the craft from whipping from side to side in the unsteady wind. It's ideal for venturing into sensitive areas of wilderness. You can come & go without a road or a trail, all you need is a strip for takeoff & landing. Flying at night is tough to navigate; flying in the rain gets you wetter.

There are tricks in the world. Just when you get to thinking that there is no way, suddenly there is.

Fly the co-op, the wood sign says. It's a colony of people belonging to the generation born at the tail end of the 1960s. They have funny names that TS will never remember—Belinda Balloon & Curious George & all the others—& the language they speak hardly sounds like English, although this has more to do with TS's ears than the words they use. He will come to know them by their faces & their voices.

[They are not too far removed from the ordinary. They are a rogue contingent of engineering students & cyclists from Oregon State University. They have given up their other pursuits to do this.]

It's a troupe just like the one TS has just left, though without Eleanor Cookee's nervous energy, a troupe just like the one who gathered at Big Muddy, only without the itchy bootheels.

No sooner does TS arrive when a group of people emerge from the lodge. They call out to greet him. So many of them—they reach their arms out to him & pull him toward them, into their group. They know why he's here. They are adjusting a helmet to fit his head & putting a vest on him. They walk with him over to a flycycle that is ready for him. His first words to them are, *I don't even know how to ride a bike.*
That hardly matters here, Love. You can learn. You have the time.

Flying by your own power is the same as being able to view your dreams while awake. It opens up new perspectives. The clear cuts of the world cannot hide from you now, you will soar above them. Hover gently over water; go lightly over the ground, teasing the pointy tops of trees. There are no monkeys in the trees to reach out & grab you by the leg. Maybe this is what we always wanted—the power of human flight & flying machines that run, not on fossil fuels, but on pancake breakfasts & spaghetti dinners & apples all day in between.

Has TS found what's always eluded him? What's always eluded all of us?

This is where TS finally arrives & for the time being, will stay. It's home to him now. Yes, we like happy endings, yes. So yes, yes, yes, a happy ending it is. TS is flying by his legs' power & in the background a U2 record plays *Pride in the name of love*.

Epilogue: Breathe

Stand in the place where you live, now face north.

Make a little birdhouse in your soul, now make two.

Walk like an Egyptian & live like a North American.

Don't fret, love, life inevitably slouches toward laughter & rainfall.

On overcast days, the clouds are barely real & are always on their way to passing. You can bring yourself up above them. The worst you'll do is fall asleep.

Remember the sun—follow.

Carry little, want not.

The best things in life are free & eternal.

Any price you pay is already marked up.

The more you expect, the less you receive.

The less you receive works out best for everybody.

The trick is getting what you want & parting with it: Bliss.

Life is strange but full of pleasant surprises—enjoy.

Know you will never return the same.

Keep your dreams close to you.

Keep your compats closer.

Stay connected. Keep in touch by phone, if needed.

Expect light & lightness—& light will shine from inside you.

Energy will come to you from other people.

Keep following gentle impulses.

Let's spin together, be together, everywhere. We are all a part of this.

Run yourself ragged.

Let go your wild sneezes.

Bring back the Buffalo.

Disable the dams.

Let dolphins swim.

Laugh yourself silly. Wander.

Live happy.